THE SEVEN STEPS TO CLOSURE

D1277514

LUSH PUBLICATIONS

SYDNEY

Published in Sydney, Australia by Lush Publications.
First Published in Australia 2012
Re-edited version printed September 2013
Copyright © Donna Joy Usher 2011
Cover design : Derek Murphy www.creativindie.com
Editor: Felicity Kay

Usher, Donna Joy
The Seven Steps to Closure
ISBN: 978-0-9873207-0-4
Pp 423

I would like to take this opportunity to thank my husband for listening patiently to my monologue, in-depth discussions on my writing, my Mother and my friends - Nicky, Kirsty, Stephanie, Tracie, Vicki, Laura and Michelle – for reading *The Seven Steps to Closure* and offering such valuable input, and my muse – for entrusting me with this story and having the faith that I would get it right.

Thanks also go to my editor, Felicity Kay, for her tireless work in re-editing this version of *The Seven Steps to Closure*, and for her in-depth grammar lessons.

But last of all I would like to thank you for buying *The Seven Steps to Closure*. I really hope you enjoy reading it as much as I enjoyed writing it. If you'd like to contact me or are interested in my other books please visit my blog site at http://www.DonnaJoyUsher.com, or follow me on twitter @DonnaJoyUsher.

Chapter One

The Hangover

'Polly want a crackhead. Polly want a crackhead.'

The voice, more piercing than any alarm, dragged me from my slumber.

'Who's a pretty boy?'

I peered blurrily at my bedside table. What time was it? What day was it? Snapshots of the night before flashed before my eyes. Dancing on a table? *Surely not.*

'Mary had a little lesbian.'

Harrumphing in annoyance I lifted my head and pummelled my pillow into a more comfortable shape. My efforts were rewarded with a spinning head and an urge to throw up.

Ahhh crap. I had a killer hangover. *What did I get up to last night?* I concentrated hard and finally more flashes of memory assaulted me - bad karaoke, skolling wine out of a bottle, falling over in a bar, telling complete strangers how my husband had left me, and finally being taken home in a taxi while I sobbed uncontrollably.

I groaned in shame.

'The money's on the dresser.'

Rolling my eyes, I turned my attention to the problem at hand. It was really no surprise Cocky had ended up at the

Animal shelter where my mother volunteered, but I was still perplexed as to why she'd given him to me.

'He talks,' she'd advised when she'd dropped him off. 'It'll do you good to have some proper company.'

'Show us your knockers.'

It begged the question: just how sad did she think I'd become if this was proper company?

Gingerly, I swung my legs out of bed and sat with my head between my knees as I made my plan. A quick dash across the lounge to the toilet, ten or so minutes of puking my heart out, and then I could deal with the bird.

He waited until I was almost at the bathroom. 'Got a fat arse.'

I spun menacingly towards the cage.

'Nice tits though.'

'Thanks,' I said, automatically looking down. I stopped and sighed, realising there was a chance that the cockatiel's compliment was the nicest thing that would happen to me that day. I had obviously reached a low point in my life.

I looked at Cocky bobbing up and down on his perch, obviously very pleased with himself. 'What am I going to do with you?' I asked. I was glaring into his beady eyes - determined to outstare him, when all of a sudden a hot sweat and waves of nausea washed over me. Breaking eye contact I rushed to the toilet just in time to relieve the contents of my stomach in a terribly undignified manner. I heard his cackles echoing around the loungeroom and into the bathroom where I lay panting on the floor, tears rolling down my face.

Quarter of an hour later, my face pressed to the cold floor tiles, I considered my options. I couldn't give him to anyone. I couldn't kill him - I mean really, I couldn't.

'Mary had a little lesbian.'

I'd have to let him go; there really was no other option.

Before I had time to rethink my decision I placed the cage on my balcony, with the door open, and then rifled desperately through my pantry searching for the Nurofen. After I had consumed two I went back to bed willing myself to sleep. But sleep wouldn't come. I sighed, letting my mind wander where it wanted to. It did an experimental poke at my heart. Ouch. It still hurt, after all this time.

Why couldn't I get over him? Last night had been the anniversary of our break up; surely now I should be able to move on. Instead I felt caught in an emotional time warp. I yearned for the day I would wake up and know that deep inside me, the wounds had healed - but at the same time I still fantasised about a reunion with him. I had become an emotional schizophrenic.

It wasn't like I hadn't tried. I'd seen a therapist, a psychologist and a palm reader. I'd read heaps of self-help books, even done an exercise from one; feeling a little stupid as I'd stared into the mirror visualising Jake's face instead of my own tear-swollen reflection, while quoting lines from different movies, sitcoms and songs.

'Tomorrow is another day.'

'Hasta la vista baby.'

'Frankly, my dear, I don't give a damn.'

'Goodbye and thanks for all the fish.'

'And that, my friend, is closure.'

I practised them again and again, but no matter how hard I tried, how much emphasis I put into it, how much I wished it and willed it, I couldn't get the thrilling feeling of power that I felt when I said them, to stick. The sad truth is - even now - after all this time, if he walked through my door

I would beg him to stay. And even sadder, I knew I wouldn't be happy. Yet it seemed I couldn't be happy without him.

'Men,' I sighed, rolling over and trying to get comfortable, 'you can't live with them.....'

And in my case, that about summed it up.

'Polly want a crackhead. Polly want a crackhead.'

I sighed, realising he was still in his cage, and then clambered back out of bed. If he didn't want to leave I was going to have to give him some encouragement. Initially I tried to grab him, intending to gently remove him from the cage and place him on the table, but the little bastard was far too fast for me. He darted around the cage, biting me as hard as he could whenever my hand got close. I stopped to rethink the situation and moved to Plan B.

Plan B quickly evolved into quite a nasty situation during which I held the cage up and shook it as hard as I could - while he clung to the bars with his little feet and squawked at the top of his lungs. 'Let go, let go', I shrieked, in time with my shaking. It all ended quite dramatically when he lost his grip and ricocheted around the cage before flopping onto the table with his little eyes closed.

Shit, I thought, *I've actually killed him.*

Filled with remorse I picked him up, cradling him in my hands. 'There, there,' I crooned softly, stroking his feathery neck as tears welled in my eyes. And then, one beady eye popped open and glared at me. Apprehensively, I tried to place him back on the table. Unfortunately I wasn't quite fast enough.

'Ayeeeee!' I screeched as he latched onto the delicate skin between my thumb and first finger and bit with all his might. Jumping up and down yelping, I shook my hand frantically trying to break his hold. Finally he launched into the air and I watched in horror as he smacked into the ceiling before thumping back onto the deck.

'Oh crap.'

I reached out a toe to nudge him and then thought better of it. I waited breathlessly, staring at him, searching for any signs of life. Finally, he shook himself violently, squawked, 'Fucking Bitch', and flew off over the balcony.

The whole episode left me feeling hollow and guilty. Pushing thoughts of my mother out of my mind, I clambered back into bed and finally fell asleep.

* * *

I was woken again at 11.30 am by the burbling of my phone. It was a text from Dinah, one of my best friends.

Wake up Tara. Don't forget Café Mudslide at 12.45

Hmmmm. I must have made lunch plans last night. I lifted my head experimentally off the pillow. No agonising pain, no head spin and no urge to puke. Fantastic. I swung my legs out of bed and stood gingerly, waiting for any nasty side-effects. All seemed to be in working order, so I texted Dinah and went to have a shower.

Natalie, Dinah and Elaine - my three best friends - were already at the café when I arrived. It was evident by the empty coffee cups they had been there a while. I wasn't sure why, but that made me nervous. I caught the eye of a waiter to order a latte and then sat down at the table.

'Give it to me gently,' I said. 'How bad was I?'

'Not as bad as me on my thirtieth,' Elaine informed me.

I felt a little better until Nat pushed her thick blonde hair back behind her shoulders and said huskily, 'You drank other people's leftovers.'

I concentrated on my few foggy memories from the night before, horrified when one of drinking remnants out of discarded glasses crystallised.

'One of them had a cigarette butt floating in it. I only just stopped you from skolling it.'

I put my hand up to stop her, my hangover still too raw to think about things like swallowing someone else's soggy cigarette butt.

'You snogged the barman,' continued Elaine, smiling cheekily.

Another slice of memory surfaced: me, kissing a stranger who stood like a statue, his arms by his side. I covered my face in shame.

'I was actually eyeing him off myself,' she said.

'It was *my* birthday,' I mumbled into my hands, 'get your own barman.' I looked up at them. 'Probably best not to go back there for a while.'

'Yeah, his girlfriend wasn't too impressed,' said Nat.

'Oh no. I don't remember a girlfriend.' I slumped a little more in my chair.

Nat laughed, her blue eyes twinkling. 'Remember that poor chick you cornered in the toilets when you were crying?' she asked.

'Nope, can't remember.'

'You were talking to her for about 45 minutes.'

I shook my head.

'You told her all about Jake and Tash.'

A vague memory of a woman with a bored expression, handing me toilet paper to blow my nose on, floated into my conscious mind.

'She was a good listener.'

'She couldn't get around you to get out.'

'That would explain it.'

Dinah was watching me with obvious amusement. Her short brown hair, flecked with reds and caramels, framed her face, giving her a cute tomboyish look. 'Do you remember throwing up in the cab?' she asked.

'Noooooo,' I said mortified, 'I didn't?'

'Nahh, just kidding.'

I punched her in the shoulder.

'Sucker,' she replied, rubbing her arm.

Nat, Dinah and I all went to school together. Nat and I had hung out in the sandpit together in kindergarten. Dinah had turned our twosome into a threesome in Grade 5 when she had moved schools. Nat and I had been hiding under the stairs behind the gym from the Grade 6 bullies when we first met her. They had increased the torture they subjected us to from simple name-calling to hair-pulling and wedgies, and just that morning we had overheard them mentioning toilets, heads and flushing in the same sentence. We had been under the stairs ever since. Unfortunately, we were ratted out by another terrified student and had been discovered. They were poking us with rulers when a new pair of legs arrived on the scene.

'What are you doing?' asked the newcomer curiously. She wore battered school shoes and mismatched socks.

'Oh look,' said the gang leader with glee. 'It's the new girl. Let's get her.'

Nat and I, torn between guilt and relief, inched out from under the stairs just far enough to watch. Dinah looked so small and vulnerable.

'Run, run,' I shrieked, hiccupping between my terrified sobs. But Dinah stayed calm. Then there was a blur of motion, at the end of which the bully was down on her back and the rest of the gang had disappeared. It's one of my favourite childhood memories.

Dinah, at five foot four and a size eight, is still petite and dangerous: she earned a second Dan Black Belt in karate a couple of years ago. Now a dentist with her own practice, she's also my boss. When I married Jake he had convinced me to be his personal assistant, a job I didn't need my business degree for. Consequently, when he left me I was out of a job. Luckily for me, Dinah had been looking for a new practice manager at the same time. Not wanting to risk our friendship we had decided to give it a three-month trial. It had quickly turned into a permanent position when we realised how well we worked together.

Natalie, blonde and beautiful, is a lawyer. She has a pert little nose, wide sensuous mouth, aquamarine blue eyes and a voluptuous body. Breasts and hips; something Dinah and I are a little short on. There are always men lining up to date her, but so far she hasn't found anyone worth having a relationship with. She has turned her eye to a partnership at the law firm she works for.

I've known Elaine for four years. We met taking a boxercise class at the local gym, which had consisted of a gay instructor jumping up and down in front of us shrieking, 'And punch, punch, punch,' as he flicked his limp wrists around. We had started laughing and then, catching each other's eyes, had laughed so hard we had to leave the class. I came very close to wetting myself. We ditched the gym, found a café and later enrolled in kick boxing classes. We've been taking various classes together since.

Elaine works in marketing. Out of all of us she is the most sophisticated and glamorous. Five-eight without her heels, (but you never catch her without them on), she has gorgeous olive skin and green eyes, and has her blonde foils maintained by the Australian Hairdresser of the Year - Tristan - who happens to be her brother. She is also a self-proclaimed cougar, being thirty-seven years old and *'vowing never to date a guy over twenty-eight'*. She says the sex keeps her lean. Her favourite man though, is her pet Chihuahua, Benny, who was just a teeny, weeny puppy when we first met. He often comes to cafés with us in her handbag.

'Tara, there's something you need to see.' Elaine started digging around in her handbag, moving Benny to one side.

Uh oh. That sounded ominous. I wondered what it was. A photo of my arse in the skirt I had worn the night before?

She finally emerged triumphantly with the *Sydney Morning Herald* and handed it to me, open at the social pages.

I glanced down with trepidation. Yep, there they were, Jake, with my cousin Tash - she looked gorgeous as usual. Just once I'd like to see a photo of her that wasn't great. Maybe one where they'd caught her at the wrong angle and she had big bags under her eyes or a huge zit on the end of her nose. I stared closer, noting how perfectly straight her nose was - remembering the day she fell off her horse and broke it - and wondering how much it cost to have it fixed.

In my mind I superimposed myself into the photo, taking her place by Jake's side.

The visual swap didn't quite work. To start with, she is a size eight; I am a twelve, maybe a fourteen on a bad day - it really depends where I shop. (All right, all right, so on occasion I've had to buy size sixteen pants. I put it down to the fact that most clothes these days are made in China. Everybody knows Chinese women are tiny.) She wears all clothes like a catwalk model; I look best in long pants and tank tops. She has blonde hair; mine is dark. She is petite; I'm tall. She has perfect creamy skin; mine is olive, with a few annoying freckles on my nose. She is naturally skinny; if I don't exercise I morph into a blimp.

Not once did Jake ever make it to the social pages when he was out with me, but Tash - who is the same age as me - has been making them since she was a little girl. While I was still an awkward, gangly, 15 year old, she was attending the races, the opera, gallery openings and even the occasional ball.

My Mum's sister - Jackie - had done very well in the marriage stakes, snaffling up one of Sydney's most desirable bachelors. I love my Uncle Edward. He's a lovely and generous man. It didn't change the fact that for our twelfth birthdays I got a cabbage patch doll, while Natasha got a pony. For our 18th's I got a silver locket, while Tash sported a diamond tennis bracelet. And for our 21st's, I got a silver cutlery set while Tash got a BMW sports car. I tried not to be jealous, I really did. I mean it wasn't like I even wanted a pony. (I wouldn't have minded the BMW.)

When we were kids we had fun playing together. But once we hit puberty she became a real prima donna and a bit of a bitch, always putting me down and assuming airs over me. I guess we were just maintaining the friendship more for our mothers' sakes than our own. Shame. If I hadn't bothered, maybe I'd still have my husband.

I looked up. The girls were watching me, obviously expecting some sort of outburst. The arrival of my coffee broke the tension. I relaxed as I took my first sip, feeling rather proud that the social pages no longer had the power to hurt me. When Jake first left me I had used it as a kind of obscure torture. On Sundays I would crawl under the doona with the paper and a box of tissues. It was a good week when he and Tash hadn't made it. Then, I could find the strength to get up and do some housework. But if they were there, I would spend the rest of the day in bed going over the events leading up to him leaving, wondering how I could have prevented it.

Everybody was still watching me. It was, to be frank, a little unnerving.

'It's just a wine tasting,' I finally said.

Elaine sighed. A look of sadness in her green eyes, she reached over and touched me on the arm. 'Honey, have another look.'

I picked up the paper and studied the picture, gasping when I saw the huge, glittery rock on her left hand. I couldn't believe I had missed it the first time.

'There's more,' said Elaine, pointing at the caption.

More than an engagement? More than the two of them getting married? More than him never, ever being mine? Slowly I read the caption unable to make sense of the words that were jumbling around inside my head.

Jake Wellington with his fiancée, the fabulous Natasha Rawson, on the eve he announces his intent to run for Lord Mayor.

What? Surely they had got the captions wrong?

'He's running for Lord Mayor? I don't understand,' I muttered.

'He's decided to run for councillor, but as an independent attached to no parties, he can also run for Lord Mayor. There's an article on page 14.'

I flipped to the page and read the short but succinct article. Jake was running for Lord Mayor and Uncle Edward was financing the campaign as part of the happy couple's engagement present. It just made me want to put my fingers down my throat and puke.

I looked at the photo again, zeroing in so I could see just his face.

I remember when I first met Jake. I remember every single detail. I remember it was a soft, balmy November evening. Nat and I had just finished our degrees and I had gone to her graduation ball with her. The University had booked out a bar and restaurant overlooking Darling Harbour for the event and lawyers from different firms had been there, romancing the new graduates.

There was a soft breeze blowing off the water and I was standing on the balcony enjoying the feel of it ruffling my hair and moving my dress against my skin. That was when I first saw him. He was inside at the bar, staring past me to the reflection of the sunset on the clouds over the harbour. He was tall - much taller than me - and had olive skin and dark brown, almost black hair. I stared into his chocolate brown eyes and studied his ruggedly handsome face and felt something uncurling inside me. It made me catch my breath and I swear, when he moved his eyes from the sunset to my face, that my heart skipped a beat. He smiled slowly - a confident smile, before swivelling back to the bar. I remembered turning away deflated, surprised by his sudden appearance as he offered me a glass of champagne. I smiled shyly and sipped while we chatted, feeling gorgeous and special.

Later we danced; slow and heated, swaying to the music, our bodies moving in sync as we entwined ourselves on the dance floor. And later still, back on the balcony we kissed; the kiss developing slowly, painfully. Our faces moving closer and closer, until finally I could feel the heat of his breath on my mouth, and then the softest brush, the gentle tug of skin on skin as our lips met and our tongues touched for the briefest of moments, the movements so slow and sensual I could feel my blood heating and rushing around my body.

We stayed for hours whispering and hugging; kissing slowly and shyly. Finally I realised it was not the sunset we were witnessing but the sunrise, and that the rising sun was washing away the magic of the night. I was torn between wanting to stay and wanting to rush away before I appeared not sexy and glamorous, but smudged and tired.

We exchanged phone numbers and Nat (who had spent the evening dancing with one of Jake's mates) and I left. I remember turning to look at him as we neared the exit, to make sure he was no dream, or phantom of my imagination. He was watching me, and when he saw me turn, lifted his first two fingers to his mouth and blew me a kiss.

'Earth to Tara, Earth to Tara.' I snapped my eyes back into focus. Dinah was waving her hand in front of my face.

'I've always felt guilty about you hooking up with Jake,' said Nat.

'Why would you feel guilty?'

'I just wish you had met someone nicer that night.'

I could feel the heat in my face. 'What do you mean nicer?'

The girls shared a look before Nat bravely pushed on. 'Well he wasn't always that supportive of your career.'

'I chose to work as his PA - he didn't make me.'

'Sometimes he didn't treat you very well,' she said.

Flashes of arguments we'd had flickered before my eyes like a slide show. I shut them tight and shook my head.

'What about the pregnancy?' she asked.

I looked at her in disbelief; tears threatening to overflow.

'I'm just trying to highlight that he wasn't very nice,' she said, sounding guilty.

'He was just scared,' I said.

'Will you please stop defending him,' Nat said in exasperation.

Elaine clapped her hands, breaking up our argument, and Benny, who had his head stuck out of her bag, barked in response. 'Enough of the self-pity,' she said. 'You've had a year to get over this and you haven't managed.' She pulled a tatty old magazine from her handbag. It had Dinah's practice stamp on the front.

'Hey,' Dinah protested, reaching out a hand to grab it.

'Oh come on. It's two years old, like you even missed it.' Elaine moved it out of her reach. 'You know you really should update your magazine collection sometime,' she said, flicking through the pages. 'Give me something decent to read while I'm waiting for you to finish work. Ahh here it is.' She handed me the magazine, tapping a perfectly manicured nail onto an article. 'Go on, read it.'

I flipped back to the cover of the magazine. '*Cosmo*?' I asked incredulously, looking between Dinah and Elaine.

'It's a reputable magazine,' said Dinah defensively.

'It's not where it came from, it's what you can get from it,' said Elaine. 'Now read it out aloud.'

'Yes Mum,' I grumbled.

CLOSURE IN SEVEN EASY STEPS.

Hey girlfriend had your heart broken? Having trouble moving on from the bad boy that broke it?

I looked at Elaine who made read-on-shushing-hand-motions at me. Rolling my eyes I continued.

Well, have I got a treat for you. Seven easy steps to closure - guaranteed to mend your broken heart and get you back out there where the wild animals roam.

'Oh please. Elaine,' I said in a whiny voice.

'Just keep reading,' she replied from between clenched teeth. Sometimes Elaine can be a little scary.

Follow these steps in order - we promise that by the end you will be so over him, you won't even remember his name.

'Well I doubt I'll forget that - what with the election and everything.'

'Tara. Just read the damned article,' Elaine said, running her hands through her shoulder length hair in frustration.

'Yeah,' said Nat. 'What are the seven steps?'

'Seriously?' I looked at her.

'What have you got to lose? Last night you were sitting on the floor of a grungy public toilet crying your eyes out. How can this be any worse?'

'Point taken, but surely there has to be a better way than this.'

'If there is, you'd think you might have tried it by now,' said Dinah as she reached over and snatched the magazine out of my hands. She concentrated on the page, taking up where I had finished.

Step number one - Get a new hairdo.

The girls looked at me, their eyes critical as they viewed my long, brown hair I had scraped back into a pony-tail.

'She has had that haircut for a long time,' said Dinah to Nat.

'Hell, she's had that haircut for as long as I've known her,' said Elaine, flipping open her phone and hitting speed dial.

'Hi Tristan darling it's me. Have an emergency. You know my friend Tara? ....Yes that is her ex running for Lord Mayor............Yes he is rather dreamy............ Anyway look, she needs a new do. Can you fit her in this week? .... Yep, that would be perfect. You're a love. Talk to you soon.'

Blowing some kisses down the phone, she hung up. '12 o'clock next Saturday,' she informed me.

'I'm working Saturday,' I said, attempting to extricate myself from this crazy ride I seemed to be on.

'No you're not.'

I stared at Dinah, unable to believe that she had dobbed me in. Damn, it sucked when your boss was one of your best friends. I pulled a face at her and she had the nerve to look all innocent.

'But you're not working,' she said, picking up the magazine to continue.

Step number two - Get a new wardrobe - clothes and shoes.

More scrutiny from my friends.

'Hey,' I protested, 'I like my clothes.'

'Yes,' said Elaine, 'but they're not very feminine.'

'Well that's just me. Whoever I end up with is going to have to like me the way I am.'

'That's not the point,' said Nat, shaking her head. 'This is about changing the energy in your life, allowing you to move on and embrace new experiences.'

'Have you been helping yourself to my self-help book collection?' I asked, causing her to burst out laughing.

I noticed Elaine look at her suspiciously, before beckoning Dinah to keep reading.

Step number three - Get a new hobby.

'Oh perfect,' said Elaine, as if unaware of the contents of the article, 'I know just the thing. I'll organise it and then surprise you.'

'It says it has to be done in order,' I protested.

'Oh don't you worry about the fine print, it'll be done in order. Go on Dinah.'

Dinah cleared her throat nervously.

Step number four - Have meaningless sex.

I let out a yelp.

'You have to have sex again *sometime*,' said Nat reasonably.

'I know that. I just don't want to be rushed into it.'

'It's been a year,' said Elaine, digging around in her handbag. She flicked open her wallet and handed me a card.

'Jesus, what the hell is this?' I squeaked. 'The phone number of a gigolo?'

Elaine laughed. 'No, it's the details of your new web-dating profile. Don't worry I'll set up the dates. You just have to sleep with one of them.'

'You are a machine,' Nat said admiringly.

'Thank you.'

'You just have to sleep with one of them.' I mimicked Elaine while screwing up my face. I was beginning to feel outnumbered.

Step number five - Travel to an exotic destination.

They looked at me.

'Well,' I admitted, 'I haven't been on a holiday for a while. That might be nice. And if I have to have sex first, at least I'll have earned it. All right,' I said to Dinah, 'give it to me, what's number six.'

'You're not going to like it.'

'What can be worse than meaningless sex?'

'Meaningful sex.'

What?' I yelled, trying to grab the magazine from her.

'Shhhh, people are looking,' said Dinah. 'It says right here.' She flicked the magazine around so I could see it.

Step number six - Have meaningful sex.

'I can't see that happening anytime soon,' I grumbled.

'Well it has to happen one day or you're going to spend the rest of your life alone,' said Dinah.

'Anyway,' said Nat airily, 'who says meaningless sex can't become meaningful sex?'

Elaine looked at her intently for a long time while I wondered what was going on. Had I become so self-centred, that I had missed something in one of my best friend's life? Then she finished her scrutiny of Nat and turning to me, asked, 'What, you'd rather spend the rest of your life with that foul mouthed cockatiel your mother gave you?'

I squirmed in my chair and muttered, 'Bird's gone.'

'Pardon?'

'The bird's gone,' I said a little louder.

'What? How?' asked Nat.

'I set him free this morning. I couldn't take it any more.'

'What are you going to tell your Mum?'

'That I woke up this morning and he was dead.'

'Don't forget to mention that you fed him last night and he seemed happy. Otherwise she may think he died of starvation,' said Nat.

'I'll tell her he sat on my shoulder while I watched TV and that I gave him a special treat to keep him occupied while I was gone. You know one of those cuttlefish thingies.'

'Christ,' said Elaine, 'this is why you have to have meaningful sex.'

I stuck my tongue out at her. 'All right, so what happens after I have meaningful sex?'

Step number seven – Obtain closure.

'What?' I asked. 'How?'

'I'm not sure about that part,' admitted Elaine. 'But I have faith that if you follow all the other steps, it will just happen naturally.'

'You just want me to have sex.'

'Yes I do dear, and the sooner the better.'

* * *

By the time I arrived home it was late afternoon and my hangover had morphed into a general tiredness. Cocky's cage - which I had placed on the sidewalk - was no longer there. I felt a momentary sadness, quickly followed by relief, and then by guilt that I hadn't returned the cage to Mum. Oh well, I would just have to buy her a new one if she wanted it back.

I rang Mum, relieved to get the answering machine, and left an over-detailed message about Cocky's death. I would see her tomorrow at my family birthday lunch; for now I just wanted to be alone to think. I hung up hoping she wouldn't smell a rat, and went to run a bath.

I love my apartment. Lily - my sister - and I had each inherited one from our great Aunt Bertha, who had died a couple of years ago. We had been overwhelmed at the generosity of the dear old lady who had spent most of her later life travelling overseas. They are in an old, red-brick building in Woollahra, which is an inner suburb of Sydney.

Lily's flat - which she rents out - is right next to mine. She has six children, and is expecting her seventh, so there's no way they could live there. When Jake and I split I had suppressed my sorrow by renovating - taking my apartment from its 1970's interior of brown and orange to a bright, modern flat.

My favourite room is the bathroom, which is large enough to fit a two metre-long spa bath. I spent a large portion of last year in that bath; initially crying, but later reading books or drinking wine - always by myself. I had hopes that one day it might be used for something more romantic - certainly not where I wanted to have my meaningless sex encounter, but meaningful sex? Well that was another thing entirely.

I dropped in a bath bomb scented with orange and lime and watched it start to fizz. Once it had finished, I followed it in - sinking into the hot water and sighing with pleasure. But just as I was starting to relax the magazine article popped into my head. I harrumphed in annoyance. Seven Easy Steps to Closure indeed. Was I really going to do this? I had to admit, it did seem like fun: my friends and I on a secret quest to find closure, but I didn't really like the idea of the internet dating, or the meaningless sex.

Had I ever had meaningless sex? I started sifting through my memories, sorting the few sexual encounters I'd had as meaningless or meaningful. The time I lost my virginity – definitely meaningful. Then about 8 months later I'd had what I thought was meaningful sex, but had turned out to be meaningless when the young man in question never contacted me again. That had taught me a big lesson. The time after that was definitely meaningless. It had been ego-driven sex - the need to be found attractive again after the previous gut wrenching experience. It had been fun, but not very rewarding and I had gone off meaningless sex after that. And then of course there was Jake. The memory flooded into my mind, shocking me with its intensity.

I managed to hold off sleeping with him until our fifth date, when the urge to feel his naked chest rubbing against mine became overwhelming. I spent the entire dinner staring into his deep brown eyes, engaging him in what I hoped was witty conversation. The whole time, all I could think about was unbuttoning his shirt and running my hands over the hardness of his stomach. During the entrée - a mouth-watering chilli mud crab which we shared, I imagined him gently teasing my bra straps off with his teeth. While we ate the main - a mixed hot and cold seafood buffet for two, I pictured him slowly sliding my skirt up my legs. By the time dessert was served - we shared a mixture of sorbets, I was visualising him throwing me onto the bed and ripping off my blouse before ravishing me with his mouth and hands.

I may have been able to resist if it weren't for the sorbet incident, which occurred after some dripped off the spoon I was offering Jake and onto his chin.

'Lemon,' I said, reaching out and wiping it off. Gently taking hold of my hand, he sucked the sorbet off my finger while staring into my eyes. Then he ran his tongue around my finger in a circular motion. If I hadn't been sitting, my knees would have given way.

(I have to admit at this point that I have a toe and finger sucking fetish. I just love having my digits sucked. It's not something I tell everyone - I am a little embarrassed by it. I put it down to my first boyfriend, when I was 15 and as innocent as a baby, sucking on my fingers while we watched a movie. He had stared straight ahead at the screen as if nothing was happening while I squirmed in my seat, experiencing feelings and emotions I had not known I was capable of.

My fetish did lead to one embarrassing moment while I was at Uni. I had played tongue hockey at a night club, with an extremely handsome rugby player. One thing led to another and we ended up back at his flat mucking around. I expressed a desire to have my toes sucked and he seemed happy to oblige. Unfortunately I had been wearing cheap, synthetic shoes, and unbeknown to me was suffering from a bad case of foot odour. The luckless fellow worked his way down my body until he got to my feet. He picked one up to start the toe ravishing, stopping with his mouth about an inch from my big toe. 'I'm sorry,' he spluttered, 'I just can't.' He collapsed on the bed, so overwhelmed by the smell of my feet and the alcohol he had consumed that he passed out. Anyway enough of that - back to the restaurant.)

I rushed off to the ladies, all hot and bothered, and examined myself in the mirror. My face was flushed and my nipples were sticking out through the material of my blouse. I splashed cold water on my face in an attempt to cool off, but some of it slid down my cleavage, only enhancing the sensual experience. There was nothing to do except grab the bull by the horn and invite Jake home for coffee. Then I would wait until he expressed a desire to take things further and calmly let myself be seduced.

The sexual tension in the car was so thick I had to think calming thoughts to stop myself leaping on him whenever we stopped at a red light. These calming thoughts were totally ruined by the left side of my brain, which is very arty and quite mischievous. One minute I would be deep breathing, picturing waves washing gently over golden sands and then pop, Jake and I would be on those golden sands, naked, with the waves washing gently over our feet. He was deep inside me, thrusting away. Christ, by the time we got home I was in quite a state.

I lasted until the front door was closed before leaping on him, pinning him to the door with my body and my mouth, while I tried feverishly to undo the buttons of his shirt.

'Here,' he grunted, buttons flying everywhere as he ripped it off.

The fabric of my blouse was a little softer and I heard fabric tear as he shredded it from my body. All I could think about was getting as close to him as possible. I had to feel naked skin moving against naked skin or I was going to go nuts. And even then it wasn't enough. I wanted to get under his skin, eat him up, and tear at him with my nails, all the time pulling him closer and closer until I got what I really wanted.

He took me there against the front door. Lifting me up so I could wrap my legs around his waist, he thrust straight inside me. I remember clutching his hair and calling out his name.

I felt weightless pinned against the door while I tried to pull him deeper and even deeper, until suddenly we both came, me bucking backwards against the door as the waves of my orgasm took me higher and higher.

When the overwhelming sensation had finally subsided, I managed to roll my eyes back to the front of my head and open them. He was watching my face, the remnants of pure lust fading from his. I was wearing my bra, undone at the back, and my skirt was up around my waist. His jeans were lying around his ankles, his boxers caught mid-thigh. His hair had been thoroughly ruffled by me running my hands through it and was standing up on top like a rooster. I don't think the whole episode lasted more than five minutes.

'Well,' he said, 'that's one to tell the grandchildren.'

And then he kissed me.

The sound of the phone ringing brought me out of my reverie. I could hear my mother's voice talking to the answering machine. 'Tara love. Sorry to hear about Cocky, I know how much he meant to you. Looking forward to seeing you tomorrow. Don't be late.'

My bath had been totally ruined by the memory of Jake. *Damn it*, I thought as I dried myself off. I didn't want to do this any more. I guess for a while I had, in a sick way, enjoyed the moping and crying. It had gotten out of hand though, and been going on far too long. Was deciding to move on enough to actually enable you to move on? Was that the catalyst I had been missing: a true desire to say goodbye to depression and self-pity? The letting go of the final tendril of hope? The acknowledgement that there would never ever be anything between Jake and me again?

I certainly hoped so. If it took a *Cosmo* magazine and 'Seven Easy Steps of Closure' to get me over the finish line, then by God I was going to do it. The hair, the shopping, the dating, the meaningless and the meaningful sex, I suddenly wanted it all. I went to bed that night feeling positive for the first time in a year.

* * *

I was, as usual, late arriving at my parent's for lunch the next day. My Mum and Dad - Elizabeth and Albert Babcock, better known as Bet and Bert - retired to Umina Beach about 10 years ago. Umina Beach is 60 kilometres north of Sydney, and is only a 75 minute train ride from town. They have a cute little cottage with a big back yard, and are close enough to the beach to hear the waves and smell the salt.

Dad is a keen gardener and spends most of his days out the back with his impressive shed, listening to sports on the radio. He has created an edible garden around the side of the house where he grows their fruit, vegetables and herbs. When you walk out the back you are overwhelmed by the sight and scent of the different types of flowering bushes he has planted. Beautiful camellias, gardenias and rose bushes are predominant. But he has also used native bushes, different types of bottlebrushes, and every morning and night the wild birds flock to the yard to feed. Fantastic red, green and blue plumed lorikeets, gorgeous galahs, and even white cockatoos have been known to drop in to visit.

Choruses of 'Happy Birthday' greeted me as I entered, and three of my eldest nieces welcomed me with a group hug. Lily, who is 4 years older than me, is like a copy of me that someone drew in different colours. We are the same height and build, but while I have brown eyes and hair, she has dark blonde hair and green eyes. I am jealous of the green eyes, but happier to have my olive skin over her strawberry and cream complexion. She just has to think about going outside to get sunburned.

Lil is married to a wonderful man called Martin. They were childhood sweethearts who drifted apart and then ran into each other again at University.

Quite literally.

Lily, late for a class, was running down the library stairs, her arms full of books. She crashed straight into Martin. Books and bags flew everywhere and they ended up in a jumble of arms and legs on the ground. According to Lily they looked into each other's eyes and, *'Bam, it was like a lightning bolt going straight through me'*.

They've been together ever since and as I mentioned previously, are expecting their seventh child. Crazy, I know, but they just love children.

All of Lily and Martin's children are girls. I'm told it has something to do with Martin being a pilot. They don't seem to have any secret yearnings for a son thankfully, because this one is a girl as well. Like Lily, all of their children are named after flowers. Initially I thought it was a bit poxy, but Martin always refers to them as his bouquet which is quite sweet. In descending order of age we have Rose, 12, Lotus, 11, Tulip, 9, Petunia, 7, Blossom, 5, Camellia 3, and they are calling number seven, Iris. I'd been all for Snapdragon but Lily had haughtily advised me that Snapdragon was not an acceptable name for a child.

'Hi Mum,' I said, watching her take a roast lamb out of the oven. My stomach started to grumble in response to the aroma.

'Hi baby.' She took her oven mitts off and kissed me on the forehead.

Lily pulled a wrapped present out of her bag and came over to give me a hug.

'I want to give Aunty Tara her present,' Rose said.

Lily shrugged her shoulders and handed the present to Rose.

'No, I want to,' said Tulip.

'I want to,' chipped in Petunia and Blossom.

The girls started to wrestle with my present in an attempt to gain control of it.

'I hope it's not breakable,' I said to Lily, well aware of what was about to happen.

'Don't be silly,' she said, easing her slightly enlarged body into a chair and settling in for the fight.

Camellia, who was too short to reach and too young to understand what all the fuss was about, started crying and was quickly followed by Blossom - who didn't have enough strength in her pudgy little hands to hold on.

'Wahhhhhhh,' wailed Camellia.

'Boohoohoo,' cried Blossom.

Petunia landed a nice shin kick on Lotus who dropped to the ground and was out of the running. Tears welled in her eyes while she rubbed her shin, but she bravely managed to hold them back.

Rose, Tulip and Petunia still had firm grips on the gift. Rose had the advantage of age and height, Tulip wasn't far behind, but Petunia had - quite by necessity - become a very cunning and dirty fighter. With her spare hand she reached out and tugged on Rose's dress. Rose was just starting to develop breasts and had unfortunately worn an elastic-topped, strapless number, which responded to Petunia's enthusiastic tugging by turning into a skirt. Rose screamed and ran crying from the room with her arms clutched over her chest.

Mum handed me a glass of wine and took a seat for the final round.

Tulip and Petunia circled each other like pro boxers in a ring. Tulip tried a lunge to the left but Petunia moved with her. Petunia tried to land a kick but Tulip, dancing like a ballerina, easily dodged the blow. I took a sip of my wine.

'This is really good Mum,' I said, holding the glass up to look at the wine.

'Thanks,' she said, 'it's Giesen.'

We both winced as Tulip risked her hold to pinch Petunia under her right arm. Petunia squealed but responded by tightening her grasp.

'Where's Giesen from?'

'New Zealand - Marlborough region.'

'Ahh, no wonder I like it so much.'

Just at that moment Petunia faked a look of horror and peered above Tulip's head.

'Spider!' she squawked, very riskily letting go with one hand to point at the ceiling.

This tactic may not normally have worked, but the last time the girls had stayed with their grandparents they had been playing hide and seek in the garden and poor Tulip had ended up with a huge huntsman spider on her head. She had come very close to knocking herself out cold with a shovel.

Tulip let out a huge 'Aieeeeeee', and releasing the gift, launched herself sideways through the air into an impressive commando roll. She bounced back onto her feet and starting searching her hair for the spider.

Lily, Mum and I laughed, watching Petunia do her victory dance.

'Oh yeah, oh yeah,' she chanted, while waving the present in the air.

Tulip, realising she had been tricked, kicked the carpet and went over to shake hands with Petunia.

'Nice play,' she said grudgingly.

Martin and Dad had arrived for the last half of the battle and both applauded Petunia's efforts. She bowed in their direction and then deposited the present in my lap.

As I was opening it, there was a knock at the front door.

'That'll be Aunt Esme,' Mum called out to Dad.

'Aunt Esme?' I asked in horror.

Mum looked sheepish. 'Sorry love,' she said, 'I accidentally mentioned your birthday when I was on the phone last week. Of course she insisted she come.'

I sighed, resisting the urge to sulk. Aunt Esme was Mum's Aunt. A tall, elegant lady with an acid tongue, she had never gained my vote for favourite relative of the year. She loved Tash of course - but Lil and me? Well I guess she loved us in her own weird little way.

Aunt Esme developed a heart condition a few years ago, which she is not scared to use to her advantage. If something isn't going her way she'll clutch her chest, roll her eyes back in her head and start moaning. Two years ago, sick of her demeaning attitude towards us, Lil and I had decided to test our theory that the heart condition was non-existent. Unfortunately we had underestimated her acting skills and her competitive nature. Consequently the whole family spent Christmas Eve at the Gosford Emergency Ward, waiting to hear if we had killed her. We still think it's all bluff, but as the wily old bat is prepared to go the whole hog to get her way, we have to concede every point.

It was during lunch that the topic I had been dreading was raised.

'So,' said Aunt Esme, watching me carefully, 'Jackie tells me that Natasha and Jake are engaged.'

'Yes,' I said, trying to keep the expression on my face neutral, 'so I've heard.'

'What?' said Lily in outrage. 'You're not even divorced yet.'

'In all fairness to Jake,' I replied, managing with super-human effort to maintain a level voice pitch, 'you have to be separated for a year before you can file for divorce. Oh wait,' I said, 'it's been a year now, so I guess I'll be getting a surprise sometime this week.' I let out a little laugh, aiming for a casual devil-may-care affect. I sounded instead a little like a chicken being strangled.

'Well,' said Mum, 'the sooner you get him out of your life completely, the better. Mind you if he becomes Lord Mayor none of us will be able to get him out of our lives.'

'Hmmmm,' I said nonchalantly, as I shoved a huge piece of potato into my mouth followed by an even larger piece of lamb and proceeded to chew noisily. My gross tactic appeared to work and Aunt Esme, who can't abide noisy eaters, was momentarily distracted.

'Really Tara,' she admonished, 'you'd think you hadn't eaten for a week.'

I gulped loudly and grabbed my wine. 'Oh look, I'm empty,' I said, after I'd skolled the remnants in my glass, 'anyone else for more?' Hopping up I proceeded to top up the still full glasses around the table.

'Jackie tells me the way he proposed was so romantic,' Aunt Esme continued. 'You don't mind me talking about it dear?' she asked me, fake sympathy fairly oozing from her voice.

I knew she was trying to get a rise out of me, so she could clutch her chest and pretend to swoon. Mum was staring at me with wide eyes - silently willing me to behave myself, so instead of pouring the contents of my wineglass over Aunt Esme's head - which would have given me a few seconds satisfaction, I replied airily, 'Of course not. I'm so over him that I couldn't be more over him.' Realising how silly that sounded I took another swig from my glass and sat back down. Lily squeezed my knee under the table in sympathy as Aunt Esme continued.

'He took her horse riding at sunrise along a beach, and there was a table set up overlooking the water. He had organised one of the top chefs from the Hilton to cook breakfast for them right there.'

I picked up a toothpick and began to clean between my teeth, thoroughly examining the end of the pick as I went for any signs of plaque.

'And then it turned out that her serviette was really a big treasure map and she had to follow the map and find the clues.'

Yawning loudly I stretched my arms above my head.

'It took her all along the beach until finally she found the place on the map where the treasure was.' Aunt Esme was really getting into her story.

'They did that once in *The Bold and the Beautiful*,' interrupted Lily, bravely attempting to stall her without causing a myocardial infarction. Aunt Esme looked at her. 'Ridge was proposing to Taylor, mmm, could have been

Brooke - I can't keep up with them. Anyway he did a treasure hunt on the beach and she found a little chest, and in it was an engagement ring.'

Pink spots the size of twenty cent pieces appeared on Aunt Esme's cheeks. '*The Bold and the Beautiful?*' she said scornfully. 'You stay-at-home Mums have it far too easy.'

Martin put a restraining hand onto Lil's arm as Aunt Esme continued her story. 'Anyway in the chest was a little heart with Jake's name on it. And when she picked it up he said, "My heart is in your hands, will you marry me".'

She looked positively teary. I, however, had a strong desire to throw up.

'And then a man appeared with a limousine and whisked them off to Tiffany and Co.'s. They had the whole shop to themselves while she picked out her engagement ring.'

'That's like in *The Bachelor*.' You had to give Lil ten out of ten for persistence.

'Huh?' The pink spots on Aunt Esme's face blossomed till they covered her entire cheeks.

Mum was making shut up hand motions but Lil ignored her and continued. 'In the show *The Bachelor*, when he is choosing between the last two girls he takes each of them to a jewellery store where they pick out an engagement ring, and then the next day when he chooses the winner he proposes with the ring.'

'I doubt very much Jake would watch a show like *The Bachelor*.' Aunt Esme's voice dripped with derision.

'Everyone finished?' I jumped up and started clearing the table before Aunt Esme could remember she had a dicky heart.

I wanted to do the dishes to take my mind off her story, but as the birthday girl I was forbidden to even enter the kitchen. I took my glass of wine and retired to the garden where there was an extremely comfortable chair. It was only normal, I guess, that I would think about how Jake had proposed to me, comparing and analysing the differences.

We had been dating for two months when I turned 22, and were just starting to reach a comfortable place in our relationship. He had taken me out to dinner and I was a little nervous, never having done any official gift exchange with him before. I was a little panicked thinking, *What if I don't like it? Or what if it's a really functional, useful present?* When let's face it, all we really want is something pretty. Or even worse... *What if he doesn't even get me a present?* Then I would have to pretend that it didn't matter, when I knew deep down I would be devastated. Not that I wanted something big or ludicrously expensive - rather just a token of his affection.

We had just finished dinner when the waiter appeared at the table with a wrapped box, sporting a big bow. It was from Jake and I could tell he had wrapped it himself because the raw ends of the paper hadn't been folded under.

So I shook it and, looking cheekily at him, said, 'What is it?'

'You're going to have to open it to find out,' he answered, quite seriously.

I unwrapped it and there was another box inside, also wrapped. And then another and another, like a game of pass the parcel, until finally I was left with a tiny box, and I thought, *Oh God he's bought me a piece of jewellery, I hope it's not a locket.* I started mentally practising my Oh-God-it's-so-beautiful-I-really-really-love-it face.

I opened it and inside was the most beautiful diamond ring I had ever seen. It was princess cut in white gold - a dainty thing with a claw setting. My breath caught in my throat, and then he was on his knees in front of me proposing.

I started crying; it was the most beautiful thing that had ever happened to me, and of course I said yes - although it sounded more like this, 'YEEEEESSSSSSSS!'

The manager of the restaurant popped the cork on a bottle of champagne, and we rang our parents to tell them the good news. I can honestly say that, apart from our wedding, it was the happiest moment of my life.

I was distracted from my thoughts by my father joining me.

'Look at that,' he said. Panther - my mother's huge black cat - was lying in the sun while the birds played around him. 'Damned thing, won't even try to catch a mouse.' Dad shook his head.

I knew what he was referring to. Panther had - a while ago - decided that his favourite game was hunting Dad. He would hide in the garden while Dad worked, waiting patiently till he could launch himself from his hiding place onto Dad's back. The first time it happened - Dad had admitted quite shamefaced - he had peed himself in fright.

I wasn't the only one ending up with animals from the shelter where Mum worked. She had personally taken on the responsibility of finding happy homes for the pets that had been mistreated by their owners. Unfortunately they were often the ones with the psychological problems. Mum and Dad had Panther and Fluffy - a huge Great Dane that thought it was a lap dog.

Right at that moment Fluffy joined us in the garden, backing up slowly till the very end of his butt rested on

Dad's knee. He lifted his hind legs off the ground and perched there happily.

'Dog should come with a reversing alarm,' Dad said gruffly, but he started to scratch him behind his ears. Fluffy groaned in appreciation and nudged further back onto Dad's knee.

'How're you holding up?' Dad asked.

'Oh just fine and dandy,' I replied brightly.

Dad was not fooled by my tone of voice. 'You've got to forgive your Aunt Esme,' he said.

I looked at him quizzically.

'She doesn't mean to hurt you.'

'Really?' I said, looking at him with raised eyebrows.

He laughed a little and looked over his shoulder to make sure she wasn't within hearing range. 'All right,' he conceded, 'she's a cantankerous, nasty old cow, who gets pleasure out of other people's misery, but she's the only relative - apart from Jackie - that your Mum has left.'

He reached out and took my hand. I was fine until he touched me, but then I could feel tears threatening to overflow. I concentrated on containing them.

'I'm going to be all right Dad,' I assured him, when I could finally speak again.

'I know you are sweetheart. I know you are.'

We sat like that for a long time, holding hands and enjoying the uncomplicated silence between us.

* * *

Dinah's surgery is on Oxford Street in Paddington. There are three working rooms, a sterilising bay, an office, a bathroom and a tearoom. She has another full-time dentist,

Mark, and a hygienist, Rana, working for her in the other two surgeries. I organise the running of the practice - the rosters, ordering and chasing up of bad debts, as well as the marketing. I also fill in when someone is sick, and have become a proficient dental nurse. The practice operates from 8am to 8pm. Dinah and Mark take it in turn to work the late shift and alternate Saturdays. Thankfully, I get to go home at 5pm every day.

The best thing about Dinah's practice is that it is situated above Beethoven's - a German teacake shop. The lingering smell of the night baking is waiting for us when we open the surgery in the morning, making you want to run straight down there and eat something. I gained a few kilos when I first started working for Dinah and now have to be very careful about how often I visit the shop. Right next door is a lovely little café called Biscuit. They do great take-out salads, so when I am too lazy to take lunch to work I eat there.

The first day back after my birthday weekend was pretty routine. I did the morning banking - being very careful not to inhale too deeply as I walked past Beethoven's. The shock of the engagement could very easily have turned into a cake feeding frenzy. On my way back from the bank though, I saw it. A life-sized picture of Jake, whizzing past me on the side of a bus with the caption, *Vote one, Jake Wellington for Lord Mayor.*

'Good to see Uncle Edward's money being put to good use,' I said, as I headed into Beethoven's.

Dinah was in the tearoom having a cuppa when I returned. She looked at my purchases and raised one perfectly shaped eyebrow.

'Just saw Jake on the side of a bus.'

'Lucky me,' she said, helping herself to a wedge of bee sting cake. 'Of course if you do this every time you see a photo of him during the campaign, we're going to be obese by the election.'

'I know. It was just such a shock.' I placed a slice of pear crumble onto a plate and then ladled some into my mouth - moaning as the custard rolled over my tongue. 'I never get over how good this is. Anyway, it's still my birthday week.'

My phone gave the little chime it does whenever I receive a text message. I could tell straight away by the terrible spelling and misused words it was from Mum. She hasn't quite mastered the art of predictive texting.

High Lara. Will bee round tonight with knew pet for you. Do you want to do diner? Love Nun.

I snorted with laughter and showed Dinah.

'Hey,' she said, 'at least your Mum has a mobile phone.'

I responded, resisting the urge to use horrible spelling.

Sure Mum. See you when I get home.

* * *

Mum had let herself in, and was having a glass of wine on the balcony by the time I got home. There was a kitty litter by the balcony door and a bag of cat food on the kitchen bench. Perched on her lap was the prettiest little cat I'd ever seen. It was white with a black patch over the right eye and ear. The front left and back right legs were also black. It had blue, blue eyes and a pink little nose.

'For me?' I asked.

Mum nodded. 'This is Princess. Princess, meet Tara, your new Mum.'

As if on cue Princess stretched, jumped off Mum's lap, and wandered over to me. She wound herself around my legs purring.

'She likes me.' I picked her up and then poured myself a glass of wine before joining Mum on the balcony. Princess turned around and around on my lap before settling down to sleep.

'Did you want to stay the night?' I asked.

'Sure love. I told your father I probably would. I brought down some beef stroganoff for us to eat.'

'Thanks Mum. I've got nothing in the fridge.'

'Yes, I noticed that,' she said in a disapproving tone. 'I took the liberty of getting you some groceries.'

'Jeez Mum, you didn't have to.'

'Think of it as an apology.'

'What on earth for?' I asked mystified.

'For yesterday, I should never have let Esme come to your birthday lunch.'

I sighed. 'It's all right,' I said. 'It's about time I get over them anyway.'

'Do you want to talk about it?' she asked kindly.

'Not really,' I said. 'All I've done for the last twelve months is talk about them and think about them. To tell you the truth I'm sick of hearing myself go on about it.'

She looked at me for a long moment before nodding her head.

'So,' I asked, 'what's Princess in for?'

'To be honest I'm not sure. I think maybe she just got lost.'

'Hmmm,' I said unconvinced, 'we'll see.'

After dinner Mum and I slumped on the couch chatting. She picked up *Breaking Dawn*, the last Stephanie Meyer's book in the *Twilight* series, which was lying on my coffee table.

'Oooohhhh,' she said, 'is it good?'

'Oh my God, Mum. You have no idea.'

I had been so keen to get the book I had queued - feeling idiotic - at seven in the morning, with the swarms of schoolgirls, the day of its release. Participating in the stampede when the shop had finally opened, I had returned home triumphantly with my copy - taken the phone off the hook - and read all day and night until I had finished. I was currently reading it for the third time.

'Hey you know that the movie is coming out in November? Do you want to go and see it?'

She nodded her head eagerly, her gaze still fixed on my copy of *Breaking Dawn*.

'Take it with you.' I nodded at the book.

'Oh no.' She indicated the bookmark half way through. 'I couldn't. You finish it first.'

'Mum, I've already read it two times.'

Faster than the eye could see Mum whipped up the book, greedily clutching it to her chest as she pretended to look at her watch.

'Oh dear, look at the time.' She stretched and yawned dramatically. 'Night love.' And with that she was gone, off to the spare bedroom and no doubt several hours of uninterrupted reading.

My mother is - if it's possible - an even bigger *Twilight* fan than me.

* * *

The next morning I was in my office doing the wages when Susan - the receptionist - brought in an envelope.

'This one's addressed to you,' she said, shrugging her shoulders. 'I didn't want to open it in case it was personal.'

'Thanks,' I said smiling at her. 'I'm sure it's just marketing brochures.'

God, I'm so stupid, I didn't see it coming.

Ripping open the top of the A4 envelope, I slid the contents onto my desk and found myself staring at a letter from the law firm Jake worked at.

'What is it?' Susan asked.

I was having trouble reading it, the letters swimming in front of my eyes. 'Oh,' I finally said breezily, hoping the words wouldn't get stuck in my throat, 'just divorce papers.' My smile now frozen on my face, I stood up and brushed past poor Susan - who was looking mortified - and into the tearoom, where I put on the jug, and got the cake boxes out of the fridge.

'What are you having?' asked Dinah when she entered several minutes later.

I hopped up, my mouth too full to talk, and poured her a coffee. Finally I managed to swallow. 'Well, I started with the crumble, which you know I can never resist, then I had some tea-cake and now I'm onto the bee sting.'

'Wow,' said Dinah, 'did I miss something?'

'Oh, nothing much,' I said nonchalantly. 'Just got divorce papers in the mail.' I nodded at the document, which had some custard smudged on the cover sheet.

'Have you told Nat yet?'

'No. I'm going to need a lawyer aren't I?'

Dinah nodded.

I guess it's normal when faced with an ending, to find yourself considering the beginning.

It was a perfect sunny day the morning of our wedding. I shared a champagne breakfast with my bridesmaids, sitting in the courtyard at Natalie's house. Part of me was excited, but the other part, exhausted from the wedding preparations, just wanted to go and lie down somewhere really, really quiet.

(We had had huge dramas the day before when Jess - Jake's twin brother who lives in India - had rung to say he wasn't coming. Jake's Mum - Juliette - had gone into hysterics and then insisted on totally rearranging the table seatings. In the process Mum and Dad had been sentenced to the far corner of the room. I had finally managed to right the wrong and unruffle the ruffled feathers, but it had left me drained and devoid of all emotion.)

As the morning progressed and the champagne flowed, the part of me that was excited gained dominance and brought along with it his old friend Mr Nerves. I was feeling positively ill by 11am when the hairdresser and make-up artist arrived. I was distracted for a while by Tash complaining that she didn't want her make-up done first or it would be ruined by 3pm, when the wedding began. Then I remembered that it was my wedding, so I told her to stop whingeing and get on with it. Of course Tash being Tash, went into a sulk until Dinah said she'd go first. I could see Nat - who was having a manicure - making rude gestures behind Tash's back - which made me laugh, and then everything was all right again.

We were in the cars and practically pulling up at the front of the church when we realised we had left the flowers at home. 'Keep going,' I screeched at the driver who sped up and whizzed right on by, with the other two cars following in confusion. Everyone's phones started ringing at once. Nat was trying to ring Dad to let him know what was happening, but he was trying to ring me. I had answered mine to explain to Tash why we had turned around, while Dinah was trying to ring Mum, because we couldn't get onto Dad.

And then my phone rang, and it was Jake wanting to know if he'd been left at the altar. I was so uptight all I could do was laugh - which pissed him off, so Nat grabbed the phone and explained that we had forgotten the flowers. Finally Dinah's phone rang and it was Mum in tears assuming I'd changed my mind, and wanting to talk to me about my pre-wedding jitters. Dinah explained that we had forgotten the flowers, and Mum said, 'But we have them in the car with us.' So all the cars did a U-turn, and headed back to the church.

Everyone from the church had crowded onto the pavement and when we got back they broke into a round of applause. Dinah jumped out first and was bowing to the audience and laughing. Then she helped me out of the car and there were oooohs and aaaaahs, before everyone realised that they were meant to be in the church when I arrived. There was a mass stampede back inside, during which, I am pleased to say, none of the children or elderly were trampled to death.

Mum and Dad handed out the bouquets and then, it was time. I could hear the organist start up and suddenly we were walking down the aisle. Light was streaming through the stained glass windows, cascading over the congregation and the masses of flowers. It was breathtaking.

Between the camera flashes I could see faces peering at me. As we moved slowly down the aisle I was looking for familiar ones when suddenly I saw Jake up the front in his tuxedo. He looked so handsome I felt like someone had put their hand around my heart and squeezed. We stared into each other's eyes, and from then on I saw no-one but him.

The rest of the ceremony is a bit of a blur, but all of a sudden we were being pronounced man and wife and he was lifting my veil and kissing me so passionately that my belly did a couple of laps around the rest of my body and my knees went weak. The next half an hour was spent greeting everyone at the church; all the time watching each other across the room disbelieving we were married.

Finally the photographer took over and it was off for copious amounts of photos. I hadn't wanted professional photos, but Jake had assured me we would be glad to have them later. (I am planning to turn mine into a dart board, so I guess he was right.) By the end, my face ached and my head hurt from all the smiling. I found myself thinking longingly of a quiet room and a big bed.

Then we had dinner and the speeches, which we kept short. I had once been to a wedding where the speeches went for four hours - the only entertaining part of the evening was when one of the Aunts fell asleep with her head on the table and dribbled all over the tablecloth.

There was a bit of excitement after dinner. One of Jake's mates had brought his sister along as a date. She was a very attractive girl, with a voice a bit like a foghorn. I could see all the other girls at the table getting disgruntled as she flirted wildly with all the men. Eventually she focused on one and started playing footsies under the table with him. Not very subtly either, as she was staring quite provocatively at him and, I heard later, running her tongue around her lips. They progressed to the dance floor where they started smooching. I lost track of them for a while after that, but apparently he persuaded her to accompany him to the cloakroom, where the real action began. Poor old Aunt Agnes got quite a shock when she went to retrieve her fur coat, only to find it being used as a mattress by the ardent couple.

He must have said something at that point that indicated he had no intention of taking their relationship any further than the cloakroom. She was devastated - probably already imagining them having breakfast in bed the next morning while they planned their week together - and rushed off to the ladies where she proceeded to spend the next two hours crying.

Meanwhile, we cut the cake and did the bridal waltz. Dad and I had a bit of a spin around the floor. I was surprised at how proficient he was. Mum giggled when I mentioned it, confiding that Dad had been quite a stallion in his day; a good athlete and deft on the dance floor, even competing in some ballroom dancing competitions. Apparently all the other young ladies had been heartbroken when she'd snapped him up. She giggled again and fluttered her eyelids at him. I saw him blush and get a shy smile on his face, and I had a feeling that the cloakroom couple would not be the only ones seeing a bit of action that night. I must admit it made me feel a little nauseous.

'Penny for your thoughts,' said Dinah, disturbing my memory.

'Just thinking about the wedding, and what a waste of time and money it was.'

Dinah nodded sympathetically.

'Who would have guessed it would come to this?' I asked, pointing at the divorce papers.

I noticed Dinah had a look of distaste on her face that spoke volumes. She had never really liked Jake, and I'm guessing she had always been pretty sure it would come to this. 'He's an arsehole Tara. Always was and always will be.'

For once I didn't even try to defend him.

'Even the way he left you. That says a lot about a person.'

'Remember when we packed up my stuff at the house?' I asked.

'Uhuh. Do you think he ever found his Rolex?'

'Only if he's had the fish pond drained. Well,' I said, putting down my spoon and changing the subject, 'I'm looking forward to getting my new hairdo this Saturday. Do you want to go out for dinner afterwards to celebrate?'

'So you're really going to do this?'

'What have I got to lose?'

'True,' said Dinah, nodding her head, 'very, very true.'

Chapter Two

The First Step to Closure – Get a New Hairdo

I was sitting in the hairdressers', resembling a large wet rat and feeling no closer to obtaining closure. To make things worse, a huge billboard of Jake had been erected straight across the street from Funk Hair - which was Elaine's brother Tristan's hairdressing salon.

'Yummy,' Tristan had commented, rubbing his hands together when I pointed out the billboard to him and Elaine.

Elaine had kindly responded by sliding one of the pot plants into the window, and positioning me with my back to the board. But if I bent down a little and peered into the mirror I could still see the side of his face, one of his legs and the words Jake Well..... yor. It was a little disturbing.

Tristan is - of course - gay. He is much shorter than Elaine, and doesn't look anything like her - probably due to the fact that they have different biological fathers. Elaine's Dad died when she was quite young. She doesn't remember him and considers Tristan's Dad - a tidy looking Italian man - to be her father. Tristan has taken his father's dark looks and combined them with their mother's good looks and the results are quite stunning. A lot of the women who come to get their hair done at Funk Hair come to enjoy the scenery.

Tristan hires a bevy of gay men and women, all of them desirable. He also won the 'Australian Hairdresser of the Year' award two years running, so the patrons are never disappointed when they leave the salon. It normally takes weeks to get an appointment at Funk Hair and months if you want to see Tristan. I was very lucky to be one of Elaine's best friends.

'Hmmmmmm,' said Tristan thoughtfully, as he lifted my hair from my shoulders and held it around my face at different lengths.

'Ahhhhhhhhh,' said Tristan contemplatively, as he pulled my hair back behind my head and played with my fringe.

'Uh huh,' said Tristan decisively, as he looked at a colour chart and held different swatches of pigmented hair around my face.

'I didn't say anything about a colour change,' I whispered urgently to Elaine, who was flipping through a magazine with Benny asleep on her lap.

She held it up for me to see. 'See this Tara?' She pointed to the date. 'A current magazine - you and Dinah should try it some time.'

I stuck my tongue out at her.

Meanwhile Tristan had stopped work and was staring at me in the mirror with one eyebrow raised.

Uh oh.

'Did you not ask Elaine to fix this appointment for you?' he asked imperiously. (Have I mentioned that not only is Tristan gorgeous, but he is also a huge drama queen?) 'Did you not beg her to get you in with me as fast as possible?'

'Well actually,' I said.

'Shhhh,' he responded, holding one finger up in the air. 'You beg and you plead and now you insult the master.'

'Oh no, no,' I gushed, 'no, it's just that I've never coloured my hair before.'

'Never?' He held the back of one hand to his beautiful forehead as if about to swoon. When he had recovered he snapped, 'Sebastian, Veronica, major hair emergency. I need you here now.' And then he started pointing at the colour chart and very rapidly giving orders. I couldn't quite make out what he was saying, and I was trying really, really hard because I was starting to feel a little panicked. What if I looked awful when he'd finished? What if he gave me a hairdo that, while nice on someone else - someone hip and chic and eighteen years old - did nothing for me at all? And then I would have to smile into the mirror, and I mean really smile. Smile so that it made it right to my eyes while I gushed about my hair - when all I really wanted to do was go home and spend hours staring at myself in the mirror willing myself to like it. Oh and worse, I would have to pretend to Elaine that I loved it. I would never be able to get rid of it. Christ what had I done?

I was just contemplating ripping off the hairdressing sheet and legging it onto the street, when Elaine - obviously noting the look of sheer terror in my eyes - intervened.

'Tara, look at me,' she commanded. I met her green eyes in the mirror. 'Good. Now breathe in and breathe out.'

'Okey dokey, breathe.' I breathed in and out while maintaining eye contact with her. Then I felt my eyes start to slide sideways, measuring the distance between my chair and the door.

'LOOK AT ME!' she commanded in a truly scary voice. 'Right,' she continued when she had my attention, 'Repeat after me. It's just a new hairdo, not a life sentence in jail.'

'It's just a new hairdo, not a life sentence in jail,' I repeated robotically.

She made me repeat it a few more times until the words penetrated my thick skull and I started to relax.

'Veronica,' she called out, 'we're going to need some of the bubbly stuff over here.'

'Ohhh goody, bubbly stuff. I really like bubbly stuff,' I heard myself garble. 'Ughh Elaine, by bubbly stuff you mean champers, and not shampoo right?' (I had once had my mouth washed out with shampoo for swearing at Lily - an experience I would prefer never to repeat.)

Veronica answered my question by arriving with two flutes of champagne. At that precise moment Dinah and Nat both entered the studio.

'Two more?' asked Veronica, looking at them.

They both nodded and sat down with Elaine who said, 'Oh good, backup. I thought I was going to have to restrain her a few seconds ago.'

Nat, her blonde hair pulled back in a French roll, looked stunning in a little navy dress. She waved at me in the mirror. I gave her a sickly smile in return. And then Tristan was back.

'Do I need to blindfold you?' he asked. I shook my head. 'Good.' He lifted his hands - which now held scissors - and began to cut my hair.

I had a vision of Edward Scissorhands and, shutting my eyes, started to pray.

About twenty minutes later the cutting stopped. I opened my right eye a teeny, weeny bit and saw Sebastian arrive with a few little bowls containing coloured paste. I peeped into the mirror for a couple of seconds before slamming my eye shut in horror. My hair was really short. Shit, I was going to look like a little boy, not the sexy minx of a woman I had been imagining in my closure scene with Jake.

(I hadn't quite worked out the fine details of the closure scene, but I had gone through a few different scenarios and come up with one I liked a lot. I varied the little things - like where we were and what I was wearing - but they pretty much all ended with him getting down on his hands and knees and grovelling, while I contemplated the condition of my nails. In one I had changed the ending by having a gorgeous guy ride up on a motorcycle and screech to a halt in front of me. He managed - of course - to slide right through a strategically placed puddle of water which splashed all over Jake. I donned a helmet and jumped on the back of the bike, and as we rode off into the sunset I yelled, 'So long sucker,' over my shoulder. That version was currently my favourite.)

I tried to concentrate on my closure scene but my haircut kept interrupting me just when I got to the really vindictive part.

'No, not that one, the other one,' Tristan barked. I could feel alfoil being applied in layers and realised I was getting foils. He finally finished and said almost kindly, 'You can open your eyes now Tara.' I opened them to see him twist a little egg timer before departing for another patron; Sebastian and Veronica riding in his wake.

'How long?' I asked.

'Thirty minutes,' said Dinah, peering at the timer. 'Ooooh I can't wait to see.'

'Maybe we should get her eyebrows and eyelashes tinted while we're at it?' suggested Nat.

Elaine nodded - handed Benny to Nat - and swept off to have it organised.

Thirty minutes later when the timer went off, I was admiring my eyebrows and eyelashes in the mirror.

Ahh shit, I thought, *the moment of truth.*

I enjoyed the shampoo and head massage, but jammed my eyes shut again when I got back to the mirror. I just couldn't make myself look. Tristan reappeared and began the blow drying and styling process. I couldn't hear much over the dryer. He was telling Elaine about some new guy he was seeing, and I could hear a few remarks about how nice the colour was, but it wasn't enough to make me open my eyes. Then Tristan was trimming again - this time around my fringe - and I had an urge to ask him to leave me with some hair, but thought better of it. He was pretty close to my eyes with those sharp scissors - I really didn't want to piss him off.

And then the feel of the soft brush on my face and neck, and the sheet being removed; I could feel them all staring at me, but nothing was being said. Oh no, did I look that ugly? Slowly, I peeled open my eyes and examined their faces in the mirror. Nat and Dinah had excited looks on their faces. Hmmm, that was promising.

Elaine hopped up and kissed Tristan on the cheek. 'Thank you,' I heard her murmur.

But it wasn't until I heard someone else in the salon ask if they could have their hair done like that, that I had the courage to look at myself.

'Oh my,' I said.

The person staring back at me in the mirror was someone I'd never met before. She was cute and classy. I raised my hand to the short layers around my face, and felt the soft silkiness of my hair. The caramel colours that Tristan had chosen set of the golden glow of my skin, and enriched the darkness of my eyes.

I had a pixie cut; short at the nape of my neck, longer on top. My fringe was cut to curve over my right eyebrow, but the edges were chipped. I loved it.

'I've got to hand it to you Tristan. You are the Master.'

'Yehhh,' he squealed, jumping up and down and clapping his hands together, 'she likes it.'

'I love it Tristan. I really, really love it.'

* * *

Back home I gave Princess a cuddle and fed her dinner before rushing to get ready for my night out with the girls. I kept getting distracted by my reflection in the mirror and took a long time with my make-up. I put on a dress I hadn't worn for a while: a beautiful, chocolate clinging number I loved because it emphasised my arms and collar bones and not my arse. I hadn't felt this good for ages and was looking forward to the night out.

I wasn't the last one to the restaurant, which was good as I already felt guilty that they had given up their Saturday afternoon watching me get my hair done. Elaine - looking amazing in a bright red dress - and Dinah - wearing her customary tailored pants and blouse - were deep in discussion when I arrived. They stopped to eye me approvingly. I did a little twirl on the spot and Dinah wolf whistled.

'What's up?' I directed my question at Dinah as I sat down.

'I got home today and there was a message on my answering machine from Doug.'

'Dr Doug?' I asked.

'The very one.'

'He's got a nerve.'

Doug Stanson, (Dr Doug, as we called him in front of Dinah, because that's how he always introduced himself. Behind her back, we called him Creepy Doug), was an endodontist that Dinah had been dating for a while. (An endodontist is a dentist who specialises in root canal therapy. Dinah once told me she'd rather blow her brains out than do root canals all day. I would rather blow my brains out than have sex with Creepy Doug.) Dr Doug was arrogant and boorish. She hadn't seen him for a while, which was great because when she was with him she was an emotional wreck - swaying between euphoria that he wanted to be with her, and misery from the way he treated her. When asked if she loved him she would just shrug her shoulders miserably, and comment that she wasn't even sure if she liked him.

One of the psychobabble self-help books I had read during the last year had talked about how our relationships with our fathers set us up for our relationships with all men. I wasn't quite sure why I was such a screw-up; I mean my Dad was wonderful. He had never raised his voice or hand against me. (Okay not entirely true, I had - as previously mentioned - once had my mouth washed out with shampoo, but it was Mum who performed the foul deed so that didn't count. But I was once smacked by Dad when I was a little girl for locking our pet cat in a cupboard. In fairness to me I wasn't trying to be cruel. I had taken all this time to dress the meowing, complaining, wiggling cat up in my Baby Alive's outfit - having gotten bored with a supposedly alive doll that did nothing, and then had to go to kindergarten for the day. I hadn't wanted Milly - the poor cat - to get the clothes dirty before I had time to play with her, so had stuffed her into the laundry cupboard to keep her safe. I had put a lot of thought into where to keep her. The laundry cupboard was full of soft towels and sheets - I thought she'd be very comfortable there for the day. You can imagine poor Mum's surprise when she'd opened the cupboard to put away the towels, only to have a shrieking cat - dressed in an all-in-one lemon jumpsuit, hat and booties - propel itself from amongst the sheets to land on her head.) Anyway you get my drift - my relationship with my Dad was something I cherished.

Dinah however - well her Dad had been a different story entirely. He had finally drunk himself to death a few years ago. She had spent a lot of time at my and Nat's houses growing up, avoiding him and his foul temper. She once said that she thought of our fathers as her Dads. Dad had pretended he'd gotten a bug in his eye when I told him that, but I knew he was actually a little teary.

'So what did he want?' I asked, annoyance evident in my voice.

'Oh just wanted to know if I was going to the dental meeting on Monday night.'

'Are you?'

'Yeah. I rang him back and said I was. He said he was looking forward to seeing me and asked if I wanted a lift.' She held a hand up to stop the angry outburst that was obviously threatening to exit my mouth. 'I told him I would make my own way there.'

I rearranged my ruffled feathers. 'And that's that?'

'Well I may talk to him at the meeting, but that's that.'

'Promise?'

'Cross my heart.'

'Hope to die?'

'Stick a needle in your eye?' Elaine finished for me.

'Stick a needle in my eye.'

At that moment Natalie turned up. 'Sorry, sorry got caught up at work with a client.'

'What between the hairdressers and now you had to see a client?' asked Elaine suspiciously.

'Yes Elaine, I do have to work you know.'

Wow. We all stopped and looked at Nat who never, ever uttered a snarky word. She squirmed in her seat, still managing to look beautiful as her red face contrasted against her blonde hair.

'Sorry,' she apologised to Elaine, who was looking thoughtful and surprisingly not at all offended. 'This case is stressing me out.'

'Oh,' said Elaine, 'what's it about?'

'Oh nothing important or interesting,' Nat said evasively, waving one hand in the air. 'Now what did I miss? Have you ordered yet?'

'Just entrees. We got you the Oysters Kilpatrick.'

'Yummy. By the way Tara, you look great. I really love your hair. When are you doing step number two?'

'Next Saturday, but I was thinking of going to the movies on Thursday night. Anyone interested?'

'Oooh, yeah. I'd love to. I haven't been to the movies in ages,' said Nat eagerly.

'Do you want to meet at mine at about 6.30pm? We can get a cab and do dinner after.'

Elaine pulled out her diary, her green eyes thoughtful. 'I have a marketing meeting that afternoon but we should be done by then,' she finally said. She made a note before flicking to the next page. 'Yep can do Saturday as well,' she said smiling.

'I can do Thursday night, but I'll be working Saturday,' said Dinah apologetically, ruffling her short hair with one hand. 'Maybe we could do dinner again to showcase your new wardrobe.'

'That's a great idea,' Elaine said, making another note in her diary. 'I'll book a restaurant.'

When I got home that night the first thing I noticed was a foul smell coming from somewhere in my flat. Princess was fast asleep looking innocent in her bed. I looked at her suspiciously.

'All right, what have you done, and where did you do it?' I asked her.

She opened one eye and stretched luxuriously, before jumping lightly to her feet and strolling over to me to wind herself through my legs. The smell was coming from my bedroom.

'Oh crap,' I said when I looked into my room, and I meant it quite literally.

There was cat poo right in the middle of my bed. And I mean right in the middle. It was almost like she had measured the bed up. I had a mental image of her pacing off my bed, before stopping right in the middle to do her steaming dump. I stepped a bit closer. Oh no, she had peed as well.

'Yes that's right Mum,' I said 5 minutes later, 'right in the middle. I got my tape measure and checked it.'

(That's true. I really had got my tape measure out and checked it. It was a little bit freaky how accurate she was.)

'And I think I'm going to have to buy a new mattress,' I whined.

'No Tara - take it onto the deck, rinse it and put heaps of white vinegar through it. Then layer it with bi-carb soda.'

'What will that do?'

'It will pull the scent out.'

'Wow Mum, where did you learn that?'

'Actually dear, it's a technique I used quite a lot when you were a little girl.'

Twenty minutes later I had managed to wrestle the mattress onto the balcony and, using my watering can, had liberally applied water and then white vinegar. I was sprinkling on the bi-carb soda when I heard it.

'Nice tits, shame about the arse.'

I knew that voice. I searched the sky but couldn't see anything in the dark. Maybe I had imagined it.

'Polly was a slut, Polly was a slut.'

Shit. I hadn't imagined it. That was Cocky's voice.

I searched high and low but couldn't find the little bastard. In the end I went off to bed perturbed by the behaviour of the animals in my life. I dreamt that I was in the hairdresser's getting my hair cut, but half way through the dream, Tristan turned into a gigantic yellow cockatiel and when he finally turned me around to look at my hair I was totally bald. I woke up in a sweat, clutching my head, wondering where the hell I was before I remembered the mattress incident and that I was in the spare bedroom. I spent a few moments calming myself before I finally managed to drift off into a thankfully, dreamless sleep.

* * *

Dinah's nurse, Tina, had called in sick on Tuesday morning. I had my suspicions about the origin of Tina's illness as I had overheard her the day before talking on the phone about a birthday party she was going to that night. My suspicions were not enough to actually accuse her of having written herself off on a work night. Maybe she had made out with some guy at the party, and picked up a really virulent bug.

I was working in the surgery, filling in for Tina, and was guessing by the fact that Dinah wasn't talking that all had not gone well at the ADA meeting the night before. It wasn't until we brought through old Mrs Smith from the nursing home that she finally took a huge sigh and I knew she was ready to talk.

'What's he done now?' I asked, referring to Creepy Doug.

'Well you know how we had that dental association dinner last night?' she said as she picked up a needle. I nodded while I held Mrs Smith's hand. 'I ended up giving him a lift,' she continued, slowly injecting local anaesthetic into Mrs Smith's gum, 'but by the time I got my handbag out of the car he was gone.'

I held off mentioning that she had said they were going in separate cars - more for Mrs Smith's sake than mine. 'What, he didn't even wait for you?'

'Nope. Straight in to mingle with all the other hoity-toity, stuffy-nosed specialists.'

'Bastard,' I murmured in sympathy, placing the suction into Mrs Smith's mouth to collect the pooling saliva. It was not the first time this sort of behaviour had occurred.

'Then, when I finally located him by the bar, he's talking to Tiffany, this new endodontist that's just graduated.' She removed the needle from Mrs Smith's mouth and patted her gently on the cheek.

'What's so bad about that?' I asked.

'If you saw her, you'd know,' she said, making huge-breast hand signals as she sat the dental chair up.

'Have a rinse Mrs Smith.' Dinah moved over to the computer to make notes. 'Then the barman deposited two glasses of wine in front of Doug,' she continued quietly, 'and I thought at least he's bought me a drink.'

'Uhh ohh'

'Yep, not for me.' She banged on the keyboard angrily as she made the patient notes. Mrs Smith shot me a worried look over her shoulder.

I moved closer to Dinah and lowered my voice. 'That stupid prick bought some other chick a drink and didn't get you one?'

'Yep. All part of his keeping things separate policy I guess.'

'So what did you do?'

'Bought my own and then stood there feeling like an idiot with a stupid smile on my face, waiting for him to introduce me.'

'And?'

'Nope. Then they called dinner and somehow he ends up sitting with her, and I end up at the end of the table next to a boring periodontist, who quite ironically enough had bad breath.'

Mrs Smith looked up at her and said, 'What's a periodontist lovey?'

'Periodontists are dentists who specialise in cleaning teeth.'

'Ohh,' she said, nodding her head.

Dinah moved back to the dental chair and hit the button to lie it down.

'It was terrible. I could hear Doug and Tiffany laughing down the table. Tee hee hee,' she mimicked Tiffany - a high-pitched girly giggle. 'Dinner was awful; I spent the whole time trying not to cry. In the end I developed a massive headache and left before dessert.'

'What about Doug?'

'I figured the stupid bastard could find his own way home.' She picked up the high-speed drill and deftly inserted a bur into its head. 'Mrs Smith, does your lip feel fat?' she asked.

'What's that lovey? Do I feel fat?'

'No Mrs Smith - not you, your lip.'

Mrs Smith tapped her lip a few times before replying, 'Yes love.'

Dinah placed a cotton roll under Mrs Smith's lip and started to remove the old amalgam restoration that had been causing problems.

'Did he ring you or anything to see if you were okay?' I asked.

'Nope nothing, nadda, zilch. Can you feel that at all Mrs Smith?'

'No lovey, it's all good.'

'I didn't get much sleep,' she continued, 'cause I was lying there staring at my phone waiting for him to phone or text to see if I was all right. I even rang my phone with my mobile and my mobile with my phone to make sure they were both working.'

'Bastard,' I reiterated, sucking water from the back of Mrs Smith's throat. 'Dinah - how long are you going to put up with this?'

She sighed. 'I don't know. I think I'm better off without him, but then when it's over, all I can do is think about him. Matrix band and etch please.'

I handed them to her. 'He treats you like shit. I don't understand the attraction.'

'Neither do I,' she admitted, rinsing the tooth. 'Bond please. Sometimes I wonder if it is more to do with the fact that my ego can't handle not being good enough for him. Curing light.'

'It has nothing to do with you not being good enough and more to do with him being a prick.' I handed her the filling material.

'You're right, you're right, I know you're right. I have to finish this.' She packed the restoration into the tooth.

'It's not healthy.'

'I know it's not. Light please.'

Right at that precise moment her mobile burbled acknowledgement of an incoming text. She flicked an interested look over her shoulder at her phone before proceeding to remove the band and shape the restoration into Mrs Smith's bite. 'There you go Mrs Smith.' She sat her up. 'Have a good rinse in the bowl. Lean right over,' she advised as she got up to check her phone.

'It's him,' she breathed in relief, as she stared at the screen.

'What's he want?' I wiped Mrs Smith's face clean with a wet towel.

'Wants to know what happened to me last night?'

'It takes him until the next day to ask you that?'

'He's very busy,' she automatically defended as she texted rapidly. 'I told him I had developed a headache.' Her mobile very quickly blipped again. 'He wants to know if I can meet him.'

'Tell him to piss off,' Mrs Smith said as she stood up.

We both looked at her, shocked.

'Yes dearie, a nice girl like you, you can do better than that. Just you remember a leopard never changes his spots - they only get bigger.' She patted Dinah on the head as she made her way out the door to the waiting room.

'Well I'll be,' I muttered as I watched Dinah reply to the text. I started to wipe down the room getting ready for the next patient. 'What did you say?'

'Well I don't want to appear too keen or eager.'

'Excellent.'

'So I told him I'd be over after dinner tonight.'

'How is that not appearing too keen?'

'Well I'm not rushing over after work.'

'You're serious aren't you? You're really going over there.'

'Don't start on me Tara,' she warned me.

I put my hands in the air. 'Fine, do what you want, but just for the record I think that he's not good enough, and so does Mrs Smith. This will only end in tears. Again,' I added.

'We'll see,' she said in a coldly dismissive voice.

* * *

'Listen to this,' I said to Dinah and Elaine. It was Thursday night and we were waiting for Nat to turn up before heading off to the movies. I beckoned for them to follow me out onto the balcony. Straight away the abuse started.

'Fucking sluts.'

'Whoa,' said Elaine. 'Who the hell is that?'

'It's Cocky. He's stalking me. I can hear him, but I can't find him. The other day all my washing was covered in bird crap.'

'So he's loose?'

'Polly is a tart, Polly is a tart.'

'He's loose. It's getting to be a real pain.'

'Maybe you should put a trap out for him.'

'Hmmm. I hadn't thought of that.'

'Ring your Mum and ask if you could borrow some sort of trap. Surely they would have them at the shelter.'

'Well therein lies the problem. Mum thinks Cocky's dead.'

At that moment Princess strayed out onto the deck and, lifting her pretty little nose, sniffed the air. Her tail started to move from side to side in a flicking motion and she crouched into a hunting position.

'Well he must be close because she can smell him. Look at her,' said Dinah.

'How is Princess going?' asked Elaine, picking her up for a cuddle.

'Jury's still out on that one.'

'Why?'

'Well she started off well. But little things keep happening which make me think she's just a little bit psycho.'

'Like what?' asked Dinah in concern.

'First it was a cushion that she destroyed. Then she weed and crapped on my bed. I've only just got the stench out of it. Then last night I woke up and found her sitting on my chest with her face about an inch from mine. It scared the shit out of me.'

'What did she do when you woke up?' Dinah asked.

'Started licking me.'

'Well,' said Elaine, scratching Princess under the chin, 'that's just telling you that she loves you.'

'I wish she would work out a different way to tell me.'

'So Dinah, how was last night?' asked Elaine, changing the subject.

I made shushing hand motions at Elaine to shut her up. It had been apparent to me, even though Dinah had a smug, *I-got-laid-last-night-smile* all over her face when she turned up to work this morning, that she didn't want to discuss Doug. Elaine saw my frantic hand motions and chose to ignore them. Sometimes she can be a little too confrontational.

'Good thank you,' said Dinah mildly. 'Where the hell is Nat?'

'Yeah where is she?' I asked, genuinely perturbed. 'We're going to miss the movie if we don't go soon.'

I picked up my phone and rang her mobile. It went straight to voice mail.

'Try home,' said Dinah

I rang Nat's home - it went to her answering service.

'I've ordered the cab,' said Dinah, 'we're going to have to go or miss it.'

I flicked off a quick text to Nat and then locked Princess back in the apartment, giving her an array of toys to play with while I was gone. Grabbing my keys, I followed Dinah and Elaine down to wait for the cab.

'I'm worried about Nat.' I voiced my concerns out loud.

'She's probably just working on that case she was talking about,' said Dinah.

'You mean the case she wasn't speaking about,' retorted Elaine.

'What do you mean?' I asked.

'Well didn't you notice that she didn't tell us anything about it? I know client confidentiality and everything, but normally she gives us a little whiff of what she's working on. I think she's up to something.'

'What? Nat? No,' I said, 'not Nat.' I paused for a second. 'Like what?'

'I'm not sure. Have you noticed lately that she's been super happy?'

'It looks like she may get her promotion,' I responded.

'Not that sort of happy - more a suppressed, excited, I've got a secret, happy. And then that stuff she said the other morning after your birthday party.'

'What stuff?'

'All that stuff about changing the energy in your life. Oh and that bit about who says meaningless sex can't become meaningful sex. It definitely triggered my suspicion bone.'

While most people have funny bones, Elaine has a suspicion bone. She is always the first to question something, find the hole in your story or confront you with a lie you've told. She's really very good. Almost like a human lie detector. For quite a while now I've been saying the FBI should employ her to question suspects. When we first became friends, I used to think she was a cruel pessimist - always the one to accuse some poor woman of murder when her toddler went missing and was found floating dead in a nearby pond. The thing was - over the years - I realised she was normally right. And without question, a few days after I had accused her of being a heartless shrew, that woman would be taken in for questioning and charged with the murder. Of course I would then have to perform a seriously grovelling apology for the heartless shrew comments. So when Elaine said she thought Nat was up to something, you had to sit up and pay attention.

'No not Nat,' I said, more out of loyalty than conviction.

But in the cab on the way to the movie, as we chatted about our week, I found myself wondering. What was Nat up to?

Chapter Three

The Second Step to Closure –
Get a New Wardrobe

Ahhhh, the joys of clothes shopping: the smell of the leather shoes, the feel of the fabrics under my fingertips, the sight of my dimpled white arse glowing in the fluorescent lighting. I was a vision to behold in the outfit I had just squeezed into. It had taken me a good five minutes to get the pants up. I had struggled and jumped up and down in the dressing room, until the sales assistant - hearing the moaning and groaning - had come to the door to see if I was all right.

'I'm just great,' I said in my best now-piss-off-and-leave-me-alone voice.

'How does it look?' asked Elaine brightly, from the other side of the door.

'Fine and dandy, if you like muffin tops.'

'How bad can it be?'

'You have no idea.'

'Are you ready to show me?'

'Promise not to laugh.'

'You know I can't promise that,' she said.

I undid the lock and opened the door just enough to give one of Elaine's eyes access to the disaster in the changeroom.

'Oh dear,' she said on viewing the pants. I had pulled them up as far as possible but the zip was only one inch long. I mean seriously how were you meant to wear these? Exactly what body shape had they been designed for?

'Jump up and down,' she said.

I jumped about five centimetres off the ground a couple of times. I could feel the part of me flowing over the top of the waistband wobbling on when the rest of me had stopped. It was disconcerting.

'Bend over.' Elaine was obviously curious as to how far we could push the limits of the shiny, disco club material.

I bent over as far as I could without ripping open the back of the pants, which was not very far. When I stood back up, a small amount of pubic hair popped over the top of the pants. I saw Elaine's eyebrows shoot up as she started giggling.

Unfortunately the shop assistant chose that exact moment to join Elaine, and pulled open the door to get a better look. I squealed in horror and held both hands over the offending tuft of hair. Elaine was doing her darndest not to laugh out loud. Her eyes were filled with barely suppressed mirth and her face was turning as red as mine felt. She probably would have made it, if the sales assistant hadn't chosen that precise moment to say, 'Mmmm. They look quite nice.'

Elaine started howling with laughter. She thumped the door with her hand as tears rolled down her face.

'Are you serious?' I asked the sales girl incredulously as I pulled the door shut.

Elaine was hanging onto the cubicle for support, struggling to get a breath around her laughter. Finally when she had it under control she asked, 'Have you got them off yet?'

'No,' I replied sullenly.

'Why ever not?'

'Tried. Can't.'

That set her off again, and I had to wait for another humiliating minute until she had gained enough self-control to come in and help me.

'Tara, how did you get them up?'

'Pure determination.'

She grabbed the top of my pants and started wrestling them down. Everything was progressing swimmingly, until she got them half way down my thighs. I had begun to sweat and they were sticking to me like the skin on a sausage. One minute I was standing there relatively calmly while Elaine huffed and puffed and pulled and pushed, and the next I lost my balance and started swaying on the spot like a tree about to fall.

'Oohahoohaahoooa,' I said, sounding an awful lot like a monkey, and then I toppled onto Elaine. We went crashing out of the changeroom door and into the aisle, where I lay flopping around like a fish, with my pants half way down.

'Well,' said Elaine, clambering up and grabbing the pants around my thighs, 'you can't say shopping with you is boring.'

I lifted my hips off the ground to assist her determined effort. The shop assistant hovered in the entry, watching us with a look of dismay on her face. Elaine swivelled around and smiled sweetly at her. 'Nearly got them,' she assured her before resuming her tugging.

'That is why I hate clothes shopping,' I informed Elaine, as we left the shop.

'Rubbish,' she said poo-pooing me, 'you just need to try on the right clothes for your body shape. No more tight pants.' Which I thought was pretty unfair, seeing as how the pants had been her idea in the first place.

'I think we should start with the shoes.' My stomach let out a huge gurgle.

'Coffee first?' suggested Elaine, turning into a café.

'And cheesecake,' I said, 'although if those pants are anything to go by I'm going to have to do a killer session at the gym this afternoon.'

'I might join you,' said Elaine, patting her own perfectly flat stomach.

We ordered our coffee and cake and then relaxed at a booth while we waited.

'Have you heard from Nat?' asked Elaine.

'Oh sorry, I meant to tell you. I had a text from her this morning.'

'So, she's alive.'

'Yep. I still can't believe she didn't show the other night.'

'I have a feeling all will be revealed tonight.'

'Why?'

'Because whatever it is, it's coming to a head. If we were to graph the events we would note that the out of character occurrences are becoming larger and more frequent; a bit like a volcano working up to a full eruption.'

'Or a serial killer,' I suggested.

We looked at each other and laughed.

'No, not a serial killer,' I said.

Our coffees and cake arrived and we were silent while we added sugar and stirred.

Elaine took a sip of her coffee and sighed. 'What are you getting Dinah for her birthday?'

'I haven't got a clue. I have however made a booking at a restaurant in Darling Harbour for dinner.'

'It's the Friday night right?'

'Yep. I hope she's better behaved on her thirtieth birthday than I was.'

'That wouldn't be too hard.'

'You know she's invited Creepy Doug?'

'Uhhuh. She told me the other night. That guy gives me the heebie jeebies.'

'Me too. I hope he doesn't ruin her birthday.'

I placed a little bit of the cheesecake in my mouth and rolled it around, trying to coat as many tastebuds at once as possible. I sighed. Baked - my favourite.

'Are you bringing anyone?' I asked curiously. I wasn't sure who Elaine was seeing at the moment. They never lasted long, and to me they all looked alike; young and handsome with good bodies.

'Most probably, I'm still considering it. I know what we can get Dinah,' she exclaimed, waiving her fork around. 'She's been eyeing off this silver cutlery set. It's lovely. Very simple and elegant, if the three of us go in together we can get it.'

'Great. I'll text Nat and see if she's interested. Maybe we can get it on Thursday night.'

Elaine nodded and took a final sip of her coffee. 'Hurry up and finish your cake,' she said, indicating her own empty plate. 'We've got a new wardrobe to acquire.'

In the end I bought three pairs of shoes (Elaine bought two). A fantastic pair of beige pumps with material that wound around my ankles a couple of times before tying in a bow, a pair of fire-engine red heels that I was secretly sure I would never wear, but Elaine had insisted I buy, and a pair of classy black evening shoes with a small chain of diamantes running around each ankle. We bought outfits to go with each of these.

For the pumps a flowy white dress that just oozed elegance. For the red heels a tight fitted, sexy little red number that had given me a squirmy belly at the thought of wearing it in public. And for the diamante shoes, a classy black dress with no sleeves, a cinched in waist and a flowing skirt that came to just below my knees. It swished when I turned and I loved it.

I also bought a few casual shirts and two pairs of pants. Elaine was finally satisfied with my purchases - for which I was eternally grateful as my back had started to ache and I had a slight headache.

As she dropped me off she said, 'Ooh. Don't forget. Step number three on Monday night.'

'Meaningless sex?' I asked in alarm.

'No silly, get a new hobby.'

'Thank God.' I breathed out a sigh of relief. 'What are we doing?'

'It's a surprise. But you know those little, black exercise shorts you have?'

'Yep.'

'Wear them.'

* * *

When I got home, I opened the front door slowly and experimentally sniffed the air, sighing in relief when I detected nothing disgusting. We had had another pooping incident the other day and I was starting to get a bit nervous about what I would find when I arrived home. I had considered calling Dr Harry, but I didn't want to be on T.V.

Princess was asleep on her bed when I walked in. Her toys were scattered, which was good as it meant she had been keeping herself occupied. I took a couple of Nurofen, gave Princess a pat and headed into my room for a sleep. I stopped, horrified. My bed was covered in big chunks of glass. I was so scared I couldn't think or move. Eventually, I realised the glass was from the picture hanging above my bed. I looked around for a stone or something hard that had smashed the glass, and then realised that all my windows were shut. Whoever had done this had been inside my apartment.

Another couple of minutes of horror-induced paralysis followed. Feeling like a victim in a CSI episode, I slowly backed into the lounge, searching the shadows for an intruder. When I was sure there was no-one in the flat I sat on the couch to think. Princess meowed and made her way over to me. She was limping. Concerned, I picked her up and found a small shard of glass in her front right foot. 'Oh poor baby,' I cooed as I pulled it out.

I started to examine her whole body and found another cut on her head. Perplexed I examined the wound. The foot I could understand, she had jumped up onto the bed to sleep and stepped on the broken glass. But her head? Well that was another matter.

I thought about it for a while as I raided my first aid kit for betadine and band aids and then stopped as a possible cause for the broken glass occurred to me.

No, surely not.

I walked back to the bedroom with Princess and looked at the height from the bed to the print. It was do-able, but why?

I rang Mum.

'Yes Mum, I think she jumped up and broke the glass on the print above my bed with her head?' I said a few minutes later.

'That's ridiculous Tara. Why on earth would she do that?'

'I don't know Mum, you tell me - you're the one that rescued her.'

'No sane animal would do something like that,' she said.

'That's what I'm worried about.'

'Maybe she hated the print.'

'Mother!'

'Well it is a bit weird. All those swirls and dots.'

'It's contemporary art,' I replied coldly.

'It couldn't have been her.'

'Well Mum, if she didn't do it then someone broke into my apartment and did it. I'm actually not sure which one of those options I would prefer. Look, I've got to go and clean up the mess. Can you just ask one of the vets from work about it? Thanks, love you.' I blew kisses down the phone and hung up. Princess was watching me with her big, innocent blue eyes. 'Don't you dare say anything,' I warned her.

Wearily I started to clean the glass off the doona. In the end I carried the whole thing into the laundry and shook it very carefully out into the tub before putting it on to wash. As I was heading in to remake the bed my phone rang. I sighed - so much for my nice long nap.

It was my sister, Lily. 'I hear you've got a psycho cat.'

'Good news travels fast I see.'

'I hope she doesn't try to smother you.'

'What?' I asked in alarm, thinking about the chest sitting incident.

'Well some cats have been known to try and smother newborn babies. Seeing as yours is such a nut she might try to smother you.'

'Cut it out Lily,' I complained. 'It's bad enough imagining her jumping up to break the glass.'

'I wonder how many goes it took her?'

'I don't want to even think about it.'

'All right, so when do I get to see your new hairdo?'

'What are you up to tomorrow?'

'Well, I'm free up until lunch time, and then I have to have Rose at ballet at 2.30pm and then Lotus does tap at 3.00pm. Then I drop Petunia at Wing Chun by 3.30pm, which thankfully goes for two hours, so it gives me time to drop Tulip and Blossom off at gymnastics. Then I pick them all up again and feed them dinner.'

'They do all that on a Sunday?'

'No, Saturday.'

'Lil,' I tried to break the bad news gently, 'today is Saturday.'

There was about ten seconds of deafening silence on the other end of the phone and then all hell broke loose.

'Rose,' she shrieked down the phone. I winced and moved the receiver away from my ear. 'Lotus, get your stuff ready. I want you in the car in 5 minutes.'

I checked my watch. It was 2.20pm.

'Martin, Martin. Oh damn it, where is he?'

'Japan?' I suggested helpfully.

There was a slight pause on the other end of the phone and then, very softly, she uttered some expletives that the girls were definitely not meant to hear.

'Gotta go,' she finally said. 'This placenta brain thing really sucks. Brunch tomorrow?'

'Sounds good. I'll bring the food. See you then.'

I hung up and headed wearily back to my bed. My feelings of pity for Lil lasted the length of time it took me to remake the bed and the sixty seconds beyond that. Then I was fast asleep.

* * *

In the end it was Elaine who cracked the Nat nut. Natalie was once again the last to arrive for dinner. When I say once again, I mean once again in recent events. I am usually the last one to arrive - although sometimes Dinah and I take it in turns. Elaine is always smack bang on time. Normally Nat is exactly 5 minutes early for everything. She says it gives her time to focus - which I guess is a handy thing when you are a lawyer.

We were onto our second glass of wine when she rushed in. Her long hair, normally perfectly coiffed, was tousled and her blouse was incorrectly buttoned.

'What happened to you?' I exclaimed in horror, thinking she'd been mugged on the way to the restaurant.

'Problem at work, all sorted now,' she mumbled as she took a seat.

'What sort of problem?' asked Elaine suspiciously, while staring at her blouse.

'Oh you know the normal type. Big emergency,' she muttered evasively, trying to tame her hair. Finishing her unsuccessful grooming attempts, she picked up her menu, staring at it intently.

'What type of emergency?' asked Dinah.

'Oh big client, I had to get his divorce documents in order. Speaking of which,' she said to me, 'yours have been submitted. You look great by the way.'

'Thanks, for the compliments *and* the divorce papers.' I patted my hair. 'I'm finally getting the hang of doing it. You should have seen me the first time I washed it. Total disaster: I looked like a mushroom. Tristan got me a hair straightener and some anti-frizzing agent and it's all under control.'

Elaine was staring at Natalie. 'Who is it?' she asked suspiciously.

'Who's who?' Nat stared even more intently at her menu.

'The big important client,' Elaine persisted.

'No one you would know.'

'I know a lot of people.'

'Look can we just drop it, it's not important.'

'Not important? You're late for dinner tonight, Thursday you didn't even show up for the movies.'

'Oh shit!' Nat looked stunned. 'I totally forgot.'

Now it was my turn to look suspicious. 'If you forgot,' I asked, 'why did you send me a text the next day?'

Nat squirmed in her seat.

'Oh my God,' Elaine said.

'What's wrong?' I asked, looking at her in concern.

'Oh My God.'

She seemed to be fine so I glanced around for a fire or some other cause for her apparent alarm.

'OH MY GOD.'

I intensified my search, now hunting for an axe murderer or a suicide bomber. And then I noticed Nat. She sunk guiltily into her seat as Elaine pointed a finger at her and hissed, 'You've been having sex!'

'Shhhhhhh,' Nat urged, flapping her hands at Elaine. 'Shut up.'

'I will not shut up. I want to know with whom, and where and for how long and well, just tell me everything.' Elaine pulled her seat in closer to the table and leaned towards Nat, eagerly awaiting the details.

'You've been having sex?' I asked Natalie.

She looked at me sheepishly, and then smiled.

'Really?' I asked. 'Anyone we know?'

She shook her head.

'Any good?'

She grinned.

Elaine called a waiter over and ordered a bottle of bubbly. 'To celebrate,' she explained. 'Now - tell us everything.'

'I can't,' whispered Natalie in a horrified voice, 'I'm such a slut.'

'Is it more than one man?' asked Elaine with glee.

'Euwwww no. Ahhh, I've been having sex with......... No I can't say it, it's just too bad.'

'Come on. It's all right we are here to support you, not ridicule you,' I encouraged.

'Okay. I'm going to say it really fast because otherwise I won't get it out.' She took a few deep breaths and then launched into her sentence. 'Itsthekleeneratork'.

She looked at us expecting some sort of response. I glanced at the others. They all shook their heads.

'Nah, sorry love we missed it. You're going to have to say it slowly.'

She put her hands over her face and said through clenched teeth, 'It's the cleaner at work.'

Collective gasps followed this outburst. Natalie having sex with a cleaner? Stylish composed Natalie, whose life was perfectly ordered? Natalie whose only interest was getting a partnership? Natalie who hadn't even looked sideways at a man for...... well forever?

I giggled nervously. 'Seriously? The cleaner?'

'You've been doing the wild thing..... with the cleaner?' asked Dinah bewildered.

Elaine, frozen in shock, suddenly burst into gut-wrenching, convulsive laughter. Everyone in the restaurant turned to look at her while she doubled over and slapped the table. 'Ahh God, this is too good.' She wiped the tears out of her eyes. 'So has he been hoovering your rug?'

She collapsed again and Dinah and I started to laugh.

'I hope he gets into all the cracks and hard-to-reach places,' Dinah said, tears coursing down her face.

'Yeah,' I said giggling. 'Is he good with his feather duster?'

'Right,' said Nat, 'all of you shut up or I won't tell you anything.' She waited till we stopped laughing - like a teacher with some wayward students. Every time we had it under control one of us would catch the other's eyes and start giggling again. Finally she began her tale.

'Well he's been cleaning there for about three months. He's very thorough,' she said enthusiastically, stopping with an annoyed look on her face when we all burst out laughing again.

'Sorry, sorry, please go on. I promise we'll behave.' Elaine was the first to regain her composure.

'It was a couple of months ago that I met him...not that met is really the right word.'

I noticed the ladies at the table next to us had gone quiet and were leaning towards us like a pack of dogs towards a tasty bone.

'I was working late trying to get some work for the Velucci family up to date. It must have been about 10 o'clock, and all I could hear was the vacuum cleaner working its way closer and closer to my office. The more I tried to ignore it the more uptight and angry I got.' She paused and we all nodded encouragingly at her while she took a deep breath. 'So when it got to the corridor outside my office I decided to ask them to move to a different area until I had gone. The place is enormous, it's not like they had to clean right there right then. I got as far as the doorway when I saw him.' She paused and shivered.

'What does he look like?' the woman at the table next to us asked.

'About six foot tall with dark hair, but really thick hair - sort of crumpled looking.'

'Like he'd just gotten out of bed?'

'That's it, like he's just gotten out of bed.' She sighed.

'I love that look,' a lady at another table whispered to her friend.

'And he has the most beautiful, buttery brown eyes. When he looked at me it was like....,' she paused to consider.

'Like he was looking into you, into your soul?' the waiter asked helpfully.

'Just like he was looking into my soul,' confirmed Natalie, totally unaware of the crowd she was drawing.

'It was like he possessed me as soon as his eyes met mine. I got such a shock that I stumbled and had to hold onto the door frame for support. And then he was there, his arms around me, supporting me. I had goose bumps all over my body, and I mean ALL over my body.' She paused.

'Go on,' said the chef, leaning over the kitchen bench to hear.

'Well then he said "Are you all right?"' she mimicked a low husky South American accent. 'At the sound of it my knees went totally out from underneath me and he picked me up and carried me to my desk. "Have you eaten lately?" he asked me, "Maybe your blood sugars are down." Which I thought was pretty funny coming from a cleaner. But I couldn't laugh because the only thing wrong with me was the effect he was having on me. And then...' She paused again, caught up in her memory.

'And then?' we all asked in unison.

'And then I looked up straight into his eyes. His face was only a few inches from mine. I could see his pupils dilate. I tried to say something but my mouth was so dry that I licked my lips.'

We all gasped.

'And then I licked them again, more slowly. It was like I could already taste him.'

'What did he do?' whispered Dinah.

'Well, as we stared into each other's eyes he tightened his grip on my waist, and I put my hands on his belt, pulling him closer. Then he licked his lips and all of a sudden I wanted him more than I have ever wanted anything or anybody.'

I saw a lady at the table next to us put her hand to her heart as if she were in pain.

'What did you do?' I was mesmerised by her tale.

'Well I pulled him closer again but my skirt was in the way. So he reached down and slowly, with the palms of his hands, pushed my skirt up to the top of my thighs, and then he moved in between my legs. His hands were entwined in my hair and I needed to get even closer to him, so I arched up bringing my face closer to his.'

She stopped, overwhelmed by the memory. We all waited while she composed herself. Finally she took a deep breath and continued. 'And then he was kissing me. Ravishing my mouth, my face, my neck - he was driving me crazy. I ripped his tank top off over his head, and the beauty of his body stunned me.' She stopped shaking her head, 'I still can't get over how perfect his body is. And then his hands were on the buttons of my blouse pulling it back off my shoulders. He paused and took a deep breath as he stared at my bra and I reached back and undid it and then threw it on the floor. He took my breasts in his hands and massaged them gently as he kissed me. It drove me wild and I started ripping at his pants, undoing his belt and zipper. And then I placed both my hands on his ...' She paused and looked embarrassed.

'Penis,' supplied Elaine helpfully.

'Yes, his penis.' She blushed as she said it. 'He went crazy, pushing me back on the table so he could get my skirt and underwear off. We did it right then and there: me lying on the table with my legs wrapped around his waist and him leaning over me, talking to me in Spanish. It was the wildest, most frightening, best sex of my life.'

She paused, and everybody held their breath, silently urging her to go on.

'Things got pretty awkward when we had finished. We got dressed and sorted out my desk, neither of us speaking, and then I left.'

She stopped, exhausted from the telling. I pushed a glass of bubbly into her hand and she took a big swig. By now the entire restaurant staff and patrons were clustered around the table.

'What the hell?' she said, acknowledging her audience for the first time. 'Everyone, back to your tables. You,' she said, pointing at the chef, 'where the hell is my dinner?'

'Uhh,' he said nervously, looking at the waiter for support, 'you haven't ordered it yet.'

'Ohh, well I'll have the garden salad and the gnocchi. Girls?'

We all ordered our meals and everyone else returned to their tables.

'So what happened after that?' I asked.

'Well I made sure I was out of the building well before the cleaners arrived for the next month, but I couldn't stop thinking about him. During the day I would think about the feel of his hands on my breasts, the weight of his body on top of me. At night I would dream that I was doing it all over again. One day I got to work and found a red rose on my desk. When I smelt it I found a little piece of paper between the petals.'

'What did it say?' I asked.

'It just said 'Sorry'. I felt bad for avoiding him so decided to stay late that night just to let him know that everything was okay but that it wouldn't be happening again.'

'And?' Dinah asked, her brown eyes wide.

Nat held up three fingers.

'Christ, three times?' Even Elaine seemed impressed.

'Yep. Once on the floor, once on my desk, and then on my couch. I didn't get home till about 1 in the morning. And ever since then, every cleaning night, I wait for him. I wasn't going to tonight because I had to come here, but I couldn't resist.'

'Well if tonight is cleaning night, where were you Thursday night?'

Natalie looked a little sheepish. 'At home.'

'But I rang you at home and you didn't pick up.'

'Hmmm, well I wasn't really in a position to pick up the phone.'

'You mean he was there with you?' Elaine asked.

She nodded. 'The thing is, when you used to talk about sex I never really got it. I mean I've never really had sex till now.'

'You've had sex,' I said.

'Not like this. Remember when I was dating Bobby?'

We all nodded.

'Sex with him was so mind-numbingly boring that I used to go through work in my head. Now it's all I can do not to pass out from the feel of him naked next to me.'

I thought about it. It was true. Nat had never really joined in our sex talk.

'They can't have all been bad,' said Elaine. 'What about Simon?'

'Didn't know the meaning of foreplay.'

'Adam?'

'Premature ejaculator.'

'Warren?'

'Used to have to watch the footy while we did it.'

'Ok. What about Richard?' I said. 'Surely he was okay?'

'Richard was the worst. He used to pull out to finish himself off.'

'Ughhhh,' we all groaned.

'Why did you never tell us?'

'Until I met Ricardo I had always assumed there was something wrong with me.'

'Well it sounds like you are making up for lost time,' Elaine said approvingly.

And then our meals arrived, cutting off all conversation for a while.

* * *

I woke a little bleary from the night out with the girls, which had turned into a bit of a champagne fest after Natalie's little confession. It had seemed like a good idea at the time to start toasting things.

Elaine had started it. 'Here's to hot sex.' She raised her glass in the air.

'Here's to multiple orgasms,' Nat said, giggling ferociously.

'Here's to new shoes,' I said, which sadly was the closest thing I'd had to an orgasm for a while.

'Here's to make up sex,' said Dinah.

'Ohh yeah,' said Elaine, 'my favourite. To make up sex.'

We had gone on like that for the rest of the night, chatting about nothing and then charging our glasses to toast things. After five bottles of champagne our toasts had lost much of the significance.

'Here's to waiters.' We toasted the waiter, who was looking distinctly nervous.

'Here's to lamp posts,' I said, walking into one as we staggered down the street.

That made Dinah laugh so hard she bent double at the waist before finally collapsing in a heap. 'Here's to pavements,' she shrieked, rolling around on it.

I stopped mid-step, staring across the road. My champagne-soaked brain slowly interpreting the new billboard that had been erected there. 'Ahh fuck.' I raised an imaginary champagne glass to the larger-than-life image of

Jake. 'Here's to cheating ex-husbands,' I slurred. 'May they rot in hell.'

I sat up in bed and paused for a second, waiting to see how my body would respond to being upright. A little hungry - a good sign. I stood up carefully waiting for any dizziness. Nope, all appeared to be in working order. I popped a couple of Advil just in case a belated hangover decided to hit, and got dressed to go to Lily's for brunch.

On the way I stopped at a bakery and bought some fresh croissants and pastries. Then I ducked into the fruit shop and bought some delicious smelling strawberries and homemade blueberry jam. It was 10 o'clock by the time I arrived and I could smell coffee brewing as I entered the front door.

'In the kitchen,' Lil yelled when she heard me.

Lily and Martin have a beautiful old terrace house in Paddington with sensational city views. They bought it about 13 years ago when they first got married. It had been a struggle for them back then to afford it, but it had been well worth the sacrifices they made in the first few years. Now it had been lovingly restored and renovated. I found Lily in the huge kitchen which opened up with bi-fold doors onto a deck. The living area - which was straight next to the kitchen - also opened up onto the deck. In summer the whole back wall of the house could be removed. In winter there were grand old fireplaces, restored to their former glory with pristine snowy white marble, to keep the house warm.

'I'm jealous,' I said to Lil for the umpteenth time, as I stared at the view.

'Yeah well, at the moment I'm jealous of you. Look at me. I'm a monster.' She gestured wildly at her belly which was beginning to bulge.

'No,' I said, looking at her, 'you're a miracle. Look at you, growing a living being. You're amazing.'

'Your haircut is amazing. And the colour is gorgeous. Maybe I should make an appointment with Tristan. Spoil myself a little.'

'I think that's a great idea. I'll babysit for you if Martin's not home. Speaking of which, when is he home?'

She examined the roster stuck to the side of the fridge with a magnet from Dinah's surgery.

'Ummm, tomorrow I think. Funnily enough he is in Japan. He's been climbing Mt Fuji.'

'What, he's on holidays?'

'Nah, they had three days off waiting for the next 767 to come through.'

'It's a tough life hey. Where are the girls?'

'Martin's parents picked them up this morning so I could have a break.'

'Geez that's nice of them.' I started to unpack the pastries.

'Yeah, I told them they didn't have to take them all, but they insisted. They're off to the movies and then out to Sizzlers for lunch.'

We moved onto the deck with the coffee and food.

'Yum, thanks for this,' she said.

'My pleasure, we should do it more often.'

'I have something to tell you,' Lil said, a distasteful expression on her face. I stopped with my croissant half way to my mouth wondering what bombshell she was about to drop. 'I ran into Tash the other day. I would have brushed her off but she was with Aunt Jackie.'

'I still love Aunt Jackie,' I admitted, taking a larger bite of the croissant than I had been intending.

'Yeah, it's not her fault her daughter is a faithless hag.'

I smiled around a mouthful of crumbs. 'So what did they say?' I finally managed.

'Well they insisted I stopped for coffee with them, and wanted to know all about the girls and Martin, even though I'm sure Mum bores her stupid with the details of my life. And then they started talking about the wedding. They've set a date, and they're having it at the country estate.'

'Jake will love that. The stupid bastard was always so impressed by the country estate.'

The country estate was Aunty Jackie and Uncle Edward's house on the Central Coast. It was a copy of a huge English Manor house, with a sweeping driveway and impressive garden of manicured shrubs. They had stables around the back for their horses; there was even a dressage circle.

'Anyway the wedding is in November.'

'He always did like a speedy wedding.'

'It was gag worthy. Tash was gushing about how much help he was organising everything, and how he'd come up with this great idea about writing their own vows, but making them cute and funny.' She looked at me waiting for the outburst.

I tried to contain it. I felt my face go bright red with the effort. But finally it burst from me involuntarily. 'That stupid jerk!' I yelped. 'That was my idea.' (I had wanted to do that at our wedding but Jake had condescendingly informed me that it was silly.) 'And where does he get off helping her with the planning when he left me to do it myself? For God's sake he's running for Lord Mayor. When would he find time to plan a wedding? Boo Hoo, poor little

Tash needs help planning the wedding.' I knew I was getting childish but I couldn't help myself. 'Can't do it by herself? For fuck's sake, she's an events organiser; you'd think she'd be all over this.' I stopped, panting for air.

'Better?'

'A little. Ahh, he's such a shit.' I threw the rest of my croissant onto the table.

Just then her phone rang and she ducked off to get it in case it was Martin. I couldn't hear her, but I could tell by the look on her face that it was. After all these years they are still stupid about each other; always exchanging gooey looks and holding hands. I only hope someday I can find something as beautiful as what the two of them have.

Lily finally hung up the phone and came back out to the deck.

'Martin,' she said beaming.

'I guessed by the stupid grin on your face.'

Laughing, she threw some of her croissant at me.

'Any other news from Bridezilla?'

'Only that she's planning to get pregnant as soon as they're married.'

I froze. 'Really,' I said slowly, 'I wonder if Jake knows about that?'

'Yeah - I was wondering the same thing.'

I tried not to think about them for the rest of the day. I spent the afternoon on the deck with Princess, reading a book and trying to ignore the abuse from Cocky. I had worked out where he was (living with the deaf old lady in the flat next door), and was concocting a plan to deal with him. I had tried confronting her about him, but hadn't been very successful. From the doorway to her apartment I could see her hearing aids lying on the sideboard, and consequently the conversation had gone as follows.

'Your bird is very rude,' I shouted, while pointing at the balcony.

'What's that lovey?' she shrieked back.

'Your bird. He's very rude.'

'Why am I in the nude?' she asked confused.

'No, No,' I shook my head, 'your bird.' I pointed to Cocky in his cage.

The door to the cage was open and, obviously mocking me, he jumped onto the table and squawked, 'Fuck off.'

The old duck smiled warmly at him before shaking her head at me. 'He's not for sale,' she advised me at the top of her voice.

'I don't want to buy him, I want to kill him,' I mumbled under my breath.

'Who do you want to kill?' she asked, backing away from me with an alarmed look on her face.

Oh great, so she could hear *that* part no problem.

'No, no,' I said, thinking rapidly. 'He's got a nice bill.'

Eventually I had given up and headed back to my apartment. I toyed with the idea of ringing Mum, but gave it up as a bad idea. I was just going to have to put up with it till a better one came to me. I just hoped it was sooner rather than later.

Chapter Four

The Third Step to Closure – Get a New Hobby

Elaine picked me up at 6.15pm sharp. I was feeling a little conspicuous in my shortie, short shorts, and was glad to see she was sporting a pair as well.

'Please tell me.'

'Nope.'

'Tell me.'

'Nope.'

'Tell me.'

'Nope.'

When we finally arrived at a large warehouse I was still no closer to discovering the truth from Elaine. The room she led me into was large, with polished wooden floors and had long, evenly spaced, shiny poles extending from the floor to the ceiling.

'Pole dancing?' I mouthed at Elaine.

'What can I say,' admitted Elaine. 'I've always wanted to try it.'

'Oh well, I guess it's far more interesting than knitting.'

Our teacher was an extremely fit looking lady in her mid-thirties. She had six-pack abs and fantastic deltoids and biceps.

'Wow,' I whispered to Elaine, 'how long till I look like that?'

Her name was Penny, and she started by giving us an idea of what we would be learning over the next eight weeks. Then she showed us what we would be able to do if we persisted and came to classes for the next year. I watched as she sprung lightly onto the pole and climbed up it, twirling around. Once she reached an impressive height off the floor she clasped the pole between her thighs and let go with her hands, leaning all the way back so her head was pointing to the floor. She sat back up and, grasping the pole with one arm above her legs and one below, proceeded to lie back and do the splits in the air, supporting her bodyweight with her arms. Then she slid down the pole upside down, just holding on with her legs, until her hands were touching the floor, at which point she did a handstand against the pole and then flicked down off it.

'Does that hurt?' I asked.

'Not any more.' She flicked me a quick grin. 'Right we're going to start with a move called a front spin.'

An hour later as we warmed down I could feel some of the muscles of my arms and back that were going to be sore.

'Thanks,' I said to Elaine.

'You enjoyed it?'

'Yep. It's the perfect hobby for obtaining closure.'

'And just think if Dinah ever fires you - you can work as a stripper.'

'Or if I decide to go back to Uni I can work nights to pay for my fees.'

Elaine laughed.

'If we hurry we can pick up that silver cutlery set for Dinah,' I said, looking at my watch.

'Excellent,' said Elaine, 'cause I have a date now on Thursday night.'

'Oh with the guy you're bringing on Fri night?'

'No silly, this is a new guy I ran into at Starbuck's last week.'

'You are incorrigible.'

'You should try it some time.'

'Yeah, maybe I should,' I said.

'Oh good - I'm glad you feel like that, cause you have a date on Thursday night as well.'

'What?' I heard my voice go up an octave.

'The first of your internet dates in your quest for fast love and a one-night-stand.'

'Elaine - I don't think I'm ready.'

'You don't have to sleep with the first one, hell you don't have to sleep with any of them if you don't want to. You just have to get yourself back out there. Look, at least this way you won't be as nervous, cause you won't have to go through the initial run into someone, feel attracted to them, hope they're attracted to you, wait for them to ask you out and then when they do stuff it up because you like them so much that your brain disconnects from your mouth.'

'I see you've studied my dating style.'

She laughed. 'Actually Dinah was telling me about it. This guy isn't important because you know nothing about him.'

'Yeah, but what am I meant to know about him, and what does he know about me?'

We were at her car by then and she pulled a manila folder out of the back. 'Here, notes I've made on him.'

I flipped it open. There was a photo of a nice-enough looking guy with a couple of pages of notes, and a printoff of the typed conversations they'd had.

'A little bit of light reading before bed time.' She smiled cheekily at me.

'Guaranteed to give me nightmares.'

'All the details of the date are on the back. Don't be late and wear something nice, maybe the black dress. He's taking you to a new Scottish restaurant.'

'Scottish? Seriously? What do they serve at a Scottish restaurant?'

'I'm not sure. Haggis probably.'

I gagged a little at the thought.

'He's picking you up at 7pm. Wait downstairs for him. I didn't give him your apartment number.'

'Thanks,' I said, reaching out to touch her arm. 'Even though I don't want to do this, I appreciate what you're doing.'

'Thank me when you've had sex again. Now that will be a cause for some celebration.'

'Well don't put the champagne on ice yet.'

'Not on ice, but it's in the fridge chilling.'

* * *

I was waiting for my date - my stomach a churning knot of nerves. I guess it was natural for me to be nervous, with the infinite number of ways this could become an excruciating experience, versus the slim chance of it actually being any good. What if I didn't recognise him? What if we had nothing to talk about? What if he saw me and kept on driving?

In the end the date was short and succinct. A beat up old Volkswagen stopped beside me and a strange man said, 'Get in.'

I peered through the window at him trying to work out if this was the same person in the little photo Elaine had showed me, or some guy who thought I was a hooker. In the end I decided it was the man in the photo with a few more grey hairs and a few more kilos. Wondering what photo Elaine had used of me, I climbed awkwardly into the car. Before I even had my seat belt on, he took off from the curb, his foot flat to the floor. I squealed in surprise and heard him snigger.

Great, I thought, *a smart arse.*

'You've cut your hair short.'

Well that partly answered the question of the photo.

'Shame - I like a girl with long hair, it gives you something to hold onto.'

'Excuse me?' I looked at him in disbelief.

'You're a bit dressed up aren't you?'

'You said we were going to a Scottish restaurant. I like to look nice when I'm out.'

He burst out laughing. 'When I said Scottish I thought you'd understand.' He beat the steering wheel with his hand as he laughed. 'Wait till I tell the boys about this.'

'About what?'

As if in answer he indicated left and turned into the parking lot of a McDonald's restaurant.

'You are joking?' I said, gesturing at the restaurant. 'You said a new Scottish restaurant.'

'Yeah, well, this one only opened a month ago.'

'You're taking me to McDonald's for our first date?'

'Who said anything about me taking you? You'll be buying your own thick shake and fries thank you very much.'

'Well,' I said with as much dignity as I could muster, 'I can see that this isn't going to work, so let's just call it quits while we're ahead.'

'Hey, you said you liked new experiences. I thought after we'd eaten we could have sex in the disabled toilets.'

'Now you have to be joking.' I looked at him in amusement waiting for him to start laughing, but there was no change in his facial expression. Okey dokey, not joking then. I opened the car door and clambered out.

'Okay, well, thanks for the ride, nice knowing you,' I said, backing away from the car.

'Where are you going?'

'Anywhere but here.'

'Oh that's just typical.' I could hear him ranting as I walked briskly across the parking lot and back to the road. 'You women are all the same. You want it all on a platter - gift wrapped. Everything for free. Well you're all sluts. Big, fat sluts.'

I could still hear him yelling as I flagged a cab and jumped in. Wow, I thought Cocky had been bad. This guy had him beat hands down.

I texted Elaine on my way back home.

DISASTROUS DATE. Call me when you get a chance.

And then I quite happily went home to my slightly psychotic cat.

* * *

I got up early the next day to decorate the tearoom for Dinah's birthday. I had booked her in for a 2pm spa treatment at a Korean Bath House in town. Then we would be heading into Darling Harbour for drinks and dinner. Nat was bringing Ricardo - we were pretty excited to finally meet him. Elaine was bringing her toy boy; I hoped he was old enough to hold a normal conversation, and Creepy Doug was coming with Dinah.

'Happy Birthday!' we all shrieked as Dinah entered the tearoom. Susan and Tina had gotten her some flowers and a cake from Beethoven's. Rana, the hygienist and Mark the other dentist, had gotten her a handbag she had been eyeing off at a shop down the road. I was sure that it was Rana not Mark who had organised that - the two had been dating for six months now.

The morning had gone well. No pain-in-the-arse patients had been allowed to be booked. Then a huge bunch of flowers had turned up from Creepy Doug, with a nice card on them saying how much he was looking forward to helping her celebrate her birthday. No mention of love I noted, but Dinah was thrilled. I packed her off to the Korean Bath house at 1.30pm and went home myself for a rest.

I arrived at Dinah's at 6pm so we could have a little drink before heading in to Darling Harbour. 'Where's Doug?' I asked as we popped the top off a bottle of champers.

'He's on his way.'

Pretty much as these words left her mouth her mobile phone burbled. She picked it up, read the text and then casually put the phone back on the table.

I looked at her.

'Doug. He's had an emergency extirpation, he'll meet us there.'

'Oh,' I said in my most nonchalant voice, and then changed the subject to how good she looked. (I feel the need at this time to let you know that an extirpation is actually the removal of the nerve from the inside of the tooth. It's done as palliative care and not as a form of torture. Well not in this country anyway.)

The traffic was bad so we had the cab drop us off at the entertainment centre and walked from there, strolling through Chinatown, peering at the ducks hanging in the windows. And that was when I saw them. I immediately panicked and tried to distract Dinah, but my body language must have alerted her and she peered through the window, past the ducks to the tables, where Creepy Doug sat with his emergency extirpation.

She gasped.

'Ahh fuck,' I said, shaking my head. 'What a prick.'

Dinah stood like a statue, staring at the two of them. Doug and a person I was assuming was Tiffany, the young, new graduate endodontist, were laughing and eating what looked like Peking duck. I winced as Doug leant over and fed some to Tiffany.

Dinah started to turn away.

I grabbed her arm. 'No way,' I said.

She looked at me miserably, her brown eyes shiny.

'No way Dinah - I let Jake walk all over me. I'm not letting you do the same thing with Doug.'

She looked uncertain.

'You're attractive, you're intelligent, you're a dentist, you own your own business, and now,' I said, 'now you're thirty. You're not some scared little girl any more. You're a woman, and I think the first task you have as a woman is to go in there, tell that arsehole what you think of him and retake control of your life.'

She looked me in the eye and took a few deep breaths while she contemplated my words. 'Right,' she finally said, and marched in the front door of the restaurant.

'Hi Doug, Tiffany.' Dinah stalked up to the table and took a seat. I maintained my distance, ready to jump in as backup if things got nasty, and had the pleasure of watching Creepy Doug, with a panicked look on his face, trying to salvage the situation.

'Dinah,' he started, 'look who I ran into on my way to Darling Harbour.'

'Hi Tiffany,' said Dinah dismissively. Her fight was not with Tiffany who - by the look of confusion on her face - had no idea that there was any type of relationship between Doug and Dinah.

'Must have been a quick extirpation.'

'Huh.'

'The emergency extirpation, must have been quick.'

'Oh you know - I've been doing them for years.'

'Yeah well, you've also been doing me for years, not that you'd know. Anyway just here to tell you not to bother coming to my birthday party tonight, because I'm sick of your shit and it's over between us.'

It was a beautiful moment. You could see Doug caught between wanting to patch things up with Dinah, and not wanting Tiffany to know the depth of his relationship with her.

'Anyhoo,' said Dinah dismissively, dumping the contents of Doug's wine glass into his lap, 'got to go, people to greet, champagne to drink. You know how it is on your birthday.'

'Umm,' said Tiffany, 'happy birthday?'

'Thanks,' said Dinah, and we walked back out of the restaurant and up the road. Finally she stopped walking and looked at me.

'Oh Dinah,' I said, 'you were amazing. It was perfect. Are you okay?'

'Need alcohol.'

'Yep, more alcohol. Come on let's go get drunk.'

By the time we arrived at the restaurant Elaine, Nat and their dates were waiting. I had texted ahead to let them know what had transpired and God bless them they had alcohol waiting for us.

I spent quite a bit of time drooling over Ricardo. Christ the guy was perfect. Gorgeous - check, amazingly sexy accent - check, intelligent - check. That had me wondering. Why was this guy a cleaner? When I asked him, he just said that he liked the hours and the peace and quiet that came with it. Nat giggled at that point, and he leant over and stroked her face while he kissed her. Elaine, Dinah and I let out a collective sigh. I didn't know till that moment that it was possible to be incredibly jealous of someone at the same time as being insanely happy for them.

I think Dinah had a nice night - even considering the Doug scene - and at the end I took her home to my place to sleep. I arranged with the girls to be at my place at 11am with a breakfast perfect for a hangover. I was sure we were all going to need it, but I also knew from experience that once the alcohol wore off, Dinah was going to feel like crap.

* * *

Dinah was already up when I woke. I could smell coffee brewing and hear the distinctive clacking of my laptop keyboard. I wondered what she was doing.

'Morning,' she said brightly, as I emerged from my room. 'Hope I didn't wake you.'

I shook my head and stared at her in disbelief. No strewn contents of the box of tissues I had placed on her bedside table last night. No huge black bags, the tell-tale sign of hours of weeping. Not even any signs of a hangover for that matter.

'Wow,' I said impressed. 'You look great. Are you as good as you look?'

'Yeah, I feel good. I drank a couple of litres of water during the night.'

'Hmmm. I wasn't referring to your hangover. I was meaning are you fine with the whole Creepy Doug thing.'

She laughed in surprise and then nodded her head thoughtfully. 'Creepy Doug?'

'Sorry, our pet name for him.'

'Don't be sorry. I like it. And in answer to your question - I feel lighter. I feel free. I feel like I can finally move on with my life. I feel like he doesn't matter one little bit. I can't believe the amount of time I wasted on him. And I'm not even angry about last night. I'm thankful that it happened.'

Elaine and Natalie had entered with grocery bags while she was talking.

'That sounds like closure to me,' said Elaine.

'Yeah, I feel like by taking back control of my life I've had closure on our relationship.'

'Ooohh,' I said jealously, 'you've had closure. That's not fair. Elaine how come she gets to have closure without having to sleep with anyone?'

'But I did sleep with someone,' said Dinah innocently, 'you, last night.'

I threw a cushion at her. 'Yeah well I slept with you, and a fat lot of good it did me.'

It was as we were eating the bacon and eggs that Dinah brought up her plans for the future. 'I'm going overseas for a few weeks,' she said casually.

'Who with?' asked Nat

'When?' asked Elaine.

'By myself, I'm not sure when. I'm still waiting for an email to see if there is any space for me. Look at this.' She jumped up from the table and grabbed my laptop. 'I've been looking into this for a while, and after last night I wasn't sure what I'd been waiting for, so this morning I emailed them.'

'Emailed who?' I asked.

'The administration of Mercy Ships, they're big floating hospitals. The one I'm looking at is called African Mercy.' She started reading off the computer. 'It has 6 operating theatres, 78 recovery beds and more than 450 volunteers manning it. They have a CT scan and x-ray and even laboratory services on board. It travels from town to town around Africa.' She looked up from the computer. 'I just feel I could do so much more to help people than I am.'

Nat took the computer from her. 'Listen to this. They do a lot of work for women who have obstetric fistula.'

Elaine winced. 'That sounds painful.'

'It's leakage of urine and faeces, caused by prolonged labour. Apparently there are between 100000 and 150000 women a year that develop this in Africa. They become outcasts, shunned by their families, divorced by their husbands and most often they die from infection and renal failure. It can be cured by a simple operation.'

'Makes you glad to be born in Australia,' I said. 'But Dinah, what can you do? Do they have dental facilities on board?'

'I think so. I remember hearing someone at a course talking about having done it and thinking how unreal it would be. It is totally volunteer - you pay your own way there and also for your food and board.'

'When will you hear back from them?' Nat asked.

Reclaiming the laptop from Natalie she clicked into her email. She gasped - an excited expression on her face. 'Already have,' she informed us, reading the email. Finally she looked up. 'I'm going next week.'

'What?' I yelped in alarm. 'But Dinah, the practice.'

'Will manage without me for a month. I have faith in your abilities Tara, and Mark is quite capable of stepping up to bat for me. You'll just have to get a locum dentist to fill in for me like you did last time I went on holiday. You know what to do.'

There were so many things whirling through my head, all of them complaints and reasons why she should not go. So I shut my mouth tight and nodded. If she had the guts to fly to a third world country and volunteer for a month on this floating hospital, then surely I could run her business while she was away.

'Thanks Tara,' she said beaming, 'you're the best.'

* * *

First thing Monday morning I contacted a temp agency regarding a replacement for Dinah. Then I picked up and filled out her vaccine script before heading back to work to finalise the flights to Benin. Dinah would have to fly via Los Angeles to Contonon which would take 42 hours. I felt tired just thinking about it. I booked the flights, emailed the information to Mercy Ships and then filled out a visa application.

By five I had everything under control and a pile of resumes from the temp agency, which I took home to peruse. I decided to have a shower first and opened the door to the balcony to let in some fresh air. When I finally emerged from the bathroom, a cloud of steam around me, I could see Princess squatting in the doorway to the balcony, the tip of her tail flicking from side to side. Cocky was sitting on the railing, taunting her. He jumped up and down squawking while Princess crept closer and closer. By the time I realised what was about to happen it was too late.

'No!' I shrieked as Princess launched her attack. She raced towards the balustrade and leapt upwards, trying to pounce on Cocky; who lifted into the air - hovering over her head as she cleared the balustrade and plummeted down four flights to her death.

'Princess!' I cried, as I hung over the balcony staring at her still body. I ran down the stairs, tears blurring my vision, and approached her slowly - wishing desperately that she would move, or meow, or hop up and come over to me, telling me with her purrs about how she had lost another life. She looked like she was stretched out enjoying the last sun of the afternoon, but I knew better. I picked up her still body and hugged it. I kissed her soft fluffy head and cried into her fur. Yes, she had been a little bit of a psycho, but she had been *my* psycho, and it was my fault she was dead.

'Oh Mum,' I cried down the phone. 'Princess is dead. Cocky was taunting her and she jumped over the balcony and now she's dead.'

'Calm down Tara,' said Mum gently. 'Now start from the beginning. What happened? Did you mention Cocky?'

'Yeah,' I sniffed. I figured with me so upset about Princess dying she couldn't possibly yell at me for letting Cocky go. 'He's been living with the old lady in Lily's apartment, and he's always saying hor, horrible things, and then he came over and he lured Pr Pr Princess to her death,' I howled.

'All right darling,' Mum said, 'I want you to go and have a lie down. I'll be there as fast as I can.'

I took Princess's body with me into the bedroom to cuddle. She wasn't a bad little cat really. I mean all animals have their wicked points. So she had freaked me out a few times in the night when I had woken to find her staring into my face. So she had destroyed all my nice cushions, and crapped on my bed and rug. So she had frequently found it amusing to attack me when I least expected it. She had still been company, and she had never criticised me or made me feel stupid.

I was ready to give her up when Mum arrived and we took her down and buried her in the little garden behind the apartment building. Mum had brought a lasagne with her and homemade garlic bread, as well as my copy of *Breaking Dawn*.

'Enjoy it?' I asked, as I whipped up a salad to go with the lasagne.

'Loved it so much I read it three times. It drove your father crazy. He couldn't get a word out of me for a week.'

I noticed a mosquito-netting covered bowl, full of water, with a little plant floating in it. 'What's that?'

'Oh sorry love, it's the best I could do at short notice.'

Curiously I went over to look at the bowl. Lying in the roots of the water plant was a bright blue fighting fish. I tapped the side of the bowl to see if he was alive. His tail made the smallest of movements.

'What's with the netting?' I asked.

'Mmmmm, well he's suicidal. It's to stop him jumping out.'

I started laughing. 'You brought me a suicidal fighting fish? Oh Mum - that's too good.'

'Well, as I said darling, it was the best I could do and I didn't want to leave you alone when I left tomorrow.'

'Thanks Mum.' I kissed her on the cheek and then wandered back to have another look at him. 'He does look a little blue,' I joked. 'What do I feed him?'

'Oh, almost forgot.' She pulled a container of fish pellets out of her bag. 'Give him two of these a day. That's all you need to do.'

I had to admit when I went to bed that night, it felt nice knowing when Mum left the next day there would be another living thing in my apartment. It was a sad state of affairs that the best I could do was a suicidal fighting fish.

* * *

Elaine had told me to keep tonight free and had rung last night with the details of my next internet date. I had thought about refusing to go, but it was the night of the election and I was eager to go out.

I had learnt my lesson and this time I met Bob - my date - at a pub in town. And no, he wasn't a builder, he was a lawyer. (I had cracked a bit of a spack about that to Elaine, who had coolly informed me that there were thousands of lawyers in Sydney and to calm down because it was, after all, just sex.)

He was a nice enough looking man. Didn't seem to be a slob and made no lecherous comments within the first 10 minutes. So far the man was in the running for an internet dating gold star. Easy to talk to, good sense of humour: the evening might not be that bad after all.

The trouble started when the bartender changed the huge sports screen over to the election. 'Oh boy, I'm hungry. Do you want to go and get something to eat?' I asked eagerly, in an attempt to get away from the T.V.

'Do you mind if we have another drink first?' he asked. 'I wouldn't mind seeing some of this.'

When he came back from the bar with another beer for himself and a cider for me, he also bought back a packet of chips. 'Here you go,' he said kindly.

And that is where we stayed. It would have been far less painful to watch it at home on my tiny television. But no, I had to watch it on the world's biggest screen, and hear everyone in the bar talking about it. I was elated to overhear someone bagging Jake, but that one brave person was booed down by the now sizeable crowd in the pub.

Shit, I thought, *he might actually win this thing.*

We were onto our fourth round of drinks and my third packet of chips when it happened. A picture of him and Tash appeared on the screen looking very pleased with themselves. But that wasn't what happened. I was used to the old kick-in-the-gut from seeing the two of them in the media. No, this was an unexpected blow that I didn't even see coming. Silly me.

'God,' said Bob, 'isn't she something?' He looked at me and nodded his head at Tash's smiling face. She looked stunning in a two piece red suit; her golden hair coiled on top of her head, her dentally enhanced smile gleaming in the lights.

'Mmm yes, she certainly is,' I replied. But my answer was layered with so many undertones that a slightly sensitive person - or maybe just a sober person - would have noticed and asked me what was wrong.

But no, Bob the Bludgeoner just kept right on going.

'Yeah he certainly is a lucky guy. God, did you see the chick he was with before this? Man, in comparison, she was a dragon. Apparently they're related, but I can't see it.'

'Really?' I said stiffly. 'Some people might think she is attractive.'

'Yeah, some people who are fuck-ugly themselves might.' He guffawed so hard he snorted beer up into his nose. 'Yes siree,' he continued when he had recovered from his coughing attack, 'she was whacked with the ugly stick when she was born. Not that Tash though. Nope, God certainly loves her.'

'What photo did you see?' I asked.

'What?'

'What photo of his ex did you see?'

'No photo, I was at their wedding.'

I stared at him in disbelief. 'The wedding?'

'Yeah, that Tash was one of the bridesmaids. Can you believe it? I wonder if he was banging her way back then.'

I had died a thousand deaths before that, but this was a new agony. To be given a total bagging by a stranger who was at my wedding was another type of torture entirely.

I stared at him harder. 'The cloakroom,' I said.

'Pardon.'

'You made out in the cloakroom.'

'Hey, how'd you know about that?' He puffed up with pride. 'Were you there?'

'Yep I was,' I said, as I stood up and grabbed my bag. 'You would have seen me; I was a bit hard to miss. I was the one all in white.'

I had the smallest of pleasures in seeing the shock register on his face before I stalked out of the pub and into the pouring rain.

He followed me to the door of the pub apologising all the way. 'I'm sorry, I didn't mean it. I was just trying to be funny,' he yelled after me.

I held one finger up in the air over my shoulder.

'I think you're very pretty too,' I heard him holler.

I kept on walking. There was no way I was going back to that. It was far too humiliating.

By the time I got home my hair was drenched, my clothes were soaked, but it was the feel of my tears mingling with the rain on my face that was the most unpleasant.

I flicked on the television, and while I stood dripping all over my rug, had the great pleasure of watching Tash and Jake hug and kiss, and Uncle Edward formally shake Jake's hand while it was decreed that he had won the election.

Poo.

I had an urge to shriek and jump up and down like a small child. In the end I decided to sulk in a much more adult fashion. I grabbed a bottle of chilled wine, stuck it in an ice bucket and ran a bath. Then I proceeded to get myself a little drunk while I soaked in the bath and tried not to imagine myself by Jake's side while he was declared Lord Mayor of Sydney.

* * *

'I'm not doing any more stupid internet dates,' I said to Elaine as we walked to pole dancing.

'Yes you are.'

'No I'm not. If I want to get abused, I'll get Mum to bring back Cocky.'

'What happened to Cocky?' she asked.

'Oh, Mum sorted it out with Esme - the old lady. Told her what he'd been saying. Esme was horrified and handed him over and Mum replaced him with a parrot. You should see this thing. It's huge and it sits on her shoulder when she goes for her daily walk.'

'So how did your Mum get Esme to hear her?'

'She took a notepad and wrote on it,' I admitted, a little embarrassed I hadn't thought of it myself.

Truth be told I was a little miffed at Mum. I get a suicidal fighting fish - who was hanging in there by the way - and the old lady next door gets this cool parrot. When I had asked Mum why I couldn't have the parrot, she had told me to stop acting like a spoilt child and I couldn't have the parrot because I would just end up killing it. I didn't think that was a very fair statement: so far only one out of my pets had actually died, and I didn't kill her, she made a poor judgement call in the heat of the moment.

'Anyway no more dates,' I said emphatically.

Elaine stopped walking to face me. *Oops*, I might have pushed her too far.

'Come on,' I said, trying to distract her, 'we'll be late for pole dancing.'

'Firstly - we are 20 minutes early for dancing, and secondly - you are going on another date in five days. It's all arranged. He's taking you out for dinner at Darling Harbour.'

'Yes Mum,' I mumbled under my breath. I amused myself by scuffing my feet the rest of the way to class, which I knew really pissed Elaine off.

It was our third lesson and tonight we were learning something more difficult.

'All right ladies,' said our teacher, 'we are going to learn how to sit on the pole.'

That sounded ominous. How do you sit on a pole?

The answer to that - I learnt over the next 45 minutes - is very painfully. You pull yourself up the pole, wrap the top of your thighs around it and then let them take your weight. It's a Chinese burn where no woman should ever have a Chinese burn, and was the most intimate I'd been with anything for the last 14 months. Our teacher promised us that with time it wouldn't hurt - I was pretty dubious about that.

After class we showered and headed out to meet Dinah and a few friends at Bar Blue for drinks. Tristan was going to be there so I had taken extra time doing my hair. I didn't feel like a lecture from a gay prima donna.

I hadn't been to Bar Blue before and had heard a lot about the decor. There were huge, blue mood lamps everywhere, including the wall behind the bar. It was mesmerising. You didn't mind having to wait to order your drink as you stared at the big blue globules breaking from the main body and floating up the wall.

'I can't believe you're going tomorrow,' I said to Dinah. She was practically glowing with excitement.

'Me neither. Thanks for all your help this week.'

'No probs, what are friends and employees for.' I laughed. 'Hey did you hear anything from Creepy Doug?'

'He sent me a text which I didn't open. I just couldn't be bothered listening to his bullshit any more.'

'So you're totally over him?'

'Let's just say when I think about kissing him I feel sick.'

'Kiss him? Is that all you used to do?'

'Urrhhh. Stop it. I'm trying to forget about everything else.'

Tristan sidled up to me and nudged me in the ribs. 'Who is that?' he asked in awe, looking at Ricardo.

'Ohhh. That's Nat's new man,' I replied.

'Ricardo, the cleaner?'

'The very one.'

'Check him out. I've got to get myself a new cleaner.' Tristan gave him an appreciative look up and down. 'I think I might go say hello.'

'Good luck, he's definitely straight.'

'There's no such thing as a definitely straight man,' he said.

'You always were an optimist,' said Elaine joining us.

We watched him saunter over to Ricardo and introduce himself.

'He's such a slut,' said Elaine, watching Tristan run his hands through Ricardo's hair. 'Look he's giving him a hair consultation.'

Tristan flicked us a wink as Nat - looking extremely amused - came over to our group.

'You do know my brother is trying to seduce your date?' said Elaine.

'Yep.' Nat took a sip of her drink.

'How's it going?' I asked.

'Great. Sorry don't mean to sound smug or anything.'

'Not smug, just happy. I'm pleased for you.'

'Thanks luv,' she replied, nudging me with her elbow.

It wasn't a late night as Dinah had an early flight the next morning. David had offered to drive her to the airport, for which I was grateful as I was looking forward to a sleep in.

Fishy Fishy was still alive when I got home, so I decreed it had been a successful day and I went to sleep happy.

* * *

The harsh ringing of my phone woke me early the next morning. 'So much for my sleep in,' I grumbled as I reached out one hand to answer it.

It was Elaine. 'Oh good you're awake,' she said.

'Of course I'm awake. The phone is right next to my bed. Who could sleep through that?'

There was silence on the other end.

'Elaine?' I queried.

'Tara?' For the first time since I'd met her she sounded uncertain.

'Yes.'

'I need a favour.'

Now I was intrigued. I sat up in bed and gave her at least 80 percent of my full attention. The rest was peering into the lounge to see if Fishy Fishy had made it through the night. I was judging the quality of my day now by whether or not my suicidal fighting fish was still alive. Great. Mind you I'd had no indication that he was actually suicidal. Depressed, yes, but hell, who didn't have a little depression in their lives occasionally? But suicidal? Well that was another kettle of fish, quite literally, entirely.

I snapped back to the present. 'Right, a favour,' I said.

'I need you to come dress shopping with me today.'

'Elaine, if you want me to go shopping with you there is no need to call in any favours. What's the special occasion? Another date?'

'I'll pick you up in 45 minutes and explain over breakfast. My shout.'

I peered blearily at my bedside clock, trying to work out if I was looking at an 8 or a 9. Ah, what the hell - it was a free breakfast. 'Sure,' I mumbled as I swung my legs out of bed. 'See you in 45.'

I was ready and craving good coffee by the time Elaine arrived. We settled in at Café Mud and I ordered the breakfast works while Elaine asked for a bowl of muesli.

'Muesli?' I asked.

'I'm not that hungry.'

Unfortunately at that precise moment Elaine's stomach released a grumble of epic proportions. I realised I hadn't seen Elaine eat much for a couple of weeks.

'Dieting?' I asked.

'Sort of,' she replied sheepishly.

'Why on earth? You're gorgeous.'

'I just need to look my best.'

I sighed. So it was going to be like that - me having to pry information out of Elaine bit by bit until I finally got to the bottom of this mystery.

'All right, we can do this the easy way or the hard way.'

'What are you talking about?'

'You obviously have something you haven't told anybody before, but you want to tell me now, and you have no idea how to begin. So why don't you just start at the beginning.'

'My 20 year school reunion is in 2 weeks,' she finally admitted.

I looked at her waiting for the rest. When nothing else was forthcoming I said, 'Well that, in itself, is obviously not the reason for your secretive behaviour.'

'There's a guy I went to school with that might be there, and I just want to look my best, all right? No secrets.'

Stunned, I stared at her. 'A guy, your own age, you haven't seen for twenty years, and you just want to look your best?' I asked.

'Not quite 20 years, I ran into him about eighteen years ago at a restaurant.'

'And you haven't seen him since?'

'No.'

'A guy your own age?'

'Yes,' she said a little tersely.

'All right so who is this masked man?' I asked when I had gotten over my shock.

'Robert Walters.'

'What does he do? Where does he live? Is he married?'

'I don't know.' She sounded agitated. 'Well, I heard a rumour that he was still single, but apart from that I'm not entirely sure. He did engineering after school.' She paused, staring into the past, a look of pain on her face. 'All right, if you want all the sordid and gory details, he broke my heart. I fell for him really hard and he cast me aside. I let him think that I didn't give a shit,' she said proudly, 'but I cried myself to sleep every night for a year.'

'And then what happened?' I was fascinated by this side of Elaine. A fragile Elaine. An Elaine I had never met.

'And then school finished and we all went our separate ways.'

'And you still hold a flame for this guy?'

'Well not exactly a flame.'

'You've hardly eaten for 2 weeks, we're going to buy a special dress so you look nice when you see him, and you're blushing. I'd say that's a flame of some sort.'

'Well let's just say I've always wondered what would happen if we met again as adults,' she said wistfully.

Our coffees arrived and I thought about what she had said, as I stirred in my sugar and took a sip. 'You didn't see him at the last school reunion?' I finally asked.

'He wasn't there.' She took a sip from her own cup and sighed.

'And you've waited another, what 5, 10 years to see him?'

'Ten years.'

I stopped asking questions while I devoured my breakfast. Elaine eyed off my eggs and bacon wistfully while she nibbled on her muesli. When I had finished, I fed my bacon scraps to Benny - who was waiting patiently in Elaine's bag - and then restarted the interrogation.

'Why didn't you ever contact him? I asked.

'That would have appeared desperate and needy. You know how much I like to appear desperate and needy.'

'You don't have a desperate or needy bone in your body. That's one of the saddest stories I've ever heard.'

'Let's hope it's going to become one of the most romantic stories you've ever heard.' She moved Benny to one side while she dug around for her wallet and then handed some money to the waiter.

'You've spent your whole adult life waiting to meet up with this guy again. Is that why you only ever date much younger men?' I asked.

She looked thoughtful while she finished her coffee. 'I've never put much stock in that mumbo, jumbo, psychobabble crap. Who the hell really knows why we do anything,' she eventually said. 'Come on.' She stood up and grabbed her bag. 'Let's go shopping.'

Later that afternoon, as she was dropping me off after a successful shopping spree, Elaine reminded me about my date the next night. I resisted the urge to stomp my feet like a small child. 'Fine,' I muttered under my breath, 'but you'll be sorry if this one's an axe murderer.'

'Wear your new dress,' she ordered.

I had bought a crisp print dress, while Elaine had bought a stunning gold number. It clung to her breasts revealing the perfect amount of cleavage, and then crossed under them. From there it was ruched down to her waist and over her hips. I could never carry off a dress like that. My breasts just weren't big enough.

'Where am I meeting him?' I asked sullenly.

'At Darling Harbour, outside the IMAX theatre. I've emailed over his details to you.'

'Thanks. I'm kind of losing enthusiasm for this whole internet dating thing.'

'What do you mean losing? You never had any to start with. Heaps of people have met on the internet.'

'Maybe that's the problem. Maybe these men would be perfect for you not me.'

'A man that takes you to McDonalds on a first date?' she said in horror. 'I think not.'

'How did that slip past you?'

'I read body language so I'm pretty clueless in a chat room,' she admitted.

'Is that how you do it? Body language?'

'What did you think?'

'Mind reading or supernatural powers - something like that.'

I stopped as Elaine burst out laughing. 'I wish. Anyway, I think that was the week I got the reunion invite. I was a little distracted.'

'Gee thanks.'

'No problems.' She smiled cheekily before driving off.

* * *

I was busy that week rescheduling Dinah's patients who couldn't or wouldn't be seen by the English locum dentist, Sarah. It wasn't till Wednesday night that I caught up with Elaine and Nat for dinner and filled them in on my latest date.

'How was it,' Nat asked breathlessly, when she finally arrived. Her face was flushed and her long blonde hair tousled. I was guessing it was cleaning night.

'Terrible,' I said, pulling a face at Elaine.

'Oh come on,' said Elaine, 'I'm sure it wasn't that bad.' She reached over and poured Nat a glass of champagne.

'He was a dog groomer,' I started.

'At least he had a job,' Elaine said cutting me off. 'Honestly Tara, you've got to stop being so fussy.'

'He was a dog groomer with a snotty nose,' I said, looking at Elaine with my eyebrows raised.

'Eueeew,' Nat said, looking a little ill.

Elaine was trying to remain serious but I could see a smile starting to twitch the corners of her mouth. 'Everybody has a bit of bogey sometimes,' she said.

'We're talking margarita glass crusty,' I said.

She started to smirk. 'Maybe he just had a cold.'

'They quivered when he laughed.' I took a sip of my champagne as I watched her reaction.

'At least he had a sense of humour,' she retorted, smiling broadly now.

'He only laughed at his own jokes,' I said.

'It can't have been all bad,' she said laughing.

'At the end, when I went to leave, he kissed me,' I said, expressing a shudder at the memory.

'See,' Elaine said, obviously congratulating herself on her match making skills, 'not all bad.'

'I could feel snot drying on my cheek afterwards,' I replied.

Nat started to laugh. 'That is horrible,' she said.

'See Elaine,' I said, 'even Nat agrees it was horrible.'

'Yes, well, Nat is having sex with someone so she doesn't have to date the dog groomer with the snotty nose,' Elaine tartly advised me.

'No more,' I said laughing.

'One more,' she bargained.

'When?' I asked, sighing.

'Friday,' she advised me.

'What are you going to do if that doesn't work out,' Nat asked, as she wrestled the cork out of another bottle of bubbly.

I don't know,' I said. 'Maybe I should hire a gigolo.'

Elaine looked at me in surprise.

'I mean really,' I continued, 'would it be that bad? At least I would be being totally honest about the situation.'

'You'd be comfortable paying someone to have sex with you?' Nat asked me.

'Not when you put it like that,' I admitted. 'It makes me sound pretty desperate.'

'You are desperate,' said Elaine. 'Desperately in need of good sex. Go on this date and if it doesn't work out we'll think of something else.'

'Thanks,' I said, thinking how sad my life had become when I had to thank a friend for promising to get me laid.

'Thank me when this is all over,' she replied.

* * *

This date started off promisingly. His name was Anthony. He was a lab technician at the Sydney North Shore Hospital. He was cute. He had a nice voice and he took me to a fancy French restaurant in King's Cross.

They were all ticks in the right boxes. Maybe I would even throw in a gold star. The problem began when we were eating dinner and I noticed the extremely long nail on the fifth finger of his left hand. We're talking corkscrew curly. It was off-putting watching him place food in his mouth with this huge nail passing in front of his face. I started to get concerned that with one too many drinks he might accidentally gouge out an eye.

And of course then I couldn't concentrate on anything else. Why would he have a nail that long? How long had it taken to grow? Would he be devastated if it broke? What was its purpose?

'Would you like to try some snail?' he asked me politely.

'What?' I yelped, having heard him ask me if I wanted to try some nail.

'Snail?'

'Oh yes lovely.' I shuddered at a vision of him stabbing it with his nail and serving it to me like a kebab.

What if he used it to pick his nose? Or his ears? Well he would really only be able to clean the left ear with it. Maybe he had grown the right one as well but it had broken during a particularly serious cleaning session.

In the end I crept off to the toilets and rang Elaine.

'It's just a nail,' she said, 'and it's just meaningless sex.'

'I can't get past the nail.'

'Why don't you ask him about it?'

'Mmm. Maybe, but what if it's really embarrassing?'

'It's just a nail.'

So when I came back from the toilets I casually brought up the topic of his long, long nail.

'My, that's a long nail.' I tried for a casual approach, but I think it came out a bit strained.

'Yes it is getting long isn't it,' he said proudly, holding it up in front of his face and admiring it.

There was an awkward silence while I looked at him with one eyebrow raised, waiting for him to disclose the reason for it. It became evident that he wasn't going to explain it unless I asked directly.

'So tell me Anthony. Why do you have such a long nail?'

I could have accepted many reasons. I was hoping for an explanation like, 'Oh when I was travelling in Tibet last year I stumbled across a village where all the children were born blind. I'm raising money - by growing this extremely long nail - for research and the possible development of a cure.'

Or here's a plausible one.

'I find if I don't grow it really long I end up with an ingrown nail which is extremely painful and very annoying,'

Hell, I would have even accepted, 'my mother's been kidnapped by an evil witch and if I can grow this nail for a year and give it to the witch I'll get my mother back alive.'

But when he shrugged casually and, looking at his nail said, 'I just like it.' I felt myself turn off. I realised at that moment there was a chance I had become far too fussy to have meaningless sex.

Later that evening when he dropped me home and leaned in for a goodnight kiss, I really did try. I let him kiss me. I closed my eyes and tried to think of England. I moved my mouth in an appropriate manner. But when I felt the end of his nail graze my cheek, my eyes popped open and I jumped out of the car with a, 'Thanks for a great night. I had a really good time. See ya.'

When I got home, (which took a few minutes as I had Anthony drop me off up the road, and I had to cut through the back yard of another block of flats and a house), I found that Fishy Fishy had finally managed to achieve his goal to take his own life.

Poor little guy, he was all dried up and hard, hanging there with his fin caught in the mosquito net cover. As I flushed his little body down the toilet I wondered how long it had taken him to come up with the idea.

'No Mum,' I repeated for the third time. 'I did not go out and leave the netting off. He jumped up and caught his fin in the netting.'

'Really Tara, do you expect me to believe that garbage?' she said.

'Yes I do expect you to believe me.'

'Well I'm sorry but after the whole Cocky debacle.'

'Hey, I only lied about Cocky because I couldn't handle him any more.'

'I don't know how you think I'm going to trust you with another pet.'

'Well maybe if you stopped getting me such deranged ones I wouldn't have this problem.'

'Good night Tara.'

'Well, goodnight to you too.'

That night I dreamt that Fishy Fishy had a huge hard curly fin which he used to pole vault himself out of the bowl. Then, when he had died and gone hard, I kept him to use as an ear-cleaning tool. It was a pretty disturbing dream and I woke feeling a little creeped out by the whole thing.

* * *

Saturday morning I got an SMS text from Nat.

Urgent. Need to talk.

R u okay?

Not okay. Bad, really Bad.

Do you want to come over?

I'm at your front door.

I opened the door to a Natalie I'd never seen before; rumpled with red weepy eyes and large black bags.

'Shit. You look terrible.'

She put her handbag on the kitchen bench, perched on one of my stools, and let out a miserable sigh.

'Natalie,' I placed a hand on her shoulder, 'what's wrong. Come on tell Aunty Tara.'

'Too bad.' She slumped down and put her head on the bench.

'You'll feel better when you share.'

'This is bad Tara, really bad. I think I may get the sack.'

I felt a prickle of alarm. Oh no. Had Nat stuffed up some huge court case? What if she ended up going to jail?

'All right talk,' I demanded.

'Last night, my boss walked in on Ricardo and me having sex.'

Not jail then. I let out a sigh of relief. 'Like actually going for it, not just kissing?' I asked.

'He was sitting in my chair and I was on top, riding him.' She mumbled the last part and blushed as she said it.

I have to say I was impressed. 'What did she say?' I asked, as I poured her a cup of coffee.

'That's the worst part of it. Nothing except, "Oh Excuse me", and then she left.' She took a big swig of the coffee, grimacing when she realised I had forgotten to add sugar.

'Sorry,' I said, handing her the sugar. 'How's Ricardo?'

'Worried I'll lose my job.'

'What about *his* job?'

'He says he'll get another job easily.'

'Yeah. Tristan would hire him in a shot.'

She smiled weakly.

'This is probably a silly question, but why were you still having sex at work?'

She squirmed in her chair. 'Sexual anticipation.'

'Huh?'

Her face reddened with embarrassment as she said, 'Knowing he was getting closer and closer to my room; it was really exciting.'

'So what are you going to do?' I asked after I had absorbed that information.

'Start looking for a new job?'

'No seriously on Monday, what are you going to do?'

'Guess I'll go face the music.'

'I feel sick.'

'Yeah, me too.'

* * *

That Sunday I made the trip to Umina for The Official Sunday Roast Lunch. I will go a long way for a roast dinner and Mum's is the best there is. Lily, Martin and the clan were already there when I arrived, and Camellia was trying to ride Fluffy, who was unenthusiastic about the idea and had decided to lie down.

'Up pony,' piped Camellia as I walked around the back of the house to the rear stairs.

Fluffy rolled one eye to look at Camellia, letting out a big whoompha of air, before putting his head back down on the ground.

'Pony, up,' she said, tugging on his big ears as if they were reins.

Fluffy closed his eyes and lay so still that for a moment I contemplated he might actually be dead. Maybe he had had a heart attack at the thought of being ridden.

'Hi gorgeous,' I said, giving Camellia a hug while watching Fluffy with concern. Over her head I saw him jump up and disappear around the side of the house. I let out an inaudible sigh of relief before jogging up the stairs to the house.

'Where pony gone?' I could hear her asking behind me.

By the way Lily and Mum stopped talking the precise moment I entered the house I knew they had been talking about me.

'What's up?' I asked suspiciously, not sure I wanted the answer.

Lily wordlessly handed me a pretty collection of layered cardboard and paper. It was a wedding invitation - Jake and Tash's wedding invitation.

'Do I want to look at this?'

Lily nodded her head at it.

Jaclyn and Edward Dubone and Juliette and Mark Wellington
are pleased to invite you to the
Union of the Lord Mayor Jake Wellington with Natasha Dubone
On Saturday 30th November
at 64 Piazza Crescent, Avoca Beach

'Blah Blah Blah Blah,' I said while I read it, torn between the urge to stick my fingers down my throat and to admire the beautiful gold cardboard they had used to print their invitations. And then I saw it.

'Are you kidding me?' I heard my voice rocket up an octave.

Mum and Lily winced.

The invitation was made out to Aunty Bet, Uncle Bert and Tara. They had fucking invited me to their wedding. What a nerve.

'Well of course I won't be going.'

Mum looked distinctly uncomfortable.

'Mum - I'm not going,' I said.

'Of course you're not love,' said my father. Thank God for the voice of reason. 'Your Mum's caught herself in an awkward situation. She told Jackie that you had a new boyfriend.'

'Mother,' I said, a little shocked, but also secretly delighted she had lied on my behalf. 'Your nose is getting bigger.' She subconsciously touched it as I hugged her. 'Thanks for not making out that I'm a big sad loser.'

'I guess now is as good a time to also give you this.' Lily handed me a hot pink piece of cardboard.

'The hen's party?'

She nodded.

'God that brings back some memories, I hope hers is as sucky as mine was.

Lily and I both laughed.

My hen's party was a complete disaster. It was the week before the wedding - just in case I ended up with the mother of all hangovers. Nat and Dinah had organised a dinner, that was all I was told. What they had failed to mention was that it was at a place that specialised in hen's parties and had a stage up the front. We sat at long tables perpendicular to, and coming off the stage, one hen's party to each table. They had to chip in and buy me a shirt that would identify me as the hen. I didn't want it, but we decided that if we were the only table that didn't do it we would look like a bunch of sad tossers.

So there we all were sitting at this table, me with my special shirt on, and I like a naive idiot am wondering what the stage show was going to be, when out comes the first stripper. I looked at Nat, who shook her head.

'Sorry,' she whispered. 'It said stage show. I didn't realise they meant strippers.'

I've never really been able to get into the male stripper thing. Maybe because they all look gay, prancing around like show ponies, groping their own packages and thrusting them into women's faces. That night was no exception. The guys were whipping off bits of clothing left, right and centre, while I tried to have a conversation about the coming nuptials with Nat and Dinah. One of the strippers, trying to get my attention, got down on his hands and knees in front of me and started wiggling his red g-stringed buttocks in my face. Everybody else was screaming, but I could see some coarse, black hair poking out from under the G-string, so I was pretty grossed out.

Then Mr Hairy Bottom insisted on dragging me up on stage. I fought pretty hard, but the girls from the table behind us grabbed my legs and threw me bodily onto the platform. I landed on my hands and knees with my bum in the air and my mini skirt up around my hips, flashing my G-string at the crowd. The girls held me down and smacked me on the bare arse, (they were pretty drunk by this stage), while Mr Hairy Bottom waggled his package about an inch from my nose. It was totally humiliating.

He sat me on a stool and started swinging his hips to 'Man I Feel Like A Woman'. Much to my disgust he held a towel in front of himself and whipped off his G-string. I, thankfully, could only see the blue and white striped towel, but he grabbed my hand and stuck it on his crotch. I could feel his sad, limp dick through the fabric of the towel, and to my dismay, the tip of my little finger missed the towel grazing his soft, waxed balls.

Now I want to get one thing straight. I am normally not that fond of penises. I mean obviously I liked Jake's, but I have never, ever had an urge to see a strange man's package, let alone feel one. I certainly didn't appreciate being forced to touch his, and given a choice I would have taken putting my hand into a jar full of huntsmen spiders over this. As thoughts of herpes and syphilis flashed through my head, I leant forward and whispered in his ear, 'If you don't take my hand off your dick this minute you'll be using a straw to pee through for the rest of your life.'

A look of horror crossed his face, and I smiled sweetly at him and raised one eyebrow. He let go of my hand pretty quickly, but not before I felt a slight hardening of his dick and I realised with a jolt that I must have turned him on. It put me right off my dinner.

The hen at the table behind us had reached a record level of desperation, bashing the other hens out of the way and commando rolling onto the stage whenever they invited one up. I could tell that the strippers were quite uncomfortable with how she was rubbing her body up against them and trying to stick her hands down their pants. By the end of the main course she was leaning onto the table, trying to grab the legs of any stripper bold enough to go near her, and yelling, 'I want to fuck you now!'

The strippers stopped going to her table after that, concentrating instead on the hen at the next one over. Obviously Mr Hairy Bottom had told the others what a nasty bitch I was, so we weren't seeing any action either, and some of the single girls from our table joined the far one. The drunken hen quickly became disgruntled with the lack of males thrusting their groins into her face, and a brawl broke out between her and the other hen. There was some bitch-slapping and hair pulling, before the not-so-drunk hen finally managed to wrestle the really-drunk hen to the floor. She had her arms pinned down with her knees and was amusing herself by pouring a beer over her face. The drunken hen was spluttering and swearing and I could hear a lot of fucks and even once the 'C' word - which I always thought was taboo among women.

The strippers came to the front of the stage, half undressed, and one of them, I think it was the cowboy, started to squeal with excitement, 'Fight Fight Fight.' The others all joined in clapping their hands and jumping up and down chanting along with him. I was watching them with amusement when Mr Hairy Bottom caught my eye and blew me a kiss. We left at that point.

I nodded my head thinking about it.

'I'm guessing there will be no strippers at Tash's hen's party,' I said to Lil, 'Are you going?'

'Nah. Petunia's birthday is around then so I'll probably have a party for her that day. Do you want to come?'

Step five of The Seven Steps to Closure flashed into my head. 'No thanks. I'm going to be holidaying in an exotic destination,' I declared suddenly.

'Ohh really,' said Mum in excitement. 'Where are you going?'

'Not sure yet, I'll let you know as soon as I do.'

The thought of being out of the country for the wedding felt right. It was going to be bigger than Ben Hur now that Jake was Lord Mayor. Christ, I wonder if the media would treat it like a celebrity wedding. Or worse, a royal wedding.

What if they decided to make them ride through town in horse-drawn carriages like when Princess Diana married Prince Charles? Yep, I was definitely going to be out of town for that one. I may as well be out of the country.

There was one teeny weenie little problem. Elaine had confiscated my passport and was refusing to give it to me till I had completed step four of the seven steps. Could I lie about the sex thing? Hmmm - lie convincingly about sex to Elaine? Absolutely not. The human lie detector would be all over me in a flash.

Shit.

That gave me 8 weeks to get laid and get out of the country. Considering the option of having to witness the wedding, I decided that if worse came to worse I would ring Anthony and his piggy wiggy nail and ask him for a one-night-stand.

I just hoped it didn't come to that.

* * *

Monday evening took forever to come. Elaine and I had organised for Natalie to come over after work for moral support. She had been planning to confront her boss that day and we hadn't heard anything about how it had gone.

'Tissues?' asked Elaine.

'Check.'

'Chocolate?'

'Of course.'

'Ice-cream?'

'Cookie Cream Commotion and Double Dutch Chocolate,' I said, checking the freezer.

'Excellent.' Elaine, took a seat on my lounge and started examining her nails.

'I can't take the pressure,' I muttered nervously, pacing the loungeroom floor and wishing I were half as calm as Elaine.

Finally there was a knock on the door. 'All right,' I said to Elaine, 'let her talk only if she wants to. We won't force her. We're just here for her no matter what.'

I opened the door to find Natalie looking surprisingly collected. If it was anybody other than Nat, that would have reassured me, but Nat was a lawyer. She was practised at hiding emotions. Hell, who am I kidding, it had nothing to do with her being a lawyer and everything to do with her being Nat. Calm and composed, no matter what. Well 99% of the time. (Even when we were hiding under the stairs behind the gym she had been composed, planning our escape. Plan A, B and C mind you. I, on the other hand, had huddled and sobbed with fright.)

'What happened?' said Elaine from behind me.

'Elaine,' I said in a we-discussed-this-and-decided-not-to-do-this tone of voice.

'What?' she asked, looking at me.

'We said we wouldn't pressure her,' I stage-whispered out of the corner of my mouth.

'No, *you* said we wouldn't.' She was technically right. She hadn't agreed with me.

'Are you going to let me in?' Nat asked.

'Sorry. Come in, sit down, put your feet up,' I said nervously. I followed her into the lounge before I broke. 'All right,' I begged, 'tell us what happened.'

She smiled at us. 'Well both Ricardo and I still have our jobs.'

'How?' I said in surprise. 'Did you have to beg?'

'Nope. I went to her office first thing and she said, "Ahh Natalie so glad you came, I was going to talk to you today." I, of course, was thinking I bet you were. Then totally out of the blue she said, "You've been doing such a great job on the Velucci account, they want to be moved entirely into your care." I was waiting for her to say, "What a pity you won't be working here any more." But instead she said, "So I think it is time to talk about a partnership."

'What did you say?' asked Elaine in surprise.

'Well I said "Excuse me?" And she said, "When our biggest account decides they want to be looked after solely by a single lawyer I would be stupid to leave you in a position where you could walk away with them." I thought I may as well take the bull by the horns so I said, "So last night is not going to affect your decision?"'

'And?' asked Elaine.

'She leaned back in her chair, kicked her shoes off, put her feet up on her desk and said, "You lucky bitch. I wouldn't mind a go myself if you get tired of him."

Elaine started laughing. 'Sounds like my type of woman.'

'Seriously?' I said. 'That was it?'

'Yup. So now you have to help me celebrate. I'm finally going to get my partnership.'

'Cancel the order for tissues,' I said to Elaine, as I opened the fridge door, 'looks like we're going to need the bubbly stuff instead.'

* * *

I still hadn't decided how I was going to do this sex thing. That's what I had started to think of it as. The sex thing. It was like a huge barricade in front of me that I had to climb before I could get on with my life.

'It's just sex,' Elaine kept telling me. 'Stop making a mountain out of a molehill.'

'I haven't had sex with anybody but Jake for a very long while,' I whined. 'What if I'm really bad?'

'Who cares, as long as you enjoy it?'

It was easy for Elaine to say that. I had a theory - formed over years of watching a bevy of gorgeous young studs pant after her - that Elaine was very good at sex.

I was lying on the couch after work idly flicking through the television channels while I mulled over the sex thing. What I didn't want to watch was exactly what I found.

A Current Affair was running an article on Jake and Tash's wedding plans. They were going to follow it through to the end doing small segments on it every week until the big day, when they would be broadcasting the entire wedding. It was all my fears come true: a royal, fucking wedding.

I reached for my phone as snippets of footage were shown. Tash and Jake - laughing and looking at crockery together, picking flowers, organising seating plans, holding hands while she stared up adoringly into his face.

Then the interviewer asked questions, while they sat in the loungeroom – *my* loungeroom that *I* decorated - and made packets of icing covered almonds.

'Ha,' I snorted, 'as if.' I rang Elaine. 'Are you watching it?' I asked as she picked up.

'Hang on. What channel?'

'Nine.'

'Oh,' she said a few seconds later, 'don't they realise those things will be stale by the wedding?'

'This Saturday night, you and me and meaningless sex.'

'Umm Tara, I think you're meant to have sex with a man.'

'Ha ha. Let me clarify that. You and I are going to go out and party until I am pissed enough to hook up with somebody and have a one-night-stand.'

'Sounds great - but can we do Friday night? I've got the reunion on Saturday.'

'Oh of course.'

'All righty, it's a date. I'll come around after work and we can get ready together. See you around 6.30ish.'

'See you then.'

I flicked off the T.V. and thought about ringing Mum, but then decided that I didn't really feel like talking. Instead I grabbed *Twilight* and headed for bed. 'Ahh Edward,' I sighed, as I snuggled under my doona and opened up to the first page of the book, 'you would never leave me for some beautiful, heartless cow.' I ignored the fact that Edward was a fictional vampire, and I was not Bella, and spent the rest of the evening blissfully entranced in my fantasy world.

Chapter Five

The Fourth Step to Closure – Have Meaningless Sex

I stood in the doorway to my walk-in wardrobe, staring at the red dress I had bought during step two. I held it in front of me, looking at my reflection. Did I dare wear it? I felt breathless at the mere thought. Would I do it justice? Could I do it justice? My front door bell rang announcing Elaine's arrival.

'Just do it,' she announced, as she walked in the front door.

'Huh?'

'The dress. I'm sure you've been staring at it for the last 30 minutes or so.'

'You're scary, you know that?' I said, shaking my head.

'Tara, wear it. You'll look great. And if a one-night-stand is what you're after, that's the dress to get it in.'

'I don't know,' I whined, 'what if I look really pathetic and everyone is sniggering as I walk past.'

'Trust me darling. No-one is going to be sniggering at you.'

'What are you wearing?' I asked.

'Little, black strapless number.' She dragged a couple of bottles of bubbly out of her handbag and, heading into the kitchen, put one in the fridge. The other she opened, pouring us both a glass.

'Come on,' she said, coming back into the lounge, 'let's pretend we're schoolgirls and do a mudpack before we get ready.'

She removed two little alfoil packs from her handbag and handed one to me with my glass of bubbly. I squished it and immediately had a flashback to the day I was getting ready for my first date with Jake.

'Stop that,' said Elaine.

'Sorry.' I put the packet down.

'Not that - although if you keep that up you're going to get it all over you. Stop thinking about Jake.'

'I did a mudpack the night I got ready for our first date.'

'Well it's a sign,' she said, sipping her champagne.

'A sign?' I asked, taking a seat beside her on the couch.

'Of new beginnings: that was a mudpack for then, and this is one for now. One for the beginning and one for the end.'

'Yeah,' I said enthusiastically, 'the symmetry in that works. Come on let's get these on and then we can do our nails while they set.'

Two hours later it was time to put on the red dress. I had consumed quite a bit of Dutch courage by then - having finished the champagne Elaine had brought with her, and was feeling more confident about my wardrobe choice. Slipping it over my head, I shimmied it down my body, zipping it up before stepping into my red high-heels. I placed some sparkling cubic zirconia studs into my ears and stepped back to examine the effect. Elaine wolf whistled from the loungeroom where she was ringing a cab.

'Well, that ought to do it,' she said in an approving voice.

I smiled at her before asking, 'Where are we going?'

'I thought we might go to Notre Dame, a new Club in Darling Harbour. We can get some food there as well.'

'Excellent. I am feeling a wee bit peckish,' I said.

'Cab's going to be here soon. Grab your bag, let's go,' she said, as she hung up.

As I closed the door to the apartment, I realised that I was excited about the possibilities that might unfold during the course of the evening. I was looking forward to flirting and letting the evening unfold around me. I just hoped the universe was holding up its end of the bargain.

* * *

The club was tasteful and modern while also being warm and friendly. I felt immediately comfortable and was able to release some of the nerves, which had been bubbling around inside me since we got in the cab. Elaine led me to the bar for a drink and looked at me questioningly with an eyebrow raised.

'Make it big, and make it strong,' I replied.

'Your drink, or your man?'

'Both.'

I have to admit that I can't remember all of that evening, but I have managed to piece together my snippets of memories. First Elaine and I were drinking wine and dancing. Then I seem to remember being at the bar drinking shots with a group of guys. I think they were part of a sports team. Hmmm - they were a soccer team, or maybe it was football. Then we danced some more - wild crazy dancing, throwing our heads back and waving our arms in the air.

After that I headed to the bar for a drink of water, but when I got there one of the more handsome footballers - or maybe he was a hockey player - asked me what I was drinking. I didn't want to say water like a big girl, so I looked up at him - he was a good six foot tall - batted my eyelids and told him I was having a Slippery Nipple.

So he and I shot a couple of Slippery Nipples, linking arms and throwing them back. And then we went and danced some more. I think Elaine was dancing with one of the hockey guys. Or maybe they were a cricket team?

After that things got pretty messy. I remember laughing loudly at a joke and having to be supported by my cricket man. Then all of a sudden, we were snogging. I don't remember how it started and I wish there were a nicer way to put it, but that was what it was: animalistic snogging. It felt extremely nice though, even more so because it had been such a long time since I'd snogged anyone.

We ended up back at his hotel - although I can't remember how we got there - and were in the lift still kissing. Things were getting more frantic and we had started getting frisky with our hands. We stumbled out of the elevator and managed to get into his room, at which point the reality of the situation imposed itself on me and I excused myself to go to the toilet. I made the mistake of looking in the mirror. Black eyes, dry scaly skin, messy hair, smudged lipstick; I resembled a drunken scary clown.

Oh God, I thought, *I can't go out there like this.*

But in the end I did, figuring it was less weird than staying in the bathroom all night. He was sitting on the edge of the bed waiting for me.

'Mmmm,' he groaned as he pulled me into his lap, 'you're beautiful.'

There's a lot to be said for beer goggles.

We began kissing again and I can remember starting to pull each other's clothes off. I can remember also that I wasn't totally turned on, it was more like a necessary exercise I had to carry out. Almost like an exorcism. I just needed to have sex with someone other than Jake.

I did enjoy the feeling of him pushing me back onto the bed, but when he started spreading my legs I thought, *Oh well at least it won't take long.* Instead of mounting me as I had expected, he leant down and licked my stomach, slowly working lower with his tongue, teasing me with the sensation; over my hips and along my inner thighs until finally taking my clitoris into his mouth and gently sucking. Christ, this was certainly more than I had expected from my one-night stand, but who the hell was I to complain? I felt my back arching against him wanting him inside me. He moved even lower and placed the tip of his tongue in my vagina wiggling it gently before darting it inside. My eyes rolled back in my head and I clenched my fingers into his hair. 'Oh God yes,' I heard my voice all throaty and husky pleading him for more. I could feel the hardness of his penis pressing up against my leg and suddenly I wanted to feel that sliding deep inside me.

'Please,' I begged, as he licked some more. 'I want you now.'

He grinned cheekily at me as he said, 'Gets them every time.'

'But,' I asked shyly, 'can we turn the light off?'

Leaning over he grabbed a condom from the bedside table and flicked off the lamp. I tried to help with the condom, but in my eagerness I was slowing things down.

His dick felt so hard and yet so smooth and soft at the same time I wanted to stroke it forever.

'Stop,' he moaned, 'I don't want to come yet.'

Then finally he was deep inside me. It felt so amazing I couldn't believe I had waited so long to do it.

The ambient light coming through the curtain gave a soft glow, showing only his outline. He could have been anyone, but whoever he was, he was moving inside me like he was made to fit. We rolled over and all of a sudden I was on top. I've always been kind of shy on top. What if my breasts look all old and droopy? What if I was pulling a strange facial expression? But he reached up and, taking my breasts in his hands, rubbed my nipples with his thumbs. It was heaven. I rode him harder and faster until I got close to coming, and then I made myself stop.

'What's wrong?' he asked panting.

'I don't want to come yet,' I muttered, a little embarrassed.

'We can always do it again,' he said.

And we did. Later in the wee hours of the morning, he entered me carefully and we moved slowly, with him deep, deep inside until finally we came together. And then we slept, taking turns to cradle each other.

In the morning he was gone. A note told me he'd had to catch an early flight and hadn't wanted to wake me. I felt sadness then of a different kind. Not so much for something I'd lost, but for something I'd never had a chance to have.

My phone started shortly after I read the note: texts from Nat and Elaine both wanting to know what had happened.

I texted back. Am alone in a strange hotel.

Nat : *What? Where are you?*

Elaine : *Was it good?*

I dragged myself to the window in an attempt to identify my location. I was relieved to realise I was still in Darling Harbour.

Novotel. Excellent. Meet me in an hour at Mudslide.

And then I searched the room for any sign of my man. Sadly, I couldn't even remember his name. Finally I had to admit that if he had wanted to see me again he could have quite easily left his number on the note. All I found was a business card for a journalist who must have been interviewing the team. For a millisecond, I considered ringing him, but luckily I paused to consider how desperate and sad it would sound.

'Oh hi, you don't know me but I found your business card in the hotel room of the man I just had unforgettable sex with, and I am wondering if you know who he is? About 6 foot with dark blonde hair and an amazing physique. What? No he didn't leave me a number. He was gone when I woke up.'

Yep - certifiably, scarily stalkerish. I put the business card in the bin and helped myself to the free toiletries in the bathroom.

* * *

An hour, a shower and two Nurofen later, I arrived at Mudslide feeling slutty in my little red dress and high heels.

'Thought you might need these,' Elaine said, with a grin on her face as she handed me a bag of clothes and my passport. Laughing I tucked my passport into my bag, before heading straight to the ladies where I struggled out of my dress in the small toilet cubicle, and into the slacks and shirt that Elaine had brought me. I felt immediately better.

They waited for me to sit and order bacon and eggs with a side serve of hash browns, (the hangover made me do it), before they started barraging me with questions.

'Ladies please.' I held up my hands. 'One at a time.'

I pointed at Nat.

'Ahh the pressure, now I don't know what to ask,' she said.

'Oh for goodness sake,' interrupted Elaine, 'just tell us all the details.'

'You mean the ones I can remember,' I said laughing.

'Ohhhhh,' groaned Elaine in sympathy. 'Was it that bad? I had a horrific one-night-stand one New Year's Eve. I stayed the night and kept getting woken up by him wanking, which was a little offensive as I wouldn't have minded a bit more myself. I've never seen anything like it. The man was a high-pressure hose. In the morning I was totally covered in dried up sperm.'

'Can somebody please cancel my egg order,' I said laughing. 'Elaine that's revolting. It was nothing like that. The truth is it was pretty good. Actually better than good, it was bloody marvellous. And the worst part is that now he has gone and I don't know how to find him.'

'Whoa, steady girl. This was a One-night-stand. Remember?' Elaine stared at me.

'Yes,' I muttered in a weak little voice.

'How do you feel about Jake now?' asked Nat.

I paused to probe at the open wound that had once been my heart. 'Still hurts, but it feels a little more distant now.' I watched in amusement as the girls high-fived each other over the table. 'No more one-night-stands though,' I warned them. 'Especially you missy,' I said to Elaine. 'Even though I have to admit it was a wonderful distraction.' I paused as memories of him sucking my clitoris washed over me. 'A simply wonderful distraction,' I repeated.

'God, I hope I get a wonderful distraction tonight,' said Elaine. She picked up her coffee and took a sip while the waiter delivered our meals. She had opted for muesli yet again.

'Oh that's right, the big reunion. How are you feeling?' I asked.

'Nervous, excited, worried, nervous, in that order.'

'You're going to look gorgeous,' Nat said, through a mouthful of eggs.

'Thanks. I just hope I look gorgeous enough.'

* * *

I spent the rest of the day with a hangover and a big grin on my face while I did the housework. I had arranged to go to Lil and Martin's for dinner and arrived at about 6pm, feeling much better after a long, uninterrupted afternoon nap.

'You look different,' Lil said.

I sat at the breakfast bar sipping white wine and watching her and Martin toss salad, cut vegies and make garlic bread.

She stopped chopping and looked at me critically. 'You look great. What have you done? No don't tell me. Your hair is the same.' She stared at me while she tried to work it out. 'It's weird you seem different but I can't put my finger on it. Martin, can you tell what's different about Tara?'

'She always looks good to me.' He flashed me a cheeky grin and I blew him a kiss.

I waited until Lil was sipping her alcohol free wine and then I said, 'I had sex.'

She snorted the wine, launching into a coughing attack. Martin patted her on the back and handed her a glass of water. 'Tara,' he said accusingly, 'you did that on purpose.'

'Just aiming for the maximum impact,' I said with a grin on my face.

Lily finally recovered enough to start asking questions. 'Who with? Where? When? Ohhh, tell me everything.' She left the kitchen and perched awkwardly on the stool next to me.

'I don't know his name,' I said.

Lil gasped. I held up a hand to stall her response and said, 'Let me clarify that statement. I can't remember his name. He did tell me but the music was really loud at the club and I was having trouble hearing him - and to be totally honest I was a little bit drunk.'

'Was he yummy?' she asked.

'Totally yummy.'

'How old?'

'I'm guessing mid-thirties. We didn't exactly swap life stories.'

'No, just body fluids,' said Martin laughing.

'Oh Tara, tell me you were safe,' Lil said in concern.

'Of course I was safe.'

'Was it fantabulous or really, really horrible?' she asked.

'I wouldn't be telling you if it was horrible. I'd be at home with my head in the oven.'

'Are you seeing him again?' she said, her eyes lighting up at the prospect.

'The point of last night was to help me move closer to closure with Jake, not to shift my emotional baggage from one man to another,' I said, quoting Elaine. I would have been very happy to see him again, but probably would have stuffed the whole thing up by talking too much, so it was probably better left just as it was - a delicious memory.

And a delicious memory was exactly what it was for me later that night while I drifted closer and closer to sleep.

* * *

Elaine was glowing when Nat and I met her for breakfast the morning after the reunion.

'How was it?' I asked.

'It was fantastic,' she gushed, 'awesome, wonderful, amazing.'

'Wow,' I said. 'So this Robert is everything you'd hoped?'

'Robert?' she sounded confused. 'Oh God, not him.' She shuddered.

We paused as the waiter delivered our breakfasts. Elaine immediately handed a strip of bacon down to Benny who was waiting patiently in her handbag.

'Was he there?' Nat asked.

'Who?' Elaine asked, patting Benny.

'Robert.'

'He was there. Loud, obnoxious, know it all. His first and only words to me were "Hey Elly, your tits look hot in that dress".' She shuddered again. 'I mean of course they looked hot, but the cheek of him to say it. I was mortified.'

'Well if it wasn't Robert that put that smile on your face who was it?' I asked confused.

'Alistair Delaine. Dr Alistair Delaine.' She emphasised the Doctor as she said it. 'I used to sit next to him in Biology. He was the school nerd.'

'Not a nerd any more?' I asked.

'So, not a nerd. Well, he might be a teeny weenie bit of a nerd, but he's a gorgeous, funny, successful nerd.'

'Did you recognise him?' asked Nat.

'No. I had decided to leave and was at the exit when a gorgeous man said, "Not leaving already? You only just got here." I looked him up and down, there was a lot of ground to cover, and said, "Do I know you?" And he said, "Not as much as I'd like you to," and then he took my hand and kissed it, and said 'Delaine, Alistair Delaine.'

'Ohhhh,' Nat giggled. 'Like Bond, James Bond.'

Elaine nodded. 'In final year I organised a school outing to see a James Bond movie, but only the two of us turned up. I wouldn't have admitted it to anyone but I had a lot of fun. Of course, I never went out with him again. That wouldn't have been cool. And honestly he was a bit of a skinny pimply dweeb. Not any more.' She smiled smugly.

'He's still single?'

'Got married when he was at Uni, then after six years of Med school and a couple of years of residency he decided to go back and specialise. She decided she wanted a life and left. He was heartbroken and threw himself into his studies. He's a neurosurgeon now.'

'Wow,' Nat said, genuinely impressed, 'I've never met a neurosurgeon before.'

'Well if all goes well you'll be meeting one soon,' Elaine said as she laughed. 'I had the most amazing night. He got me champagne and we talked on the balcony for hours. Before we knew it, the reunion was over and we were being kicked out. We went to a bar nearby and continued talking. He is so interesting.'

I had never heard Elaine praise a man for being interesting before. Rock hard body – yes. Huge penis - yes. A truly talented tongue - sadly, also yes. But never interesting.

'Was he good in bed?' I asked.

'I wouldn't know. I'm not that kind of girl,' she said prudishly, and then burst out laughing. 'Well not at the moment I'm not. He's taking me out to dinner next Friday, so maybe I'll know after that. Maybe not though; I'd like to ride this pony as far as I can. Hey when does Dinah get home?' she asked, suddenly changing the subject.

'Late Thursday evening. She wants to meet us for breakfast on Saturday. Can you come?'

'Can we make it brunch?' asked Nat. 'Ricardo is making me dinner on Friday night. He dropped some candles off at my house yesterday so I may be sleeping in.' She blushed prettily.

'No worries, I'll let her know when I pick her up on Thursday. Brunch it is.'

* * *

That afternoon I decided to pop up to Mum and Dad's.

'Want to stay for dinner?' Mum asked, looking up from the carrots she was picking in the garden.

'Sure, why not.'

'So,' she said, as I kicked off my shoes and relaxed into a deck chair near her, 'I hear you've had sex.'

I let out a startled yelp and turned to look at her. She had an amused expression on her face. 'Bloody Lil,' I muttered.

'Oh, don't blame her,' said Mum, dusting off her hands and coming to join me, 'I pumped her for the info; she didn't stand a chance. You know I can be very persuasive when I want to.'

'What did it take?'

Mum tried to look innocent. She lasted for a few seconds before caving. 'I offered to babysit all the girls for two weekends.'

'Two whole weekends, I'm impressed the information was worth so much.'

'It was a bet actually, after Jake left you. I bet you'd be back in the saddle within four months. Lil said that it would take you at least a year. I was feeling pretty safe with my bet thinking you'd have a drunken, anger bonk.'

'Mother!'

'What? I read books, I watch telly. I blame it on *Twilight* personally.'

'Blame what?'

'You hanging on so long - all that unrequited love. Anyway don't blame Lil, she didn't so much ring to tell me, as to smugly organise the dates for the babysitting.'

My anger at Lil subsided just a little. Then I thought about her with her swollen belly and her six children and husband – who, although wonderful, was not always there - and my anger vanished. Hell, I was happy I'd managed to win her a couple of weekends alone with Martin.

'So tell me about it.'

'Mum I'm not telling you about it.'

'Why not? I'm sure you told the girls all about it.'

'Not all about it, just that it was good.'

'Just good?'

'Well better than good actually if you really must know.'

'Well that's all right, as long as it wasn't terrible.'

'I've never had really terrible sex.'

'Me neither,' she said smugly, opening her mouth to continue.

I shoved my hands over my ears and started saying, 'LALALALALALALALALA,' knowing that Mum's only sexual encounters were with Dad, and not wanting to know any more than that.

Mum laughed and held up her hands in defeat.

'All right, all right, I'll leave the subject alone.'

Just then, a cute, reddish bunny with enormous ears, hopped into the garden and started nibbling on Dad's greens.

'Ah Mum, there seems to be a rabbit eating Dad's vegies.'

'Oh,' she jumped up, 'bad bunny.' She scooped him up and sat back down with him on her lap. He looked at me and twitched his cute little nose.

'Awwwww,' I said, 'he's adorable. What's he in for?'

'Actually nothing, he was just so cute I brought him home. Unfortunately he's taken a real liking to your father's garden.'

'Mum, he's a rabbit. He eats vegetables.'

'Actually darling he's a Belgian hare. Although technically a Belgian hare is a rabbit.'

'How can a hare be a rabbit?'

'They're rabbits that have been bred to look like hares. None of it makes any difference; I'll have to take him back.'

The words hung there like a cloud between us.

'Really?' I said nonchalantly, resisting the urge to reach out a finger and see if his coat was as silky as it looked.

'Yes, such a shame, he's toilet trained and everything.'

'How do you toilet train a hare?'

'Same way you do a cat. He uses a kitty litter we leave in the toilet.'

'But you leave the toilet door closed.'

'He thumps on it with his hind leg. He's freaked your father out a few times.'

I laughed. Dad liked to disappear into the toilet with a book. It was a survival technique I believe he had developed from being the only male in the house while we were growing up.

'I wonder how long Martin has to stay in the toilet to maintain his sanity?' I asked.

'I think being away kind of does it for him,' Mum replied. 'If he didn't travel for work he'd probably have to get a toilet put into the library.'

We both laughed.

I plucked a piece of grass and held it out to Bad Bunny. He grasped it with his little paws and nibbled it into his mouth. It made me think of a typewriter.

'Mum,' I said in my best weedly voice.

'Yes dear?'

'Can I have him?'

'Who? Martin? I think you'll have to take that up with Lil.'

'No silly.' I nodded my head at the rabbit in her lap. 'Him.'

'Oh,' she said innocently, 'I hadn't even thought of that.'

And suddenly I knew he had been mine when he was brought home from the animal shelter.

'Thanks Mum.' I leaned over and threw my arms around her neck, before picking him up off her lap and placing him on mine.

'Bad Bunny,' I said, patting him on the head. I leant over and sniffed him. 'He smells gorgeous.'

'I washed him this morning. It's his leave-in conditioner.'

'He has leave-in conditioner?'

'Yes, but best not to wash him too much, it's not good for his skin. Everything you need is inside. I'll go through it with you after dinner. He has quite specific dietary requirements and a very high metabolism, so you need to look after him well.'

Later that night as I drove back to my apartment I looked over at Bad Bunny, who was asleep on his bed, and I smiled as I realised I was content.

* * *

I was on my way to the airport to pick up Dinah with Bad Bunny riding shotgun. I had advised him quite firmly that once Dinah got in he would have to retire to his bed in the back. He had sulked about it for a little while, but had eventually agreed. He loved the front seat. I had put the window down and he was standing on his hind legs with his little face stretched towards it, his nose twitching and his long ears blowing crazily in the wind. He looked adorable.

I had missed Dinah terribly over the last few weeks, and was looking forward to hearing her adventures as well as giving her my good news. Since my one-night-stand, my reaction to Jake and Tash had changed from a deep ache to an irritated disdain. I would humph in annoyance, at having them suddenly intrude into my life, and then change the channel. I wasn't at all tempted to watch the nightly snippets on *A Current Affair* so that I could wallow in my misery. It was a huge step in the right direction, and a bit like a snowball rolling down a hill, was gaining momentum. The better I felt, the less I cared. And the less I cared, the better I felt.

I parked at the International Terminal, wincing at the thought of the parking fee and hoping her flight was on time. Bad Bunny fitted easily into my huge handbag and, after his exciting car trip, he curled up and went to sleep.

It felt like forever before Dinah finally cleared customs. 'I'm sorry,' she exclaimed, as she fell into my arms. 'I had shoes that had soil on them and they had to take them off and clean them for me, and I had a wooden carving I bought that needed checking, and God, I'm so tired.'

I just laughed and hugged her and slowly became aware that there was a strange woman watching us. Geez, what was her problem? Hadn't she ever seen two women hugging before? Maybe she thought we were lesbians and was having a good old gawk. Or maybe it was someone I knew and had forgotten. Bad Bunny chose that exact moment to stick his head over the top of my bag and the strange woman said, 'Dinah, you didn't tell me she had a bunny. How gorgeous. Can I hold him?' she asked me.

'Sorry, time for introductions,' Dinah said as she let me go. 'Tara, this is Gloria Johnson. She was one of the doctors on the ship. Gloria, this is Tara.'

'So pleased to meet you,' Gloria gushed. 'Dinah's told me so much about you.'

She smiled at Dinah who said, 'Gloria does the most amazing work on the Mercy Ships. She spends a month every year in Africa operating on women with Obstetric Fistulas.'

'Right, ' I said, 'the thing they get from prolonged labour.'

'Oh, you know about it. That's amazing, hardly anyone knows about it,' said Gloria excitedly.

I squirmed a little, wanting her to believe that I really was that clever. 'Nah,' I finally admitted, 'I read about it on the Mercy website when Dinah first decided to go. I'd never heard about it before then.'

'Oh.' Gloria looked a little disappointed, but then she smiled and said, 'well you know about it now. That's the important thing.'

'Here.' I handed her Bad Bunny. 'He loves having his belly rubbed.'

Squealing she scooped him up.

'Tara, when did you get a rabbit?' asked Dinah.

'Actually he's a Belgian hare,' I corrected her. 'Mum gave him to me last weekend to replace Fishy Fishy, who committed suicide, who was to replace Princess, who plunged to her death while trying to kill Cocky.'

Dinah started laughing. 'It looks like I've missed a lot.' She reached out and rubbed Bad Bunny's belly and she and Gloria shared a smile.

'What's his name?'

'Bad Bunny.'

'Why Bad Bunny?'

'Mum was calling him Bad Bunny because he was eating Dad's garden. It sort of stuck.'

'What's his problem?' she asked.

'As far as I can ascertain his only idiosyncrasy is that he really, really likes humping things.'

Dinah burst out laughing then explained to Gloria, 'Tara's Mum, whom you have to meet, works at an animal shelter and tries to find homes for the psychologically disturbed animals.'

'Oohh,' said Gloria, 'maybe she could get us one.' And then she blushed and said, 'I mean me one.'

I watched while Dinah reached out and touched Gloria's face. Whoa, what was going on here? I was standing there with a stunned expression on my face while the pieces started to fall into place, and then the clincher occurred. With Bad Bunny still in her arms, Gloria pivoted towards Dinah, who wrapped her arms around her and kissed her. Not a chaste peck on the cheek either, but a full-on smooch on the lips. It gave me such a shock that I let out a little squeal.

Dinah turned to me in concern. 'Sorry, a bit too much too soon?'

'No no,' I lied, clutching my face, 'a bug just flew into my eye.'

'Here,' said Gloria, handing Bad Bunny to Dinah and suddenly becoming all business. 'Let me have a look.'

'Isn't she great?' said Dinah.

I tried to nod my head at her while Gloria prised open my eye and examined it. 'Can't see anything, which is great as it means it didn't scratch your eyeball. You should be fine,' she finally announced.

'Gee, thanks, it feels better already,' I garbled in embarrassment.

Dinah stuck her tongue out at me from behind Gloria's back, knowing full well I had had no such thing as a bug in my eye. I stuck mine back out at her and then I smiled. I saw Dinah sigh in relief and realised how worried she must have been about the whole coming-out-to-your-best-friend thing.

'So,' I said, as we finally arrived at my car, 'how long have you guys been an item?'

'Well,' said Dinah, 'we were on the same plane on the way over. They told Gloria to look out for me at the gate.'

'We asked if they could move our seats so we could sit together and I could fill Dinah in on what to expect,' continued Gloria. 'I couldn't believe my luck when I saw how cute she was.' She winked at Dinah before continuing. 'I didn't want to freak her out, but I just couldn't stay away.'

'It only took her a week to break me down. She was pretty convincing.' Dinah chuckled. I decided that I didn't want to know exactly what form the convincing had taken.

'And we've been inseparable ever since,' finished Gloria.

'Right, so whose house am I heading for?'

'Mine,' said Dinah. 'Hey Tara, please don't tell the others before Saturday. I want to be the one to do it.'

'Hell, be my guest. I want to be there to see it.'

'Do you think they'll mind?'

'No, of course not - I think they'll get a bit of a shock though.'

I pulled up in front of Dinah's little, red brick cottage in Randwick and helped them unload their things.

'Brunch on Saturday,' I told Dinah. 'Is that all right with you?'

'Yeah brunch's great.' She opened her mouth in a huge yawn.

'Come on Gloria. Let's go get some sleep.'

I doubted though from the look Gloria threw her that she would be getting much sleep for a while.

'See you guys on Saturday,' I said as I hopped back in the car.

Dinah threw me a grateful look and I knew she had been worried about Gloria's acceptance into our little group.

Picking Bad Bunny up, I waved his little paw at them and then moved him back to his shotgun position.

'Well BB,' I said as we drove off, 'looks like it's just you and me kid.'

Bad Bunny, however, was trying to hump the armrest of the passenger seat and wasn't at all interested in my moment of self-pity.

* * *

Nat, Elaine, Benny, Bad Bunny and I were at the Mudslide Café waiting for Dinah to turn up. I was struggling not to say anything that would give Dinah's secret away and was grateful that Elaine had been on a date with Alistair the night before.

'Where'd he take you?' I asked, while mentally chanting, *Don't say anything about Gloria. Don't say anything about Gloria.*

'Villa Diora.'

'Oh, that fancy Italian restaurant. Any good?' asked Nat.

'The food was fantastic, the wine was wonderful and the company was even better.' She looked like the cat that had gotten the canary.

'So did you…?' I asked thinking, *Don't mention the word lesbian.*

'We had a very passionate embrace on my front doorstep. And then I wished him good night and told him I'd see him tomorrow. We're having a picnic.'

'Wow. So you weren't even tempted to invite him in?' asked Nat.

'Of course I was,' said Elaine. 'I had to go straight upstairs and have a cold shower.'

Just then Dinah turned up, which was a huge relief as I was so overloaded trying not to say anything about her and Gloria and kissing and lesbians, that I had got to the point where I couldn't say anything at all.

We all jumped up to give Dinah a hug. When it was Elaine's turn, she held her out at full arm's length, looked her in the eye for a few seconds and then clasped her into another embrace.

'Thank God,' she exclaimed. 'You've finally come out. It's about time.'

'Tara,' admonished Dinah, 'you promised.'

'You are super scary,' I said to Elaine. 'You knew Dinah was gay?'

'Dinah's gay?' Nat asked.

'Is that a problem?' Dinah said defensively.

'No, no, not at all, a bit of a shock,' Nat paused. 'A big shock actually,' she admitted. 'But I'm sure I'll get used to it.'

Dinah squeezed her hand.

'Well,' said Elaine, 'thank God that's finally out in the open. Now where is she?'

I had been wondering the same thing myself. Where was Gloria? Had they had a spat already and broken up? But no, I watched as Dinah blushed - definitely not broken up.

'I'm guessing she's somewhere nearby waiting to see how we respond to your big news before you introduce her, and that you're going to give her some sort of prearranged signal. Ahh a text,' Elaine amended, 'when it's safe to come over.'

'You sure you didn't tell her?' Dinah asked me.

'Hell, even I didn't know that,' I said.

'Well go on,' said Elaine, 'I'm dying to meet her.'

'All right, as long as you're all comfortable with it, I'd love you to meet her.'

'Wow,' said Nat a little dumbfounded, 'you're really gay.'

'Of course we're all comfortable with it.' Elaine leaned over and shoved Nat. 'Aren't we Natalie?'

'Hughhh? Oh yeah right. I'm fine with it. I'm cool with gay, you know I love Tristan,' she said to Elaine. 'I'm just in shock that's all. I had no idea.'

'All right,' said Dinah as she rapidly punched the keys on her mobile and fired off a text.

A few moments later Gloria appeared around the corner and sauntered up the road to us. Her shoulder-length hair fell in soft curls around her face, giving her an angelic look that suited her huge blue eyes. That's where any resemblance to an angel ended. She had on low cut, tight fitting leather pants and a t-shirt that showed us a flash of smooth brown belly. Over the shirt was a matching leather jacket.

'Wow,' said Elaine to Dinah approvingly, 'she's hot. What does she do?'

'She's a doctor.'

'Ohhh,' squealed Elaine in excitement, 'so's mine.'

'Great,' said Nat laughing, 'they both get doctors and I get a cleaner.'

'Yes, but a hot cleaner,' said Elaine.

'Hey, at least you're getting something,' I said, poking her. 'All I've got is a nymphomaniac hare.' I patted Bad Bunny's head, which was poking over the top of my bag.

Gloria arrived at our table and stood there shyly while Dinah introduced her. Once the introductions were finished, we pulled up an extra chair and began to fill each other in on what we'd missed in each other's lives.

It was several hours later that Dinah finally said to me, 'So Tara, what happens now?'

'What do you mean?'

'What step are you up to.'

'Oh, step five. Travel to an exotic destination. I'm going to go overseas while the wedding is on.'

'Ooooh,' exclaimed Gloria. 'Can we please, please, pretty please look after Bad Bunny while you're gone?' She reached over and rubbed his head.

'Sure,' I said. 'Dad will be thrilled.'

'So where are you going?' Dinah asked.

'I don't know yet. I'm waiting for the universe to supply the destination. I'll let you know as soon as I do.'

I stretched my arms over my head and said, 'I need an afternoon nap.'

'Yeah, I'm whacked,' admitted Dinah. 'This jetlag thing sucks.'

'All right,' said Elaine, 'the meeting of the girlhood is officially over and will reconvene at Tara's as soon as she's ready to fill us in on her travel plans.'

'I'm not sure I can handle the pressure,' I gasped. 'Where to go, what to do? Any takers on a joint trip?'

'This is something you have to do by yourself,' said Elaine, effectively nipping the idea in the bud.

I looked at Natalie for support but she just shrugged her shoulders and nodded her head as though to say, 'Sorry, you're on your own here.'

'How long have I got to come up with a destination?'

'Everybody free Wednesday night?' asked Elaine. 'All right Tara,' she continued, once they had all checked their diaries, 'you've got till Wednesday night. We'll be at your place at 7pm - don't stress, we'll bring dinner.'

As I lay in bed later that afternoon, listening to the rhythmical humping of Bad Bunny giving my old teddy a bit of a session, I contemplated different holiday destinations. What if I chose the wrong place? What if something was meant to happen while I was away that would change the course of my life, but I missed it because while it was happening in Turkey I was sunbaking on a Greek Island? In the end, I came up with an idea that would take the decision out of my hands and allow the universe to provide me with my destination. I drifted off to sleep peaceful and happy with my decision.

* * *

The girls had arrived at 7pm sharp on Wednesday night and taken over my kitchen. Benny and Bad Bunny were having a Mexican standoff: Bad Bunny towering over Benny, they sat like statues, eyeing each other.

'What's he eat?' Gloria asked.

'Hay,' I said.

'Hay?'

'Yep, grass hay. I get it from the pet store. It keeps everything moving so it's very important. Plus I give him three cups of greens and 3 tablespoons of carrot or fruit a day. He loves strawberries, but I can only give him a tiny bit of that because it's so high in sugars.'

'What can't he eat?'

'Lots of things, but in the vegetable world potato and corn are too high in starch, and cauliflower, broccoli and cabbage can give him wind and kill him.'

'Right, no broccoli, cauliflower or cabbage,' she said, sounding a little stressed.

'Don't worry, it's all written down for you.'

She wandered off to watch Bad Bunny and Benny who were now sniffing each other carefully.

'So,' I said as I sidled up to Dinah, 'have you told them?'

'Told who what?' she asked nonchalantly, as she sliced up a tomato.

'Your Mum and David, about Gloria.'

'Yes I told them. Mum's meeting her next week.' She placed the tomato in the salad bowl and picked up an avocado.

'And?'

'And what?' she asked, flicking the seed out of the avocado.

'I know you're doing this just to annoy me,' I said.

She laughed. 'They were fine about it.'

'Just fine?'

'More than fine, Mum was relieved.' She put her knife down and turned to face me.

'Relieved?' I asked confused.

'That I had finally worked it out,' she said, shrugging one shoulder. 'She said she had been worried that my relationship with Dad had made me choose abusive men as partners.'

'Do you think that was the case?' I asked thinking, *Damn well you chose abusive men as partners.*

She looked at me and shook her head. 'Tara you and I both know that's exactly what I was doing. When I had that showdown with Creepy Doug at the restaurant, it was like gaining closure from my father. It left me free to be who I really am. It was a bit annoying though. There I was all worked up to tell her, wondering how she was going to take it, and she just throws her arms around me and says, "Thank God".'

'And David?'

'Said, "Whatever makes you happy sis. When do I get to meet her?"'

'Has he met her?'

'Funnily enough he knows her. They were working in the same ward at the hospital last year.'

Gloria wandered over with some garlic bread, which she held out to Dinah. 'He tried to crack onto me in the tearoom,' she said.

I laughed. 'That sounds like David.'

When we had all eaten, I decided it was the right time to let the universe reveal its chosen destination for me. 'All right then,' I said, hopping up to prepare my decision-making tools. When I had them ready and the girls were seated on the lounges in front of me, I began. 'Thank you all for coming tonight. As you are aware the Wedding of the Year is next month, and I have come to a decision that it would be better for my mental health, and everyone else's, if I was nowhere near Sydney during this time.'

Elaine raised her wine glass. 'Hear, hear,' she said.

'So I have decided to finally take Dinah's advice about the psychological benefits of travel and will be venturing overseas for a few weeks during this time.'

The girls broke out in a round of applause, as if it were the first time they had heard this.

'Where are you going?' Elaine asked.

'Well Elaine, that is why you are all here tonight.'

'You don't know do you,' she said, shaking her head.

'No, but I will very soon. I am going to allow the universe to make the decision for me.'

'I knew those self-help books were a bad idea.'

'No seriously, I am opening myself up to the energies of the cosmos and I will let them guide my hand in determining my fate. Here you see before us the prepared tools of divine intervention.' I picked up a world map and, unfolding it, tacked it onto a cork-board I had previously placed on the wall. I was momentarily distracted by how big the map was. Wow, there were a lot of different countries I had never heard of.

'Are you just going to look at it and choose somewhere?' asked Nat.

'No, I am going to throw this at it.' I held up a dart I had borrowed from Martin and Lil the night before. 'Wherever it lands is where I go. Your job is to witness the honesty of the process and make sure that I allow the energies to guide me forwards. I am distancing myself from the decision-making, because let's face it, up until now my decisions have been crap.'

'Clever, clever,' said Dinah enthusiastically.

I picked up the dart. Looking at the map had made me realise there were a lot of areas of the world that I didn't want to visit, and I was starting to get a little nervous. Closing one eye I lined the map up with the end of the dart, and propelled the dart in what I hoped was the direction of Hawaii. The dart missed the map completely, thudding into the wall.

'Looks like you're staying right here,' said Gloria, laughing as I examined the hole I had created.

My next throw hit the Pacific Ocean and we clustered around the map examining it, searching for a teeny, tiny island.

'There's nothing there,' Nat announced officially.

'Bugger, I wouldn't have minded a relaxing holiday lying in the sun by the ocean,' I said pouting.

'Well, why don't you just go to Bali?' asked Elaine.

'No, no, if I don't do this right, the rest of my life will be a disaster. I just know it,' I said.

'Well you could hang around in a lifeboat at this location waiting to be rescued. Who knows, the rescuer may be hot.'

I stuck my tongue out at Elaine. 'You know I get seasick,' I said.

'Honey, you threw up on the ferry to Manly, that's not seasick, that's flat water sick.'

'There was a big swell that day,' I said defensively, as I pulled the dart out of the board.

The third shot landed right at the top of Mongolia. They looked at me expectantly.

'I don't want to go to Mongolia,' I whined. 'It's cold there and I saw Ewan McGregor in *The Long Way Round*. He had to eat sheeps' balls in Mongolia.'

'Look on the bright side,' said Dinah, smiling cheekily, 'maybe you'll meet Ewan McGregor.'

'That would be nice,' I said thoughtfully, 'but he's probably not there any more, and anyway he's married.'

'Maybe this is like in *Who Wants to Be a Millionaire* where you get three lifelines, but in this you get three chances to say no,' suggested Gloria helpfully.

I smacked my hand to my head and then pointed at her. 'That is exactly what this is like. I'm using up the first of my lifelines.'

After a brief conference, they all agreed that that was only fair, so I took up my position again. The next throw saw the dart bury itself deep in the middle of Greenland.

'Greenland?' I yelped. 'I'll freeze there.'

'Or get eaten by a polar bear,' suggested Elaine.

'Second lifeline?' asked Nat.

'Definitely.'

'Only one more lifeline though,' she warned.

My next dart smacked into Africa before falling to the ground.

'What does that mean?' I asked them.

'Maybe it means that you shouldn't even consider going to Africa,' said Nat, pulling her long blonde hair over one shoulder.

'Does it count as a lifeline?' Elaine asked Gloria.

'No,' she replied, 'that was the universe sending Tara a big warning about the dangers of going to Africa.'

'There are lions in Africa,' I said.

'And hippopotamuses who kill more people a year than lions do,' said Dinah.

'And there are these worms,' said Gloria, who was an African expert, 'that dig through the soles of your feet into your blood stream. They grow about a metre long before sticking their head out through your skin. The only way to get rid of them is to wrap them around a matchstick and turn them a little every day. It takes about a year.'

'Well,' I said, shuddering at the thought of having a worm wrapped around a matchstick attached to me for a year, 'that's settled. I'm not going to Africa.'

'You still have a lifeline,' Dinah said officially.

I threw again.

'New Zealand,' announced Elaine.

'I've already been to New Zealand. I want to go somewhere new,' I said, stamping my feet childishly.

'Do you want to use up your last lifeline to not go to New Zealand?' asked Dinah.

It was a tough one: New Zealand or the unknown. I pondered it for a while. What if I hit Antarctica next? But there was also a chance of Tahiti. Oh well, I had started this to have an adventure, so what the hell.

'I am going to use up my last lifeline,' I announced finally, staring at the map. *Bali*, I willed the universe, *Bali*. My probability of ever hitting it was pretty slim, but a girl can only hope. 'I give myself over to the will of the universe,' I shrieked, as I launched my dart at the map.

'India,' cried Dinah. 'God you are going to love it. I can lend you my *Lonely Planet*. Hey, isn't that where Jesse lives? Maybe you can stay with him when you get there.'

Jesse was Jake's twin brother. The two were as alike as night was to day.

'Won't Jesse be coming to Jake's wedding?' asked Gloria, once we had explained who he was.

We all burst out laughing.

'No,' I advised her, 'Jesse and Jake hate each other. I always got on well with him though. Jake hated that,' I admitted.

I sank down onto the couch as I considered the option of going to India. It was something I had never thought of before. Going to stay with the brother that Jake hated, while he married my cousin certainly had agreeable symmetry. I could see why the universe had offered it up. I rolled it around my mind. Maybe he could get some time off work and travel with me. Finally, I nodded my head at the girls. I was going to go to India and I was going to love it.

Chapter Six

The Fifth Step to Closure –
Travel to an Exotic Destination

To say that I loathed India would be an understatement. All right, so I hadn't been there very long - three days to be precise, but already I was hot and flustered, and nothing had worked out how it was supposed to. I felt so guilty even thinking that, given everything that had happened since I had gotten here, and all the pain and suffering there had been. At least I was alive and safe. But I'm getting ahead of myself. Let's start with the plane ride over.

Ahhh, the plane ride over: one squeamishly embarrassing moment after another. I had found my seat and squeezed into it, wondering who I was going to sit next to. It was a bloody long way to Mumbai and I was hoping I would get someone very small and petite, who didn't hog the armrests. Even better, someone with no arms. *Oh and God,* I prayed, *please no sneaky farters.*

I picked up the Qantas magazine while keeping an eye on the people filing towards me, breathing a sigh of relief as a man bordering on obesity waddled past. After a few minutes had passed, and my neighbour hadn't appeared, I began to have hope that the seat next to me would be vacant.

I flicked to the entertainment section of the magazine to see what movies would be shown on the flight.

'Do you mind?' a low, husky voice asked from beside me.

I started at the feet and worked all the way up his long, hard body to his face, which was every bit as pleasant to look at as the rest of him. He had to be at least six foot tall. His brown hair, long enough to be fashionable without appearing girly, was sandy brown. His bluey-green eyes, stared at me intensely, intelligence evident in their depths.

'Woof,' I said as I stumbled out into the aisle to let him in, blushing profusely when I realised I had just woofed out loud. Christ, how embarrassing.

'Pardon?' he said, looking at me. 'It sounded like you said Woof.'

I blushed harder. 'Why would I say Woof?' I asked defensively, wishing I hadn't consumed those Dutch-courage, pre-flight drinks.

'My mistake,' he said.

He brushed past me and, squeezing into his seat, shifted trying to get comfortable. His long legs looked very cramped.

Yummy yummy yummy, I thought to myself as I wriggled in next to him, making sure to keep it inaudible this time. 'Thank you God.' Oops, out loud again.

He looked at me.

'Thank you God,' I repeated thinking furiously, 'for the food we are about to receive. I like to get it over really early,' I explained, 'in case I forget when they bring out the food. I get really hungry sometimes and before I know it I'm halfway through my meal and have forgotten to say Grace.' I giggled nervously, while resisting the urge to put my head in my hands.

'Well, is it possible to just say one big Grace that could last you the whole day or month, why not your whole life?' he asked.

'Very good question, I shall be sure to ask the minister next time I see him,' I said, picking up the Qantas magazine and staring intently at it.

I was saved from having to say anything else by the appearance of a flight attendant with a lifejacket and a whistle. Watching intently as she explained what to do in the event of an emergency and how to brace if we were going to crash, I felt a small ball of panic starting to unfurl in my stomach. I mean really, how was I going to remember all of this if there were a real emergency? Frantically, I counted rows to find my closest exit and felt under my seat for the lifejacket. Then I noticed my neighbour watching me with an amused expression on his face.

'First time flyer?' he asked. He really was very cute.

'Absolutely not. I flew to New Zealand a few years ago,' I said, staring at him. He reminded me of someone. Who the hell was it?

He looked, if anything, even more amused. 'Ah, New Zealand,' he said, smirking.

I looked at him suspiciously. Was he mocking me? Surely not.

Finally locating the lifejacket, I settled down for take-off, trying to appear calm and relaxed. *Do not grip the armrests*, I told myself severely.

The plane began to taxi down the runway gathering speed; going faster and faster until all of a sudden, like magic, we were airborne. I felt the acceleration of the plane push me back into my seat, and just when I was starting to feel comfortable, I heard a funny noise and felt the plane shudder.

'Jesus,' I yelped, grabbing the armrests.

I could feel my neighbour staring at me. I mean seriously, this guy was starting to get on my nerves. What was his problem?

'What?' I said rudely.

'It's just the undercarriage retracting,' he said.

I looked at him stupidly.

'That bump you felt, it's just the wheels retracting back into the plane. It's nothing to worry about,' he smiled reassuringly, his eyes crinkling at the corner.

'Oh,' I said.

'Do you think I could have my hand back?' he said a few moments later.

I looked down and realised that instead of the armrest on my left, I was in fact gripping his hand.

'Sorry,' I muttered letting go. I could feel my face heating up.

To hide my embarrassment I picked up the on-board information card, examining the menu options for the flight.

'Saying Grace again?' he asked.

'Pardon?' What the hell was he going on about?

'Well, you were staring so intently at the menu that I thought you might be trying to get another Grace in before they brought out the meals.'

Belatedly, I remembered my previous slip up. 'Grace, right,' I said enthusiastically, nodding my head.

I heard the rumble of the trolley down the aisle as they announced over the intercom they would be serving pre-dinner drinks and snacks. I couldn't believe my luck when they also informed us that the dinner movie would be

Twilight. Finally, I settled back with my sparkling wine and tiny bag of nuts to enjoy the movie.

About ten minutes into it, my neighbour shifted uncomfortably in his chair and bumped me, causing a large slurp of wine to miss my mouth and end up on my lap. 'So sorry,' he said sincerely.

'Don't worry about it.' I dabbed at my black t-shirt with my serviette.

I didn't think much the second time it happened either. I mean the man was obviously too big for the seat, but the third time I started to have a suspicion that it had been no accident. I glared at him. He raised both hands in the air in a gesture of helplessness.

Hmmphhhhh.

Halfway through dinner, a sharp kick in the back of my seat from the girl sitting behind me caused a large forkful of korma to end up in my lap. I glanced over to see my neighbour fighting to contain a smile. He had a cute dimple in his cheek. 'Did you pay her to do that?' I asked grumpily.

'Pardon?' he asked innocently.

'Oh never mind,' I said.

I tried to concentrate on *Twilight,* but he would have none of it.

'You really like this crap?' he asked.

'What?' I glanced frantically at him. 'It's my favourite book,' I said, wishing he would be quiet.

'He's a vampire. I mean it's not very realistic is it?' he said. 'It's nearly finished,' I said. 'You can be annoying afterwards if you want.' As I turned my attention back to the screen, I heard him laugh a low, throaty laugh.

'If it's your favourite book then you already know how it ends. I'm curious as to why you are so nervous?'

'DO YOU MIND?' I roared at him.

His laugh this time was not so quiet.

Finally, when the credits were rolling up the screen I turned to him. 'Seriously what is your problem? Do I know you?'

'You really don't remember?' he said, crossing his arms.

'No. Please explain.'

'Hi, I'm Matthew King.' He held out his hand to shake mine.

'Nope. Still means nothing to me.' But I had to admit there was something faintly familiar about the name.

Looking disgusted, he shook his head. 'So how many men have you gone home with?' he asked, before muttering into his wine, 'Maybe I should get some blood tests.'

I stared at him for a few seconds as the few shady memories of my one-night-stand from last month came back to me.

'The cricket player?' I asked him.

'I'm a journalist.'

'Well I'm sorry. I have only gone home with one person, other than my ex-husband, in the last 6 years and he was in a sports team.'

'Your husband was in a sports team?'

'No, not my EX, ' I stressed the ex, 'my one-night-stand.'

'What was his name?' he asked.

'I don't see what my ex-husband's name has to do with any of this?' I said huffily. God the last thing I wanted was a journalist writing some incriminating article about me being a tart, and how lucky Jake was to get rid of me.

'Not your ex-husband, your sportsman.'

'I can't remember,' I admitted defiantly. 'It was great, but I was drunk and I can't remember his name. Now do you mind?'

'One in the last six years?'

'What's it to you?'

'I am a journalist who was interviewing a cricket team a month ago and went out with them afterwards.'

It took me a little while for it to sink in, but when it did, it hit me like a tonne of bricks. Ahh, the shame, I was sitting next to my dreamy one-night-stand guy and I hadn't even recognised him. This guy had gone down on me.

'Does that make me a slut?' I asked blushing.

'I don't think one guy in 6 years would classify anyone as a slut.'

'No, not that part. I'm sorry I didn't recognise you. It was dark and I was drunk, but you were great,' I gushed. 'Really great, and then in the morning you had gone and I wanted to ring you, but you hadn't left your number so I couldn't.'

'I left you my business card.'

'No, there was a card for a journalist which I threw out. Oh.' I stopped. 'Oh shit. I didn't realise it was you.'

'Because you couldn't remember my name,' he said.

'Yes.' I cringed as I admitted it.

'And you thought I was a cricket player.'

Part of me was mortified; the other part was doing a little song and dance.

Ratatatata yeh, he left me his number yeh. Ratatatata yeh.

I could feel my ego congo-ing around my head.

'Sorry,' I muttered, 'always have been a little bit of an idiot,' I admitted.

'Just a little bit?'

'Sometimes just a little bit, sometimes a really big one.' I smiled at him. 'Forgiven?'

'Forgiven for seducing me and doing crazy things to my naked body and then throwing out my number like a heartless shrew?'

'Yeah, for all that stuff.' I was pretty sure he wasn't mad. I smiled again encouragingly.

'Oh what the hell, forgiven.'

After that there was a bit of an awkward silence. It lay there between us like a black hole, getting bigger and bigger with each passing second. I cleared my throat in an attempt to fill the silence, and saw Matthew look up from the book he was reading. Oh good. So he was actually reading, and it was just me feeling the embarrassing silence.

'If two people are talking, and then they stop and one thinks there is an embarrassing silence, but the other one is quite content reading, does that mean there actually was an embarrassing silence?' I asked before I could stop the words rushing out of me. Oh crap, he was going to think I was a right weirdo now for sure.

'Do you always say exactly what you're thinking?' he asked.

'Most of the time, I can't seem to help myself.'

'Have you had many embarrassing moments?'

'Yes, but it means I normally don't have any embarrassing silence issues.'

'Sometimes silence is a good thing.' Ouch. I guessed that was his way of telling me to shut up. 'But I must say I find conversation with you refreshing. You don't pretend to be something you're not. You say what you're thinking and not what you think I want to hear. And you don't come up with pompous statements, while secretly hoping I'll quote you in my next article. You have no idea how nice that is.'

'Well if you find my foot in mouth disease nice, then I'm happy for you.'

'Now, I'm going to read my book. But I don't want you to think that I'm doing it just to ignore you. I'm up to a really good part and once I arrive in India I'll be doing more writing than reading so I want to get it finished.'

'That's all right; I've got a book to read as well.' I pulled out the book I had been advised to buy by the pimply, little book clerk at that airport, thanking God I had let him talk me into it. He had raved that it was the best book he had ever read and I really wouldn't regret carting it around India.

As I opened up the cover Matt glanced over to see what I was reading. 'No,' he said.

'What?' I asked alarmed. Did I have a spider on me somewhere? I frantically checked my shirt.

'Look.' He held his book up so I could see the cover. *The Girl With The Dragon Tattoo.* It was the same book I had purchased.

I smiled at him and flicked open to the first page. 'I hear it's very good,' I advised him, 'and that everybody who's anybody is reading it. And you can quote me on that.' As he laughed, I made a mental note to find the pimply book clerk youth and give him a large gift.

After a few glasses of wine, I fell asleep and woke with a start wondering where the hell I was. I hoped I hadn't been snoring. Matt was still reading beside me, and I decided to duck off to the toilets to check on my make-up and hair. I was almost back at my seat when Matt glanced up at me and started laughing. It couldn't be a bad case of bed head, I had just checked it in the bathroom. Did I have a bogey hanging out of my nose? No, I would have seen that. In the end it turned out that he was extremely amused by the 'I Love Edward' t-shirt I was wearing.

'My Mum has one too,' I told him coldly as I regained my seat.

That had only made him laugh harder.

The rest of the flight passed quickly. Probably because I nodded off again and slept through most of it. Finally, the crew announced our descent into Mumbai and we were off the plane and heading through customs. Matt and I walked in silence until we cleared customs.

'Where are you staying?' he asked me.

'With an old friend,' I said, not wanting him to know who I was staying with. I didn't have time to explain the current situation I found myself in.

'Here's my card,' he said, handing it to me, 'don't lose this one. Maybe we can catch up when we're both back in Sydney.'

'That would be nice,' I said, disappointed I would have to wait till then.

'What are you doing tomorrow?' he asked suddenly.

'Not sure, my friend is still working tomorrow.'

'Well,' he said smiling, 'do you want to meet up and I'll show you a bit of Mumbai.'

I tried to restrain the broadness of my smile but I could feel it threatening to crack my face in two. 'That would be lovely,' I said, as I spied an Indian man outside the terminal holding a card with my name on it. Jesse had sent his driver to pick me up.

'11am at the Gateway to India,' said Matt. 'Call me if you can't make it.'

'Oh, I'll be there,' I assured him. Hell, I'd be there if it meant walking through a pit of snakes to get there.

'See you then.' I smiled back at him as I followed my driver to the car.

* * *

There were people everywhere. People in cars, people on foot, people on bikes. Cars were jammed together moving along the road with seemingly no order, and yet amazingly, there was not the sound of metal on metal I kept expecting. I shoved my right foot into the floor for the umpteenth time in an attempt to stop the car, as yet another daredevil driver on a motorbike dashed through the traffic directly in front of us. The sound of car horns was continuous. It seemed that everybody drove with one hand on the wheel and one on the horn.

We had been driving for 45 minutes and I was finally starting to relax. Initially it had been a combination of the terror of dying in a terrible car accident, combined with the fear of this not being my driver that had caused my tension. I mean what if someone associated with the illegal sex trade had mugged my driver and I was about to unwittingly start a new occupation? I shuddered at the thought.

I took some calming breaths in and out and watched the scenery flick past the window. It was so different from what I was used to. Sydney was clean in comparison. Clean and yet strangely sterile - everywhere here there was something interesting to see; women washing clothes, children skipping and playing, people preparing food on fires, goats and cows just hanging around. And everywhere the bright colours of their clothing stood out in stark contrast against the browns and greys of the city.

After an hour and a quarter of driving - some of which involved dodging cows resting in the middle of the road, and a lot of which involved sitting still in traffic while my driver held his hand on the horn - we burst from the sprawl of suburbia to a road arching around a bay. My feeling of claustrophobia began to diminish as I watched the vast expanse of water disappearing into the distance.

'Not far now,' my driver informed me.

Fifteen minutes later, we turned up a little side street and stopped outside a building, before walking up three flights of stairs to what I desperately hoped was Jesse's apartment and not my new home as a prostitute. The driver knocked on the door, which opened, and there on the other side was Jesse. I fell into his welcome embrace.

'It's so good to see you,' he said, when we'd finished hugging, 'I can't believe you're here in India with me. When was the last time we caught up?'

'Ummmm, I think it was Christmas two years ago. Far too long.' I gave him another hug.

'Wow. Time travels fast,' he said. 'Here bring your stuff through to your room.'

He grabbed my bag and carried it into a room opening off the lounge. There were two single beds in it. 'Is this all right?' he asked. 'I could push them together and make it a double if you want.'

'I prefer them apart. I once spent a whole night trapped between two single beds. I suspect Lil had something to do with that.'

Jesse laughed, 'How is Lil?'

'Pregnant.'

'Again? What is this, number five?'

'Number seven,' I corrected him.

He whistled, 'Seven. Don't tell me?'

'Yep, all girls.'

He shook his head in disbelief before continuing, 'And Bert and Bet?'

'Really good thanks. Mum's still bringing home crazy pets. I am now the proud owner of a nymphomaniac hare.'

Still laughing about my nymphomaniac hare, he showed me where to store my things and then he asked me the magic question. 'Do you want to have a shower before we head out to dinner?'

'Ooh, yes please,' I said. In reality, it hadn't been that long since I'd showered, but after such a long flight and the drive in the heat I was feeling pretty disgusting. 'Is this the shower in here?' I asked, looking into a room containing a toilet and a basin. There was a shower nozzle sticking randomly out of the wall next to the toilet.

'Yes. Best to leave the toilet seat down while you shower,' he said. 'Oh and don't forget to wear these while you're in the bathroom. There's a bit of an electrical current running through the walls and things can get a little hairy if you don't.' He handed me a pair of rubber thongs.

I looked at him with my eyebrows riding so far up my face I could feel them disappearing into my fringe. He didn't start laughing and punch me on the shoulder and say 'Gotcha', like I was really hoping he would.

'You're serious.'

'Deadly serious.'

'Okey Dokey,' I said bravely.

Five minutes later, I was standing in the door to the bathroom, wearing only the rubber thongs. I had been standing there for four of the last five minutes, too scared to enter. I lifted my left foot and gingerly touched it down on the bathroom floor. When nothing happened I rested my full weight on it - still nothing. So far so good, now for the right foot. I advanced slowly into the room all the while waiting for an electric shock. Reaching out, I lightly rested the back of my hand against the tap, squeezing my eyes shut at the last second in anticipation and fear. I opened them slowly as I realised I was still alive. Things were looking promising. I turned on the water and cautiously stepped under it, but the feel of the warm water rushing over me was divine and I immediately relaxed. *Mmmm*, I could stay in here forever.

'Tara,' I heard Jesse yell through the closed door.

'What?' I yelled back.

'Don't drop the soap.'

All feelings of relaxation gone, I washed as quickly as I could with an iron grip on the soap and emerged from my room feeling human again. I positioned the rubber thongs in the middle of the door to the bathroom and after some consideration placed a chair there as well so I wouldn't forget in the middle of the night.

Jesse was sitting on the couch with a glass of red wine in one hand, looking handsome and relaxed. It was a good thing that he and Jake weren't identical twins. Where Jake was dark, Jesse was light, with golden blonde hair and freckly skin. He smiled when he saw me and poured me a glass of wine. 'I know you prefer white,' he said, holding the glass out to me, 'but trust me, in India stick to the red.'

I took the glass from him and wandered around the room looking at his things. 'Shabby chic,' I said approvingly.

Jesse's furniture was an eclectic mix of beautiful Indian and Asian woodcraft. The shabby part was the walls. Cracks ran haphazardly through the creamy plasterwork, yet through the soft glow of his lamps it looked cosy, not creepy. The one piece of modern furniture he owned was the huge couch on which he currently reclined.

'Who is she?' I asked, nodding at a photo of a pretty lady.

'Oh,' he said, 'that's Tahlia.'

'Details, I need details,' I demanded. 'What does she do? Where is she from? How old is she? How long have you been dating? When do I get to meet her?'

'She's a journalist, from England. She's 32 and we've been dating for 5 months, but I've known her for about eighteen. I thought just the two of us could go out to dinner tonight and then tomorrow night I'll introduce you to some friends of mine.'

'Sounds great.'

I snuggled back into the lounge and sighed, luxuriating in the feeling of being on holidays and at the start of an adventure.

'Sorry I can't spend tomorrow with you,' he said.

'That's fine,' I said, smiling inwardly as I thought of my plans tomorrow. I'm not sure why I didn't mention it to him. Part of me didn't want him to think I was a desperate slut. But the real reason I didn't tell him was because it was still far too delicate to discuss. Yeah, we had shagged. But that had been meaningless. Now we were in the meaningful part of the department store and it was a whole different ball game. I felt as if this almost non-existent thing we had between us might disappear if I talked about it too soon. A little like a fragile artefact that would disintegrate into nothingness if it were handled too much.

'I thought I'd go into town and do all the touristy things.' I waved Dinah's *Lonely Planet* in the air, which was littered with bookmarks.

'That's a good idea,' he said nodding. 'Where do you want to go after that?'

'I'm not sure. What were you thinking?'

'Well we could go north to Rajasthan, or we could go south and do some safaris.'

'Safaris? I thought that was just an African thing.'

'We do have elephants and tigers you know.'

'I guess you do,' I said laughing. I stopped to think about his question. 'Do I have to make up my mind now?' I finally asked.

'No. But the day after tomorrow we'll have to start organising things. Are you hungry?'

My stomach chose that precise moment to let out a huge rumble.

'Guess so,' he said, climbing up and extending a hand to me. 'Come on let's get dinner.'

A few hours later I collapsed into bed stuffed and exhausted. I would like to say that I sighed with the pleasure of lying down, but the bed was as hard as a rock. *Christ, what did they make their mattresses out of?* I spent the next 10 minutes trying to get comfortable before I gave up and headed for the lounge.

'I'm sleeping on the lounge,' I called out to Jesse.

'You'll be sorry.'

'Why?'

'You'll see.'

Thirty minutes later, I was heading back into the bedroom.

'Told you,' he yelled smugly.

'What the hell is that?' I asked.

'It's an alarm on the elevator. It plays if the door is left open.'

'It plays *Here comes the Bride?*' I clarified.

'Yep. Annoying isn't it.'

'I'm taking the cushions,' I informed him.

Finally, I snuggled into the ornately embroidered cushions I had layered onto my bed, and sighed in comfort. Jesse had taken me to an Indian seafood restaurant where the food had been fantastic. Just thinking about the garlic crab made my mouth water. Well, if nothing else, I was sure I was going to love the food in India.

As I drifted off to sleep I reminded myself, 'Don't forget the rubber thongs.'

That was the last thing I knew until the morning.

* * *

I woke with a start, struggling to find my watch and wondering where the hell I was and what had woken me.

'Thank God,' I moaned, looking at the time.

It was 8.30am. I must have heard Jesse departing for work. I had been terrified I had slept through my meeting time with Matt. That would be terrible. First I don't ring him and then I stand him up.

Jesse had informed me it should take 25 minutes to get to the Gateway of India in a cab. He had warned me to be careful of the cabbies ripping me off, (no big surprise there), and to make sure I ask to see the tables that convert the old method of meterage to the new method. I wasn't quite sure what he meant by that but when we arrived at my destination the cab driver waved his hand at the meter hanging off the side of the car. The little box showed a big five and a little 60. I assumed he was asking for 560 rupees.

'The table,' I said. He looked at me like I was a little simple and waved his hand around again. 'No. The sheet,' I insisted, holding out my hand in return.

Mumbling under his breath, he dug around on his front seat and finally handed me a crumpled piece of cardboard, which had large numbers down one side and little ones on the other. I found the 560 and ran my finger across to where it read 120. The little shit had been trying to get me to pay over four times the proper cab fare. I threw the correct money at him - Jesse had lent me some smaller notes than what the ATM at the airport had coughed up - and jumped out of the cab, resisting the urge to slam the door.

I had had little butterflies fluttering around inside my belly making me feel all squirmy and nervous. The cab ride added a squirt of anger and adrenaline to the butterflies. Now I felt positively ill.

I wandered through the market area towards the water and saw the picturesque Gateway to India rising up in front of me. I had read in my *Lonely Planet* that it had been built to commemorate the 1911 visit of King George V and was finished in 1924.

I was 15 minutes early for my rendezvous with Matt and was admiring the Gateway when I saw him approaching me. My adrenaline rush went into overdrive at the sight of him. Christ, how was I going to appear even slightly normal with these emotions crashing around inside my body? I felt like a teenager with her first crush and was sure I was about to behave like one as well. Then, as I was schooling my face to what I hoped was a pleasantly-surprised-to-see-you-here-so-early-how-are-you-going expression, he was in front of me.

'Hi,' he said.

'Hi yourself,' I responded, inwardly groaning. I hoped I wasn't going to keep repeating what he said right back at him. I read once that men liked that. It makes them feel important or something. I had a feeling it would just make me look like a moron.

'Been here long?'

'Nope you?'

Ooooh Yeah. This was going to be bad. I shifted nervously from one foot to the other and wiped my sweaty palms on my camouflage pants. Finally I broke.

'I'm sorry,' I garbled embarrassed. 'I sound like an idiot but I am, for some reason, absurdly nervous. I think it has something to do with the cab drive.'

'The cab drive?'

'Yeah, the guy tried to rip me off and it made me angry. Now I'm all emotional.'

He burst out laughing. 'If that's the worst thing that happens to you while you're in India, you're doing well. Have you eaten?'

'No.' My stomach chose that second to let out a huge grumble. 'I'm hungry,' I admitted laughing.

'Let's go to the Taj Mahal Palace and have a high tea. My treat.'

He led me to a beautiful old building overlooking the Bay. 'This is the Taj Palace. It was built by a local man in the early 1900's after he was refused entrance to one of the European hotels.'

'Wow. Egging the hotel in the middle of the night would have done it for me.'

'Yeah or a brick through a window,' he said laughing.

We joined a queue of people passing through the security at the front of the hotel. First, we walked through a metal detector, which appeared to be beeping at everybody. I paused waiting to be searched but was waved on by the security guards who seemed unconcerned and a little bored.

'Maybe they think if it doesn't beep there's something wrong,' I whispered to Matt.

Then they wiped each of us down with a small swab of material, which I can only assume was part of a bomb-sniffing machine. I looked around for the machine thinking this was going to take an awfully long time if they tested each one of us, but they seemed to have forgotten it. I noticed a pile of swabs lying discarded on a table and watched in amusement as another one was added.

'What are they going to do with them?' I asked Matt.

'Nothing,' he said, 'that's it.'

'You're kidding, right?' I asked as he shepherded me through the front door.

'Bureaucracy gone mad. Unfortunately nobody seems to have ever explained the equipment to them. I was having a chat to some of the locals out the front. Two weeks ago they found a bomb in front of the Gateway and waited so long for the police to turn up that in the end one of the locals disarmed it. I guess that's why they've added the security precautions.'

Noticing the alarm on my face he stopped. 'Sorry. I've scared you.'

I nodded nervously.

'Tara, I'm sure there is nothing to worry about. Come on, let's get something to eat. You'll feel better then.' He led me past the reception and down the hallway to an elevator. I paused before stepping in and looked at him. 'It's all right,' he said, holding a hand out to me. I looked at his hand and then reaching out, gripped it and stepped into the elevator. I figured I could spend my whole life worrying about things that would probably never happen or I could just get on with it.

I was feeling a little self-conscious holding onto Matt's hand by the time the elevator doors opened again. It was one of those how long can I hold on and not look like a sad tosser moments. Had he actually expected me to hold it or had he just offered it to be nice? Was he right now wondering how he could get me to let go? Would it be funny if I let go for no reason, or should I wait till I was getting out of the elevator? It had obviously been offered as a comforting gesture not a romantic one, so I felt a little dirty getting any sort of pleasure from it, but it did feel nice having his large warm hand wrapped around mine. I wondered if he was thinking how nice it was to be holding my small sweaty one? I doubted it very much. By the time the doors finally opened, the silence between us was deafening and I was exhausted by the marathon my mind had just run.

'This way,' he said, releasing my hand and stepping through the doors.

He led me to an elegant room with water views. It was like something out of an old movie. All the waiters, dressed in white, moved efficiently through the room, weaving around the tables, which were decorated with large silver pots of tea and coffee, and tiered plates of tiny cakes and sandwiches. It was gorgeous.

'I've never had high tea before,' I said. The sight of the cakes had totally driven any fear of terrorists away.

The waiter led us to a table and Matt asked him something in Hindi. Nodding his head the little man moved us to a different table beside a window with a fantastic view out over the bay.

'That's better,' Matt said as he sat down. The waiter held my chair out for me and I tried as gracefully as possible to sink into it. I hadn't brought a lot of clothing with me to India, and nothing at all nice. I didn't feel much like a lady in my walking boots, camouflage pants and I Love Edward T-shirt, which had survived the sniff test that morning.

It wasn't long before we had our own pot of tea and towering platters of sandwiches, crust off of course, and little iced cakes. Our hands bumped as we both reached for a cucumber sandwich. Smiling he gestured for me to go first.

'These remind me of my grandmother,' we said at the same time.

'Sunday afternoons,' I added laughing.

'Saturday mornings,' he said. 'I used to take her shopping and she'd show me off to all her friends before taking me home and making me cucumber sandwiches.' He sighed. 'I really miss her. She had a wicked sense of humour.'

'Yeah, I miss my Grams too.'

I chose a little cake off the platter. It had pink icing and a cherry on top.

'You can expect to be ripped off regularly while you're in India,' Matt said. 'Some of their schemes are so elaborate that you don't even know you've been had. But at the end of the day, everything here is so much cheaper than at home that it doesn't really matter. If you pay a little bit more for something than it's worth, it's still normally a bargain.'

'That's true,' I admitted. 'I just don't like being taken for a fool.'

'Everybody's a fool in India,' he said. 'Just in this little area around the Gateway there is the milk scheme and the big balloon scheme. Hell there's probably a heap of other schemes I haven't even worked out.'

I raised an eyebrow giving him what I hoped was a how-interesting-please-do-go-on expression, and not an, I've-got-a-terrible-pain-in-my-gut-and-I-think-I'm-going-to-fart one.

He continued so I was guessing I had pulled it off.

'In the milk scheme the mothers ask you to buy milk for their family. They take you to a shop where you buy them the milk, but what you don't know is they take it back and get a cut of the money.'

'Seriously? I hate to think what the big balloon scheme entails.'

He laughed. 'We can do it after this if you want. It's quite amusing but you end up with an awful lot of balloons.'

'Sounds like fun. It's not every day that you get ripped off in a balloon scam.'

'Big Balloon scam,' he corrected me.

About an hour later when I had crammed in so many delicious little cakes and sandwiches that I thought I would burst, I declared myself officially ready to be scammed. I felt a little guilty letting Matt pay for the high tea, but he insisted and I agreed on the condition that he would let me shout the next meal. We strolled back down to the market area, having first admired the gorgeous hotel, and proceeded to drift around waiting to be approached by the big balloon people. It didn't take long.

'Big Balloon?' an Indian man said as he shoved a packet of balloons under my nose. He was carrying a huge balloon tied to a stick. I mean this thing was ginormous. It was every child's dream come true.

'Yes, very big,' I advised him smiling.

'You buy.' He shook the packet under my nose and Matt handed him a 100 rupee note.

'So where's the scam in that?' I asked Matt, after he had received his change.

'Just wait, you'll see,' he said mysteriously.

We wandered further, stopping to look at some leather goods. I was admiring a handbag when another man with a humungous balloon approached us.

'Big Balloon?' he enquired.

'Oh thank you,' I said, 'but we've already got some.'

'No, not big balloon,' he said.

'Yes, big balloon,' I assured him.

'You show me,' he insisted.

I pulled the packet of balloons from my bag and showed them to him.

'Oh no,' he said dramatically, pressing his hand to his head, 'not big balloon.'

'Yes big balloon,' I assured him looking around for the other big balloon man who was nowhere to be seen. I noticed Matt had a big grin on his face.

'No, this big balloon,' said the concerned man, pulling a different packet of balloons out of his bag.

I examined it. Yep the balloons in this packet did appear to be bigger than the lot I had purchased. I looked at Matt, who was pulling another 100 rupee note out of his pocket. He handed it to the man who smiled happily and departed, leaving me with the packet of balloons.

'So that's the big balloon scam,' I said to Matt.

'Just wait, there's more.'

About five minutes later yet another man with a big balloon approached us.

'Nooo,' I said to Matt, who just laughed.

'Big Balloon?'

I took a deep breath. 'No thank you,' I said politely, 'I already have small and big balloons.' I felt like I was in a play and the only person who didn't know the script was me.

'No, not big balloon,' he informed me.

'How can you be so sure?' I asked suspiciously.

'Only I have big balloons,' he informed me proudly, touching his hand to his chest.

'So what are these?' I asked, pulling out my packets of balloons.

'Small balloons,' he pointed at my first packet, 'medium balloons,' he pointed at my second packet. 'These are big balloons.' He pulled yet another packet out. These did indeed look like they had the potential to become truly, very large balloons.

I rolled my eyes at Matt who was handing more money over.

'Is that it?' I asked him.

'Yep. Congratulations you have been officially scammed.'

'So,' I said, slowly working my way through it, 'they were all working together?'

'Like a tag team, it's annoying if you actually want the big balloons. You have to insist they bring the final man to you. But they make great gifts for the kiddies at Christmas.'

I thought of Lil and the girls and realised I had officially begun my Christmas shopping. 'Do you have nieces or nephews or kids?' I added the last option realising I knew nothing about this man.

'No to all of the above. I have a sister but she doesn't have any kids either.' His face darkened for a minute and I thought he was going to say something. There was a play of emotions across his face and then he obviously changed his mind. 'My Mum is gagging for grandkids. She's all over her grand nieces and nephews. I keep telling her, "one day".'

Hmmm, so he wanted children. I filed the sliver of information away for future examination. Sad sack that I was I would probably use it later when I fantasised about the two of us together.

'So,' he said, changing the subject, 'what shopping are you planning on doing while you are here?'

'Shopping? I must admit I didn't even think about the shopping options of India. It was kind of a knee jerk reaction to come here.'

He looked at me quizzically.

'Long story,' I told him. I really, really, really didn't want to talk about Jake to Matt. Bless him, he just nodded his head. So now, we both had a secret. 'Well, what's good to buy in India?' I asked.

'Leather products, handbags.' He nodded at the bag I had been looking at. 'Leather jackets, antiques - mainly fakes. Silver products, silk rugs, shoes, clothes, and jewellery; the shorter answer would be what things aren't good to buy in India. You just need to know the best places to go. And this,' he swept his hand around the market area we were currently standing in, 'is not a good place to shop. This is a tourist trap and there are much cheaper places than this. Listen, I have to do some Christmas shopping for the women in my life and I was wondering if maybe you could help me?'

I tried to keep a bright smile on my face as I said, 'Sure, sounds like fun. And then I can buy you lunch.' But inside I was thinking, *Women in his life? How many are we talking about?* Had he met someone since our night of horizontal tango-ing?'

'I need something for my Mum, my aunt and my sister. Would that be too much trouble?'

'No no,' I gushed in relief at the absence of the mention of a Paris, or a Tiffany, or worse still a Portia, just casually thrown in like I was meant to know he had a girlfriend. 'Where to first?'

Let's go to the Chor Bazaar. It's got the leather and the antique districts. Mumbai is split up into districts; like if you were looking for a second hand car you would go to an area with all the second hand car shops.'

He led me back to the main road and hailed a cab as he was talking. We jumped in and he fired off a series of rapid instructions that I didn't understand.

'When did you learn to speak Hindi?'

'I worked here for about five years when I first graduated from Uni. Couldn't get a job in Australia, and I had a friend already over here. I did a bit of work in Afghanistan and won a couple of awards, which pretty much guaranteed me a job in Sydney. But after all that I found that I didn't really like working for the major newspapers. So now I survive on freelance work. That, and I do the traffic reports for Sun FM in Sydney when I'm around.'

'That's a little obtuse isn't it?' I said in amusement.

'A friend of mine runs the station. Thinks it's funny to have me flying around in a helicopter doing the traffic. They call me The King.' He paused and looked at me. 'It's really embarrassing.'

I was obviously looking at him with a stupid look on my face.

'Matthew King,' he said, probably wondering if I was clever enough to get it.

'Ohh, the King, right.' I laughed. 'Yeh that would be bad. Do they make you sing the report?'

'No thank goodness. I don't think they'd get many listeners if they did that.'

The cab driver pulled up and after paying him, we jumped out.

'Come on,' said Matt, 'let's go shopping.'

He led me down a dirty little street to a tiny shop, which had its windows stuffed with leather jackets. It was just one shop among many along the road. As we entered, I inhaled the scent of the leather, and brushed against the material with my hands.

'It's so soft,' I said.

'It's calf leather,' said a man as he approached us, 'we only use the best leather.'

'We'd like to get some jackets made,' said Matt. 'What does something like this cost?' He pointed to a knee length jacket and the haggling began.

'How many jackets do you want Tara?' he asked me a few minutes later.

'Ummm. I'm not sure, how much do they cost?' I asked.

He lowered his voice and said to me, 'the more we buy the cheaper they'll get.' In the end I got three short jackets; cream and red for myself and olive green for Lil, and a chocolate brown three quarter length jacket with a belt for myself. I helped Matt pick out a jacket for his sister - whose name I found out was Gina - and we got a chocolate brown and a cream one for him. They measured us up and promised they would be ready for delivery the next afternoon.

From there we wandered through the antique area; tiny shops crammed with brass pots, wooden statues and copper ornaments and streets lined with refuse and inhabited by goats. After browsing for a while, I picked out a couple of brass elephants and Matt bought an enamelled brass vase for his Aunt.

After that, we hailed another cab and headed back to the water area.

'There's a great restaurant down here that I want to take you to, but I don't want you to pay for me as it's an expensive one,' he said. 'But the food is fantastic - you've got to try it.'

'A deal is a deal,' I said. 'You can take me out when we get back to Sydney.'

God, it came out of my mouth without me even thinking it through. I had relaxed so much with him - he was excellent company - and now I had this cringefully embarrassing sentence just out there in the air somewhere between us doing God knows what sort of damage to the fragile relationship that had been building. I had practically asked him out on a date. No, worse, I had told him he had to take me out when we got back. I resisted the urge to put my face in my hands and groan. He was probably already sick and tired of me and looking forward to never ever having to see me again. I opened my mouth to retract the sentence but couldn't think of a graceful way to do it.

'I'd enjoy that,' he said thoughtfully and smiled at me. 'Here we are,' he paid the cab driver and leapt out, leaving me sitting there with a stunned look on my face.

A slow smile started to replace my stunned look. *He'd enjoy that hey? Well, there you go.*

He stuck his head back in the cab, 'Tara?' he said questioningly. I realised that the cab driver had pivoted around and was also staring at me, looking slightly annoyed that I was still in his vehicle.

'Yep sorry,' I said, unable to wipe the grin off my face, 'just checking I had everything.'

'You don't want to leave anything in a cab in India,' Matt agreed.

The food at Trishna – the restaurant Matt had suggested - was out of this world.

I groaned as I lay back in my chair and undid the top button of my pants. 'The heart is strong but my stomach's too small. It seems such a shame to leave any of it.'

'I know,' he said, as he also leaned back groaning, 'just wait about ten minutes and we'll be able to keep going.'

I laughed. 'I don't think I'll need any dinner.'

'I always think that in India, but come dinner time I'll be ready to go again. You just don't get proper Indian food anywhere but India. So when I'm here I tend to gorge myself.'

I looked at my watch. It was 3pm. Jesse had said he'd be home at 6pm and we'd head out at 8.30pm. Matt's mobile phone burbled and he glanced at the screen, laughed and then rapidly fired back a text.

'Old friend of mine,' he explained. 'I emailed him a couple of weeks ago to let him know I was coming to town and he gets back to me now to see if I can meet up with him tonight for a drink.' He shook his head. 'Typical. What are you up to tonight?'

Was that a what-are-you-up-to-tonight-maybe-we-could-meet-up question I wondered, or just a question that had absolutely no underlying meaning at all?

'I'm going out with my friend.'

Nodding his head, he reached out for more food. 'I think I can do it,' he told me smiling. 'I never can resist a challenge.'

Later - while I got ready to go out, I found myself analysing every part of our conversation from that day. Every look, every glance, every laugh was taken out and given the once over before being packed carefully away in my mental archive. We had agreed we would meet up for dinner in Sydney, but I wasn't sure under what capacity we were meeting up; as friends who helped each other shop or as two people with potentially something between them?

Only time will tell, I told myself firmly. It wasn't worth not enjoying the rest of my holiday because I was wishing I was already back in Sydney. That wasn't fair on Jesse or myself, so I pushed Matthew King to the back of my mind and decided to enjoy the rest of my holiday.

* * *

We were in the cab on the way to a nightclub at Juhu Beach called Vie Lounge, which Jesse assured me, was THE place to be. I had met Tahlia earlier on in the evening, and in response to her English rosebud gorgeousness had ended up back in the bathroom - with my rubber thongs, applying more makeup. I think I had achieved an exotic look; my eyes darkened up with some kohl powder I had bought that day, and a lick of mascara and voilà - gorgeous, sexy, smudged. Unfortunately, on my first attempt, I had poked myself in the eye with the kohl applicator stick and ended up red, watery, smudged, which - let me tell you - does not have the same effect. A packet of ice and a glass of wine later Tahlia showed me how to do it properly. She also loaned me a skirt, and I was feeling a little more feminine than I had in my cargo pants.

It was 8pm when we reached Vie Lounge. There was a warm breeze coming off the ocean and I luxuriated in the feel of it rustling my hair and stroking my skin. I relaxed on a lounge, sipping my cocktail and listening to the pleasant chatter and joking of Jesse's friends. The sound of the waves crashing onto the beach was soothing and I could feel myself starting to unwind.

Jesse's phone blipped indicating the arrival of a text. He looked at it and then laughed. 'The bastard's turned up,' he said, as he beckoned to me.

I stretched lazily before climbing off the lounge. 'What's up?' I asked him.

'I need your help getting another friend in.'

'No probs.'

In Mumbai men can't gain access to clubs unless they are accompanied by a female. Jesse had used me to ferry in a few friends already. The bouncers seemed to be either turning a blind eye to me having several boyfriends or just very unobservant. I followed him and Tahlia out to the street where I noticed a dog with a large ulcer on its paw looking for food.

'I wouldn't,' said Tahlia, as I started to move towards it. 'It could have rabies.'

'Ohh,' I replied, snatching my outstretched hand back to my side.

'Mate,' I heard Jesse exclaim, as I watched the dog snuffle through an empty plastic bag.

'It's been far too long,' said a voice so familiar I gasped in surprise as I swung around.

'Matt, this is Tara,' said Jesse.

I felt my face split into a wide grin. 'Hello Matt. Nice to meet you,' I said, extending my hand.

'Lara,' said Matt, shaking my hand formally.

'No, no Tara,' I corrected him emphasising the T.

'Let's go in,' said Jesse, 'all the old gang are here.'

Matt and I followed Tahlia and Jesse back to the entrance where I reached out and took his hand. 'For the bouncers,' I advised him.

'Your friend?' Matt asked, nodding towards Tahlia.

'No. Jesse,' I corrected.

'You and he?' He looked between the two of us.

'Oh no,' I exclaimed, 'no, he's with Tahlia.'

As soon as we entered the club all of Jesse's friends closed in on Matt, so it was a while before we were able to converse again. I tried to concentrate on the conversation I was having with Tahlia and her friends but I found myself watching Matt out of the corner of my eye. Just when I thought I wasn't going to get to speak to him at all that night there was a surge in the crowd and we were pressed close together next to Jesse and Tahlia.

'So how do you two know each other?' Matt asked Jesse.

'Oh,' said Jesse, 'you wouldn't believe it, but this is Jake's ex-wife.'

Matt shot me a startled look. 'Tara is Jake's ex-wife?' he asked Jesse, looking at me with a strange expression on his face.

I should have realised he might have known Jake, but I had thought his and Jesse's relationship was purely work orientated.

'Yep. This gorgeous girl used to be married to my brother.' Jesse reached out and threw an arm around my shoulders. 'She's over here to escape the circus of a wedding Jake's organised with Tara's cousin Tash. It's all very messy, awful and boring, so she thought she'd pay Uncle Jesse a visit.'

Matt looked at me with what could only be described as profound disgust. 'Excuse me,' he said, brushing past and storming off to the bar.

'What was that about?' I asked Tahlia and Jesse.

Jesse looked thoughtful, but before he could answer, his mobile rang. Immediately, the phones of all of the other journalists started to ring as well. I could hear pagers going and different ring tones everywhere. There was a split second during which they all froze staring amongst themselves. Something profound had obviously happened. Then that second passed and they were all action; mobiles jammed up against ears, the murmur of their voices urgent.

'What, you're kidding!' I heard Jesse exclaim.

'When, when did it start?' barked Tahlia down her phone.

'Just now?' I heard Tom, another of Jesse's friends say.

And I could hear the urgency in my voice, 'Jesse, Tahlia, what's going on?'

Jesse grabbed me by the arm and dragged me towards the door. I saw Matt sprinting in our direction as he talked into his mobile.

'Leopold Café's been bombed,' Tahlia informed me as she rapidly punched numbers into her phone.

Leopold Café bombed? God, Matt and I had walked past it that afternoon.

'They've stormed the Taj Palace.'

'There are shooters and bombers.'

'They've taken the Chatrapati Shiraji Termanus.'

'And the Oberoi Trident.'

'They've killed some tourists at Leopold's.'

'There are hostages at the Taj.'

They talked on their phones and shouted information to each other, while we searched for our drivers. It was mayhem with pushing and shoving as the rest of the crowd started to react to the news they were overhearing.

'Quick get in,' Jesse said, pushing me into the car and firing off some rapid instructions to Raj, the driver.

Tahlia jumped in behind me, still talking.

'Get down,' Jesse barked at me between mouthfuls of phone conversation. I noticed that Tahlia had already slid down in the seat so she was barely visible from the street and suddenly I realised what was happening. All right, so I was a little slow. But one minute I'm enjoying myself at a club by the beach, and the next I'm caught up in the blow-by-blow details of a widely spread terrorist attack across Mumbai. I stifled a gasp and slid down in the seat as far as I could. Jesse nodded approvingly at me as he flipped a notebook out of his back pocket and continued talking.

The drive back to Jesse's was tense as the two of them made notes, and I sat terrified - waiting for a gunshot or a bomb to be directed at us. By the time we got to Jesse's I had worked myself into a state of near hysteria. It wasn't until we were safe, locked inside his apartment, and I had drunk the measure of whisky that he had pressed into my hands, that I could feel myself starting to relax.

'Are you all right?' asked Tahlia in a concerned voice.

God, I was such a weener. It wasn't like we had driven through the area under attack, but I had felt my insides wind tighter and tighter as I stared out the window with panicked eyes. My hands were tired from being scrunched into little balls of fear.

I nodded my head, 'I'm fine.'

'Here.' Jesse topped up my glass and handed another one to Tahlia.

'Not for me,' she said hopping up and heading to his bedroom. 'I've got to get down there.'

'You're going down there?' I exclaimed. 'Are you crazy?'

Smiling at me she said, 'No Tara, I'm a journalist.'

She re-emerged shortly dressed in long black pants and a black t-shirt. Her hair was pulled back in a bun and she had a cap on.

'You look like Lara Croft,' I informed her.

'I wish I had her weapons,' she said as she crossed to Jesse and dropped a deep kiss on his lips. 'And her boobs,' she added with a grin. 'Don't wait up,' she said, disappearing through the front door.

'She's really going?' I asked him aghast. 'Aren't you going to stop her?'

'Tara. I couldn't stop her if I wanted to.'

'How's she going to get there?'

'Raj is waiting to take her in.'

'What about you? Do you have to go?' I asked, suddenly terrified that I would be left alone. What if they took over the city and searched the buildings room by room?

'No. I write commerce articles for the *London Financial Times*. No doubt I'll be busy over the next few days writing bit articles on this, and I'm sure there'll be a profound effect on the Indian stock market, but there is no need for me to go in. Guess it makes me look like a bit of a jerk letting Tahlia go when I'm not...but my paper wouldn't thank me for getting myself killed over this. They have other writers, much more experienced at this sort of thing - like Tahlia. I guess Matt will be in there as well. Probably get some scoop and win another award.'

He flicked on the TV and started roaming through the channels until he found one covering the attack. There was a night scene, with what I identified as the Taj Mahal Palace in the background, and a tousled looking journalist talking in a hushed voice.

'The attacks seemed to be co-ordinated,' he whispered in an English accent.

'No shit Sherlock,' Jesse muttered.

'They started at the Leopold Café at 9.30pm, where locals and tourists were having dinner. We haven't yet confirmed the mortalities, but we know that at least one tourist and four locals were killed in the attack - many others have been injured. What you can see behind me is the Taj Mahal Palace. Gunmen reportedly stormed the hotel shortly after 9.30pm.'

Just then, a small group of people appeared around the corner of the building and ran for their lives up the street towards the reporter, who appeared overjoyed at his luck. The sound of gunshots could be heard as the reporter beckoned to them: one fellow, braver - or perhaps more voyeuristic than the others, scuttled towards him.

'Can you tell me what's going on?' the reporter asked him.

'We heard gunshots so we hid in the bar.' He stifled a sob and continued. 'We could hear them moving towards us, so we broke the window with a chair and climbed out.' He stopped and looked nervously over his shoulder. 'You should get out of here,' he informed the reporter, before racing off.

'So far nobody has claimed responsibility for this terrible attack,' the reporter whispered.

Jesse flipped open his phone and stared at a new text. 'It's the Lashkar-e-Taiba, stupid,' he informed the reporter.

As if on cue, the reporter pressed a hand up to his ear, 'This just in,' he said urgently, 'the Pakistani-based militant organisation Lashkar-e-Taiba has just claimed responsibility for this terrible travesty.'

Jesse flicked off the television with an irritated harrumph and, stalking to his computer, switched on the monitor. As it warmed up, he looked at me and said, 'Tara, I'm sorry, but there's no way they're going to let me take leave now. I'll be covering the economic effect of this for weeks. Shit.' He put his head in his hands.

I walked over to him and put my hand on his shoulder. 'That's all right Jesse,' I said. 'I won't be going anywhere for a few days I'd imagine. And then I'll sort something out.' A thought crossed my mind. 'Hey Jesse,' I said, 'I know this is pretty frivolous considering what's happening,' I paused almost too embarrassed to continue, but Jesse was giving me his full attention so I finished my question in a rush. 'Why did Matt brush me off when you told him I was married to Jake?'

Jesse looked at me for a few moments before answering. He got up and sat on the couch gesturing for me to follow.

'Why do I get the feeling I'm not going to like this story?' I asked.

'Because you're not,' he said. 'Jake, Matt and I all went to school together. We were like the three musketeers, doing everything together. We were in the same sports teams, the same classes and we hung out together when we weren't in school. When we were in our first year of University, Gina - Matt's sister - turned 16 and invited us to her party. She always was a pretty little thing, but by the time she turned 16 she was starting to really blossom. Unbeknownst to Matt and me, Jake started a relationship with Gina after her birthday party, and seduced her.'

I gasped and held my hands over my face suspecting where this was going. 'He didn't,' I said quietly.

'Yep, he got her pregnant and then refused to have anything to do with her. It almost destroyed her. She ended up having an abortion, which had complications. Now she can't have children. Matt has never forgiven him and neither have I.'

'That bastard,' I said, surprised by the venom in my voice. I could feel a weird unravelling in my mind. It was like someone had lifted the veil fogging my eyes - had cut the ties imprisoning my mind. Suddenly I could see Jake for the manipulative beast that he was. I felt something shift inside me and realised that my desire for him had gone. In its place were feelings of repulsion and revulsion.

Jesse reached out and put a hand on mine. 'I never told you this before,' he said, 'but I'm really sorry about your miscarriage.'

I sat, lost in thought. 'I'm not,' I finally said.

He left me there on the couch, staring into space, drowning in my memories.

* * *

We'd been married for eight months when my period was late. I had no nausea, no tenderness, and no moodiness, so I was not suspecting pregnancy, but I did a test just to rule it out. And there they were, the two pink lines.

After the initial shock had worn off, I was pretty excited. And why shouldn't I be? I was in love and married, and I was sure that once Jake got used to the idea he too would be excited. I spent the afternoon picturing us shopping for baby stuff; little clothes, bassinets, prams. By the time Jake got home, I had worked myself into a frenzy of excitement. I left the test on the kitchen bench with a note asking him what he thought, and then I sat in the lounge waiting for him.

'What the hell is this?' It wasn't the response I had been hoping for. 'Tara is this some sort of joke?' He emerged into the lounge waving the test result around like some sort of weapon.

'It's no joke,' I said.

He stared at me incredulously. 'How could you let this happen?'

'Pardon?'

'You heard me.' His voice went up a couple of decibels, 'How could you let this happen?' He enunciated each word slowly, angrily.

'I didn't plan this Jake.' I felt my fantasies of shopping hand in hand for maternity clothes dissolving.

'Like hell you didn't. You've been planning this all along haven't you? Haven't you?' He grabbed me by the shoulders and shook me as he said it.

Ripping myself out of his grasp I said, 'I don't know what you're talking about. It was an accident.'

'Sure that's what they all say,' he snarled. 'I know your plan. Get the guy, rope him into marriage, get pregnant and then have the easy life.'

I was getting upset. Firstly, he had proposed at the two-month mark. Secondly, I had been planning to go back to work at least three days a week once my maternity leave had finished. And thirdly, I don't think being a mother is an easy life at all. From what I have seen of my sister and friends that have children, they have it far worse than me. I get to go home and put my feet up. I can skive off to the hairdresser's or for a massage whenever I want. I can go out to dinner, or the movies with a second's notice. Fourthly, I think the whole pregnancy emotional hormonal thing had finally caught up with me.

'Jake, you're in shock. Everything is going to be okay,' I said, fighting back tears.

'No it's not. We decided we weren't going to have children and now you've gone and gotten pregnant on purpose. I can't believe you would do something so low and devious. I don't think I know who you are any more.' He turned and walked out the front door. He didn't even shut it.

I think the shock from his outburst was worse than the shock from the pregnancy. I couldn't ever remember having a conversation that included the words, 'We won't have children'. I think we had said we would wait. And the thought that I had done this on purpose was so preposterous I was speechless; just sitting on the couch like a giant fish, my mouth opening and closing soundlessly, as I tried to digest exactly what had happened.

In the end I went to Nat's. I felt I should be celebrating and I couldn't do it alone at home with the echoes of Jake's words going round and round in my head. Nat almost wet herself with excitement when I turned up on the front door with the news I was pregnant. That quickly turned to indignation when I told her Jake's reaction.

'He's just getting used to the idea,' I defended him.

She didn't look convinced. 'Come on, let's celebrate.' She cracked open a bottle of orange juice and we toasted my foetus. Then we toasted the glowing mum-to-be, and of course the soon to be Godmother. And although it was lovely, it couldn't take away the sting from the fact that I should have been having a romantic dinner with my husband as we celebrated the conception of our first child.

Jake didn't come home that night. As I waited for him on the couch, I thought about all the wonderful things he had done for me. The first time I had stayed over at his place I had gone into the bathroom and found a new, fluffy pink bathrobe with matching slippers waiting. He routinely made me breakfast in bed on weekends, and I often had flowers delivered to me at work. He showered me with jewellery, for no special reason, and often ran a bath for me when we got home from work. I was having trouble assimilating the two Jakes; the hard angry one and my doting loving one.

The first sign of problems began the next day. I had turned up to work hoping that Jake would be there, and was surprised to be told he was in court all day. I just smiled and pretended I had forgotten. When I went to the toilet at lunch I had some slight spotting. I told myself it was nothing to worry about, but I was dying to ask Trish, one of the other PA's about it, as she had three children. I love Trish, but she has a pretty big mouth, so I was sure she would squeal, and I didn't want to risk that at the moment. I did however make a doctor's appointment during my lunch break for the following day.

Jake was there when I got home from work. My relief rapidly turned to dismay when I met him in the kitchen carrying a small overnight bag.

'Where are you going?'

'To Garry's, I can't be near you at the moment.' The look he gave me spoke volumes. I was a piece of dirt.

'Please don't go. Can't we talk about this?'

'There is nothing to talk about.'

'What, so, that's it? I get pregnant and you're just going to run away?'

'You expressly went against my wishes. I never wanted children, and I still don't. If you want me back you know what to do.' And he was gone.

I staggered to the couch and sat with my head in my hands. An abortion? Jake wanted me to get an abortion. It made me realise that I wanted this child, but whoever that stranger was in the kitchen - the cold hard angry man, I wanted him gone.

Exhausted and utterly depressed, I climbed into bed, fully clothed, and slept until my alarm woke me the next morning.

I didn't bother going to work that day. It was all I could do to make myself get up and pull a comb through my hair. I was tired and miserable and confused. The spotting was a little heavier, but now I wasn't sure if I cared. Jake had left me. Part of me was sure he would come back when he got over his little tantrum, but another part was already imagining me with a crying baby - or even worse, twins - in one of those big double pram contraptions. In my mind, I was walking home from the grocery store, pale and fat, with two babies and the small amount of food I had been able to afford when I see Jake. He's sitting at the lights in a convertible sports car with his arm around a blonde skinny woman, who I recognise off the cover of the latest Vogue magazine I had read at the checkouts. If that isn't depressing enough, he looks up and sees me standing there at the lights trying to shut up Jake junior - who hasn't stopped crying since we left home two hours ago, and rather than say hello, look a little guilty and ask me if I'm all right, he leans over and whispers something in the model's ear. She looks at me and I distinctly hear her say, 'Her?' He nods, the lights turn green and I can hear her peals of laughter as they speed off up the road.

I know it would never happen, simply because Mum and Dad would take me in well before I ever got to the stage of poverty, but it still terrified me. And the thought that Jake would be fine without me, well it had never crossed my mind before.

The doctor took a blood test to confirm my pregnancy. The results wouldn't be in for a few days. He also made an appointment at the hospital for me to get an ultrasound to see how advanced I was. He told me that spotting can be normal, and not to worry unless I had some cramping as well.

The cramping began that night. I hopped up and made myself a hot cup of milk with honey and waited to see what would happen. The stabbing pain started an hour later. Intense sharp pain in my abdomen, radiating up into my shoulder and neck, it buckled me in two and left me gasping for breath. I rang Natalie and then I rang for an ambulance. Dinah and Nat beat the ambulance, and found me on the floor in the lounge, clutching my stomach and crying. I wasn't sure if I was crying out of fear of losing my child, or fear of losing Jake.

I passed out before the ambulance arrived. The last thing I remember is a gush of blood and Nat rocking me and telling me that everything was going to be all right.

I regained consciousness a few hours after the surgery. The doctors told me it was an ectopic pregnancy. They managed to save my fallopian tube, but told me that my chance of another ectopic occurring was increased due to the scarring.

Nat, Dinah, Mum and Dad were all there; but there was no Jake. Turning my face into the pillow I cried softly, my sorrow so absolute that I didn't hear him enter the room.

'Why didn't you tell me she was awake?' he demanded.

'Where the hell were you? She needed you and you weren't there.' I heard Dinah, angrier than I had ever heard her. But all I knew was that he had come back and now everything would be fine.

'Shhhh.' I beckoned him to me and held him at arm's length staring into his face. I wanted so desperately to hug him, and yet at the back of my mind was a niggling thought. Where the hell had he been? He should have been with me, and maybe if he hadn't left, this never would have happened. What if his ill thoughts had caused the little foetus to get trapped? Maybe it could sense that it wasn't wanted. I knew it was a stupid thought even when I was thinking it, but it persisted.

Tracing one finger down my cheek he whispered, 'My God I thought I had lost you. I love you so much.' And then he kissed me.

A little voice in my head was shrieking, *'Well if you love me so much where the hell did you go? What was all that crap about you don't know who I am any more.'* But I told it to shut up. This was my wonderful Jake kissing me, and I wanted to hold him forever and never let him go.

We never spoke of the pregnancy. It was like a fragile shell that we walked around but did not touch. Sometimes I looked at it and examined my feelings. I realised that I wanted children one day, but I was too scared to mention it to Jake in case I would be forced to act on the information. So I told myself that I was too young anyway - I was only 24, and that when the time was right we would have children and Jake would be excited about the prospect.

* * *

You know when you wake first thing in the morning feeling great, then you remember something you had managed to forget in your dreams, and you feel the world come crashing down around you? That was what happened to me the morning after the bombings. I woke and stretched in my bed of cushions feeling wonderful. And then I remembered, and I felt my body tense with remnants of last night's fear. I felt guilty for having slept so soundly. And then I remembered Matt and I wanted to cry. He hated me. He hated me because I had been married to the person he detested most in the world, and I couldn't find it in my heart to blame him.

'If you're married to a bad person, does that make you bad by association?' I asked Jesse, when I staggered into the lounge. I had been relieved to catch a glimpse of Tahlia asleep in his bed.

Looking up from his computer, he scratched the growth on his face as he pondered my words. 'Are you talking about the terrorists?' he asked confused.

'No, me,' I said, running my hands through my tangled hair in an attempt to tame it.

'Being married to Jake?' he clarified.

'Yeah.'

'Does that make me a bad person being his brother?'

'No, you didn't choose to be his brother. I chose to love, honour and obey the son-of-a-bitch.'

'It doesn't make you a bad person - naive perhaps, but not bad.'

Tahlia stumbled into the lounge in her nightie and croaked, 'Coffee.'

I poured both of us a cup from the pot Jesse had brewing. She took a sip and groaned in appreciation.

'If it makes you a bad person for marrying him, what does it make Sydney for electing him to be their Mayor?' she asked. She managed to look beautiful even with smudged make-up and bed-head hair.

'Sin City,' I answered. 'So what happened last night?'

'It was mayhem. Unfortunately the heads of the police force were taken out fairly early on so there was no real leadership.'

'The police station was attacked?' I asked dismayed.

'No, they were out to dinner together when some of the terrorists drove past. They had a shoot-out and were all killed.'

'But they got the terrorists?'

'Unfortunately no.' She shook her head sadly.

'But it's all over, isn't it?' I asked.

'No,' said Jesse, looking up from his computer, 'the Taj Palace is still under attack. They've also found out that they came in on boats from the bay to launch the attack.'

I had goosies thinking that while Matt and I had been sitting in the Taj Palace having high tea, terrorists had been hiding out on the bay strapping bombs to their bodies.

'What's the body count at?' mumbled Tahlia through a huge yawn.

'100 dead, another 150 wounded,' Jesse informed her.

100 people dead? I couldn't fathom it.

'I've got to get back out there,' she said, heading to the bedroom. 'Want to come?'

For a second I thought she was asking me, and for half a second I considered it. I imagined myself commando crawling behind her up the streets of Mumbai while bullets whistled over our heads and Tahlia stopped to check people for pulses.

'This one's alive,' she'd say and yell 'MEDIC' like in the movies, before flicking open her notebook and saying to the victim, 'So tell me, what happened in there?'

And then the next half a second my brain froze up with the sheer terror of what it had been contemplating - and then I realised she was talking to Jesse, not me.

'Sure, why not?' he said, hopping to his feet and stretching. 'Tara, you should spend the day contacting your friends and family. Use my computer to email them, or there's Skype set up on it you can use if you want.'

'Thanks,' I said, wondering how you use Skype. I didn't want to appear a total eejit, so I refrained from asking and decided that emails would work well.

I finished my coffee and jumped in the shower before I sat down in front of Jesse's computer with some toast.

Flipping on the small television so I could keep an eye out for any developments, I logged into my Hotmail account and was overwhelmed by the increasingly frantic emails. Poor Mum was going ballistic. By the sound of it, she practically had my funeral planned. I logged into Windows Messenger and saw Mum's icon waiting.

Calm down Mum. I typed. *I'm safe at Jesse's apartment, why didn't you ring me here?*

She must have been sitting on the computer because within a few seconds I had a response.

Oh Thank God you're safe. They said some tourists had been killed and I thought it was you.

Mum there are thousands of tourists here in Mumbai. Why didn't you ring?

I tried but I couldn't get a line to Mumbai. Maybe they're damaged.

Or overloaded.

What are you going to do? When are you coming home?

I'm not sure. Just staying indoors till it's all over and then I'll make up my mind. Don't worry about me. You know I'm too much of a chicken to put myself in danger!

Love you.

Love you too Ma. I'll let you know when I know.

I flicked off an email to Lil and the girls that had way more information - information about a certain Matthew King - but it was hard to be enthusiastic about that with thoughts of terrorists killing hostages whirling around in my head.

I was bored by the time Jesse and Tahlia got home. Having emailed everyone and responded to numerous questions from them, I cleaned up the kitchen and tidied up the loungeroom. Then I watched the English news channel for updates and did my nails with some of Tahlia's stuff I found in Jesse's bathroom.

(Yes, I had been snooping. And yes, I know snooping is wrong. But as I mentioned earlier, I was bored.)

I had some more toast for lunch with some cheese I discovered in the back corner of the fridge, and tried to nap on the couch – but the annoying tinkling of *Here comes the Bride* from the elevator soon drove me into my bedroom to sleep. Finally I heard the front door open. I was eyeing off the area under the bed wondering if I could make it before I was discovered, when I smelt the unmistakeable wafting of Indian cuisine. Surely terrorists wouldn't be luring out foreigners with curry? They wouldn't be that clever.

It was Jesse and Tahlia. I don't think I'd ever been so pleased to see two people.

'Thank God you're safe,' I said, launching myself at them.

'Bet you're hungry,' said Jesse.

'Starving. You're out of bread by the way.'

He laughed and put the curry on the table while Tahlia grabbed the cutlery and plates.

'How is it out there?' I asked, digging my fork into my pile of butter chicken.

'Getting better,' Jesse answered, around a mouth full of curry.

'So it's still going?'

'You can hear gunshots at the Taj Palace and occasional groups of tourists are still escaping,' he replied, once he had swallowed.

'I got great photos of some climbing down curtains they had tied together,' said Tahlia. 'They were trapped in the conference rooms. It's going to make a great story.'

'I've always wanted to do that,' I said.

'What, get trapped in a conference room?'

'No tie the sheets from my bed together and climb out through the window.'

'Seriously?'

'Haven't you?'

'Maybe just a little,' she admitted laughing.

It was after we had finished eating that they dropped the bombshell on me.

'We ran into Matt today,' said Jesse.

'He's good isn't he?' Tahlia said to Jesse.

'He's on another level totally.'

'What did he do?' I asked.

'God,' Tahlia continued, 'I couldn't believe it when he ran into that burning building.'

'I could have saved those kids,' Jesse said defensively.

'I'm sure you could have,' Tahlia said soothingly, reaching over and rubbing his arm.

'He went into a burning building?' I asked, when I had managed to get my mouth to function again.

'An orphanage caught on fire,' said Jesse. 'They thought they had everybody out and then these two little faces appeared at a window on the top floor. It was awful.'

'Heart wrenching,' said Tahlia. 'They were crying and clutching each other.'

I shivered at the vision, trying not to remember the other tear jerking images I had seen in the last 24 hours.

'The authorities wouldn't do anything, so Matt went in to save them.'

'I thought he was dead for sure,' said Tahlia.

'So what happened?' I asked, feeling more like I was asking about an action movie plot than a real-life event.

'Well, about a minute after he went in we could see him through the window talking to the kids,' said Jesse.

'You should have seen it,' gushed Tahlia, 'he just swept them up and threw them over his shoulders.'

'It did look pretty heroic,' Jesse admitted. 'But of course when they didn't come back out, well, I thought that was it.'

'It was horrible, wasn't it?' Tahlia said to Jesse.

I was sitting on the edge of my chair, my hands clenching the armrests. 'And?' I finally asked, unable to take the suspense any more.

'He went out a rear door,' Jesse said. 'We didn't realise it for a few minutes though, but he and the kids are fine.'

I sat there shell-shocked. I had been hiding all day while Matt was out saving lives. I could see now that even if he didn't hate me, he was far beyond my reach.

'Anyway - it turns out that he's going to Rajasthan to do an article for a travel magazine and he said you could tag along if you wanted,' said Jesse.

'What?' I asked, thinking I had totally misheard them. 'Pardon?'

'Matt,' said Tahlia, 'he's going up to Rajasthan for a couple of weeks, and we thought since Jesse or I can't go with you, that you might want to go with him.'

I tried to get my head around the information. 'But,' I said, 'won't he be here covering the story?'

'He's been paid in advance for this article by *Travel Abroad* so he has to go,' Tahlia explained. 'Lucky you,' she sighed.

'You know I can just step aside and give you and Matt a little space,' said Jesse teasingly.

'Nah,' Tahlia said, 'you'll do. Besides I think I'd have some competition.' She looked at me meaningfully. 'I saw the looks you were shooting him last night.'

I tried to look innocent, but I was also dying to ask if she'd seen him shooting me any looks. I managed to maintain my air of nonchalance with extreme effort. I thought I'd gotten away with it until Jesse piped up.

'Yeah,' he said, his journalistic instincts kicking in, 'for two people who've never met, you two seemed quite chummy.'

'What are you talking about?' I said, examining the job I had done on my nails.

'Oooooh goody,' said Tahlia, 'a secret. I love secrets.'

'She's relentless,' said Jesse, 'just spill your guts now and save us all an evening of persistent questioning. Just when you've lowered your guard, bam, she'll slip in another one. She'll get you in the end.'

'I don't really know him,' I said weakly.

'You've admired him from afar? You've been stalking him? He's an old flame from before you were married? He's a one-night-stand?'

I was sure my facial expression didn't change at all - I certainly didn't flinch or do anything obvious.

'A One-night-stand!' she yelped in excitement. 'When, where, details... I need details. God was he fantastic?'

'I told you,' said Jesse apologetically. 'She's like a heat-seeking missile.'

'She reminds me of my friend Elaine,' I admitted. I could feel myself blushing.

'Tell me,' said Tahlia, in a pathetic, girlish voice, batting her long eyelashes at me.

I grimaced and bit my tongue, but she came and sat behind me on the couch. 'You look so tense,' she said, starting to give me a back rub. Groaning I leaned into her; she had hands of gold. 'You don't have to tell me,' she said after a few minutes, 'but if you feel like sharing, I'd love to listen.'

'All right, all right,' I said, breaking away from her. 'I'll tell. But just to shut you up. '

'Oh thank God,' said Jesse from his computer, 'I thought I was going to have to put my ear muffs on.'

'It was a few months ago. I was out with Elaine, she's the one you remind me of,' I informed Tahlia, 'and the aim was to have a one-night-stand to help me achieve closure from Jake. I've been doing this stupid Seven Steps to Closure thing and it was step number four.'

'What's step number five?' she asked, fluffing up a cushion behind her.

'Travel to an exotic destination.'

'Tick.' Tahlia mimed a big tick as she nestled back into the cushion and crossed her legs. 'You're almost there. What's step number six?'

'Have meaningful sex,' I said, trying not to blush again.

'I'm confused. Wasn't that step number four?' said Jesse.

'No, that was to have meaningless sex,' I explained.

'You had sex with Matt?' Tahlia clarified.

'Yep.' This time I did blush.

'Wow,' interrupted Jesse. 'That's totally out of character for Matt.'

'What to have sex with someone like me?' I asked, a little offended by the implication.

'No silly, to have a one-night-stand. It's really not his thing.'

Hmmmm, I filed that one away as food for thought later.

'So you two hadn't seen each other since you did the wild thing?' Tahlia asked.

'Well...'

'What, you've been seeing him in Sydney?'

'No. Quite coincidentally we ended up sitting next to each other on the plane.'

'Noooooooo,' said Tahlia in an excited voice.

'Yeeees,' I said, getting into the story. I hadn't realised how much I'd been missing the girls. 'Only I didn't recognise him.'

'NOOOOOOOOOO,' screeched Tahlia. 'Oh this is too good.'

Jesse laughed and said, 'I would have loved to have been there for that. So then you met up last night?'

'Well. No, we actually spent yesterday together in town.'

'Ahhhhahahahahhahahha.' Tahlia was rolling around on the floor, kicking her heels in the air. 'Thanks,' she said, when she sat up, 'I needed a really good laugh after the last couple of days.'

'Glad to be of service.'

'Ohh, you so have to go travelling with him,' she said breathlessly. 'This was meant to be.'

'But,' I said in a pathetic little voice, 'he hates me.'

'No he doesn't,' said Jesse, as reassuringly as he could, 'he hates Jake. And,' he added cunningly, 'Jake hates him. Imagine the look on Jake's face if the two of you ended up together.'

I paused to add that to my favourite fantasy. My dream guy/Matt rides up on his motorbike, removes his helmet and says, 'Bugger off Jake, you had your chance and you blew it. Tara's with me now, and I won't be letting her go.' Yep. I definitely liked the way that all fitted together.

I was interrupted from my daydreaming by Jesse. 'Tara, the way I see it, these are your only two options. You either go home in time for the wedding, or you go to Rajasthan with Matt.'

'Or I could just stay here and hide until the wedding is over. Or I could travel by myself.' I stopped and thought about it. I knew there was no way I was going to travel by myself.

'You wanted to go to Rajasthan anyway,' said Jesse, in his most convincing voice. 'Think what a great chance this is. *Travel Abroad* will be footing most of the bill.'

'When do I have to let him know?' I asked.

'As soon as possible, we'll have to book you a plane ride to Delhi for Saturday.'

I thought about it while I helped do the dishes. I remembered how much fun we'd had on Wednesday and how it had been good until he had learnt who I was. If he didn't mind taking me, then he couldn't totally hate me, so that was promising. It was while I was brewing the tea that I realised this was a once-in-a-lifetime opportunity the universe was handing me: I would be stupid to let it go.

'All right,' I said suddenly, disturbing the two of them from their frantic writing, 'I'll do it.'

I lay in bed that night torn between sadness at the horror of the Mumbai massacre and nervous nausea at the thought of travelling with Matt, praying intently that the universe knew what it was doing.

* * *

The next day passed a little too quickly for my liking. I spent most of it watching the television, feeling morose at the senselessness of the tragedy. Jesse rang to let me know that everything was under control except the Taj Palace. I couldn't believe it was still going. It was a tragedy of huge proportions, and the Indian people as a nation were going to doubly suffer for this through a lack of the tourism they so desperately relied on. I was glad I had decided to stay.

My leather jackets turned up that afternoon. I felt guilty as I admired them, wishing there was something I could do to make a difference but knowing that there wasn't.

Tahlia, Jesse and I risked going out to a local restaurant that evening, and then it was time for bed. I had a bit of trouble sleeping. To say I was nervous would have been an understatement, considering the many different levels of emotion I was functioning on. I was nervous of flying at the best of times. Now I was nervous of flying because of the terrorist attacks. Actually on a scale where one is slightly nervous, and ten is I'm-so-terrified-I-might-actually-pee-my-pants, I was on the pee-my-pants end of the scale. I was nervous of travelling with Matt, and I was also excited at the thought of travelling with him. So when I finally woke in the morning, I was nervous, terrified and excited all at once. The combination had me in the toilet with my head over the bowl, but the thought of being electrocuted made me too anxious to puke, so instead I put up with the nausea. I figured if we were confronted by any terrorists I could throw up on them, which would hopefully distract them long enough for Matt and me to get away.

Then I was on the way to the airport, with Matt sitting in the front seat talking to the driver. I was a little disappointed that he hadn't sat in the back with me, but I knew I was being ridiculous, and that it was much better he couldn't see my nervous twitching or sweaty brow.

The security at the airport was out of control - which should have made me feel better, but I kept thinking of the security that had been on the Taj Palace Hotel the very day it had been attacked. We x-rayed our luggage, had them opened and inspected, and then put them through yet another x-ray machine. Then we checked in our backpacks. (I was glad I had borrowed one from Dinah. The thought of lugging a suitcase around Rajasthan in front of Matt was unbearable.) We walked about 50 metres and then had a body search while our carry-on bags were x-rayed again. Another 100 metres we had to go through the whole routine again. Finally, after one last bag check we were through to the departure lounge.

I must have looked a little peaky because Matt took one look at me, sat me down and went for coffee. He came back with a sticky bun each, which was delicious but very hard to eat without getting crumbs stuck all over my face. All of this had progressed without Matt and me really saying anything at all to each other. I was starting to feel drained with the tension between us - none of it sexual unfortunately.

Matt picked up a local newspaper and started flicking through it. I got out my copy of *The Girl with the Dragon Tattoo* and continued reading. Finally, I could hear them calling our flight and Matt and I squeezed into the cabin. He very kindly let me have the window seat and I sat – terrified - counting the rows to the exit and trying to guess where the lifejacket would be.

'You wouldn't need one.' It was the first whole sentence Matt had directed towards me.

'Huh?' I asked him confused.

'The life jacket, you won't need one.'

'Why not?' I asked, hoping he would tell me something really reassuring like, 'these planes can't crash, it's physically impossible.'

'We won't be flying over water,' he answered.

'Oh.' Not the answer I had been hoping for.

Then we were rolling down the runway gathering speed and I could feel the acceleration of the plane accelerate my fear. I grasped the armrests tightly and clenched my teeth together.

'Look,' said Matt, pointing out the window.

I stared out over a huge slum city. It was built right up to the edge of the airfield.

'Can you imagine trying to get to sleep down there?' he said, pointing to another runway where the walls of the shacks were leaning against the airport fence.

As we climbed over the city, I could see the slums stretching away into the distance. 'More than half of India's population lives in slums,' he informed me. 'Even those who have jobs can't afford the exorbitant rent and end up living there. Did you notice the people asleep in their cars the other night?'

I nodded my head, 'I thought they were drivers waiting for passengers.'

'Some might have been. But mostly they are people who have nowhere else to sleep.'

He flicked open a book and started taking notes. Guessing that was my signal that the conversation had ended I watched the view of the city for a few more minutes until we were too high to see anything, and then recommenced reading my book. Eventually I fell asleep with my head resting on the window.

The motion of the plane commencing descent woke me and I groaned as I straightened my head with my hands. Matt was watching me with an amused look. He indicated the side of his own face and I realised he was trying to tell me I had something on mine. Hoping it wasn't crumbs from that damn bun, I experimentally dabbed my cheek with my fingers and discovered I had slobbered. Oh Christ. He must think I'm some sort of special person. I looked down and was dismayed to find a wet patch on my shirt. Wow, I had really drooled.

'I was a St Bernard in my last life,' I told him, indicating the wet patch on my shirt.

He burst out laughing and I could feel some of the tension between us dissipate.

Finally, we were off the plane and out of the terminal into the not so fresh air of Delhi. Like Mumbai it was chaos, people and cars everywhere.

'The hotel will have sent a car for us,' Matt informed me. 'Ahh there they are.' He led me towards a man holding a placard with Matt's name on it.

Within a few minutes, we were safe in the air-conditioned car and off to our hotel.

'We'll be staying near the train station,' Matt said. 'We've got an early train to catch the day after tomorrow and a lot of sightseeing to do. Are you up to it?'

I nodded my head as I wondered if I were. My previous emotions had burnt out leaving me drained and hollow. I watched as the slums slipped past, feeling sad for all those people born into poverty. India apparently has the most new millionaires a year. It was hard to correlate that information with what you saw when you were looking at the other end of the scale.

And then, there was Mumbai. All those people killed and maimed in that terrible event. The images of the wounded - the burnt and bruised, torn and twisted bodies I had seen on the local television still haunted me. Believe me when I tell you that the local Indian news pulled no punches when they were covering the massacre. Bodies lined up in the streets, relatives keening and mourning their loved ones. It had moved me on a level I hadn't known was possible. It had left me morose and empty. What sort of world did we live in where people could do such terrible things to each other?

We arrived at the hotel and while I sat in the foyer, Matt organised our check-in. He indicated for me to follow him up the mosaic-lined stairs to our room.

'Look I hope you don't mind but we'll be sharing a room for the trip.' He looked a little nervous as he said it. 'But look at the bright side, *Travel Abroad* are footing the bill, and we've got a twin room.'

He opened the door and I saw, somewhat to my relief, that there were indeed two double beds in the room.

'I can't thank you enough,' I said, entering the room and slumping onto one of the beds.

'Are you hungry?' Matt asked, looking at me with concern.

'A little, why?'

'You just don't seem to be your normal chirpy self.'

'I'm feeling a little emotional,' I admitted, and then to my shame I felt tears well in my eyes. 'I'm all right,' I said, 'just so much pain and suffering. I feel like such an idiot to have ever complained about anything in my life.'

He sat down on the bed opposite me. 'Don't let it pull you under,' he said. 'Yes, there is a lot of pain and suffering in India. But there is also laughter and joy. You see those kids living in the slums? They are capable of happiness. So don't get caught up in the tragedy of India, but instead learn to embrace the life here.'

It was the most he had said to me all day.

There was a light knock at the door and the porter arrived with our bags. I saw Matt slip him a note and made a mental note to myself to learn about the correct tipping here in India. I couldn't keep letting Matt do it. They conversed together and the porter left with a slight bow to Matt.

'He's gone to get us some menus,' he told me. 'I thought we could have lunch here while we freshen up and then head out to see some sights.'

'Sounds good to me,' I said, hopping up to use the bathroom.

The porter had delivered the menus while I was on the toilet and Matt handed me one as I sat on the bed.

'What's good?' I asked him.

'Have you tried the egg rolls yet?'

I shook my head.

'All right we'll get a couple of them. Do you want a fruit lassi, some coffee or Marsala tea?'

'Marsala tea thanks.'

I listened while he phoned through our order and then feeling a little braver I said, 'You know Matt, I'm not Jake.'

I was watching his face closely so I saw the muscles around his jaw bunch up. A hard, scary look came into his eyes, and then he took a deep breath and consciously relaxed his face.

'I know you're not. I just can't believe you were married to him. Please,' he said, 'try to help me understand how a nice girl like you ended up with a total ....' He paused while he rethought his choice of words. 'Pig like him,' he finished.

'Well,' I began slowly, 'I was still at Uni and very naive. He was older and so dashing. I couldn't believe that someone like him wanted to be with someone like me. Hell, I was deliriously happy that anybody wanted to be with me.'

Matt looked at me quizzically. 'Why wouldn't someone want to be with you?'

'Well let's just say my dance card wasn't full. It was Uni, and guys at Uni didn't seem to be big on the commitment thing.'

He looked thoughtful and then laughed. 'Yeah, I guess I wasn't really into commitment while I was at Uni.'

I resisted the urge to ask him if he was into it now and instead continued. 'Anyway I guess he swept me off my feet. And then he proposed so quickly.'

'But he's such an arse.'

'I know that now. But back then if something went wrong, or wasn't how I liked it, or didn't feel right, somehow he would twist it and it would be *me* that was the problem. Do you know what I mean?'

'Yes. He can be very manipulative.'

'I found that out the hard way.'

'That's when you broke up?'

I nodded.

'Why did you leave him?'

'I didn't,' I said.

He looked surprised.

'Well I guess technically I did leave him, but in reality he left me first. He just didn't let me know about it.'

'Sounds typical of his behaviour.'

'Look Matt, Jesse told me about Gina. I'm really sorry. If it makes you feel any better he pulled a similar stunt on me after we were married. But I had a miscarriage.'

Matt shook his head. 'She tried to kill herself after the abortion,' he said in a broken voice. 'The combined loss of someone she thought had loved her, her baby, and then the ability to have children was too much for her. It took her years to get over it.'

Our lunch turned up and we were silent while we ate.

'You're right,' I said, picking up my Marsala tea and sipping, 'these are really good.'

'So tell me about when you left him,' he continued, when he had finished eating.

'You're not going to use this in some article are you?' I asked suspiciously.

He laughed. 'No, I swore to never write a word about him.' He paused and looked speculative, 'So Tash is your cousin?' he asked.

I nodded.

'But she's such a bitch.'

I burst out laughing, coming very close to snorting Marsala tea through my nose all over Matt.

'It's amazing how the press never mentions you,' he continued.

'I know. It's like I never existed. I used to get offended by it, but then I realised he's such a press darling that if they were to post pictures of me, none of them would be flattering. And believe me, it's not hard to get an unflattering photo of me.'

Matt laughed, his greeny-blue eyes crinkling at the corners. I noticed he got a cute dimple in his left cheek when he laughed. 'All right, so I promise not to use anything that you are about to tell me in any written or verbal form. Satisfied?' he said.

'I guess. So you really want to know how it ended? Just warning you though, once I start I may not stop.'

'That's all right, I'm a good listener. So shoot.'

'Well,' I said thoughtfully, 'the beginning of the end began about two weeks before my 29th birthday. In reality it probably began before that, I just didn't know about it.'

Matt punched a pillow into a ball and stuck it under his head, stretching out to get comfortable. 'Most endings begin without one party knowing about it,' he said.

I nodded. 'He had been really nit-picking at me. It seemed I couldn't do anything right. I thought we were just going through a rough patch. He was so stressed with work at the time, and what with us spending our working hours together as well as our non-working it was all getting a bit much.'

'Working hours?'

'Oh yeah. I should have told you. I used to work as Jake's personal assistant.'

'So when you broke up, you lost your job as well?'

'Bummer hey. Mind you after what I've seen here the last few days I feel like a bit of a shit ever finding anything in my life to be sad about.'

'It's all relative,' Matt said. 'You can only relate sad and happy to what you already know. Anyway go on.'

'He was criticising me continuously and I finally reached breaking point. So we had a discussion and we decided it would be best if I stayed at my parents' for a couple of weeks to have a break. Just until my birthday.'

'Who made the decision?'

'We both did. Well he suggested it and I agreed it would be a good idea.'

'Manipulative bastard,' Matt snorted. 'And whose idea was it for you to leave?'

'Well, it was just easier for me to go and spend time with my parents. He had nowhere to go.'

'Really? What about his parents?'

I sighed. 'It was just easier. So I waited the two weeks, thinking that without me there to cook and clean and run round after him he would be gagging to get me back. Unfortunately I missed the one small flaw in my plan.'

'That he already had someone else to run round after him?'

'Exactly. So I was at Mum and Dad's and the first Sunday morning we were all in the garden reading the papers and there they were in the social pages.'

'Jake and Tash?'

'Yep. In fairness, they actually mentioned that Tash was Jake's wife's cousin. So I wasn't suspicious at that point - just hurt that he seemed to be having a good time without me. All right - and a little jealous that he had been with her, even if it was just for the photograph. After I had recovered from my initial shock, I managed to convince myself it was a coincidence that they had been at the same social event. I tried to ring him but he didn't pick up that day, or the next, or the next. If it weren't for the fact that he kept turning up in the paper I would have believed something terrible had happened to him. Finally the two weeks were up, and it was my birthday and I decided I was going home.'

I stopped, the pain of my betrayal and abandonment still raw after all this time. Taking a deep breath I continued, determined not to cry about this ever again. 'The problem was that it didn't really feel like my home when I got there. Any articles that had been mine had been removed and Jake's stuff had been spread out further to cover the gaps.'

'All of them?' Matt sounded outraged. It was really nice.

'I hadn't had that much stuff anyway, cause Jake and I don't really have the same taste, but my vases, my throw rug and even my photos, all gone. I found them all stuffed into boxes in the spare bedroom. The prick had started to pack up my things.'

'What did you do?' Matt asked.

'I rang Mum and Dad, and my three best friends, Elaine whom I think you met, Dinah and Nat. I waited for them to arrive and then we started to pack. I figured he'd come home and find me totally gone and realise how stupid he'd been. As I said, I was pretty naive.'

'So when did you realise he already had someone else?'

'While Mum and I were packing up my clothes. It was so clichéd. We found a leopard print teddy with matching G-string stuffed into my top drawer. Once I started to look, I found other signs as well. An extra toothbrush in the bathroom, two wine glasses left on the sink to drain and a pair of shoes kicked off by the front door that weren't mine.'

'Not your style?'

'I would have broken my neck if I'd tried to wear them. That was if I could have fitted into them.'

'Please tell me you did something really good,' he almost begged.

'Hell hath no fury like a woman scorned?' I asked him.

'Yeah. Tell me you did something, anything in retaliation.'

'I had my petty revenge.'

'I'm all ears,' he said, smiling broadly.

'I cut the straps off the teddy and slashed some holes in the front of the material. Mum was a bit shocked at first, but then she said "Hang on. I'll get the G-string." And I knew it was all systems go. Dad stood watch at the front door while the girls, Mum and I wreaked subtle havoc. I didn't want what we were doing to be too obvious. I was hoping they would be discovering things for weeks.'

'What did you do?'

'Apart from the teddy, I scrubbed both the toothbrushes around the toilet bowl. I found a bottle of lubrication in the top bathroom drawer and tried to put super glue in it, but Mum stopped me.'

'Why?'

'She didn't think it would work. So she suggested we punch holes in the condoms she had found. I mean we all know how much Jake wants to be a Daddy.'

'Remind me not to get on the wrong side of your mother.'

I laughed, 'Yeah - the only thing worse than a scorned woman is the scorned woman's mother.'

'I'll try to remember that.'

'We did silly stuff. We short-sheeted the bed - I cut an arm off his expensive Armani jacket and turned off the fridge at the wall. We found a bottle of Möet in the wine fridge and drank it, keeping the foil and cork so we could refill it. Dinah had wanted to fill it with urine but we couldn't find a funnel, so Dad was the only one who could do it, and he refused.' I started laughing thinking about it. 'You should have seen Mum trying to convince Dad to spend the afternoon pissing into the Moet bottle. It was priceless.'

Matt was laughing as well. 'I would have done it. It would have been a great pleasure.'

'In the end we used soda water. Nat shaved the cork down so we could get it back in the bottle. And we re-assembled it and put it back in the fridge. Then I placed all his work shirts in the washing machine to soak with some clothes dye I had left over from a tie-dying experiment. We packed up as much as we could into all the cars, and Dad had the foresight to bring his big trailer, so I got some of the furniture, and we left. I broke my key off in the front door on the way out, and that was that. I never went back.'

'What did he say when he got home?'

'I don't know. I never spoke to him again.'

He looked amazed.

'I know. Weird isn't it? But he never called, and I never called him and then one day a year later I look in the paper and see that he's engaged to my cousin and running for Lord Mayor. Then the divorce papers turned up and it was all over.'

'So you haven't spoken to him since you went to stay at your parents'?' he asked in amazement.

'Nope.'

'He's such a coward. How could he just let a marriage end like that?'

'I know, I was angry at first. I mean shit - you think he'd have the decency to at least make it official. But as time went on I think I preferred it that way: It was hard enough always having to see him in the social pages. Anyway, I am sure he would have managed to turn it around somehow to be my fault, and frankly, I don't think I would have been able to handle that. Anyway, that's it. The end. Kaput. Sayonara.'

Matt jumped up to go to the toilet leaving me sitting on the bed thinking about the unspoken part of the story. The part of the story where I thought I had been going mad with grief; when I thought I would never get over it.

That first night I had dreamt of his touch on my skin, of lying sheltered in his arms. When I woke, I had hovered in the eye of the storm for the briefest of moments, before the reality of his betrayal came crashing down. I had rocked rhythmically for hours, my head in my hands, trying to block out the memories. Emotional and physical pain had crashed into each other, rolling over me, threatening to drown me. Finally, I disappeared inside myself looking for a place to hide. Deeper, still deeper until I was a little core in my empty shell, where the agony was muted and breathing suddenly possible. And then I had heard it. My heart; still pumping so quietly, so softly, so sadly inside me, and I grasped onto its rhythmical beating, counting desperately, in my attempt to stay sane.

With time, it had become easier to pretend that I was fine, to function in a semi-normal manner. To smile; even though it didn't reach my eyes. To laugh; even though it didn't touch my heart. But I found myself continuously wondering. What could I have done differently? Why wasn't I enough? And self-doubt had become a shadow, following my footsteps and shaping my decisions.

I was brought out of my reverie by Matt emerging from the bathroom.

'It's not the end,' Matt said shaking his head, 'it's a new beginning.'

'A new beginning and a lucky escape,' I said, relieved to find that I actually meant it.

'Are you ready to go sightseeing?' Matt asked, looking at his watch.

'Yep.' I jumped to my feet. 'Feeling much better thanks. That egg roll was to die for.'

'It's so nice to meet a woman who enjoys her food.'

I shot a look at him to see exactly how he meant that comment. Was he staring at my arse as he said it?

'No offence meant,' he said, correctly interpreting my look and holding his hands up in a gesture of peace. 'You are definitely not fat. What I mean is that too many women you meet are so concerned about their waistlines that they don't eat enough. They look like scrawny little string beans - like your cousin Tash. She looks like she's just escaped from a prisoner-of-war camp.'

I laughed, wondering if he really meant it. I had always felt enormous next to her. I was having trouble fathoming that any male would think she was too thin.

'No seriously,' he continued, 'so many times I've gone on a dinner date only to have my date eat hardly anything. They spend the whole time moving their food around the plate rather than eating it. Am I meant to be impressed by their willpower? I'm never sure. It's such a waste. Food was meant to be eaten and enjoyed, and it's nice to be with a woman who appreciates good food.'

'I've always been a little too fond of food,' I admitted, picking up my hat and bum bag and getting ready to leave the room.

'Nonsense, you look fantastic,' he said as he opened the door and gestured me through ahead of him.

I felt my head puff up a little with his compliment. 'If you keep that up my hat won't fit on my head any more,' I told him.

Laughing he said, 'Well it's India. I'm sure we'll be able to buy you a new one that will fit. And if not, we can always get one made.'

* * *

'Have you ever been in a tuk tuk?' Matt asked five minutes later.

'Can't say I have.'

'It's hot and smelly, but really the only way to go sightseeing. You get a much better feel for the place roaring around in the back of a tuk tuk than in an air-conditioned car.'

'I'll take your word for it,' I said dubiously, eyeing our mode of transport.

It was a motorbike with a box on wheels attached to it. It had open sides, which, while good for letting the breeze through, had me checking on the whereabouts of my bum bag.

'Good idea,' Matt said, as he saw me repositioning it to my front.

I slid into one side of the back and Matt jumped in the other, and then we were off. I let out a squeal of surprise. I hadn't expected it to be quite so fast.

'They have good acceleration, but the top speed isn't so hot,' said Matt, grinning at the look on my face.

I clutched the side with one hand, and sent up a silent prayer for our safety. 'Where are we going?' I yelled over the traffic noise.

'I thought we'd go and see the Red Fort and Humaryun's Tomb. Then tomorrow we can see the Lotus Temple and The Lodi Garden and visit some markets. The night markets around the corner from where we are staying are meant to be excellent.'

I clutched tightly onto the side of the tuk tuk and watched Delhi whiz by.

'Part of the negotiations on the tuk tuk involved us having to go to an emporium,' Matt said.

'What's an emporium?' I asked.

'It's a collection of shops showcasing products made in India. Pashminas, silk rugs, tapestries, wooden artefacts - those sorts of things. You don't have to buy anything, but if you do, the driver gets a cut.'

'I can see why he would want us to go there.'

Feeling braver, I let go of the tuk tuk long enough to pull out my *Lonely Planet* and flick to the section on the Red Fort.

'Look I hope it's not going to be too boring for you,' Matt said, 'but I'm going to have to spend a portion of each day writing.'

'I'm just happy to be travelling,' I said. 'Don't worry about me. I'll read, or write postcards, or I'll sleep. I'm very good at sleeping.'

The Red Fort was a huge sprawling red building surrounded by an impressively long wall. It was hard to concentrate on the sightseeing with the hawkers hassling us continuously to buy things. Matt, obviously used to this behaviour seemed oblivious, but I was filled with guilt watching their smiling faces turn sad when I rejected them. I finally caved and bought a whole series of postcards from a little boy at the front gate. I had never really been a postcard writer. I mean apart from my trip to New Zealand I hadn't really been anywhere postcard-worthy. Now however, I found the thought of relaxing in the evenings, sipping Marsala tea and writing postcards to be an appealing idea.

We stopped at the emporium on the way to Humaryun's tomb, wandering though aisles of soft silks and pashminas, rows of exquisitely carved wooden animals inlaid with semi-precious stones, and room after room of lush, silk rugs - all of them well out of my price range.

'Four thousand dollars?' I gasped to Matt, after having converted the asking price for a small silk rug to Australian dollars.

'This place is really expensive,' he said, 'tomorrow we'll find a cheaper one.'

To get to Humaryun's Tomb we walked through a manicured garden full of canoodling, Indian couples. The ladies - carefully coiffured in brightly coloured silks - looked like exotic birds amongst the foliage.

'Oh excuse me,' I said as I rounded a corner and ran into a couple in the middle of a particularly arduous cuddle. She smiled shyly - her kohl-lined eyes standing out like beautiful jewels, and ducked her blushing face behind her beau. I could hear Matt chuckling and shot him a venomous look.

'Sorry,' he apologised, 'but that was really funny.'

Finally, we reached the tombs and stopped to admire them from afar. They were obviously shadows of their former glory, but I found a rugged beauty in their decaying surfaces.

'The *Lonely Planet* said that elements of the design of this building were refined over the years to eventually create the magnificence of Agra's Taj Mahal,' I informed Matt, who was busy taking photos. 'A squat building with high arched entrances, topped by a bulbous dome,' I read as we moved to a better position for his camera.

'They must have been spectacular when they were new,' he answered, looking at the position of the sun in relation to the tombs.

The exposed stonework was wondrous in its variety of colours and shapes, but if you looked closely, you could see the remnants of what used to cover the stonework; patches of shiny, peacock brilliant blues and greens.

'It must have been magnificent,' I agreed.

Moving closer to the building, the fine detail became evident. Carved writing cascaded over the arches of the doorways and wound around the windows. We wandered through the buildings taking photos and admiring the changing colours of the stones in the setting sun.

'I like this much better than The Red Fort,' I said to Matt.

'It was kind of hectic wasn't it, this is much more peaceful.'

Later that evening, after we had eaten, we sat in our room and wrote. Matt downloaded photos, and tapped away at his laptop while I started to compose what I like to think of as 'The Indian Postcard Collection'

Dear Dinah and Gloria,
I hope Bad Bunny is behaving himself and not shagging too many of your fluffy toys. This morning we arrived in Delhi. And when I say we, I don't mean Jesse and me. I mean Matt, my one-

night-stand guy, and me. Stop squealing - I can hear you all the way over here. Today we went to The Red Fort, impressively massive but slightly boring, and Humaryan's Tomb, which was awe-inspiring. Believe it or not I've only just realised that.... (to be cont. on Nat's postcard.)

Dear Nat and Ricardo,
(Cont. from Dinah and Gloria's card). ......I will be going to see the Taj Mahal. I know sometimes I'm a bit of a thicky, but when Matt said we would be going to Agra I just thought it was another town, NOT the home of the Taj Mahal. I always thought that it was in Mumbai, didn't you? Who would think it was a 2-hour plane ride, and then a 2-hour train ride from Mumbai. Hmm that was confusing. It's two hours to Delhi by plane from Mumbai and then 2 hours by train to...... (to be cont. on Elaine's card.)

Dear Elaine,
(Cont. from Nat and Ricardo's card) ....Agra from Delhi. Tomorrow we are seeing another temple and a garden and will be doing some shopping. Apparently the night markets near where we are staying are fantastic. Hey Elaine just in case you haven't read Dinah and Gloria's card yet, Guess what? I'm travelling India with my yummy one-night-stand guy. Who would have seen that coming? That dart thing really worked! Hope you are all well and that your Doctor is being a good boy, or a bad boy, whichever you prefer. Love you, miss you, and wish you were all here. Xxxxx

I made sure I hid these postcards in my bag before I started on the one to Mum and Dad.

Dear Mum and Dad,

Well, as I said in my email I have decided to travel up through Rajasthan rather than come home. One of Jesse's good friends, who is a likeable and very polite sort of fellow, has offered to take me travelling with him while he writes an article for 'Travel Abroad'. We arrived in Delhi today and did some sightseeing. Tomorrow we will be doing some more things in Delhi, I am hoping to buy something nice to remember my time here. Then on Monday we are off to Agra to see the Taj Mahal. I'm really excited about that. We will be catching a train, which Matt informs me is quite an experience in itself. Love you both. Xxxx

Matt was still typing rapidly, so rather than disturb him by using the phone I snuck down to the front desk and asked them to send up a couple of Marsala teas. They told me it would be about twenty minutes as they had a high level of room service orders, so I had a shower and washed my hair while I waited.

'Likeable and very polite sort of fellow?' Matt asked me as I exited the bathroom.

'Hey, no peeking,' I said, grabbing the card from him. I took the other cards out of my bag and placed a rubber band around the bundle - making sure the card for Mum and Dad was on top.

Shit, I thought. *Thank God I hid the others.* I'd have to be more careful in the future.

'Sorry,' he said laughing. 'I saw it out of the corner of my eye. I've never been described like that before.'

Clutching my confidence around me I said, 'Well, I couldn't very well tell her that you were an extremely gorgeous and yummy bachelor whom I once shagged in

Sydney now could I? She'd have been on the next plane over.'

'What to protect you?' he asked laughing.

'No, to make sure I don't make a fool of myself and scare you away. You know I'm over thirty now. I've got a better chance of being killed in a terrorist attack than meeting an available man.' I stopped as I realised what I had just said. 'Hey, I almost did that,' I said.

There was a knock at the door.

'I hope you don't mind,' I said to Matt, who was standing there smiling and shaking his head at me, 'I got us some tea.'

'Marsala?'

'Of course.'

'You're a mind reader.'

After the porter had left, we relaxed on our prospective beds sipping our tea.

'How's the writing going?' I asked.

'Good. Not really much to write about yet. I'm roughing in a storyline, trying to get a unique angle.'

'I can imagine that would be difficult. I mean this must be one of the most written-about places in the world.'

'Yeah, one of them.'

'So what's your angle?' I asked curiously.

'Haven't got one yet, but it will come to me - it always does.'

I let out a huge yawn.

'Have I been keeping you up?' he asked, looking at his watch.

'No, it's only 9pm. Anyway I told you I could compete for Australia in sleeping. If I get tired I'll just go to sleep.'

'With the lights on?'

'With the lights on, so don't worry about me. You do what you need to do.'

'I'm finished for the night anyway.' He also let out a huge yawn.

'It must be all that fresh air making us tired,' I said laughing.

'Either that or coating our lungs, depriving us of oxygen and making us sleepy,' he said smiling.

'More likely that,' I agreed.

Grabbing my toothbrush and bottle of water I headed for the bathroom. I was determined not to go getting any Delhi Belly in front of Matt. God, can you imagine?

I jumped into bed while I heard Matt in the shower and tried unsuccessfully not to think about his long, tanned, lean body with water cascading down it. I was a bit jumpy by the time he came out of the bathroom and all of a sudden realised we were sleeping in the same room. Well of course it wasn't the first time I realised it, but the full importance of it hit me. What if I snored? What if I talked in my sleep? Or worse, what if I farted? The myriad of ways in which I could cause extreme embarrassment to myself without even knowing it were endless. I thought I would lie awake the whole night - but one minute I was lying there staring at the ceiling, and the next I was waking to light streaming in the window and the sound of Matt back in the shower. It was a little disorientating. I closed my eyes and was quickly sound asleep once again.

* * *

'Tara, Tara.'

I could hear my name being called and dimly feel someone shaking me. I clawed my way upwards towards consciousness and opened my bleary eyes.

'Wow,' said a familiar voice, 'you really could sleep for Australia.'

'Matt?'

'The one and only.'

'Is that coffee I smell? Cause, I'm only opening my eyes if there's coffee.'

'Open your eyes sleepyhead. I have coffee and some fruit and pastries.'

'Oh goody.' I opened my eyes and sat bolt upright in bed.

Matt had obviously been up for a while. I helped myself to my coffee and a pastry.

'First,' he said, 'I was trying to be really quiet, tiptoeing around and everything. And then I accidentally let the bathroom door slam and I thought that would wake you for sure.'

'It would have to be something more substantial than a door slamming,' I said around a mouthful of pastry.

'Yeah I figured. So then, I started trying to wake you - talking loudly on my phone, opening the cupboard doors and closing them hard. Man you didn't even flinch.'

'What time is it?' I asked him, concerned I'd slept through the day.

'9am.'

'Oh thank God. I thought it might be midday or something like that.'

'You had twelve hours sleep. '

'I'll be right for the night markets tonight. Give me fifteen minutes and I'll be ready to go,' I told him as I headed to the bathroom with my coffee.

True to my word, fifteen minutes later I was dressed and ready to rock and roll.

'When you said fifteen minutes, I was thinking more like an hour,' said Matt.

'Yeah I've never understood what takes some women so long to get ready,' I said as we headed out the door. 'I mean really, shower, dry, moisturise, deodorise, put your clothes on, brush your teeth and comb your hair. How long can you make that last? Admittedly,' I said, 'I don't look as good as the women who take an hour to get ready, but seriously I wouldn't want to. If I had to spend an hour getting ready every time I went somewhere, I wouldn't bother leaving the house. I mean for a special occasion or a date, well of course you want to look your best. But day-to-day, all you need is a whip of lipstick and some eyeliner. Then again, Jake used to complain that I didn't spend enough time on myself. He said it looked like I didn't care about him if I went out without a full face of makeup. I never really understood the logic behind that.'

'Yeah, but we established yesterday that Jake is a complete arse.'

'Yes we did, didn't we?' I laughed. 'I have to admit, the makeup thing was a relief when we broke up. I didn't wear makeup at all for about 9 months. But that was probably because I was too depressed.'

'Wow,' said Matt laughing, 'you're like a wind-up doll in the morning. I woke you up and you haven't stopped talking since.'

'Hey. That's not true. I wasn't talking while I cleaned my teeth.'

'Actually,' he said, 'you were. It was pretty disgusting.'

'Was I? I'm not normally like this in the morning.'

'Really?'

'No. I don't normally start talking till about ten-thirty. Up to then I just grunt and nod. I wonder how much caffeine was in that coffee.'

'Obviously a lot.'

Matt pulled over a tuk tuk driver and started chatting to him. After a few minutes, he gestured for me to jump in and introduced me.

'This is Fahad. Fahad this is Tara. Tara and I have been married for a couple of years Fahad so I'd appreciate it if you didn't try to hit on her.'

Fahad let out a loud, deep chuckle. He turned around to look at me and I realised he sounded and looked like an Indian version of Fat Albert.

'No worries Mr Matt,' he boomed. 'I look after your wife like she was one of my sisters.' He hit the accelerator pedal and we shot off into the traffic.

'Would you mind telling me what that was all about?' I stage-whispered to Matt out of the corner of my mouth.

'Some of these men can be a little frisky with their hands, just making sure.'

'What about the man that drove us around yesterday?

'Well, if you noticed he wasn't very friendly. I could make you my sister next time if you prefer?'

Damn. He had check-mated me, and I bet he knew it. I was pretty chuffed at the thought of pretending to be his wife, I certainly didn't want to be downgraded to a sister. But then if I admitted that to him I was pretty much telling him that I fancied him. Let's face it though, I would have to be a deaf, dumb, blind, mute with no sense of smell, and no imagination to not fancy him. But did he know that? Did he realise just how desirable he was? I was guessing the answer to that was no.

All of that flitted through my head at the speed of light and then I found a loophole in his theory. 'Better not make me your sister,' I said quietly, '*then* Fahad could still hit on me.'

Matt nodded his head as if considering this seriously, but I could see a smile playing around the corners of his mouth.

'Mr Matt, Mrs Tara,' said Fahad, looking at us in the rear vision mirror, 'where do you want to go first?'

'Well,' said Matt to the mirror, 'we want to go to the Lotus Temple and the Lodi Gardens. Is there somewhere there that is good for lunch?'

'Oh yes,' he continued, in his singsong Fat Albert voice, 'the Garden Restaurant at Lodi. They do very good Indian food there.'

'Sounds good.'

'Yes, very good Sir,' said Fat Fahad. 'We'll go to the Lotus Temple first. It is very beautiful Ma'am,' he informed me.

I was wishing, just quietly, that he would watch the road a little more, and the rear vision mirror quite a bit less, so I didn't respond. I just nodded, hoping he would get the hint and start watching where we were going.

He spent the next 30 minutes practising his English while driving haphazardly through the streets of Delhi. Finally, he pulled over at the side of the road near some street vendors.

'There,' he said waving his hand, 'the Lotus Temple. I wait here for you.'

Matt handed him a note and told him to get himself a drink. Fat Fahad was happy with that and after helping me out of the tuk tuk, took himself off to the street vendors.

I stepped around to the other side of the tuk tuk and got my first view of the Lotus Temple.

'My,' I said.

'Is that it?' Matt asked.

'Wow. Is that better?'

'A little.'

After having driven through the built up suburbs of Delhi, the vast expanse of manicured lawn and trimmed hedges were impressive enough, but in the midst of them, opening like a giant white flower, was the Lotus Temple.

'What sort of Temple is it?' I asked Matt as I fumbled around in my bag for the *Lonely Planet*.

'It's a Baha'i Place of Worship,' he informed me.

I was thinking he was pretty clever until I saw a sign just near the entrance gate to the garden that said, 'Baha'i Place of Worship.'

I stood and admired the beauty of the giant flower before me, while Matt took photos of the Temple, the vendors and the crowds.

'The Bahai philosophy revolves around universal peace and elimination of prejudice,' I read as we began the walk down the long pathway to the Temple. 'No speaking is allowed inside the temple,' I advised him.

'Has your caffeine hit worn off yet?' he asked.

'I think so, why?'

'I'm not taking you into a temple where speaking is not permissible unless it has.'

'I'll be fine,' I assured him.

We began to queue as we approached the temple and I realised everybody was taking off their shoes. 'I'm not taking off my shoes,' I whispered to Matt.

'Why not?'

'What if someone steals them?'

'Look, you hand them to that lady and she gives you a number for them,' he said.

'Are you sure?'

'You'll be fine. Trust me.'

I took off my trusty reef sandals and handed them to the lady who gave me a wooden token in return. Then we headed up the steps and into the Temple. I must admit I had expected there would be more to the interior. I mean the sweeping ceiling was certainly spectacular in its flowery form, but the temple was just a large room with heaps of fold out chairs. There was a sprinkling of people sitting in the chairs in silent contemplation. Of course as soon as we were inside the Temple, I had an urge to start talking. It was like an itch that I couldn't scratch. I could feel the pressure building inside me, threatening to come out as a huge bellow. I looked at Matt who smiled at me smugly and held one finger up to his lips in the universal sign of silence. I had an urge to hold up a different finger, in a different way, for a very different universal sign. We shuffled slowly around the edge of the Temple until finally we were free. I let out a huge explosion of air and took a huge breath.

'Did you breathe at all while you were in there?' Matt asked. 'You've gone all red.'

'That was terrible,' I exclaimed, 'as soon as I couldn't talk I had the hugest urge to start yabbering at you. And now of course I have no idea what was so important that I had to say.'

'Guess that caffeine's still working its way out of your system,' Matt said chuckling. 'Come on let's get our shoes and visit the information centre.'

We headed back to the shoe storage area where I handed my little token to the lady. She promptly handed me a pair of shoes. The only problem was they weren't my shoes.

'Excuse me,' I said trying to back up in the queue and get her attention. There was, however, an overwhelming large number of women all trying to get their shoes, and I found myself being jostled further and further from the front row.

'What's wrong?' asked Matt, coming over to see what was taking me so long.

'Oh,' I said, looking down at his feet, 'that'd be right. You get the correct shoes, of course you do. Look what I got.' I dropped the shoes to the ground and shoved the front half of my feet as far into the teeny golden sandals as they would go. 'What do you think?' I said as I tottered around.

Matt shook his head. 'Unbelievable,' he said. 'Why do I get the feeling that these sorts of things always happen to you?'

'Why do you think I didn't want to hand my shoes over?' I asked in response.

Matt laughed and held out his hand. 'Hand em over,' he said and waded back through the crowd of women to the shoe lady. I could see him gesturing and pointing at me and then he filled out what appeared to be a form before finally heading back.

'Thanks,' I said in relief, holding out my hand for my shoes.

'You're welcome,' he said sheepishly as he deposited the gold sandals back in my hand.

'Nhhooooooo.'

'You're not going to believe it,' he said.

'Oh yes I think I am,' I said. 'Let me guess. She gave them to a small Indian lady?'

'She gave them to a small Indian lady. I filled out a form though. They said they'd post them to us if they turned up.'

I shut my eyes and started counting to ten. And then I remembered Mumbai. 'Well I think we both know the chances of that happening are somewhere between zilch and impossible but it's okay,' I said as I reopened my eyes. 'I'll just have to get some more.'

'I'll get you a new pair,' said Matt.

'Why should you get me a new pair?' I asked confused.

'Cause I'm the one that told you to hand them over,' he said.

'But we didn't have a choice,' I argued.

'I said to trust me.'

'You're serious aren't you?'

'Of course.'

'Matt, I am not letting you buy me new shoes. I'm a big girl, I can handle it.'

'Weeelll, at least let me buy you lunch.'

'Fine. I never say no to someone buying me lunch,' I conceded graciously.

We had been heading back to the information centre as we argued and were stopped at the door by a well-garbed security man.

'I'm sorry,' he said, wobbling his head from side to side as he talked, 'but I cannot be letting you in like that.'

'Like what?' I asked.

'You be having no shoes on,' he informed me.

'Really?' I asked sarcastically. 'Well that would be because one of your fellow employees gave them away,' I informed him.

'Oh deary, deary me. That is indeed a shame,' he said.

'Yeah, big shame. Now, are you going to let us in or not?'

'If it was up to me madam,' he continued with the head waggling, 'I would let you in. But unfortunately it is not.'

I looked around. There didn't seem to be anyone else who was in charge here.

'Well, who is it up to?' I asked stupidly.

The man waggled his head a little and looked up to the heavens. I looked up as well, trying to find an office where the person in charge was working. I spun slowly around looking up for someone, somewhere, but it was a single storey building.

'Tara,' Matt whispered, 'I think he means God.'

I started to giggle. 'Are you talking about God?' I asked him.

'The one and only,' he informed me gravely.

I backed away from him dragging Matt with me. 'I'm confused,' I whispered. 'I thought the Indians had multiple Gods.'

'Not the Baha'i,' he whispered back. 'They're monotheistic.'

'Meaning?' I asked, feeling a little stupid.

'They believe in one God.'

'Oh.' I thought about it for a moment. 'So how do they differ from Christians or Muslims?' I asked.

'They believe that the major religions are part of a progressive revelation from God, and that all the major figures, like Buddha, Jesus and Mohammed are sent by God to guide the world's spiritual development.'

'Right,' I said, dropping the gold sandals to the ground and shoving my toes into them. 'Do you think God would be happy with this?' I asked, turning back to the security guard.

He broke into a huge smile of relief. 'Oh yes madam,' he said, 'God is very happy with that.' And he opened the door for us.

I shuffled through in my dainty gold sandals with Matt following me, his face screwed up with his attempts not to laugh.

'If you laugh,' I warned him, 'I'm going to get God to throw you out.'

I navigated to the first display and started to read about the Baha'i beliefs. Matt finally regained control of himself and joined me there.

'Hey, what's with all the head waggling?' I asked him.

'It's a cultural thing.'

'It's hypnotic. I felt like he was trying to exercise his mind powers on me through his head waggles.'

'I think you might be onto something there. The head waggle could actually be a form of hypnosis.'

'Did I bark like a dog?'

'No, but you ran around clucking like a chicken.'

I laughed out loud, earning a look of intense annoyance from some browsers nearby. 'Oh,' I whispered to Matt, 'I didn't realise we weren't allowed to talk in here either.'

One of the browsers looked at me and catching my eye pointed to a 'no talking' sign.

'Oh for goodness sake,' I said to Matt, earning me a look that could kill from the browser. 'Come on, let's get out of here.' I shuffled back down the stairs and out the door with as much dignity as I could muster.

'Here,' I said to the doorman, 'I'd like you to have these.' I kicked off the sandals which were beginning to rub. 'I'm sure you'll find a good use for them.'

'Oh thanking you very muchly Ma'am. I have a daughter who will love these.'

'Here,' said Matt, pulling what appeared to be an Australian colouring-in-book out of his backpack. 'Maybe she'd like this as well.'

The man went as red as is possible for an Indian man, with very dark skin, to go.

'You are very kind,' he said. 'God bless you both and your marriage. May you have many, many children.'

'Thanks,' I said, and then we headed back out to Fahad.

'We have got to get you some shoes,' said Matt.

'Will there be anywhere around here I can buy some.'

'T i i,' said Matt.

'Pardon?'

'T i i. This is India.'

'Oh right,' I said laughing, 'Tii indeed.'

Fahad was extremely dismayed when I returned without my shoes. As he took us to a shoe shop he kept turning around to apologise, which - while very sweet, was also terrifying as we zoomed blind through the Delhi traffic.

He pulled up outside a small run-down shop and insisted on haggling for the shoes on my behalf. There were so many pretty sandals I couldn't make up my mind. In the end I bought five different pairs - at rock bottom price thanks to Fahad - and returned to the tuk tuk with my package.

'I've unleashed a machine,' Matt said, laughing as I ummed and ahhed over which ones to wear.

When I had finally settled on a pair, Fahad took us to the Lodi Garden Restaurant for lunch.

'I'm starved,' I said to Matt as we sat down.

'Let's get thali.' He rubbed his hands together.

'What's thali?'

'It's a tasting plate of Indian food. You get a platter with three or four different dishes, curry puffs and chapatis.'

'Yummy.' I could feel saliva pooling.

It turned out thali was the Indian version of an "all you can eat" meal. I ate so much, I considered undoing the top button of my pants, but I didn't want Matt to think I was a fatty.

'Fancy hanging around the pool this arvo?' he asked when we had finished.

'Sure. I can work on my non-existent tan,' I said.

'I'll get some writing done, and then tonight we can hit the markets.'

I clapped my hands together enthusiastically and said, 'Yeah, more shopping.'

Although the Lodi Gardens had been relaxing, I was happy to get back to the hotel. The heat, the noise, the smells and vibrant colours of Delhi created a huge sensory overload which was tiring. Plus I was sticky and hot and the thought of the pool water was extremely enticing.

'I'm going to get some photos of the hotel so I'll meet you down there,' I heard Matt call through the bathroom door, where I was struggling to get my bikini top down my sweaty skin. Finally, I was ready and, grabbing my book, headed down to the pool area. I was delighted to find that I had it all to myself. Using my towel and sarong I bagged a couple of deck chairs before slipping into the water, gasping at the temperature change. I swam a few laps and floated for a while before deciding to read my book. It wasn't long before the sun's rays lulled me to sleep.

Water drops splashing across my skin woke me and I opened my eyes to see Matt towelling himself down. Sunlight glinted off his body showing the perfection of his muscles. I felt my stomach tighten into a knot as I watched him moving and flexing in the act of drying himself. As if he could feel my gaze, he stopped and turned till our eyes met. Flashes of memories from our night together danced before my eyes: him lifting me onto his lap and kissing me deeply, him working his way down my body with his tongue, him pinning me down with the weight of his body and slowly sliding inside me.

I could feel the heat in my face and every cell in my body was urging me to reach out to him. Only the thought of his rejection enabled me to restrain myself. I didn't think I'd be able to bear the utter humiliation.

I smiled stiffly and said, 'Get what you wanted?'

'Not really,' he answered and his eyes travelled - for a second - down my body. Did his voice sound a little husky? I'm sure my fevered brain was imagining it, trying to create a situation in which it could have what it wanted: Matt, inside me, again.

Shit, if I didn't stop thinking about it I was certainly going to do something embarrassing. I hopped up and headed for the pool.

'I'm hot,' I said.

'I know,' he replied.

Whoa. Did he mean gorgeous, sexy, desirable hot or sweaty, sticky, uncomfortable hot?

I glanced at his eyes but they were dark and unreadable. After diving in, I swam the length of the pool under water, still feeling aroused and confused when I finally came up for air. A few laps later, my frustration had eased. When I finally felt I had myself under control, I headed back to my chair.

Matt was already asleep, my sarong bunched under his head as a pillow. I stopped to admire him lying there like a golden god. So perfect, so funny, so sexy, so desirable, so sweet - so out of my league. I sighed and, hopping into my chair, was finally able to release my sexual tension enough to slip back into sleep.

* * *

After our afternoon nap, we headed to the markets. I took a little longer than 15 minutes to get ready, applying foundation, lip gloss and the Kohl around my eyes. I had picked up some colour at the pool and my skin had a healthy glow about it.

Initially, things were a little strained between us.

'Is everything all right?' I finally asked him.

'Sure. Why?'

'You seem a little distracted.'

'Just thinking about the article.'

'Oh.' Bugger. I had been starting to think that maybe I hadn't been alone in my fantasising that afternoon.

We were half way down the markets when we found the rug shop.

'Right,' said Matt. 'We're going to play good cop, bad cop.'

'Am I the bad cop?' I asked hopefully. I'd always wanted to be a bad cop.

'No, you're the good cop. We're married and I'm a tight arse.'

'All right,' I said. I was disappointed at having been allocated the good cop role, but sadly excited by the prospect of pretending to be Matt's wife again.

The shopkeeper - Sahir, a tall, skinny man - was happy to educate us about rugs. The most expensive were the silk on silk. They were soft and shiny; I was fascinated by the way they changed colours. One end showed you the soft muted colours, and the other the strong vibrant ones.

Finally, I found one that I loved. Pointing at it I said to Matt, 'That one's not too awful.'

Matt screwed up his face as he walked around it and said, 'It's all right, if you like that sort of thing.'

Sahir clapped his hands and a young boy emerged from behind a rug. I started to laugh at the absurdity of the boy standing behind the rug waiting to be summoned. When he disappeared behind the same rug and returned with a tray ladened with different assortments of beverages, I realised it hid a doorway leading to another room.

Coffee, Marsala tea, beer?' Sahir offered us.

'Beer,' Matt said.

We sat with our beers while Matt commenced negotiations over the rug. It took him thirty minutes to bargain Sahir down to half his starting price and throw in free shipping to Australia.

After that, I bought Matt dinner to thank him for saving me so much money, and then we returned to our room to try and get a good night's sleep before our early morning train.

It was the crack of dawn when Matt shook me awake the next morning.

'Sorry,' he apologised. 'I hope I didn't hurt you. You're so hard to wake up.'

'S'all right,' I mumbled as I stumbled into the bathroom to splash some water on my face.

Once I had woken up sufficiently, we grabbed our backpacks and walked to the train station. Compared to last night the streets were empty. It was eerie.

When we got there, the train station floor was scattered with bodies covered in sheets. *Christ*, I thought, *there's been another terrorist attack.* I backed nervously out of the building; searching for men with guns.

'What's wrong?' Matt asked.

I indicated the bodies with a look of terror on my face.

Matt burst out laughing and said, 'They're just sleeping.'

'Last time I saw bodies lying in a train station with sheets over them it was on the news,' I replied tersely, feeling like an idiot.

'Sorry, I should have warned you,' he said, still smiling. 'Come on or we'll miss the train.'

The train to Agra was luxurious compared to what I had been expecting. (Being jammed into the carriage like a sardine in a can, while the locals groped my arse and tits.)

'Oooh,' I said, reading the card in the seat pocket, 'we get a six-course breakfast.'

'Don't get *too* excited,' Matt warned me.

'A six-course breakfast is a six-course breakfast,' I insisted.

An hour later, I was trying to work out what the six courses had been.

'Do you think they count the milk that goes on the cornflakes as a course?' I asked Matt.

'Possibly. And I'm assuming that the orange juice was a course of its own.'

'That still only makes it four. Maybe the tea or coffee?'

'Or if you count the egg as one course and the sausage as another you've got your six.'

'That must be it,' I agreed, relaxing back into my seat and looking out the window as the sun rose. The passing fields were slowly becoming visible. I peered into the shadows perplexed. The fields were covered with men. Some squatting and others arriving and departing.

'What are they doing?' I asked Matt. 'Is it a morning prayer ritual?'

'Sort of,' said Matt, sounding amused.

I watched as field after field slipped by. As it got lighter I realised what I was seeing. 'They're going to the toilet,' I said aghast. It raised a whole series of questions. 'Where are the women?'

'They aren't allowed to go during the day.'

'Why not?'

'I'm not sure.'

'What if they can't go when they're meant to? What if they have to go later?' I was thinking of my own very irregular needs.

'They've been doing it like this since they were children. I think they're pretty well trained.'

'What if they get an upset stomach?'

'I'm sure they're allowed to go if they need to.'

'Do they do it in the fields for the fertiliser aspect of it?'

'They don't have a sewerage system.'

'Hmmmmmmmm.'

'That's it?'

'No, I'm thinking.'

'Take your time.'

'Do they have a set rule of how close they can be to each other?'

'I'm sure they have their own etiquette.'

'Where do they wash their hands?'

'I don't know.'

'Do they use toilet paper?'

'Tara, sometimes being with you is like being with a small child.'

The part of my brain that was hoping to get laid by him again one day - 99.9999 per cent - shuddered to a halt. The other 0.0001 per cent was still asleep or it too would have been shuddering with the want-to-get-laid-by-Matt group as well.

'That doesn't sound very good,' I said, grimacing.

'No, it's refreshing.'

Refreshing? Not a bad thing surely?

'Frustrating, but refreshing.'

Oooops, frustrating. That wasn't good.

I lapsed into a slightly depressed silence.

'What no more questions?'

I shook my head.

'Hey,' he said, reaching out to touch my arm, 'I was kidding about the small child thing. I enjoy being with you. You make me laugh more than anyone else I know.'

He thought I was funny. That should have made me happy, but I had a flashback to school when I was the fat funny girl all the guys liked to hang around with, the fat funny girl who they told their girl problems to, and the same fat funny girl who would sit alone and watch while the pretty popular girls got asked out.

(I know I hadn't told you I was fat when I was at school. It's something I try not to share. Of course at my twenty-first birthday party all the fatty photos came out - something everybody but me found hugely amusing. And of course the old nickname came back to haunt me. But I guess that's what twenty-firsts are all about so I tried to take it in good spirits. I admit though that I had to restrain myself from punching Tash as she had danced around me chanting, 'Ten tonne Tara,' over and over again. I wish now I had have given into the urge.)

Realising what I was doing, I gave myself a mental shake. I was on the way to the Taj Mahal and here I was choosing to let myself slump into a pool of self-pity. Pulling myself together I said, 'Thanks, while you're nowhere near as funny as me, I enjoy being with you too.'

Matt smiled, looking relieved.

We sat in a companionable silence watching the fields slipping by. Gradually they turned into villages and then we were entering the city.

'We're here,' I said excited.

Matt had organised for a guide to meet us at the train station. We were escorted to a waiting car and bustled off to the Taj Mahal.

'This is my wife Tara,' Matt told the guide. 'She decided to come with me at late notice.'

'Managed to find a babysitter,' I informed the guide.

'How many children do you have?' he asked me. His English was very good.

'Six.' I had the pleasure of hearing Matt make a choking little gurgling noise.

'That is a lot of children for one so young.'

'We started really young,' I said, patting Matt on the arm. 'I was still in school wasn't I honey?'

Matt had a timely coughing fit, which conveniently prevented him from having to answer.

The driver stopped the car next to a long walkway leading down to a huge arched gate. 'That is the south gate entry to the Taj Mahal,' the guide informed us. There were long queues of people at the beginning of the walkway. 'You will have to queue in the women's line,' he said, gesturing to the far line.

The woman's queue was miniscule compared to the men's. I admired the arching gate to the Taj while I waited for Matt and Daha, our guide. After that, we had a bag search. I was amused when they found my iPod and insisted that Daha take it to a cloakroom from where we would pick it up later.

'But why?' I asked Matt, confused as to what threat my iPod was.

'Tii baby,' he replied, smiling at me.

I couldn't help remembering my poor late departed shoes and hoped that my iPod didn't suffer a similar fate.

Finally we were approaching the South Gate; a red sandstone structure inlaid in areas with the same marble and semiprecious stones as the Taj Mahal. Daha informed us that it was also inscribed with verses from the Koran. I was thinking how beautiful the gate was when through the arch I glimpsed the snowy whiteness of the Taj Mahal rising mystically before us. I felt a tingle run over me as my breath caught in my throat.

'It's amazing isn't it,' Matt said, stopping beside me to admire the contrast of the red sandstone arch against the distant marbled building.

'Awesome,' I whispered.

We continued through the arch until we could view the whole of the Taj Mahal. The hazy air cloaked the building, amplifying its majesty. I gazed at it, soaking up the atmosphere while Matt took numerous photos.

'I'm expecting copies,' I informed him.

'Of course,' he said, without taking his face away from the lens.

'Let me take one of the two of you,' said Daha.

We looked at each other and shrugged.

'You stand here,' he said, lining us up in front of the pools of water leading to the Taj Mahal. Looking through the lens, he indicated for us to move closer. We shuffled towards each other a little. Daha flicked his hands again to move us closer still. We shifted until our bodies were touching.

'Now put your arms around each other,' he said.

Matt looped an arm over my shoulders and I put mine around his waist. It felt really nice.

Daha took a photo and then looking over the top of the camera said to Matt, 'Now you kiss your wife. It's very good luck for your marriage.'

I looked up at Matt. We had told the man we were married with six children, he was going to think it mighty odd if we didn't want to kiss for the camera. Matt shrugged a little and then leant down to kiss me. I thought he would go for my cheek so when I felt his lips touch mine I responded a little too ardently, arching up against him and tightening my hold.

'Very nice,' I vaguely heard Daha say, as I pressed my lips to Matt's.

Unaware of the effect he was having on me Matt abruptly let go and, stepping away from me, reached for his camera.

I felt dazed and disorientated by the loss of contact.

I could hear Daha begin his tourist guide speech and tried to concentrate on what he was saying. I caught the part about the central Taj structure being made from marble inlaid with 43 different types of semiprecious stones. And then I vagued out for a while hearing only random words. Emperor's second wife. Died in childbirth. Heartbroken. Token of his love.

I started as I realised that Matt and Daha were walking towards the Taj and hurried after them. Matt stopped to take a photo of it reflected in one of the pools. And then Daha was talking again. I tried to listen, I really did. But all I could think about was that kiss; the feel of Matt's arms around me and his rock hard body pressed against mine. I wandered around the Taj Mahal admiring it, but thinking about Matt. I was frustrated by my patheticness.

Finally we were back in the car and on our way to the hotel.

'Do you mind if we hang out this afternoon while I work?' he asked me.

'Of course not.' I patted my bag, which contained postcards of the Taj Mahal. 'I've got some writing of my own to do.'

Dearest Elaine,

Today I saw the Taj Mahal can you believe it. Photos don't do it justice. I am having a great time with Matt, (not that kind of good time unfortunately.) But today at the Taj the tour guide made us kiss for a photo. He thought we were married you see - long story, and the feel of .....cont. on Nat's card.

Dearest Nat and Ricardo,

....cont. from Elaine's card - his body pressing against mine was enough to make me delirious for the rest of the day. No Nat, it wasn't a good thing, just a pretend thing. Matt kissed me at the Taj Mahal, but for a photo, not because he wanted to. One thing I have learnt in India is that .....cont. on Dinah's card

Dearest Dinah and Gloria,

......cont. from Nat's card - beggars can't be choosers, so I guess I'll just have to be happy with that one night in heaven. Hi guys, saw the Taj Mahal today. You were right Dinah, it's unbelievable. Hope you guys are all well and not missing me too much. Seems like I've been gone ages. Lots of Love, Tara. Xxxxx P.S. Love to BB.

Dearest Lil and Martin, all the girls and the foetus,

I am having a really great time in India. Wait till you see what I've bought you Lil. Today we caught the train to Agra and saw the Taj Mahal. It really is a very spiritual place. All the more so for me cause I got to kiss Matt. Only for a photo for the guide who thought we were married, unfortunately. You guys would love it and maybe one day, if you're nice to me, I'll babysit and you can come and see it. Miss you all. Tara Xxxx

I hid those cards and then started the one to Mum and Dad.

Dearest Mum and Dad,

Today I saw the Taj Mahal. Can you believe it? It is even more beautiful than it looks on television. We are having a great time and are staying in Agra for the night and then tomorrow continuing to a fort that is on the way to Rajasthan. We'll be there for a couple of nights. Love to all the animals and big kisses to you both. Miss you. Tara. Xxxx Xxxx

* * *

We had dinner at the hotel and collapsed ridiculously early. The last thing I remembered, while drifting off to sleep, was hoping that I wasn't going to talk or snore. I woke before Matt and for the first time had the luxury of watching him sleep. He looked so peaceful lying there, his hair all tousled. It made me want to reach out and run my hands through it.

I had been staring at his face for a while when all of a sudden his eyes popped open. Just like that. One minute he was asleep and the next wide-awake. It gave me such a fright that I leaped out of bed yelled, 'I bags the shower,' and bolted for the bathroom.

Shit. I sat on the toilet with my head in my hands while I waited for the hot water to come through. I hoped he didn't think I'd been watching him - which I had, I know - but I didn't want him thinking I was some creepy stalker. He might decide to leave me behind if he thought I spent the whole night watching him. I was starting to feel a little like Gollum.

'My precious,' I whispered softly to myself.

I took my time in the shower partly because it felt so damned good, and partly because I was too embarrassed to face Matt. Eventually I realised I couldn't stay in there forever, so I held my head high, stuck what I hoped was not too-fake a smile on my face, and re-entered the bedroom.

Matt was nowhere to be seen. Oh crap. A quick examination showed me that his bag was still there. That was something - at least he hadn't done a runner. I dried my hair, packed my things and was sitting in the bay window admiring the view, when he finally returned.

'No room service this morning,' he said. 'I had to go out for coffee.'

A quick look at his face revealed no hidden agendas, no concern for his own well-being, and indeed only the normal relaxed happy Matt I had come to know. I let out an internal sigh of relief.

'Smells good,' I said, picking up one of the cups.

'Curry puff?' He handed me a brown paper bag.

'Yummy.'

'The driver should be here in about thirty minutes to take us to the fort. It's meant to be a long drive so we may want to grab some nibbles.'

'I'll go and get that sorted while you have a shower,' I offered.

'That'd be great, thanks.'

'No, thank you,' I said, saluting him with my curry puff.

Six hours later, we were still driving. We had already consumed the chips, nuts and fruit that I had bought and I was starting to get hungry. I was also starting to have a sneaking suspicion that the driver might be lost. He had at one point pulled over and spoken to some locals. I was guessing he had asked for directions.

It was, however, interesting watching the landscape changing around us. Monkeys were starting to pop up on the side of the road; hanging around, cleaning and grooming each other. And the women were becoming more exotic. I watched as a group of them with huge baskets resting effortlessly on their heads, walked towards us. Their faces were draped with brightly coloured, gauzy material, which billowed around them, swaying in the light breeze. Matt told me it meant they were unmarried.

I was watching some monkeys play in the trees when I noticed the barricades stretched across the road in front of us. As the driver slowed, a group of young men rushed out from behind a building and surrounded the car.

'Fuck,' I said eloquently.

'That about sums it up,' Matt replied.

The driver wound down his window while the men yelled and gestured towards us. I made myself as small as possible, squashing into the corner of the car. Matt looked concerned but calm. This was the man who had run into a burning building to save orphans, he probably saw things like this all the time - but I was terrified. Visions of us being dragged out of the car and shot in the head danced before my eyes. I could feel myself starting to hyperventilate.

And then Matt held his mobile phone out for the youths to see. 'Policie,' he said calmly. He waved his hand from side to side so they could all see his finger on the call button and said it again. 'Policie.'

I could see them looking at him and the phone and then at each other. They started talking amongst themselves and I tried to look braver - but I have a feeling I looked like I wanted to puke, which was pretty much how I felt. Slowly they backed away from the car and moved part of the barricade.

'Fuck,' I said again, as we drove through the gap.

Matt looked at me in concern. 'Are you all right?' he asked.

I tried to answer but couldn't because I was clenching my teeth together so hard I couldn't move my jaw. He smiled reassuringly and, reaching over, took my hand. I gripped it tightly and took a deep breath. We continued like that for a while, not talking, just holding hands and watching the landscape slip by.

One hour later we finally arrived at the Hill Fort Kresoli; an old fort that had been transformed into a hotel. I had by this time managed to unclench my teeth and let Matt have his hand back. I had seen him surreptitiously massaging his knuckles after I had finally released it.

It was starting to get dark and I was hungry, tired and a little disgruntled. I was sure we had driven past the same hill at least three times before the driver, at Matt's insistence, finally stopped and asked for directions. I suspected we were really only about four hours from Agra, not the seven it had taken to get there.

A porter showed us to our room and it wasn't till we both put our bags on the same bed that we realised there was, indeed, only one bed in the room.

'Hmmmm,' I said, looking at Matt.

Matt just smiled and went back to reception to ask for a room change. A few minutes later, he was back. 'Do you want the good news or the bad news?' he asked me.

'The good news,' I answered from the doorway to the bathroom.

'They have cold beer here.'

'Excellent. And the bad news is.....?'

'No other rooms available.'

I nodded my head thoughtfully. 'But they definitely have cold beer?' I asked.

'Yep.'

'Well, I guess we'll live.'

'How about I go and get us a table outside,' he said, picking up his camera, 'and you take your time and have a shower. I'll have a cold beer waiting for you when you're ready.'

'It better be cold,' I said, smiling brightly as I headed back into the bathroom.

I locked the door and looked at myself in the mirror. 'Good Lord,' I said to my reflection. I was a mass of confused emotions. Nervous, but also slightly excited, which only made me feel guilty - like I was some sort of letch trying to take advantage of the poor guy.

Jeez, he had just wanted to come to India to write an article and now he had to lug me around with him. Meanwhile, here I was lusting after him and no doubt making it all very inconvenient and uncomfortable for him. Plus we'd already had sex, which made it just that little bit more awkward. I mean he had seen my tits. Seen them, held them, licked them, kissed them. You named it he had pretty much done it to my breasts. And well the things he had done to my hooha, they made me blush just thinking about them. And thinking about them was not going to do me any good.

'Pull yourself together,' I told my reflection, which stuck its tongue out in response.

Did I take a bit more care over my make-up? Did I spend more time selecting my outfit for dinner? Did I make sure my hair was just right before I went outside? Damned right I did. I might have decided to behave myself, but it didn't mean I wanted him to find me undesirable. A girl can only try after all.

I emerged from our room into a fairy wonderland. The rambling gardens of the fort had been transformed with little lights while I had showered. Tables and chairs were scattered throughout the garden, giving the guests privacy within the magical setting. I stood admiring the effect and then noticed Matt at a little table for two. True to his word, he had a beer waiting for me.

'I hope that's cold,' I said to him.

'Frosty,' he informed me.

'Did you get some good photos?' I said once I had seated and sampled the beer. It was, indeed, very cold.

'A couple; I caught the last of the sunset from the top of the Fort, but I'm having trouble getting my focal field with all these lights.' He picked up his camera, took a photo of me, and then looked at the result. 'Nope,' he said and sat the camera back down.

God, I wanted to see that photo so badly. I felt that whatever was on that camera was what he saw when he looked at me. But I couldn't ask - he had just said that the focal field was all wrong so it would probably be blurry.

I relaxed back into my chair, aiming for nonchalance. 'Here's to dodging bullets,' I said, raising my glass to him. I immediately felt stupid because it occurred to me that that was a line from *Mrs and Mrs Smith*, and while he could very well be a John Smith, here under cover to assassinate the Indian Prime Minister, I was certainly no Jane Smith. But bless him, he just raised his glass, looked me in the eye, gave me his cute little smile, and said, 'To dodging bullets.'

'What's for dinner?' I asked, after I had taken a long slurp.

'Buffet.' He nodded his head to a long line of platters where a cluster of Indian men were busy.

'Yummy,' I said. 'I love buffet. Although I always eat too much, and then I have to sleep on my back.'

'Why do you have to sleep on your back?'

'If I eat too much I get a pain when I lie on my side.' And then I remembered that I would be sleeping on my back right next to him and I desperately wanted to change the subject, but be buggered if I could think of anything else to talk about.

'Nice night,' I said, looking around the garden. I could see stars twinkling through the leaves. Hearing the click of a camera I looked back at Matt who was examining the settings again.

'Still no luck?' I nodded at the camera.

'Nahhh.' Shaking his head he placed the camera on the table, leaving me wondering exactly what he had taken a photo of. The lights? The buffet? Me? I guess I would never know.

'That was an interesting day,' Matt said as we ate dinner.

'I nearly shat myself when the try-hard bandits surrounded the car,' I admitted, taking a sip of my beer.

Matt burst out laughing. 'Try-hard bandits,' he finally said, wiping tears out of his eyes, 'permission to use that in my story.'

'Permission granted,' I said magnanimously.

In the end, dinner was more relaxed than I had thought. I was worried it would be awkward as we both thought about the sleeping arrangements. I was prepared to fake a huge yawn and "turn in early" so that I could pretend to be sleeping when he finally hopped in beside me. I would, however, be wide-awake, aware of his every movement, hoping just hoping that he might reach for me, but knowing damned well that he wouldn't.

The buffet had been cleared away and we had lingered in the garden far past the other diners. 'Need to wee,' I said standing.

'Wee Willy Winkle?' he asked.

'No, just wee,' I said smiling.

'Yeah we had better turn in. Do you want me to get us some tea.'

'That would be great.'

We drank our tea sitting on the bed and then Matt headed for the shower, at which point I took the opportunity to jump in my side of the bed and plump up the pillows. I sighed with the luxury of lying down and before long was giving way to the overwhelming tiredness that had descended upon me. I was thankfully asleep before Matt finished in the bathroom.

I woke in the middle of the night, lying flat on my back, holding Matt's hand. I could hear him breathing deeply, and told myself that I wasn't letting go because I didn't want to wake him. But I knew that it was really because I liked the feel of it way too much. As I slipped back into sleep I wondered who had reached out for whose hand. I guessed it was just one more question to which I would never know the answer.

* * *

The sun was cascading over the bed when I was woken by the sound of the door closing.

'I hope he's gone for coffee,' I said to the ceiling, before bouncing out of bed and into the shower. I washed my hair and dressed, humming to myself as I went. It was while I was giving my teeth a quick scrub to relieve any morning breath that I did it. I rinsed my mouth with tap water. I realised as soon as it was in my mouth what I had done and spat the water straight out. Then I dashed to the bedside table, being very careful not to swallow any saliva as I went, grabbed my bottle of water and swished some around before spitting it out again. I ravaged frantically through my toiletry bag finally emerging triumphantly with my Betadine throat gargle.

Matt must have entered during my gargling because I didn't hear him until he popped his head into the bathroom to ask me if I was all right. He gave me such a fright that I swallowed some of the Betadine. The rest I spurted all over the bathroom wall while I retched convulsively from the foul taste.

Once I had myself under control, I said to him, 'Fine thanks, why?

'All that gargling and swishing, I thought maybe you weren't feeling well.'

'I rinsed my mouth with tap water,' I admitted, embarrassed by my own stupidity.

Matt screwed his face up. 'Good luck with that,' he said. 'Here, this coffee will kill anything.'

'I can only hope.'

We moved out to the garden, which was dripping with flowers, and settled down to breakfast. Then we spent the day exploring the fort and the small village that lay in its shadow. I took photos of Matt as he played cricket with the children. We ate lunch in the cool of the garden and snoozed in the deck chairs. I wandered the rambling ruins, exploring its nooks and crannies until I found the roof top terrace where I sat, admiring the view.

I felt good until pre-dinner drinks, when my stomach started to feel squirmy and I realised the smell of the cooking food did nothing for me. I pressed on with my beer trying to ignore what my body was telling me.

'Not hungry?' Matt asked when I put my fork down with food still on my plate. It must have been an unusual sight for him having watched me stuff my face at every opportunity.

'I'm feeling a little off,' I admitted.

'Uhohhhh, not enough betadine?'

'Obviously not.'

An hour later my stomach commenced audible gurgles. Matt looked at me with his eyebrows elevated after one particularly loud grumble.

'I know,' I said, 'it's not going to be pretty.'

We had retired to our room by the time the full onset occurred. I went to the toilet a few times with no result and started to feel more confident.

'Maybe it will self-resolve,' I said to Matt, the third time I emerged from the bathroom.

He looked at my pasty, sweaty face and shrugged his shoulders. 'I don't like your chances.'

The words were just out of his mouth when my intestines started making sounds indicative of liquid travelling at high speed while negotiating tight bends. I gasped at the sudden pain accompanying the noise.

'Uggggh ohhh,' I said as I raced back to the toilet.

I made it just before the liquid exploded from me. The noise was impressive and if I had been at home by myself I would have been quite proud of it. As it was, I cringed with embarrassment. Maybe he hadn't heard it.

'Are you all right?' he called out.

Well so much for my maybe-he-didn't-hear-it theory. He was probably ringing reception right now to see if another room had become available. That, unfortunately, was when the real fun began. My body had turned into a spray-painting machine and it wasn't about to stop. I felt the waves of excruciating pain preluding each burst. After about 5 minutes I was past all shame, leaning over my knees, panting with exhaustion.

'Ummm Tara.' I heard Matt at the door.

'Don't come in,' I squealed in horror. 'Unless you have goggles and a gas mask,' I amended.

As he chuckled, my bottom let out a foghorn-like blast. I put my head in my hands. Oh, the shame.

'I was just wondering if you wanted your book. It might help with the pain,' he said.

God bless his little cotton socks, he'd obviously been in this predicament before. I gasped, tears forming in my eyes, as my intestines completed another complex, gymnastic move. I could hear the commentator's voice in my head, *With a difficulty score of 5.6, she's going to perform a triple back flip with a half twist.* 'How long is this going to last?' I asked.

'A while yet. Do you feel like you want to vomit?'

'No.'

'Well that's something. It's usually best to hop in the shower when both ends go.'

I laughed weakly at the mental vision. 'So does this happen to you often?'

'It used to, but I think I've built up a tolerance. I'm impressed you've made it this far.'

I tried to feel pleased that he was impressed, but right at that moment my body let out a noise that sounded like my arse had ripped in half. I yelped in surprise and could hear Matt laughing on the other side of the door.

'Maybe you should go outside for a while,' I suggested hopefully.

'I tell you what. I'll open the door just a tiny bit and slide your book to you and then I'll turn the T.V. up really loud.'

'Okay. Just don't breathe in when you open the door.'

'Believe me, I'll be trying very hard not to.'

The door inched open just far enough for my book to be passed in and then with a flick of his wrist he slid it across the floor to me.

'Did you get it?' he asked.

'Yes,' I lied, looking at the book sitting a good metre from me. The last thing I wanted was him offering to come in and actually hand it to me. God knows he was nice enough to give it a shot.

'Thanks,' I said, reaching out my foot towards it. I heard the television turn on in the bedroom. 'Louder,' I yelled, still eyeing off the book. In the end, I managed to snare it with one end of a towel and drag it towards me.

The reading helped take my mind off the intestinal spasming, but occasionally the pain was all-consuming. During those moments, I rested my head on the wall next to me while I tried not to pass out.

Eventually I could stand up and move around without fear of spraying the walls. I flushed and then viewed the remaining mess in the bowl. That would never do. I flushed again and scrounged around under the sink looking for a toilet brush, breathing a sigh of relief when I found one. After I had finished cleaning, I jumped in the shower, relishing the feel of the warm water on my body. My poor stomach was still tender and I had pain radiating into my back.

When I finally emerged sheepishly into the bedroom, Matt was fast asleep with the light on and the TV blasting. His laptop lay open next to him. I turned off the television, closed down his computer making sure I saved everything and climbed in next to him. He stirred as I turned off the light and I felt him reach across the bed to me.

'You all right now?' he asked, touching my shoulder.

'Better thanks, I think I'm done.'

'I put a new bottle of water on your bedside table. Make sure you drink it during the night.'

'Thanks.' I took a bit of a slurp from the bottle and then nuzzled thankfully into my pillow. It felt great to be lying down. I was so exhausted I passed out straight away and for once slept the dreamless sleep of the dead.

* * *

I was feeling a bit better when Matt woke me. 'Sorry,' he apologised. 'I let you sleep as long as I could but the driver's been here for a while.'

'Ohh,' I said, sitting up in bed.

'Are you well enough to travel?' he asked concerned.

I paused to consider his question. 'My stomach's a bit sore but compared to last night I feel great,' I finally answered.

'Up for breakfast?'

'Not breakfast, but black tea might be good.'

'I'll go get it while you get ready.'

I was up and dressed by the time he got back. We drank the tea sitting in the garden and then left the beautiful fort behind us. I trailed my hands over the vine-covered stone as we descended to the car.

'Smile,' I heard Matt say, looking up in time to see him snap a photo of me.

Then we were back in the car and heading for Jaipur. It seemed to take hardly any time to get there but the sun was starting to set when we arrived. I suspect I slept most of the way.

'I can see why they call it the Pink City,' I said, as we drove past building after building all painted the same shade of pink.

'Can you believe they painted it pink to welcome King Edward VII when he came to visit?'

'Wow, that's quite a welcome. I wonder why pink?'

'Maybe it was his favourite colour.'

'What? You think he was gay?' I asked.

Matt laughed in response but didn't answer.

The driver pulled up in front of our hotel and I gingerly clambered from the back of the car. I slumped on a couch in the foyer while Matt completed our checkin.

Matt and I had a beautiful room looking over the city with - yes - two big beds. I collapsed gratefully on to one, telling myself I would rest just for a little while. When I woke, it was dark except for the bedside lamp on the far side of the other bed. Matt was sitting on his bed typing rapidly and staring intently at the screen. I rolled over and was soon fast asleep again.

The next morning I was back to my old self. I woke before Matt, absolutely starving. I tried to be patient. I read my book for a little bit, but in the end, the ravenous hole in my centre needed to be filled. I threw a pillow at him and when he opened his eyes said, in a pitiful little voice, 'I'm hungry.'

He rubbed his eyes sleepily as he processed the information and then smiled.

'I'm not surprised,' he said, 'you didn't eat anything yesterday. What do you feel like?'

'Everything.'

'Breakfast buffet?'

'You just used my two favourite words in one sentence. How very clever of you.'

He laughed and sat up in bed. God, he really was gorgeous.

'Do you want to have a shower first?'

Hmmm, if the question had been - Do you want to have a shower with me first? - I certainly would have taken him up on the offer. Just watching him ruffle his hair had given me an entirely different appetite. But I was guessing that he wasn't on the breakfast menu.

'Nah,' I said, 'does that make me disgusting?'

'After about a week it starts to get disgusting. Actually at the one week mark it stops being disgusting. I've never really understood it. Maybe you stop being able to smell yourself. Anyway I wouldn't call 24 hours without a shower disgusting.'

'That's the longest paragraph I've ever heard you say.'

'I think you're starting to rub off on me.'

'I'd like to rub off on you.'

(Just kidding, I didn't really say it. But I wanted to. Considering in the past 36 hours the man had heard my body make more noises than a brass band, I was guessing he didn't find me sexy.)

What I really said was, 'Excellent. I've never really liked the strong, silent type.' I hopped out of bed and disappeared just long enough to pull on some clothes. 'Ready?' I asked eagerly when I reappeared.

About thirty minutes later - when my hunger pains had finally subsided enough to think, I asked, 'So what are we doing today?'

'The City Palace and museum, Hawa Mahal, which used to house the Royal ladies, Jantar Mantar, Nahargarh and Galta, but not in one day. We'll need a few days to do it all.'

'I have no idea what you just said,' I replied around a mouthful of pancake, 'but it all sounds very interesting.'

We spent the next few days in our old routine. Sightseeing in the morning, I rested and read in the afternoon while he wrote, then out to dinner or the markets or both.

I was about to start creating the next chapter in my postcards from India series when Matt surprised me.

'I bought this for you at the markets,' he said, pulling out a brown paper bag.

Mystified I took it and pulled out a beautiful, teal-green pashmina.

'It's lovely,' I said, holding it up to admire the silky material. 'When did you get this?'

'Tonight, while you were looking at the wooden carving.' He looked a little embarrassed as he said it. I stared at him wondering if he were blushing or if it were just my imagination.

'Thank you,' I finally said, running the soft material through my fingers. 'It's gorgeous.' I swung it around my shoulders and hopped up to admire it in the mirror.

'I was right,' he said from behind me. 'It looks lovely on you.'

I pirouetted in front of him - embarrassed and unsure what to say.

'I bought my mother one as well,' he said, pulling out a dove-grey one.

'That's nice too,' I said, 'but I like mine better.'

He smiled and went back to his typing, leaving me sitting on the bed a little speechless. After a few minutes, I picked up my postcards and began to write.

Dearest Nat,

We are having a lovely time and are in Jaipur. I had my first bout of Delhi Belly the other night. Not at all a fun experience I can assure you. And pretty embarrassing as Matt could hear everything through the bathroom door. No vomiting thankfully. But the combination of that, and the bandits that tried to hold us up on the way to the fort we were staying at, (Don't worry we're fine,) seems to have done something good between us. .... cont. on Dinah and Gloria's card.

Dearest Dinah and Gloria,

.........cont. from Nat's card. Tonight he gave me a gorgeous pashmina he bought for me. Said he thought it looks lovely on me. That has to be good, right? And it makes me wonder if maybe, just maybe, he may like me a little bit as well. I mean I like him a hell of a lot more than just a little bit. The man is pretty much perfect. Too good for me by far. And then again maybe he just hates the clothes I wear .... cont. on Elaine's card.

Dearest Elaine,

.......cont. from Dinah's card. But we did have to share a bed at the fort and I did wake up to find us holding hands in our sleep. So that also has to be a good thing. I know Elaine, you think I should have woken up holding a lot more than just his hand but it's not like that. It's new and fragile and special. Well, to me it's special. And now I have hope that it might be to him as well. I'm

pathetic I know. Wish you were all here to chat. Miss you heaps. All my love Tara. Xxxxx

Dearest Lil and Martin,

Missing you both, but having a great time here in India. The other day Matt and I were held up by some bandits on the way to the fort we were staying at. I hid in the back seat while Matt handled them most efficiently. (Best not to tell Mum about the bandits.) I have also had my first bout of diarrhoea. Lil, do you remember when we went to the Easter Show and I ate my whole liquorice show bag in one sitting? Well it was far worse than that. Love you, Tara. Xxxx

Dearest Mum and Dad,

Well we have made it to Jaipur, which is called the Pink City because the whole city was painted pink back in 1876 when Prince Edward came to visit. They are still doing it to this day. We have spent the last three days here sight-seeing and tomorrow night we are catching an overnight train to Udaipur - The Lake City. Matt assures me we will be perfectly safe on the train so nothing to worry about Mum. Love you all, Tara. Xxxx

Chapter Seven

The Sixth Step to Closure – Have Meaningful Sex

'**D**o you think all the pervs live at the train station?' I asked Matt while we waited for the train to Udaipur. There had been a continuous stream of strange men staring at me since we arrived and it was starting to get a little unnerving.

'It certainly looks that way,' he replied as he shooed away another curious onlooker.

Finally, our train arrived and we clambered on. It was a sleeper train and we had managed to get beds one above the other, but I was still feeling a little vulnerable as we squeezed our way through the carriage with our bags.

'Here we are,' said Matt, stopping in front of two bunks. 'Top or bottom?'

'Top please,' I said, nervously looking around. There seemed to be an inordinate number of men in the cabin all showing an interest in my appearance.

We slid our backpacks under the bottom bed and then I climbed up to my bunk, pulling the little curtain around to give me total privacy. I sighed in relief and relaxed back onto the mattress.

I was, however, unable to sleep, even when the rocking motion of the train should have been lulling me into unconsciousness. I kept expecting someone to open my curtain to get a better look at me. Or worse - what if I fell asleep and woke to find someone climbing in with me? I was doing a pretty good job of freaking myself out and finally I gave up on sleep and clambered down to stand outside Matt's curtain.

'Matt,' I whispered, looking nervously over my shoulder.

'Matt,' I said a little louder.

'Matt!' This time I poked what I hoped was his back through the curtain.

I heard a grunt accompanied by some movement and then his curtain pulled back a little. He peered at me with sleepy eyes.

'Yes?'

'I'm scared,' I said pitifully.

To his credit, he didn't mock me. He just stared at me for a few seconds and then peered out past me. Most of the other passengers had climbed into bed and pulled their curtains, but there were still a few strange men sitting around on their bunks. He patted the side of the bed closest to the wall and said, 'Get in.'

I clambered over him trying not to stick my knees or elbows into any really sensitive parts. 'Thanks,' I said as I lay down. 'I don't suppose we'll be getting a six-course breakfast on this train.'

'I don't think we'll be getting any breakfast.'

It was a little cramped for the two of us - we could only fit if we both lay on our sides, but I immediately felt safer lying there next to him.

'This is only going to work if I put my arm over you,' Matt said. 'Do you mind?'

'No that's all right,' I said, trying to sound nonchalant when in reality my heart had started beating a little faster.

He slid one arm over me and I tensed, trying to stay as still as I could.

'Okay?' he asked.

'Ahuh,' I said, a little nervously.

I found myself thinking that the last time we were in this position we had been naked. Damn. That didn't help in the getting to sleep department either. If anything, every fibre of me was aware of the weight of his arm and the feel of his body. My skin had come alive and I could feel lust unfurling in my belly. Oh great, I was totally turned on. I lay there for what seemed like forever waiting for some movement from him, some little noise that would indicate that he wanted me as badly as I wanted him. In the end I realised I was listening to the soft noises of his breath as he slept.

It certainly wasn't the most comfortable train ride I have ever had - well before morning my body was screaming to be allowed to stretch out in all directions - but it was by far the most enjoyable one. Matt woke me when we arrived in Udaipur and it took me a while to get the kinks out of my neck and back. I noticed him stretching as well.

'Sorry.' I smiled ruefully at him indicating his neck.

'Sadly I have to do this every morning,' he told me.

'So it's not because I turned your bed into a sardine can last night?'

'Well maybe a little,' he admitted as he helped me down from the train and onto the platform.

There was a hotel car waiting for us at the front of the station. It drove us past a huge lake which had a number of buildings built in it.

'Wow,' I said, looking out of the window.

The buildings seemed to emerge from the lake. It wasn't like an island had been made and then the building built, but the walls actually disappeared down into the lake.

'Do you think they have rising damp issues?' I asked Matt.

'Probably. I guess to them it would be normal.'

I was delighted to find that the hotel we were staying at was near the lake.

'Can you see the lake from our room?' I asked the porter as we followed him up the winding staircase.

'Madam, from your room you have excellent views of the Lake Palace Hotel,' he informed us proudly. The tone in his voice stopped me from asking what the Lake Palace Hotel was. I didn't want to disappoint him and I had my trusty *Lonely Planet* in my bag. 'And,' he continued, 'today we are running complimentary cooking courses for all house guests. You will come, yes?'

'Of course,' I answered, looking at Matt for confirmation.

He was correct about the view from our room. It looked out over an area of the lake, which housed a spectacular white building.

'Lake Palace Hotel?' I asked Matt.

'The one and only. I might have a shower before the cooking course. Did you want to go first?'

'No, you go. I want to read about the Lake Palace Hotel,' I said, staring out the window.

I heard the water in the shower turn on and a noise I associated with a zipper being undone. Good God - I could actually hear him undressing. Grabbing my *Lonely Planet* I moved onto the deck where I tried valiantly to concentrate on the words on the page and not the sound of Matt in the shower. I wasn't very successful.

The cooking course, consisting of us and two other girls, was excellent. I took notes while Matt took photos, and then we all made chapatti - a type of Indian bread. When it finished the four of us had lunch together.

I hadn't paid much attention to the other two girls during the course - being quite intent on my note-taking - so I didn't notice them noticing Matt. It did, however, become quite apparent during lunch, just how much noticing of Matt they had done.

'So how long have you two been dating?' Angie - a blonde, busty English girl – asked, while staring longingly at Matt.

I had a sudden, intense urge to scratch out both her eyes so she would stop looking at him like he was a lollipop waiting to be licked.

'Oh about 10 months now,' Matt said as he dragged my chair closer to him and threw an arm over the back of it.

She pouted a little and I smiled sweetly at her. It took all my willpower not to poke out my tongue.

'But, like, you're not engaged or anything?' asked Victoria, twisting wisps of her brunette hair around her finger while she stared at my ring-less left hand.

I could feel blood rushing to my head and battle lust kicking in. So it wasn't enough that we were dating - not that we actually were, but you know what I mean.

'No, we're not married yet,' I said as I looked her in the eye, 'but we've just found out we're expecting our first child.' I placed one hand over my belly.

'Oh,' said Angie tartly, 'is that why you're eating so much?'

She looked primly at her own plate, which had hardly any food on it, to mine which was covered with the smeary remains of a large lunch.

I smiled inwardly knowing how much Matt detested fussy eaters.

'Yep,' he said, reaching over and patting my belly, 'she's eating for two.'

Victoria looked confused. 'So, like, you've only been dating for 10 months and you're already having a baby. And you're happy with this?' She directed the question to Matt.

Matt shrugged and said, 'The first moment I laid eyes on Tara I said to myself "that's the woman I want to spend the rest of my life with".'

He was looking straight into my eyes as he said it and I could feel blood rushing to my head.

'What about you?' the blonde asked me.

I was, truth be told, feeling light-headed from the intense eye contact Matt and I were sharing. 'Well,' I said slowly, 'I had come out of a bad relationship, so I was a little cautious at first.'

'She played hard to get,' Matt smiled as he said it, reaching out and stroking my arm.

'But the next time we ran into each other, it was like a bolt of lightning had struck me and I knew without doubt that he was the one for me,' I said.

Angie pouted and slouched back in her chair, chewing on the end of some hair. 'So it was, like, love at first sight?'

'Pretty much,' said Matt. 'I didn't believe in love at first sight until I saw you.' He tucked a stray piece of hair behind my ear.

Whoa. Were we still make-believing? He was so convincing that I was having a bit of trouble with my brain - which was leaping around inside my skull high fiving itself, and my lungs - which were refusing to breathe properly. As we stared into each other's eyes I could hear pieces of a puzzle clicking into place inside my head. The trouble was I wasn't sure if I was playing the right game.

'I'm bored,' Angie complained to Victoria.

'Come on hon,' Matt said, gallantly helping me to my feet, 'we should do some sightseeing before you have your afternoon nap.'

'What? Oh yeah. I get very tired now,' I told the two of them as I climbed to my feet.

'Wow,' I said to Matt, once we were clear and I could think straight, 'they were tigers.'

'I don't like cats much,' he said. 'I'm allergic to them.'

We spent the afternoon getting lost in the back alleys of Udaipur. We shopped, and admired the view of the city, and as the sun was setting we found ourselves at the City Palace overlooking the lake, where we had a couple of beers. Then we stumbled across a quaint little restaurant called The Secret Garden.

'My,' I said as we entered the rambling garden with its sprawling lounges and many cushions.

We drank more beer, and then ordered some thali. They brought out one huge platter for both of us, full of steaming food.

'Dahl,' I said, dipping some naan bread in one of the dishes. 'Yummy. Here.'

I held out some naan filled with dahl for Matt, expecting him to take it. He leaned forwards and the feel of his lips grazing my fingers sent a bolt of electricity through me. My nipples were immediately rock hard.

Matt held some chicken masala out to me. 'Here,' he said.

I leant forward, hoping he couldn't see my nipples through my shirt, and he placed it in my mouth. Indian food had never tasted so good.

We ordered some more beer and kept eating in silence except for our murmurings of appreciation for the food.

I took a bite of a curry puff and held it out to him to try. He fed me some butter chicken and laughed when I ended up with it on my chin. I wiped it off and slowly licked my finger looking into his eye as I did it. Had his pupils widened slightly? I couldn't be sure.

The combination of the heat, the beer and my need to be closer to him was making me giddy. I stood up to go to the bathroom and stumbled a little.

'Whoa,' I said giggling. 'Matt, I think I'm a little drunk.'

'Me too,' he said as I walked unsteadily off to the toilets.

I had a really good talk to myself while I was in there. It went along the lines of, *Okay Tara let's just take it down a notch. I think the alcohol is affecting your judgement if you really think that he is into you. So let's just be cool and if there is any move to be made, let him make it.*

When I exited the toilets, it was to find Matt with the two tigers from lunch all over him. Shit, just when things were going really nicely between us.

'Ahh here she is,' he said, sounding relieved. 'Ready to go, love?' he asked jumping up.

'Sure sure,' I said and then looked at the table and the pile of tallies we had drunk. 'I think you've had quite enough to drink young man, time to get you home to bed.'

'It's good to have a designated driver,' said Matt, taking my hand and letting me lead him to the exit.

We staggered up the street leaning on each other.

'Do you think they'll follow us?' I asked looking over my shoulder. Instead of finding Angie and Victoria, I found myself staring straight into the eyes of a cow. I looked down to check and corrected myself. I was staring right into the eyes of a bull.

'Matt,' I whispered, 'there's a bull behind us.'

'Yep,' he said, 'there's a lot of bull behind us.'

'No really Matt.' I looked again to be sure. He was following us, and he was scary. Someone had painted his horns bright red. 'There's an actual bull following us up the street.'

Matt stopped and looked over his shoulder. 'By George I think you're right,' he said. Then he flapped his hands at it and said, 'Shoo.'

'Shoo?' I asked incredulously, starting to giggle. 'He's a bull, not a mosquito.'

'How about, "go away you big bad bull"?' he said in a high-pitched girly voice.

Given the circumstances - it was one of the funniest things I had ever seen. The alcohol and my fear blended, leaving me with nervous hysteria. I started laughing and then I couldn't stop. I watched the bull plod closer to me.

'Stop,' I gasped, gulping for air as I inched my way back up the hill.

Matt continued to back with me while shoo-ing his hands at it.

'That's the best you've got?' I asked, after a particularly feeble bout of hand shoo-ing.

'Fraid so,' Matt said, 'I can't seem to stop him. What we really need is a stick,' said Matt.

'Good idea,' I replied, looking around desperately for one as the bull got closer. 'Are you going to hit him with it?'

'No, I'm going to throw it for him.'

'Matt, he's a cow not a dog.'

'Oh right.'

'He's going to get me,' I gasped as he lumbered even closer. Normally in times like this, my fright-or-flight mechanism took over allowing me to break Olympic records for sprinting short distances. This time I was having trouble getting my legs to do what I told them. I think it was a combination of the alcohol and the laughing.

'Hey, do you think it might just be walking up the hill?' Matt asked.

I darted to the side, holding my breath while the bull plodded on by.

'I guess he was,' I said, leaning over and laughing so hard I couldn't stand up straight. 'I really thought he was going to attack me.'

'I don't think he had enough speed up to do any real damage,' gasped Matt between laughs.

'Ohh.' I straightened up and wiping tears from my eyes, stepped straight into a huge pile of steaming cow dung. I could feel the warmth of it wrapping over the end of my toes. 'Oh no,' I said as I felt my foot slipping out from underneath me.

I was like a cartoon character with my arms and feet peddling backwards in an attempt to regain my balance: finally losing the battle and collapsing with a huge 'whoompf', straight into the pile of dung.

'Oh dear,' I said. I could feel it seeping through my clothes.

'Oh dear?' asked Matt, thumping his hand onto his knee as he buckled over with laughter. 'Oh dear?' he said as he slid to the ground next to me. And then he saw the remnants of poo oozing out from underneath me. 'Oh dear,' he said. And then we both lost it.

'Stop. Stop,' I begged him as I howled with laughter. 'I think I'm going to wet myself.'

'Go ahead,' said Matt, gesturing at my pooey pants. 'It won't make any difference.'

'It's a matter of pride,' I tried to explain. But he only laughed harder.

Finally, he clambered to his feet. 'Come on,' he said holding out a hand, 'we have to get you home and into the shower.'

'Yucky,' I said as I walked up the street. I was leaving pooey footprints behind, and my pants were stuck to my arse. I reeked.

'Don't make me look,' said Matt, 'or I'll probably wet myself.'

I took my shoes off when we got to the hotel. 'After you,' I said politely gesturing at the stairs to our room.

Matt led us into the room and I headed straight for the bathroom.

I looked at myself in the mirror and started to giggle. 'I'm disgusting,' I called out.

'I know. I can still smell you.'

I stripped the filthy pants off and then looked at my shoes. They had been pretty satin slip-ons I had bought in Delhi; now brown liquid poo stained the shiny material.

'I don't think my shoes can be saved,' I said.

'I'm not surprised. I'll go and get a laundry bag for your clothes,' he called out as I hopped into the shower.

A few minutes later, I was clean again. I wrapped a white towel around me and then realised I had no clothes to put on. I'd have to duck out and get them before Matt got back from downstairs.

Darting into the bedroom towards my bag, I stopped in fright when I saw movement in the door to the balcony. I gasped and then realised it was Matt - standing there, staring at me.

'I didn't hear you come back,' I said, realising just how short the towel was. It only just covered my bottom.

Matt stood still in the same spot, seemingly transfixed by his view of me. I could feel my breathing getting heavier as I met his eyes. I licked my lips nervously. He moved towards me, stopping just short. 'You're so beautiful,' he said, reaching out a hand to my face. I felt myself moving towards him as if in a dream.

He trailed his fingers down my face as if mesmerised by the feel of me. In their wake I could feel tingling spreading out and dancing across my skin.

'Matt,' I whispered as his fingers reached my neck, 'I think you need to kiss me.'

He pulled me closer and bent his head to mine, and finally I got to feel his sweet lips - once again - caressing mine. I melted towards him, into him, distressed when he pulled away. 'I've wanted to do this to you ever since I saw you on that plane,' he said, running a hand through my wet hair.

I stared up into his beautiful eyes. 'Do what?' I asked breathlessly, hoping it was to rip the towel off my body and have his wicked way with me.

'This.' He picked me up easily, laying me on the bed in my towel. Then he proceeded to unwrap me. First he unwrapped my body as he peeled back my towel, and then he unwrapped my mind as he caressed me and kissed me, driving me crazy with my need for him. I writhed in ecstasy beneath him as I clutched at his clothes trying to shred them from his body.

'Not fair,' I complained in between frantic kisses, 'you've still got your clothes on.'

He hopped off the bed and let his pants fall to the floor.

I groaned in anticipation looking at him in all his glory. And I mean all of it. He had an erection that would have made King Kong proud.

'Is that for me?' I asked teasingly, watching him roll on a condom.

'It's all yours baby,' he said, smiling as he climbed back onto the bed to kneel over me.

If I had thought I had felt good up till then, it was nothing compared to how good I felt when I finally felt him slide inside me.

'Oh - my - God.' I could feel my eyes rolling back in my head. 'I've wanted you to do this to me ever since you stopped doing it to me the first time.' I gasped as he thrust further and further into me. I wrapped my legs around him and clasped his rock hard buttocks in my hands. The feeling of his body on mine, his lips on mine, his tongue in my mouth and his hands on my body - I was having trouble breathing with the overwhelming sensuality of it. I groaned and urged him on harder and faster as I moved my hips to match his rhythm.

'I think I'm going to come,' he said, sounding dismayed.

Lifting my pelvis up, I encouraged him even deeper inside me. 'Then come,' I said as I dug my nails into his back. And he did.

'Sorry,' he apologised. 'You feel so amazing and I've been imagining doing this to you for weeks now, I couldn't stop myself.' He started kissing and caressing me, moving slowly down my body. 'I've also been imagining doing this to you,' he said huskily as he placed his tongue on my clitoris and licked it.

'Jesus Christ,' I moaned, as he also stroked my nipples. I could feel the knot of tension inside me tighten even further. 'Oh please,' I heard myself cry, as I started to move rhythmically against his mouth. 'Oh yes,' I said, as I felt myself riding higher and higher towards an orgasm.

And then he stopped just before I peaked and I let out a frustrated yelp.

'Look what I found,' he said, reaching for another condom as he nodded towards his erection.

'Oh my,' I said admiringly, 'come to Momma.'

He slid inside me and this time we came together. I bit his neck to stop from screaming as my body spasmed with my orgasm. I'd never felt anything like it. He shuddered inside me, in time with my climax, and then we both collapsed, exhausted onto the bed.

I held him to me to stop him from moving, enjoying his body pressing me down; his naked skin on mine. I tried to memorise the feel of it but he started to kiss me lazily, nuzzling my neck and tickling my ear, and all of a sudden, I could have gone again, right then, right there.

Eventually when we had both emerged from the cloud of lust he said, 'To think, we could have been doing this the whole time.'

I smiled at him and said, 'Yes, but we wouldn't have gotten any sightseeing done.'

'I know what I'd rather be doing given a choice between sightseeing and making love to you.'

'It's all right,' I said teasingly, 'the lake is pretty spectacular.'

'Hmm yes,' he said, rolling over and kissing me, 'but not as spectacular as you.'

Then we made love again.

* * *

I opened my eyes to the clear blue skies of Udaipur and the soft warmth of Matt's chest against my back. *Mmmm*, so it hadn't been a delicious dream. I moved my body experimentally. Yep, it certainly felt like it had had a night of passion. I smiled unable to believe my extremely good luck that this man wanted me, wanted to be with me. It all seemed too good to be true.

'Good morning,' he said, raising himself up and kissing me on the shoulder.

I wriggled around in his embrace so I could kiss him on the lips and then said, 'Right back at ya.'

The kissing continued for several minutes, getting more and more intense until suddenly I screwed up my nose and pulled away.

'Phew,' I said. 'What's that smell?'

'I think,' said Matt laughing, 'that you'll find it's your clothes.'

'Oh no.' I had totally forgotten about the dung covered clothing left deserted on the bathroom floor.

He swung his feet out of bed saying, 'I'll take them down to the laundry and get us a coffee.'

'I could kill for a coffee,' I admitted, wrapping a sheet around me and climbing out of bed. 'And I think the place needs airing.' I opened the windows onto our balcony as far as they would go in an attempt to look busy, but really I was waiting for Matt to leave so I could commandeer the bathroom. I desperately wanted to check my hair and give my teeth a quick brush. I was sure I had morning breath.

We were on the balcony drinking our coffee and enjoying the vista of the lake beneath us when I remembered something I had noticed the day before and wanted to ask him. 'Hey what's the deal with the whole *Octopussy* on the rooftop thing?' I said.

'Haven't you seen *Octopussy*?

Hating to seem ignorant, I shook my head.

'Not a James Bond Fan?'

'I don't mind the latest one,' I said.

'So Daniel Craig is my competition then?'

'Him and Edward.'

'Edward?'

'From *Twilight.*'

He laughed. 'Well I don't think I have much to worry about there.'

'I don't think you have much to worry about with Daniel Craig either.' I leant back on my chair. 'So *Octopussy* is a James Bond movie?'

'Yep. It was filmed right here. They show it at the roof-top restaurants in the evening. Did you want to go tonight?'

'Sure. But why the roof-top restaurants?'

'You can see all the places in the movie while you're watching it. Tomorrow we can go sightseeing and visit them.' He smiled cheekily at me as he said it.

'Tomorrow?' I asked hopefully. 'What are we doing today?'

He smiled and pulling me onto his lap kissed me. 'I thought maybe today we could stay in our room,' he said as he pulled my sheet apart and kissed the top of my breast.

'I like the way you think,' I said, gasping at the feel of his tongue on my nipple.

'Well, at the moment I think we both need a long hot shower.' Lifting me, he carried me effortlessly into the bathroom where he deposited me gently. He flipped the shower on and pulled his shirt off over his head. Eagerly I reached out and undid his pants, sliding them down to the floor. I stood, admiring the beauty of his form, unable to believe it was being offered to me. Then shyly I let my sheet go. He kissed me deeply as he pulled me into the water with him. The combination of the hot water streaming over me and his body pressed up against mine, was divine.

'I think,' I said, 'that today is going to be my favourite day of the holiday.'

'Well,' he said, 'as your tour guide, it is my job to make sure of it.'

Many, many hours later hunger finally drove us up to the rooftop. The sun was setting and a sprinkling of lights had started to sparkle across the city. I walked around the rooftop admiring the night-lights. 'Look at the City Palace,' I said to Matt, snuggling my back into him as he wrapped his arms around me. The whole building wasn't so much lit as glowing. It was a breathtaking site.

We watched *Octopussy* on a television which was positioned so we could also see the lake. Roger Moore worked his way through the tourist attractions of Udaipur, many of which twinkled below us like large floating candles.

'Wow,' I said to Matt when it had finished, 'that Lake Palace Hotel is something to behold.'

'Yeah, it certainly is,' he agreed.

I stretched my arms above my head and faked a huge yawn. 'Bed time?' I asked him cheekily.

'Sure is babe,' he said smiling.

We headed back to our room where I found, to my delight, that we weren't tired at all, and instead had to find some other way to entertain ourselves. It wasn't very difficult.

* * *

Once again, I woke to the glory of an Indian blue sky and Matt's arms around me. I sighed. I could get used to this. After a lazy breakfast on our balcony, we spent the morning at the City Palace Museum. From there we strolled down to the water's edge where there were children swimming and playing in the water.

'Fancy a boat ride?' Matt asked me.

'It's not one of those pedal boats we saw those people using the other night?' I asked suspiciously.

He laughed, 'No, I promise this boat uses an engine.'

The breeze coming off the water was a welcome relief to the humidity of the morning. I relaxed against Matt as I enjoyed the feel of the boat gliding around the lake. Eventually it docked at the Lake Palace Hotel and I watched enviously as some tourists departed the boat.

'Shall we?' asked Matt.

'What? Get off here?' I asked in confusion.

'Well, it is where we're staying tonight.'

I stared at him, stunned. He laughed and shooed his hands at me shepherding me off the boat. 'It's not often that I see you speechless,' he said.

'I don't know,' I advised him primly. 'I was pretty speechless when you did that thing last night with your tongue.'

He laughed again and stroked my face before enveloping my hand with his. At that moment it wouldn't have mattered where we were staying; I was the happiest woman in the world. I floated beside him up through the magnificent surroundings to the reception where we were given a welcome Masala tea before being taken to our room.

I have never experienced anything like our suite at the Lake Palace Hotel. Huge silk rugs covered the floors. The walls were intricate murals, the plasterwork so ornate I continuously saw more detail. The bed was huge; a sumptuous banquet of silk and cushions. The bathroom had a freestanding claw-foot bath by a bay window; the simplicity of the enamel only enhancing the beauty of the surrounding mosaics.

'I don't ever want to leave this room,' I said, slowly turning to experience its full glory.

'I know it's gorgeous,' said Matt, taking some photos. 'But I am sure the rest of the hotel is amazing as well. We really should go exploring.'

I looked at the bed, imagining the fun we could have in it, and then out the window to the glorious day that was waiting. 'All right,' I said, sulking just a little, 'but we're going to have an early night right?'

'An early night,' he agreed, also looking hungrily at the bed.

The hotel was built around the edge of the island leaving the middle as a large courtyard. On one side of the courtyard was an ornate garden with a huge lily pool. It was breathtaking.

'There's a lot here to photograph,' said Matt apologetically. 'Did you want to go to the pool bar and get us a drink? I promise not to be too long.'

'You do what you need to do,' I said, standing on tiptoes to kiss him on the lips. 'What sort of drink do you want?'

'Surprise me.'

I headed to the pool bar and, at the barman's recommendation, ordered some cocktails and assorted Indian bar snacks. By the time Matt turned up I was relaxing in one of the deck chairs by the pool.

'Perfect timing,' I said, viewing the bar snacks and cocktails heading our way.

We munched and slurped contentedly before laying the deck chairs back flat and stretching out in the sun.

'Matt.'

'Hmmm,' he said sleepily.

'I don't think I've ever had as good a time as this.'

He opened one eye to look at me.

'Seriously - I know that may seem sad to you, but I am so happy at the moment I feel like I'm going to burst.'

'I'm glad,' he said. There was a few seconds pause and then he added, 'I think this would also be one of the best times I've ever had.' He reached over and squeezed my hand, before closing his eyes again. Still holding his hand, I drifted off to sleep.

We ate dinner at the hotel restaurant, ordering room-service dessert before heading back to our room. Sitting in the huge window seat, we admired the sparkling lights of Udaipur while we fed each other dessert. Then Matt pulled out his laptop. 'Sorry babe,' he said, 'gotta work.'

'Well you haven't done much over the last few days, so I guess I can excuse you.'

'Yeah,' he grinned cheekily, 'I've been a little distracted.'

'Never fear.' I pulled some more postcards out of my bag. 'I have work of my own to do.'

'Are you going to tell your mother that you've been shagging the polite young man you've been travelling with?'

'No. Not yet,' I said. 'But I'm going to tell the girls.'

He laughed while he booted up his computer.

'Have you found your angle yet?' I asked.

'Pardon?' He looked a little confused.

'When we first started travelling you said you were trying to think of a unique angle to write your story from.'

'Oh that. Yes I'm working on an idea that seems to be coming along nicely.'

'Can you tell me what it is?'

'Nope. You're going to have to wait till it's printed.'

I stuck my tongue out at him and started on my first postcard.

Dearest Elaine,

It finally happened. And when I say it, I really mean IT. Yep Matt and I have finally given into our mutual lust and have spent the last few days in bed together. I know you'd be proud of me, because I have now completed Step Six of the Seven Steps to Closure and had extremely meaningful sex. I have decided to laminate and frame the magazine article. I hope you and Dr Alistair have been having meaningful sex as well. We are staying at the Lake Palace Hotel in Udaipur. It is to die for and I recommend it if you ever...... cont. on Dinah's card.

Dearest Dinah and Gloria,

cont. from Elaine's card. ....go on a honeymoon. Everything here is so beautiful. I nearly cried when I saw our room for the first time. We are sitting in it at the moment enjoying the night lights in Udaipur out our window while Matt works. Hey guys, if you haven't read Elaine's card or spoken to her yet, Matt and I finally got down and dirty. Well first I got really dirty when I slipped over in cow poo, and then I had a shower, and then Matt and I finally did what I've been wanting to do since I saw him on the plane. It was even better than our one-night-stand. Possibly because he was still there in the morning, and also because....cont. on Natalie's card.

Dearest Natalie,

cont. from Dinah's card. ....we have been doing it multiple times a day ever since we started. I have to say that I can understand Bad Bunny a little better now, continuously wanting to shag. So Nat, I'm guessing that you have guessed by the limited context of your postcard that Matt and I finally got it on. We are having the best time and are staying in the nicest hotel in the world at the moment. Well it may not be THE nicest hotel in the world, but it is no doubt the nicest one I am ever going to stay in.

I must send my thanks to Travel Abroad when I get home. Love to you all. Tara. Xxxx

Dearest Lil and Martin,
There is a magnificent Lily Pond here that reminded me of you Lil. We are staying at the Lake Palace Hotel which is extraordinarily sumptuous. India is such a country of contradiction. Today I was sitting at the hotel pool drinking cocktails, and I could see in the distance a building with steps leading down to the water. Women were washing their clothing while their children swam. They were like a bunch of bright flowers clothed in bright pinks, yellow and oranges, contrasting beautifully against the white marbly surroundings of the Lake Palace Hotel. Love to all. Tara. Xxxx P.S. Lil, Matt and I finally had sex. Yehhh!

Dearest Mum and Dad,
We are in Udaipur which is a city built around a lake. Octopussy with Roger Moore was filmed here, and it is fast becoming my favourite destination. The shopping, food and scenery here is all amazing. Tonight we are staying at a luxury hotel on an island in the lake. You should Google it Mum, it's called The Lake Palace Hotel. It used to be the Royal Summer Palace of one of the Maharajas. There are heaps of palaces in Udaipur. The City Palace still houses the Maharaja, but the Monsoon Palace is empty. (Except for when Roger Moore was held captive there, in Octopussy) Can't wait to fill you in on everything when I get home. Love to you both Tara. Xxxx

* * *

The next afternoon we departed The Lake Palace Hotel to wander Udaipur, one last time. We ate dinner before heading to the bus station where we would catch our overnight bus to Jodhpur.

I was led into a false sense of security by the toilets on the overnight train to Udaipur and had a large bottle of water with dinner as well as some beer. I mean really, who would believe they would invent an overnight bus with no toilet? (I know, I know, Tii and everything I shouldn't have been surprised.)

We clambered onto the bus searching for our sleeper seats, amused when we realised the overhead baggage area had been converted to the sleeping quarters. They were awkward to climb into, especially when you are as tall as Matt, and, when you are as tall as Matt, impossible to fully stretch out in. But at least we were lying down, right? Which would have been lovely if the road had been nice and flat and smooth; not the four-wheel-drive-only road that we took to Jodhpur.

The outside wall of our compartment consisted of two sliding windows, so initially I amused myself by watching the night scenery slip by. That was before the road deteriorated and Matt and I started jumping and bumping uncontrollably around the floor. It was also before I started to need to go to the toilet. After a while it became difficult to control my bladder while also bracing my limbs against the walls.

I let out a whimper as we went over a particularly large rut.

'Are you all right?' asked Matt from behind me. We had quickly discovered that the only way for him to be even slightly comfortable was to spoon.

'I need to go to the toilet,' I whispered.

'Oh dear,' he replied. 'How bad?'

'Pretty bad.'

'Number one or two?'

'Number one.'

'Well that's something.'

I had a vision of me trying to hang onto a Number Two while doing uncontrollable silent farts that fogged up the compartment we were squeezed into. Or worse, what if they weren't silent but loud and deadly, so that you couldn't even pretend it was a putrid smell from outside leaking into the bus that was threatening to suffocate both of us. I mean it was India so the putrid smell thing was actually possible. Because it was India, it was also possible that those loud and deadly farts could end with a tell-tale follow through sound, obvious to all within hearing range that the fart hadn't been entirely dry. I shuddered at the thought. Would Matt still find me attractive if he had to spoon me knowing I had shat in my pants?

So even though I was ecstatic it was just a number one I was hanging onto, it certainly didn't help with my current predicament.

'Why don't you turn around and stick your bottom out the window?'

I wiggled around to look at him. Was he serious? Although he did have a small smile on his face I think he actually was. I tried to imagine myself doing it. Even if I made Matt turn around so that he couldn't see, I knew I couldn't. Not unless it was the last option open to me.

I felt the bus starting to slow down and realised it was about to stop.

'Quick,' I said, desperately trying to clamber over him to get out of the compartment. I could feel my elbows and knees squishing into soft tissue.

'Stop,' he said, wincing in pain.

Rolling over on top of him I pushed the little curtain aside as far as I could and slithered out head first.

'Help,' I whimpered as I hung from the compartment.

'Tara,' said Matt laughing, 'stop wiggling.'

He grabbed my legs and lowered me to the floor where I landed quite inelegantly.

'Excuse me,' I said politely to the little Indian man whose lap I had narrowly missed. Pushing myself to my feet I sprinted towards the front of the bus. 'Toilet,' I yelled as I dived off the bus. Some passengers waiting to alight gestured to a nearby building. I sprinted around it, staggering in the pitch black, trying desperately to get my pants down.

'Don't think about it,' I told myself sternly as I struggled with my belt, but my brain had already engaged the go button and all of a sudden I was in a race with my bladder to get my pants down. I squatted in relief as I managed to win the race.

It went on and on and on and on, until finally I could hear Matt whispering into the night. 'Tara. Where are you?'

'Stay there,' I said urgently, still in the throes of a Guinness-Book-worthy pee.

I could hear the bus driver honk his horn.

'Why didn't you go in the toilet?' he whispered.

'What?'

'Why didn't you use the toilet?'

I finally finished and redressed myself. 'What toilet?' I asked, emerging from behind the building.

'This one,' said Matt, pointing at the worldwide woman's symbol for toilet on the door closest to me.

'Hmmmm,' I said, trying to think of some really clever answer.

'You didn't realise it was a toilet.'

'No. I didn't realise it was a toilet. It's probably disgusting anyway,' I said as I entered to wash my hands.

'Is it disgusting?' he asked from outside.

'Yes,' I lied as I activated the electric hand dryer.

'Liar,' he laughed. 'Come on, the bus driver is getting impatient.'

Five minutes later, I was back in our compartment sighing with the relief. I took off my shoes and wiggled back against Matt trying to get comfortable.

'Tara,' said Matt, 'I wouldn't do that if I were you.'

'Why not?' I started to ask and then I felt it, large and hard digging into my back.

'Oh,' I said, 'you got me a gift.'

'Yep, but you can't unwrap it until tomorrow.'

I sulked for a bit but finally conceded that the physical probability of us being able to have sex was small. Plus it was only a curtain separating us from the rest of the passengers. It would just have to wait.

We finally managed to catch a few hours' sleep before arriving in Jodhpur early in the morning. The conductor woke us, gesturing for us to get off. I peeped outside making sure that we were indeed in Jodhpur, and noticed the end window had become loose and bounced open during the night. I shoved it shut with my foot before looking around for my shoes.

'Oh no,' I said as I realised what had happened.

'What's wrong,' Matt asked, sticking his head into the compartment.

'My shoes.'

'What? They got dirty in the field last night?'

'No. They're gone.'

'Gone where?'

'Out the window during the night.'

Matt looked at me with a stunned expression before chuckling and shaking his head. 'What is it with you and shoes?' he asked.

While Jaipur had been the pink city, Jodhpur was the blue one, named because the majority of the buildings were painted the exact same lilacy blue.

After we had checked in, I placed my bag in the corner of the room and, turning to Matt said, 'Now where's my present?'

'You're insatiable.'

'You're just too damned sexy,' I replied, looking at him. His crumpled clothing and tousled brown hair made me want to throw him on the bed and have my wicked way.

'Well,' he said, unbuckling his pants and letting them fall to the floor, 'here's one I prepared beforehand.'

'I knew I could rely on you.'

We were quite busy for a while after that and when we were both finally satisfied; we curled up and went to sleep.

* * *

We spent a couple of days in Jodhpur, sightseeing in the mornings and resting/working in the evenings. I did the resting and Matt did the working. He seemed to be getting into his magazine article, but try as hard as I could he wouldn't let me see any of it. I tried walking past behind him really slowly. I tried creeping silently up behind him. I even tried hiding behind the curtain in the room hoping to stealthily emerge and get a look before he realised I was there. Unfortunately for me, the man had a sixth sense and seemed to always know where I was.

Then all of a sudden, we were on the plane heading back to Mumbai. I couldn't believe how fast the time had gone. I had assured Matt that Jesse wouldn't mind if we both stayed with him. I couldn't wait to see the look on Jesse's face when he found out we were together.

'Tara and Matt,' Jesse said, when he opened the door for me.

'Hi,' I said, bouncing into the room. 'Miss me?'

'Hell yeah. It's been a right pain in the arse having to work while I know you've been gallivanting around Rajasthan with this big freak.'

'You don't mind if the big freak stays tonight?' Matt asked.

'Sure. You can sleep on the couch.'

'That won't be necessary,' I said, smiling like a Cheshire cat. 'He can bunk with me.'

Jesse looked from me to Matt and then back again and then he slapped him on the back. 'You dirty dog,' he said. 'I leave her in your care for a few weeks and you go and seduce her.'

'Can you blame me?' Matt asked, causing me to blush.

'No. But now I owe Tahlia 1000 rupee. You could have held off till you got back to Sydney.'

'What, so you could win a bet?' I asked indignantly.

'A bet's a bet,' said Jesse.

'Well I definitely wanted Tahlia to win that one,' I replied.

'Me too,' Matt said, smiling at me.

'So you guys on the same flight home?' Jesse asked.

'I changed my flight,' Matt said.

'I thought you would be staying to write about Mumbai,' Jesse said.

'I have this thing I have to get back for,' Matt said.

It was the first I had heard of it and I was as curious as Jesse. 'Thing?' Jesse asked.

'Stupid radio comp,' Matt replied, looking sheepish.

'To do with the traffic report?' I asked, referring to his job for Sunshine Radio.

'Something like that,' Matt said, looking uncomfortable. 'As I said, it's stupid. I'll tell you about it later. More importantly, tell us about what's been happening in Mumbai.'

We relaxed on the couch while Jesse filled us in and then we told him about our adventures. We had been chatting for about an hour when Tahlia got home.

Hey,' she said as she burst through the front door. She stopped and looked at me and then Matt, who was sitting on the far end of the couch from me.

'Ah ha,' she said triumphantly to Jesse, 'you owe me 1000 rupee.' She held out her hand.

'Damn, I was hoping to convince her otherwise,' said Jesse.

'Well I think I would have realised something was going on tonight when there were monkey noises coming from the other bedroom.'

I burst out laughing. 'I promise no monkey noises,' I said.

I was sad that this was my last night in India, but excited about going home with Matt and seeing where this thing between us was heading. Somewhere really good, I hoped.

'You weren't lying about that bed,' Matt said to me the next day on the way to the airport.

'I know. A rock,' I said.

'Nervous?'

'About the flight?'

'Yeah.'

'Nope,' I said. And it was true. I felt that while I was with Matt nothing bad could happen to me. He was my personal good luck charm.

The flight passed pretty uneventfully. We watched a couple of movies, had some dinner and then I pushed up the armrest, snuggled into Matt, and with his arm wrapped around me drifted off to sleep.

After we landed, we picked up our bags and queued for customs. It wasn't long before we were through the sliding doors and into the arrival terminal. We were on the way to the taxi rank when I saw a large contingent of media milling around.

'Look,' I nudged Matt excitedly, 'there must be someone famous coming through.' I pointed to the group.

Matt examined them for a second. 'Oh no,' he said in alarm.

'What?' I asked, turning around to see if the famous person was right behind us. I certainly didn't want to be swamped. I didn't recognise anyone, but by the way the crowd surged towards us I was guessing I was right.

'If we stand to the side they'll go right past us,' I said, giggling as I thought of the red-horned bull from Udaipur.

'I don't think so,' he replied. Turning to me he said urgently, 'Tara, I'll explain later.'

I only had time to ask, 'Is this to do with the radio comp?' before they reached us. It was immediately obvious by the way they were slapping him on the back that they knew Matt. They surrounded him, squeezing me out the back of the group.

One of the journalists cleared his throat and speaking into a microphone said, 'We are here with 'The King' at the Sydney International Terminal where he has just returned from India. Did you have a good flight?'

'Yes thanks,' said Matt, twisting around to look for me. I waved, smiling reassuringly.

The interview continued. 'And Matt, may I call you Matt?'

'Of course,' growled Matt, sounding like he had held back a, you idiot, on the end of the sentence.

'So Matt, how does it feel to know you are getting married in just a few short weeks?'

Whoa. Not the question I had been expecting. What the hell was going on?

'Not too good at the moment,' said Matt through clenched teeth, trying to catch my eye.

I backed away slowly as the words bounced around my head. Married? In a few weeks?

'Are you excited about meeting your bride to be?'

He hadn't met her? What was she? A mail-order bride?

'Where do you think you'll go for your honeymoon?'

'Will you be having a buck's party?'

'Yeah, are we invited?'

Like a frightened horse I shied away from them. I had waited as long as I could; waiting for him to say something that would tell me this was just some weird joke. But he hadn't denied it. Not one little bit.

He met my stare, a tortured look on his face as tears burned my eyes. Cursing myself for a fool, I ran as fast as I could for the taxi rank. I could hear Matt call my name but I ignored it, too devastated to go back and hear the explanation.

I jumped into a taxi and barked out my address; angry foolish tears coursing down my cheeks. As we roared away from the curb, I saw Matt burst from the terminal. He didn't see me, and I didn't tell the driver to stop.

By the time I got home, I was absolutely, utterly and emptily exhausted. I had sobbed quietly in the back of the cab until the driver had asked me if I wanted to borrow his hanky; politely declining the piece of cloth being waved in my direction.

Leaving my bags by the front door, I dragged myself into the shower where I sat on the floor letting the water course over me. Sighing, I finally hopped up and trudged to my room, where I took the phone off the hook and climbed into bed. I didn't want to talk to anybody - didn't want to answer any silly questions about my wonderful holiday. I mentally kicked myself for all the postcards I had sent raving about Matt and me. Now I was going to look like a big fat fool. Again.

I thought I wouldn't be able to sleep. I thought I would lie there for hours staring at the ceiling. But I fell asleep as soon as my head touched the pillow and didn't wake until the banging on my front door breached my subconscious barrier, bringing me back to consciousness.

Chapter Eight

Obtain Closure

I lay still getting my bearings. There it was. That confounded noise. Why couldn't the world just let me sleep? It took a few more seconds to realise that it was my front door being pounded on. I shot out of bed. What if it were Matt? A surge of hope burnt through my chest, quickly followed by dismay. I didn't know whether or not to open the door. Then I heard my name being called by a female voice. It was Nat. I charged to the door and opened it. We fell into each other's arms, both of us crying.

'Welcome home.' She sniffled as she finally pulled away.

'Thanks,' I smiled grimly.

She followed me into the kitchen where I switched on the coffee machine.

'You first,' I said, pointing to the box of tissues on the table.

She smiled and helped herself.

'Let me guess,' I said. 'It's Ricardo?' She nodded. 'You've had a fight?'

She blew her nose noisily and nodded again. 'We broke up,' she croaked, starting to cry again.

'What happened? I asked, shocked.

She sighed. 'It started about a month ago.'

'The fighting?'

'No, that only happened last night. The secrets.' I waited for her to continue. She sighed again. 'I understand now how you felt after Jake. One minute you had everything and the next nothing.'

That just made me think about Matt. 'You didn't understand that before?' I asked, stifling a sob.

'No. I've never been in love before.'

'I guess you have to have gone through it to appreciate it.' Sighing, I led her to the lounge where I slumped into the cushions. 'So tell me about the secrets,' I said when I was comfortable.

'His phone would ring and he would leave the room to answer it. A few times he came home all dressed up but didn't tell me where he'd been. Finally, last night, I demanded to know what was going on.'

'And?'

'He wouldn't tell me. All he would say was that he was working on something good, and he wanted to surprise me with it. But I had to press it of course; I think I'm a little hormonal at the moment. So I said that if he trusted me he would tell me now.'

'What did he say?' I asked.

'That if I trusted him I would wait.'

'Stalemate.'

'Yep. But of course I couldn't wait. So I pushed and pushed, finally accusing him of cheating.'

'Ouch. Do you think he is?' I asked.

'What else could it be?' she said, pulling another tissue out of the box and blowing her nose.

'I don't know - a surprise for your birthday?' Nat's birthday was in between Christmas and New Year's Eve.

'All the meetings in the suit?' she said.

'Yeah, maybe not,' I agreed. 'How did he take it?'

'It was awful. He said in a really quiet voice, "Well I can see that the trust in this relationship only goes one way. Without trust there can be nothing." And then he went and packed a bag and left, and I just watched him walk away.' She started sobbing, only just managing to say, 'I didn't want him to go.'

I pulled her into my embrace as she cried, rocking her gently while resisting the urge to join her. Finally - when she had stopped - I asked her, 'Why did you let him?'

'I didn't want to continue only to find out in a year that he had been cheating the whole time.'

'I just can't see him cheating on you,' I said.

'Really?' She looked up at me, hope shining in her beautiful blue eyes.

'I mean I might be wrong of course, but he just doesn't seem like the cheating kind.'

'Well what could it be?'

'Maybe he's setting up a big business deal?'

'He's a cleaner,' she reminded me.

'Yeah, in Australia, what was he in South America?'

'I don't know. See that's another thing. Every time I tried to talk about his past he would change the subject.' She paused for a second looking thoughtful and then exclaimed, 'Oh God, you don't think he was setting up a drug deal or something?'

'Don't be silly. Maybe he's immigrating his family?' I suggested.

'What, his wife and ten children?' she said grimacing.

I smiled weakly at her. 'Do you think he'll come back and explain?'

'He's very stubborn. And I hurt him. I could see it in his eyes.' She sighed. 'That's the worst part. Knowing that I hurt him, and not knowing why.'

We were interrupted by more knocking which turned out to be Elaine, Dinah and Gloria, with shopping bags and Bad Bunny.

I squealed in delight as Gloria reluctantly handed him over. He looked, I think, pleased to see me. It's a little hard to tell with a hare, but he turned around a few times, thumped me in the stomach with his hind leg, and settled down for a nap.

'You owe me a new cushion,' said Dinah.

'Did he pee on it?' I asked.

'No, he humped it to death.'

'We thought you might need these,' said Elaine as she dumped the groceries in the kitchen.

'Wow. Thanks,' I said, feeling blessed to have such good friends.

'Bacon and eggs?' asked Dinah giving me a hug. She held me at arm's length, eyeing me critically. 'You look terrible,' she said. 'You're meant to be all happy and glowy.'

'Yeah,' said Nat, 'what were you crying about when you opened the door?'

'Why don't you fill them in on yours first while I jump in the shower,' I said to her.

Nat nodded and, as I closed the bathroom door, I could hear her telling them about the break-up.

I took my time in the shower, not really wanting to breach the wound yet, but knowing I had to talk about it sometime. Breakfast was ready when I re-emerged and I felt a little better after filling my belly with bacon, eggs and thick slabs of toast with melted butter. I noticed my pants were a little tight.

'Damn.' I undid my top button. 'I'm going to have to go on a diet. Elaine, do you want to go kickboxing tomorrow night?' I asked, mentally planning a week of intense exercise to take my mind off Matt and the flab off my belly.

'I would love to, but Alistair and I are going to a work function,' she said, smiling smugly.

'So that's all good?' I asked her.

She smiled happily. 'Oh yes, very good thank you. Now tell us about what happened to you.'

'Well you know some of it right?' I said, perplexed when they looked at me blankly. 'From the postcards,' I clarified.

'What postcards?' asked Dinah.

'You haven't got the postcards?' I asked, unable to believe my good luck. They looked at each other for confirmation and then shook their heads. 'So you know nothing about my holiday?' I said.

'Apart from you being alive after the terrorist attacks, nothing,' confirmed Elaine.

'I might just leave it at that,' I said.

Elaine threw a cushion at me. 'As if we're going to let you get away with that. I demand details.'

There was silence while they all stared at me. After a few moments the pressure became too much. 'All right, all right, but I'm giving you the speed version,' I said. I waited till they all nodded before proceeding. 'After the attack Jesse - unable to leave work - organised for me to travel through Rajasthan with Matt. You all remember who Matt is right?'

Gloria shot her arm up into the air. I pointed at her and she said, 'Dreamy one-night-stand guy, with whom you spent that day in Mumbai.'

'Correct. So it turns out he was going to Rajasthan to write an article for *Travel Abroad* and he agreed to let me tag along.' I stopped.

'Please tell me there's more to it than that,' said Elaine.

Nodding I recommenced. 'Things were going well until we got to Udaipur, where they got really good. Then when we got home last night there were a heap of journalists waiting at the airport to interview him about his up-and-coming wedding.'

'Whoa,' Elaine said, shaking her head. 'You just summed up your holiday in two sentences. I think you owe us a bit more detail, especially about the 'it got really good' part.'

'Nu uhh, you agreed to the speedy version,' I said stubbornly.

'I didn't realise it would be the *Reader's Digest* abridged version.' She collapsed back onto the couch with a thoughtful look on her face.

Gloria put her hand in the air again.

'Yes Gloria,' I said. I really liked her.

Smiling she asked me, 'So he's really getting married?'

'He didn't deny it?'

She put her hand up as high as she could. 'Did he ring you to explain?' she asked when I nodded at her.

'No, because she has the phone off the hook,' said Elaine as she stood up and rehung it.

'What about your mobile?' Gloria asked.

'That's turned off as well,' Nat said, passing it to me so I could switch it on.

We all waited while my phone turned on. There was a beep indicating a text had arrived, and then a few more beeps in rapid succession.

'Some of them are from me,' said Elaine.

'I sent one,' said Nat.

'So did we,' added Dinah.

I waded through the texts until finally I could see one with Matt's name attached to it. 'There's a text from him,' I said tentatively.

'Well read it,' Elaine demanded.

'Tara call me. It's not what you think,' I said in a wooden voice.

'How could it be not what you think?' asked Nat.

Elaine had the look she gets when she's ferreting through information in her brain. Her eyes were slightly squinty and she had an intense look of concentration on her face.

'What's Matt's last name?' she finally asked.

'King?'

'The King?'

'Apparently yes,' I said.

'Ah huh,' she said triumphantly.

'What?'

'It's a radio competition.'

'What's a radio competition?' I asked.

'The marriage thing.' Elaine said it slowly, sounding out the syllables.

'Oh my God,' said Gloria. 'As in 'The King' on Sunshine Radio?'

'Yes. Why?' I asked, still none the wiser.

'Sunshine Radio is running a radio competition looking for a bride for 'The King'. Kind of a crossy spin on those stupid reality shows where the winning girl gets to have a date with a prince or marry the bachelor. Every weekday they'll have a new competitor. He asks them three questions, and at the end they announce the winning girl and they get married.'

'But Matt is 'The King',' I said stupidly, remembering him talking about a radio competition he had to be back for. I wondered when he had been planning to tell me. After his new bride was pregnant?

'Yep,' said Gloria excitedly.

'So he's getting married to someone he hasn't ever met?'

'Yep,' she said again, a bit more uncertainly.

I sat stunned, trying to take it all in. 'But what does he mean by it's not what it seems?'

'Well,' said Nat, 'it's just a radio comp.'

'But he's getting married,' I said. 'So he's still unavailable, right?'

I looked around at them and one by one they nodded their heads.

'Maybe he'll get it annulled,' suggested Dinah helpfully.

'Yeah, well if he does he can come and find me.'

* * *

After the girls left I decided it was time to ring Mum. If she hadn't been receiving any postcards from me she would be frantic by now.

'You sound calm,' I said, after she'd picked up.

'Hang on,' she said, 'let me put you on speaker. Now what did you say?'

'I said you sound quite calm.'

'Well, after the first couple of weeks I didn't hear from you I figured the Australian Embassy would ring me if you were dead. You know what they say, no news is good news.'

'Sorry. I sent you some postcards. I didn't realise how long they'd take to get here. How was the wedding?' I finally broached the subject I had been dreading.

'Trashy and boring.'

'Really?' I asked hopefully.

'Do you really think your Aunt Jackie would organise a trashy wedding? It was a little boring though. They disappeared for hours getting photos done. Sold the rights to *Woman's Weekly*, for $200000 and donated all the money to charity.'

I resisted the urge to stick my fingers down my throat.

'She was a vision in white,' I could hear Dad yell out in the background.

'Really Bert,' said Mum annoyed, 'why don't you go and play in the garden?'

'Play in the garden? I'm 60 not 6,' I heard him say.

'And the rest. I thought I saw some weeds near the petunias this morning.'

'Really?' he asked in dismay.

'That got rid of him,' my Mum chuckled. 'You know how he feels about his petunias. Anyway, the speeches were long and windy. All these important people got up - they do love the sound of their own voices don't they? I got quite tipsy waiting for them to finish so we could eat something.'

'How was the food?'

'Your Dad was complaining about the portions.'

'Big white plates with dainty little amounts?'

'Yes, you know the ones. We had to go through the McDonald's drive-through on the way home to top up.'

'How did she look?' I asked, not really wanting to know the answer.

'Beautiful of course. What did you expect - that the only day in her life she'd look less than stunning would be her own wedding day?'

I sighed. 'I guess it was too much to hope for.'

I could hear Dad in the background mumbling about something.

'What's that dear?' Mum called out.

'I've put up with your steroid-filled cat playing hide and seek with me and your dog trying to smother me, but I think when your horse starts to use my vegie patch as its own private buffet enough is enough.'

'But darling,' I heard Mum say, 'I don't have a horse.'

There was a pause, during which I could imagine Mum and Dad sharing an astonished look, and then Mum said quickly into the phone, 'Gotta go Tara. We're expecting you tomorrow for lunch.' And with that she was gone.

* * *

Mum rang me just as I was about to walk out the door. 'There's been a terrible accident on the freeway. A truck has overturned and is blocking both directions. You'll have to catch the train,' she informed me.

It wasn't so much that I minded catching the train, it's just that I didn't like leaving my car at the train car parks. It's not much of a car - a dinged up old Datsun was all I could afford to buy when Jake and I split - but it was mine.

Dad picked me up from the station in Woy Woy so we got a chance to have a little one-on-one time before the mayhem of Lil's family.

'How's it going?' I asked.

'Can't complain. You?'

'I've been better. I've been worse too,' I said, realising it was true.

'Well as long as you're better than your worse you can't complain,' he said wisely.

We rode the rest of the way in a companionable silence.

I always find being at Mum and Dad's a soothing experience. Today was no different. Even though it was total chaos with children and animals running everywhere, (Mum seemed to have managed to banish the horse), at the core, there was a calm that I could tap into. There was always somewhere in the house that you could curl up in a patch of sunlight and relax. I sat with a glass of wine listening to the kids play and Mum and Lil chatting about school and homework.

'What's happening for Christmas?' I asked. Mum had the good grace to look uncomfortable. 'Oh no, you didn't,' I said.

'Well darling it was at the wedding, and I'd had a lot to drink, and as I said before not a lot to eat, and it just seemed like such a good idea when Jackie brought it up.'

'How bad is it?' I said to Lil.

'Bad enough that we'll be having Christmas dinner with Martin's family.'

'Muuummmm,' I whined. 'I don't want to spend Christmas by myself.'

'You could always come.' I gave her a look that could have curdled milk and she sighed. 'No, I guess not. It's not till the evening anyway.'

'So I can come up for Christmas eve and breakfast?'

'That would be lovely,' she said, nodding her head.

'We might come up for the morning and then go to Martin's family,' said Lil.

'So what exactly are you doing for Christmas dinner?' As I asked her, Dad stomped into the kitchen to get another beer for himself and Martin. He shot Mum a dirty look and harrumphed before leaving. 'I take it Dad's not happy either?' I said.

'No. It's a black tie event at the summerhouse. Jake's family will be there as well.'

'Black tie?' I giggled. 'Seriously? Oh poor Dad. He's going to enjoy that about as much as a hole in the head.'

'I'd rather have a hole in my head,' Dad yelled from the balcony.

'So,' I said to Lil, 'any dirt on the wedding?'

'Not on the wedding, but I did hear something about the honeymoon.'

'Ooooh. Tell me, tell me,' I said eagerly.

'Lil,' Mum interrupted us, 'it's not nice to tell stories.'

'But Mum, *you* told *me*,' Lil said.

Mum looked a little embarrassed.

'You know she's going to tell me anyway Mum,' I said, 'so you may as well make sure she doesn't embellish it too much.'

'I guess you have a point there,' Mum said. 'It would be wrong of me to let you turn this into a Chinese whisper. Okay go on Lil.'

'Well, apparently Jake organised the whole honeymoon as a surprise,' Lil said.

'He wouldn't tell her anything about it,' cut in Mum.

'She found brochures for different countries and overheard him talking on the phone. He mentioned an around-the-world plane ticket.'

'She was so excited that he was going to so much trouble for her,' said Mum.

'You should have seen her at the wedding gloating about it,' Lil said.

'Lil, that's not very nice.'

'Well, she was Mum.'

'It was her wedding; she can gloat if she wants to.'

'Please, just get on with it,' I begged.

'No need to get snitchy Tara.'

'I'm not snitchy Mum, I'm dying to hear what happened.'

'Well, he whisked her off overseas and she found herself in China,' Mum continued.

'China could be interesting,' I offered.

Lil shook her head. 'Not when she was hoping for the Bahamas.'

'Tara, it's not the fact that they were in China that was the problem. They were in Guangzhou,' Mum informed me. When I looked blankly at her she said, 'Honestly, don't they teach you youngsters anything in school these days?'

'Mum, school was a long time ago. They may have taught me about Gongzoo.'

'Guangzhou.' She pronounced it with a fake Asian accent that made me giggle. 'It's a sister city of Sydney.'

'Ohhhhhhh.' I began to see where this was heading.

'And then after that they went to Nagoya,' said Lil.

'It's in Japan,' Mum informed me.

'I do know where Nagoya is Mum. So let me guess. Nagoya is also a sister city of Sydney?'

'Uh huh. And then to San Francisco,' said Mum.

'That wouldn't be so bad.'

'Yes, but they didn't get to do any sightseeing. Well not unofficially,' Mum said.

'Oh no. So he had organised this all politically?'

'One of his assistants organised it,' Lil said. 'Official meetings with the Lord Mayors of the sister cities, official dinners, ribbon-cutting events, balls, one event after the next. No private time and certainly no romantic time.'

'He even had one of his administrators accompanying them,' said Mum indignantly.

'And translators with them,' said Lil.

'After San Francisco?' I asked.

'Somewhere in the United Kingdom,' said Lil.

'Portsmouth,' supplied Mum. 'Then Florence and finally Wellington in New Zealand.'

'Although she didn't go to Wellington,' Lil informed me. 'She got the shits in Florence and insisted they go sightseeing by themselves.'

'They had a huge fight about it. She accused him of being a selfish pig,' Mum said in a scandalised voice.

'Touché,' I said.

'And he accused her of not caring about his political career,' Mum continued.

'She told him that she was going to stay and have a proper honeymoon with or without him,' said Lil.

'And he said it would have to be without him.' Mum shook her head as she said it.

'Ouch.' I actually felt - for the very first time - a fleeting feeling of pity for Tash. I tried to banish it, much more comfortable with my feelings of distaste for her, but it persisted.

'So she came home alone, and he went to Wellington,' Mum finished.

Lil sniffed disdainfully. 'Of course it was all flowers and chocolates when he got home.'

'So they made up?'

'Of course,' said Mum.

'It's so hard to see through his bullshit.' I sighed. 'Poor Tash.' I realised that both Mum and Lil were staring at me in disbelief. 'What?' I asked, 'It's not like I want to be her best buddy or anything. I still think she's a shallow cow. But I know what he's like, and I realise now that if it weren't for her, I'd still be in an unhappy marriage. I'm thinking of sending her a thank you card.'

'That's nice dear,' Mum said vaguely, as she raced off to check on dinner.

'Wow,' said Lil, when she was out of earshot. 'What happened to you in India?'

'Long story, but let's just say that I am finally over him. How ironic. We had our first ever fight on our honeymoon.'

'Really, what was it about?'

'I don't know.'

'How can you forget what your first fight was about?'

'No, I haven't forgotten. I didn't know at the time why we were fighting.'

Lil looked at me with a perplexed expression on her pretty face. 'How can you not know what you were fighting about?' she asked me.

I paused while I tried to work out how to explain it to her. 'You know how when you had that fight with Martin the other night about whose turn it was to put the kids to bed?' She nodded at me. 'Well our fights were never like that. They were never about anything black and white.' I could tell she was still confused, and I struggled to explain it better. 'Our first fight was about something that I thought was funny and he didn't.'

But why would you fight about that?' she asked.

'Exactly,' I said. 'With anyone else I wouldn't. But he thought I was being stupid, and I wanted him to see the funny side of it. In the end we had a huge argument and he stormed off, leaving me to find my own way back to the hotel.' Talking about it still hurt. 'Every time I argued with Jake I lost a little piece of myself,' I finished quietly.

She reached out and touched my arm. 'Why didn't you ever tell me?' she asked.

I smiled as I said, 'I didn't want you to hate him any more than you already did.'

'I didn't hate him,' she said.

'You didn't like him,' I replied. As we looked at each other I realised something I had been too blinded by my obsession with Jake to see. While my loyalty had been with Jake, Lil's had been with me. 'It's okay,' I said, finally understanding. 'I wouldn't have liked him either.' I reached over and squeezed her hand, thankful for her love.

'So did you want to tell me about India?' Lil said, when we had both wiped the tears from our eyes.

'As I said, long story.' Mum had finished checking the roast and was heading in our direction.

'Come over for dinner on Tuesday night and fill me in,' Lil said.

'Sure, why not.'

I found myself thinking about Jake and Tash on the train home. I had always believed Tash had premeditatedly seduced Jake. It was far less painful than admitting he hadn't wanted to be with me. I had enough distance now to see that the opposite had probably been true, and I realised that I really did feel sorry for Tash. It was a unique and refreshing feeling.

* * *

It was dark when I departed the train; dark and deserted. I had stayed at Mum and Dad's till late in the afternoon playing Monopoly with Rose, Tulip, Lotus and Petunia. Blossom and Camellia were too young to understand the finer points of the game.

I was still thinking about the whole Jake/Tash thing; revelling in my uncomplicated feelings, so I wasn't really paying attention to my surroundings. I was nearly at the car when I noticed the youth, with his spray can, squatting down with his back to me. I watched in amazement as he proceeded to graffiti the driver's door.

'What the hell do you think you're doing?' I yelled, expecting him to jump guiltily away from my car.

But instead he turned slowly to face me and replied insolently, 'It's art.'

'It is not fucking art,' I screeched, 'it's my *car*.'

'Nooooo,' he replied, pretending to be shocked, 'this here is your car?' He aimed his can at the windows and sprayed a long red line along them. I watched dismayed as some of it dribbled towards the door.

'Stop that,' I yelped.

'What are you going to do about it?' he asked as he squirted a cross on the bonnet.

It was a very good question. What was I going to do about it? The smart thing would have been to walk away and call the cops, hoping that they would get there in time to apprehend the little shit. Not that he was that little - he towered over me. But I have never been good at doing the smart thing, and I'd had a couple of rough days - what with the whole Matt marrying a total stranger thing never far from my mind, and having to hear about Jake and Tash's wedding. Without even thinking about it I found myself charging him, yelling like a mad woman. I saw the look on his face change from smugness to alarm as I barrelled into him; punching and kicking and screaming. He dropped the can and grabbed a fistful of my hair.

'What the hell are you doing? Get off me you crazy woman,' he yelled.

He held me out at arm's length while I punched the air in front of me. All those years of kickboxing classes finally paid off as I instinctively ball-kicked him in the groin. (Please note that a ball-kick is a kick using the ball of your foot, not a kick to the balls. Although in this case it was both.)

I watched in satisfaction as his eyes rolled back into his head. He let go of my hair and bent over holding his crutch, at which point I palmed him in the face. He collapsed to the ground, one hand on his face the other cradling his crutch.

I hadn't finished though. 'It's art?' I screamed crazily, grabbing the can off the ground. 'I'll give you fucking art.'

I spray painted him from the tip of his head right down to the end of his Nikes. I don't think I've ever had so much fun. I felt like I was finally striking back at every shitty thing that had happened to me over the last few years.

'Take that,' I shrieked as I sprayed his hair bright red. 'And that.' I kicked him in the back, rolling him onto his stomach and sprayed a bull's eye right over his butt. It looked so funny I doubled up laughing.

'Have you finished?' a calm voice asked me from behind.

I started guiltily up and peered over my shoulder. *Oh great a cop.* 'I guess so,' I said, handing him the spray can.

'I don't know,' he said pointing at the youth's head. 'I think you missed a little there.'

'You know,' I smiled, 'I think you're right. You'd better close your eyes,' I said to the kid, before spraying a big cross over his face.

'I've always wanted to do that,' said the cop jealously.

'Do you want a go? I asked magnanimously.

'Nah, better not, maybe when I'm off duty.'

The boy looked up at the cop and said, 'This crazy bitch attacked me,' and then he spat out a bit of his front tooth. I must have done it when I palmed him.

'Hmmmm,' said the cop looking at me. 'That's not good.'

'No.' Up until that point I was thinking I had gotten away with my momentary madness. But a broken tooth? Shit. It just stunk of an assault case.

I whipped out my mobile and dialled Dinah's number. 'Don't suppose you're sober enough to go to work?' I asked hopefully.

'Just opened a bottle of wine, why?'

'I have a little problem I was hoping you could help me with.'

'What is it?' she asked cautiously.

'It appears I have broken someone's tooth and well, it would be really good if you could fix it.'

'What, now? It's 6.30pm. Can't it wait till tomorrow?'

'Believe me when I say no.'

I heard her sigh into the phone. 'All right bring them down. How far away are you anyway?'

'Oh, about 15 minutes,' I lied.

'See you then.'

I hung up and looked at the cop hopefully. 'Hi I'm Tara,' I said.

'Constable Turner,' he replied, nodding his head at me.

Uh oh, CONSTABLE Turner. That's not good.

'But you can call me Eddie,' he continued.

'What are you going to do about my tooth, Eddie,' asked the youth.

'You get to call me Constable Turner,' Eddie replied.

I smiled and stuck my tongue out at the kid, who was sitting in front of us feeling the edge of his broken tooth.

'All right kid,' said Eddie, 'this is your lucky day. If you didn't have a broken tooth I would be hauling your arse down to the station and writing you up for graffiti to personal property. However since this lady seems to have accidentally broken your tooth, I'm not. What we are instead going to do is take you off and have your tooth fixed - at no cost to you - and then we are all going to forget this ever happened.'

The kid looked up at Eddie, then at me, and then he swivelled to look at my car.

'Sounds fair,' he said grinning.

Dinah was waiting when I pulled up twenty-five minutes later.

'You said 15 minutes.'

'Sorry, slight complication,' I said.

'What the hell happened to your car?' She stared in dismay at the drying paint.

'Graffiti artist.'

'Did you see him?'

'You could say that,' I replied.

Just then, the cop car pulled up and Eddie climbed out.

'Your friend is a cop?' Dinah asked.

'I never said it was a friend and no.'

Eddie helped the kid - whose name it turned out was Julio - out of the car.

'You're kidding?' Dinah said, staring at him.

He did look pretty funny with the big cross on his face and bright red hair.

'That's not the best bit,' said Eddie. 'Hey numb nuts turn around. Check out what she did to his arse.'

Dinah stared at my bull's eye. 'You did that?'

'Uh huh.'

'Wow. I hope that's quick drying paint or he's not getting anywhere near my dental chair.'

'Thanks so much,' I said to Eddie, once Dinah had finished and Julio had departed into the night. 'I don't know what came over me.'

'Hey, it was fun. Maybe we could do it again sometime.'

'What, graffiti a kid?'

'Well if you want to, but I was thinking more along the lines of coffee, or dinner.'

'Gee,' I said, suddenly speechless. 'Hmm, that would be nice.'

'But?' he asked.

'But what?'

'The way you said 'that would be nice', there was a definite 'but' there.'

'You're very perceptive.'

'It's the cop training,' he said, humbly. 'I'm trying out for detective.'

'You'd be good at that,' I replied.

'Thanks. So I'm guessing it's a no to dinner.'

'At the moment it wouldn't be fair on you to say yes.'

'Someone else?'

'Yes. No. Maybe.'

'It's complicated?'

'Very.'

'Well here's my card. If it becomes uncomplicated give me a ring.'

'Thanks, I will.'

'Wow. You don't mess around,' said Dinah after I had showed Eddie out.

'I said no.'

'Why?'

'I'm not sure,' I said sighing.

'The competition starts tomorrow,' Dinah reminded me.

'I know. I don't want to hear it.'

'We'll have to put a ban on that station for the next couple of weeks. Did you want to come over for dinner?'

'Nahhh. You and Gloria have fun. I think I'll go take a bath.'

'You're going to need one to get all that paint off your hands,' she said grinning.

* * *

The small tearoom was crowded the next morning as we munched on an apple teacake I had accidentally bought on the way back from the bank, and waited for Sunshine Radio's newest, hottest-ever competition. (The radio station's words, not mine.) Turns out, I had been unable to resist the temptation to hear Matt's voice when the others had suggested we listen.

'Do you want to go Christmas shopping tonight?' I asked Dinah, attempting to distract myself from the butterflies doing circuits in my stomach.

'Done and dusted.'

'What, wrapped and everything?'

'Yep.'

'Wow.'

'Another one of the many benefits of dating a woman.'

'Shhhhh,' said Sue, 'it's starting.'

A smooth male voice on the radio said, 'And today we have contestant number one on the line.'

'How many contestants will there be?' I asked.

'Five,' said Dinah before she was shushed again.

'Contestant number one, is there anything you'd like to ask 'The King' before he interviews you?'

'Ummmmm,' she giggled ferociously, 'what size shoes do you wear, your majesty?' She giggled again, making me wish I could stick an arm through the radio and slap her.

'Is she referring to the size of his...?' I asked in outrage.

'I think so. What size does he wear?' Dinah asked me.

'Shhhhhhh.'

Then we could hear another voice on the radio, but it was all warped and distorted, 'Six,' said the voice.

I burst out laughing and they all looked at me. 'He's an eleven,' I explained.

'Impressive,' said Mark.

'All right contestant number one, 'The King' will now ask you his three questions.'

There was a long silence, some static and then that voice, which I could not associate with Matt asked, 'Why would you want to marry someone you don't even know?'

'Ummmmm.' Contestant number one sounded confused. 'So I could be his Queen?'

'Good answer,' said the chirpy radio announcer. 'What is your next question for contestant number one?'

'If you were to slip over in cow poo, what would you do?'

I gasped out loud but the look Sue shot me kept me quiet.

'Dahhhh, is this a trick question?' said contestant one, in a ditsy little voice.

'No it's not a trick question. Why?'

'Well, it's just that I would never go anywhere I could slip in cow poo.'

'What? You would never go to a farm or a country where there were cows in the streets?'

'Is this question number three?' asked the radio announcer.

'Yeah, let's make this question number three.'

'There are countries where there are cows on the streets?'

'Christ,' said Rana, 'where did they get this bimbo from?'

'Well there you have it,' said the announcer, trying desperately to wrap it up. 'Contestant number one has finished her interview with 'The King'. What did you make of her?'

There was a few seconds of silence before the announcer said, 'We seem to have lost 'The King'. Tomorrow at the same time we will be interviewing the lovely contestant number two.'

'What's with you and the disgusting cow poo question?' said Sue, as she turned down the radio.

'The night we got together I slipped over in cow poo,' I explained, sighing at the memory.

'You guys got it on while you were covered in cow poo? That's some pretty kinky stuff.' Sue sounded impressed.

'No, I had a shower and then we got it on.'

'Ooooh, that sounds much more fun than wrestling in dung.'

'It was,' I said smugly.

'So what do you think he meant with the poo question?'

'I don't know.'

'Do you think he'd like her to slip over in poo so he can get it on with her?'

'What, you think that's his usual method of seduction? Take a girl somewhere there's cow poo, wait for her to fall in it, and then seduce her after she's clean? May I remind you the first time we had sex there was absolutely no cow poo involved.'

'I guess that crushes that theory.'

'I don't think it was ever a theory.'

'Maybe he's trying to send you a message,' said Dinah.

'What sort of message would that send her?' asked Rana.

'That he's thinking of her, remembering that night.'

They all looked at me, but I just shrugged my shoulders while I ladled more teacake into my mouth.

'Too much to hope for,' I eventually said, although it sounded more like 'Ooo uch to ope or'.

I swallowed before asking, 'Shall I get the pear crumble or the beesting tomorrow?'

The vote went three for pear crumble and two for beesting. I voted for the pear crumble so I was pretty happy with the result.

* * *

I didn't have much time during the day to think about the radio competition. I was frantically trying to catch up on the three weeks of work I had missed, so it wasn't until I started my Christmas shopping that night that my mind was free to wander. What had he meant by the cow poo question? Was he trying to send me a message? Was he comparing them to me?

It was distracting, trying to shop with these questions bouncing around in my head. I would reach out to pick up a toy only to find myself staring into space instead. Lil had kindly given me a list of suggested gifts for each of the girls as well as a list of Don't-You-Dare presents, which contained anything requiring a large number of batteries or making an annoying sound. With her help I managed to find each of the girls a suitable gift, but I was too distracted to buy anything for anybody else.

I rang Nat as I was heading out to the car. 'What are you doing?'

'Lying in bed crying,' she sniffled. 'What about you?'

I felt a moment of guilt. I had been so self-absorbed with the radio comp and my own misery, I had forgotten about Nat. 'I'm attempting to shop, but I can't keep my mind on the job?'

'Thinking about cow poo?'

'You heard it?'

'No, Dinah told me. I had a deposition all day. I should have only taken the morning but I had to keep excusing myself to go to the toilets to cry.'

'Do you want me to come over for dinner? I've just given up on the whole shopping thing. I can pick up something on the way.'

She blew her nose really loudly. 'Can you pick up some ice-cream as well?'

'What sort?'

'Something disgusting, surprise me.'

'Okay. And pizza?'

'Perfect.'

'What are you doing for Christmas?' I asked Nat, in between mouthfuls of cheesy pizza.

'Well, Ricardo and I were going to spend Christmas morning at home and then go to my parents' in the evening.' She paused to regain control and then sighed as she picked up a large slice of extra cheese pepperoni pizza and took a huge bite. 'Don't you just love comfort food?' she finally said.

'Yeah, but if I keep up all the comfort food I'm going to be the size of a house: today I ate three pieces of apple teacake. Do you want to come to Mum and Dad's Christmas Eve and then go to your parents in the evening?'

'Group Christmas function involving Tash and Jake?' she asked.

I nodded my head. 'Black tie event at the summer house.'

She smiled sympathetically. 'Mum and Dad will be pleased to see you. Mum was complaining last time I was there that she hadn't seen you or Dinah for ages.'

Thinking I had better buy her parents a present, I grabbed a notepad and wrote Mr and Mrs Green on it.

'What are you doing?' she asked.

'Tonight was such an abysmal failure that I have decided to start a Christmas shopping list.' I thought for a moment and then wrote Big Box of Chocolates, next to their name.

'At least you've started your shopping. I was planning to start on Sunday, but you know how that worked out.'

'I'm going again on Friday, do you want to come? We can help each other.'

'That would be great. So what time is this competition?'

'Ten o'clock, why?'

She typed it into her phone. 'Just setting it up as an appointment so I can listen to it. It will help distract me.'

'I doubt he'll mention anything else to do with me,' I said, secretly hoping that he would.

'You never know.'

It wasn't until I got home, had a shower and was heading to bed, that I noticed there was a message on my answering machine. I hit retrieve and walked to the kitchen assuming it would be Mum or Lil. Instead I heard Matt's voice. It was hard to understand as it was breaking up, but it was definitely Matt. I raced back to the phone and hit replay, but be buggered if I could make out what he was saying. All I could hear for sure was my name and something about India. After about the tenth attempt at replaying, I gave up trying to work it out and sat, depressed, on the edge of the lounge. He had rung me, but what for? Was it to say that he was sorry and he could never see me again, or was it to tell me that he missed me and wanted to see me? I was just going to have to bite the bullet and ring him to find out.

Nervously, I dialled his home number and got the answering machine. I hung up. I wasn't ready to commit anything to an answering machine. Knowing me, I'd get so nervous I'd end up leaving some mortifyingly embarrassing message like, 'Hi it's me. Umm that's Tara. You know from India. Anyway ring me. If you want, or not, whatever thanks. Speak soon. Hopefully, but only if you want to yeah, okay, bye.'

So I tried his mobile phone number but got a message telling me that the number was currently unavailable. The word unavailable brought me back to my senses.

The radio competition.

It was real and it was happening. He was indeed unavailable to me. Angry with myself I hung up the phone and headed for bed.

* * *

I arrived at Lil's with a tub of Baskin and Robbins chocolate and peanut butter ice-cream, which we hid at the back of the freezer so the girls wouldn't see it. When they were finally all asleep we retired to the back deck with a coffee and the tub of ice cream.

'I'm going to miss the comfort food when you get over all of this,' said Lil as she licked some ice-cream from her spoon.

'Don't worry. Comfort food has become an important part of my life. I've had ice-cream every day this week.'

Lil laughed before saying, 'So tell me about India.'

I sighed. 'You might want to get comfortable,' I advised her. I waited till she had put her feet up and then filled her in on what had happened while I was away.

'Whoa,' she said when I had finished. 'So your Matt, is 'The King' from Sunshine Radio?'

'Uhuh.'

'That guy is seriously hot.'

'Tell me about it.' I had spent a lot of time staring at the promotion boards that had been erected to advertise the radio competition.

'This is the guy that jumped your bones in Udipudi.'

'Udaipur. And yes.'

'So why aren't you all depressed and weepy?'

'I was on Saturday.'

'What, just one day?'

'And then on Sunday I got to spray-paint a graffiti artist who had decorated my car and since then I've been feeling all right.'

'Back up a little. Spray-paint a graffiti artist?'

'Hmmm. I guess I had better fill you in on that too.'

When I had finished she looked thoughtful. 'That still doesn't explain why you aren't all depressed and weepy.'

'I think that by acting on my anger, rather than suppressing it like normal, I've freed something inside me.

'Tara, this whole acting on your anger thing....'

'Don't worry, I'm not about to become a raging, super-aggressive chick that picks fights in pubs.'

'Phew.'

'When Dinah caught Creepy Doug in the restaurant with Tiffany and acted on it rather than walking away, she said she felt like she had healed something. I feel like that a little. Maybe I should have confronted Jake last year, but I wasn't in a state to do it, so I don't think it would have worked.'

'Probably would have had a negative effect.'

'Yeah, he would have had me apologising for making him sleep with Tash.'

Lil giggled. 'Do you think that works? Dinah healed herself by confronting Doug. How can you fighting the graffiti guy have helped you heal?'

'No, Dinah was healing her issues with her father when she confronted Doug.'

'Oooohh.' Lil pushed a wisp of brown hair behind her ear.

'I don't think it was really us using one person to confront another. I think it was more about us reseizing control of our lives, control we had given to another person.'

'So Dinah was attracted to Creepy Doug, because of her relationship with her father?'

'Yep. She chose men that made her feel like crap, like her father had.'

'So why were you attracted to Jake?'

'He was charming and good looking. I saw you and Martin, and Mum and Dad and I wanted what you guys had. You all made it look so easy I assumed it would be like that.'

We sat in silence for a while, eating ice-cream and thinking.

'Do you think it's bad that I don't need to heal myself or regain control of my life?' Lily finally asked in concern. 'Maybe there's something wrong with me?'

I burst out laughing. 'I can't believe you just said that. You're so lucky. But it's not so much luck,' I corrected myself, 'you've made wise decisions to get where you are now. I didn't. That's all.'

'When did you work all this out?'

'I had a lot of thinking time in India.'

'Do you know what I think?' said Lil.

'What?'

'I think we both need more ice-cream.'

'I think that's the wisest thing you've said all day.'

* * *

Over the next week the radio competition progressed like this:

Contestant number two.

'What is your favourite colour?'

'Ummmm. Pink.'

'What is your favourite drink?'

'Pina Coladas.' (Followed by heaps of giggling.)

'If you were in the back of a car that was pulled over by bandits, what would you do?'

'I'm sorry..... I don't understand the question.'

Contestant number three.

'What is your idea of a perfect date?'

'Walking hand in hand along a beach while the sun sets.' (Said with slight lisp so it was really thun thets, not sunsets.)

'What is your favourite continent?'

'Ummmm. Italy.'

'What's your favourite James Bond movie?'

'*Mission Impossible.*'

Contestant number four.

'What is your greatest fear?'

'Oh golly, that's a hard one. Yeah, I would have to say – ahhhhh - yeah spiders.'

'What is your star sign?'

'Gemini.'

'What would you prefer to eat for dinner, Indian or Thai?'

'Neither. I hate foreign food.'

Contestant number five.

'What is your favourite movie?'

'Gosh, it would have to be *Breakfast at Tiffany's.*'

'What is your favourite song?'

'*Moon River.*'

'If you could go anywhere on your honeymoon where would it be?'

'New York.'

***

Natalie and I were Christmas shopping. By her red eyes, I had surmised she was still frequenting the ladies at work for her spasmodic crying sessions. She told me she had started taking her laptop in with her so she could get some work done while she cried. I guess that was why they had made her a partner - total dedication.

'What did you think about contestant number five?' I asked.

'Do you think she wanted to go to New York so she could go to Tiffany's?'

'Probably.'

'I wish he had asked her what her cat's name was.'

'Probably Cat.'

'So is that it for the contestants?'

'Yep. They have a week off over Christmas and then they'll announce the winner.'

'I'm breathless with anticipation. Where the hell did they find these girls?'

'I guess it's the type of girl who would enter such a competition. I mean, would you ring up and go into a competition to marry someone you don't know?'

'No, it would be horribly demeaning. I guess in their defence they sort of know him from the radio?' she said.

'What, listening to him doing the road reports from the helicopter?'

'And seeing his photos on those advertising billboards.'

'That would be enough to make them ring up. He looks hot in those photos,' I said sighing.

'Yeah, hanging out of the helicopter like that. He looks like a real Indiana Jones.'

We both paused while Nat looked at some perfume for her Mum and I thought about Matt in those photos. Yummy.

'Oh look,' said Nat, holding up another bottle, 'Ricardo bought me a bottle of this.' She looked at the price tag. 'He would have had to clean forever to buy it.' Tears flooded her eyes.

I handed her a tissue.

'Thanks,' she said. 'I went through a whole box today at work. I've started buying those man-sized tissues, they last a lot longer.'

'I love those tissues. All tissues should be man-sized.'

She blew her nose noisily.

'What do you want to do for your birthday?' I asked, changing the subject. Thinking about Matt was making me start to get a little hot under the collar.

'I don't know. Go out to dinner? I'd be happy to do nothing.' She sounded quite glum as she said it.

I decided to bite the bullet. 'Have you heard from Ricardo?'

'No. I think I've blown it.'

'He'll come round,' I said it more for reassurance than because I believed it. The truth was, I didn't know Ricardo enough to know what he would do. Maybe she *had* blown it.

'Why don't you ring him?' I asked.

'Why don't you ring Matt? He's obviously not into this competition.'

'I did.'

'What? Why didn't you tell me? What did he say?'

'Nothing. I got the answering machine.'

'What made you ring him?'

'When I got home from your place the other night there was a message from him on the answering machine.'

'What did he say?'

'I couldn't understand him,' I said frustrated. 'It was all staticy. He said my name and something about India.'

'So you left a message for him?'

'No. He's currently unavailable Nat, that's what his phone told me.'

'What, his phone told you he was unavailable?' She looked at me concerned, as if maybe I was going crazy.

'No, the message on his answering machine was that he was currently unavailable.'

'Oh,' she sighed. 'At least he rang you.'

'He could have been ringing to tell me that there was nothing between us.'

'He could have been ringing to say that he loved you.'

The total unexpectedness of the thought of him saying he loved me made my heart clench painfully. I stopped and steadied myself with a hand on the slipper selection. Bright lights flashed before my eyes and I had to remind myself to breathe. When I had myself under control, I continued. 'I guess we'll never know. Now do you think I should get Mum the blue slippers or the purple ones.'

'You're really not going to ring him again?'

'I tell you what - I'll ring him if you ring Ricardo.'

'I think the purple ones.'

'Great.'

And we left it at that.

* * *

I love the lead up to Christmas. Even though I was lonely and morose - and missing Matt like crazy - I couldn't help but be caught up in the festive season. Nat and I were hung-over and officially late for the 1pm departure time to my parents, as we sat on the floor in my lounge, frantically wrapping presents. We had gone out for some Christmas cheer the night before and had ended up having a double celebration when Mark had pulled out an engagement ring and proposed to Rana.

'Just wrap the ones for tonight,' I advised Nat as I passed the sticky tape. 'We can finish it up there.'

'Hang on,' she said, clambering to her feet. 'I need to vomit.'

'Feeling better?' I asked when she finally returned.

'There's probably much more where that came from.'

I chuckled, happy that for once it wasn't me doing the vomiting.

The drive to Umina was a nightmare. It seemed everybody in Sydney had joined the freeway at once. Nat took advantage of the traffic jam to get a couple of hours' sleep and was feeling better by the time we arrived. She must have still looked a little peaky though, because Dad took one look at her and handed her a glass brimming with champagne.

'Hair of the dog,' he said. 'Merry Christmas gorgeous.'

'Oooiiiiii,' I said, 'where's *my* hair of the dog?'

'Sorry beautiful.' Dad handed me a glass as well.

'What's with all the beautiful and gorgeous?' I asked Mum.

'Your Dad started the hair of the dog quite a while ago.'

'Is it just the four of us tonight?' I asked.

'Jake and Tash said they might drop in to say hi.'

'What?' I asked in alarm.

'Gotcha.' She laughed merrily.

'I think someone else might have started the hair of the dog a while ago as well,' I said grumpily.

We had a merry evening, pulling bon-bons and singing Christmas carols with our paper hats on. I found myself remembering last year, when I had still been almost comatose with grief. I had put in what I had thought was a good effort, but in retrospect I must have been a bit of a Christmas Grinch. It was amazing how far I had come in a few short months. The first part of the year had been an uphill slog, but it seemed I had been on the downward slope for a while.

Would I have come this far without Matt? I doubted it. He had shown me there was life beyond death. The question was, would I have come this far without The Seven Steps to Closure? Would I have been open to the experiences that had allowed me to move on from Jake? Would I have been in the right place at the right time?

In the end I decided that it didn't really matter about the what ifs and buts of the situation. I was where I was, and even though I was upset about the whole Matt situation, the emotions involved were a lot less convoluted and didn't involve the excruciating confusion that had accompanied my breakup with Jake. So yes, I was sad and depressed, but I still held on to my newly restored sense of self, and with that I would just have to be happy.

* * *

'Wake up, wake up, wake up,' I said, bouncing up and down on the end of Mum and Dad's bed. 'It's Christmas and guess what?' Mum opened one eye and stared at me. I took that as an invitation to keep on going. 'Santa's been.'

'What time is it?' Dad groaned, feeling around on the bedside table for his alarm clock.

'It's ten o'clock.'

Mum shot bolt upright in bed. 'Oh no, I have to get the turkey in the oven, scrub the potatoes and make the salads. Bert, we need to get some ice for the drinks.'

I sat with a huge grin on my face. 'Just kidding, it's only eight.' Mum flopped backwards onto her pillow. 'I've scrubbed the potatoes, the oven's preheating and Nat's started on breakfast. We still have a few hours till Lil and Martin get here so I thought we could have breakfast on the deck.'

Dad lifted his head into the air and sniffed. 'Mmmmmm, what's that I can smell?'

'Bacon cooking and coffee brewing.'

'Good enough for me.' He threw back the sheets and clambered out of bed. 'I'll just have a shower first.'

'You're mighty chirpy,' Mum said to me when Dad had departed.

'I'm feeling good.'

'So you're finally over Jake?'

'I think I am. I guess I won't really know till I see him again, but I can't see that happening in the foreseeable future.'

'So does this Matt have anything to do with it?'

'How do you know about Matt?' I asked, thinking *Bloody Lil*.

'Oh a little birdie told me.'

'Bloody Lil,' I grumbled out loud.

'Now dear, don't go blaming Lil, you've only got yourself to blame for this one.'

'What do you mean?'

'The postcards.'

'What about them? They never showed up.'

'Actually they did. All of them. Here.'

'You got all the postcards?' I could hear my voice going up a couple of notches. 'How could that happen?'

'You bundled them with rubber bands.'

'I thought they would take them off,' I said, remembering placing the bands around the postcards with Mum and Dad's on top in case Matt saw them.

'They made for some very interesting reading.'

I put my head in my hands and groaned. Oh the embarrassment, my own mother reading about how I had got it on with Matt.

'I don't know why you're so mortified,' she said, 'you always tell me these things eventually.'

'Yes, but not quite in the same way.'

'I wish you would. It's much more amusing, and easier. Normally I have to pry all the nitty gritty bits out of Lil. So, back to my original question - does it have anything to do with Matt?'

'Yes and no. Yes he helped me rediscover what it was to feel attractive. But more importantly I've been able to find *me* again. I hadn't realised how much of myself I had sacrificed to be with Jake. I gave up my identity.'

'You were too lost to realise you were lost. It made me so sad watching you. You got smaller and smaller and then one day you stopped shining.'

'Mother,' I said saddened, 'why didn't you say something?'

'Some things you have to realise yourself, and until you do, you drive anyone who tries to tell you away. I'd already lost so much of you I didn't want to lose all of you.'

We sat in silence holding hands.

'So this Matthew,' she finally continued, 'he lets you be yourself?'

'Even better, he likes who I am.'

'I like him already. When do I get to meet him?'

'You're not.'

'What?'

'Didn't Lil tell you about the radio comp?'

'Yes. Surely you're not going to let a little thing like that get in your way?'

'Mum, he's getting married.'

'Married, Shmarried. It'll all work out, just you wait and see.' She kissed me on the forehead and climbed out of bed leaving me sitting there bemused.

* * *

It was 6pm on the eve of Nat's birthday and Nat, Dinah, Elaine and I were at the Sydney Convention Centre waiting for a medical convention Alistair and Gloria were attending, to finish. Gloria had met us out the front and advised us that it had run over time.

'Alistair has to present certificates to the newly registered doctors,' she advised us as she ushered us into the conference room.

What she had failed to mention was that the speaker before the registration ceremony was attempting to break a Guinness Book record for the longest and most boring lecture ever given.

'Blah blah blah blahblah blah,' he said as I fought my sinking eyelids. 'Blah blah blah blaaaaaaaaaaaaaaaah.'

Elaine elbowed me in the ribs as I felt my head rolling forwards. 'Wake up sleepy,' she whispered.

I straightened up my head with my hands and then said, 'Why does Alistair have to hand out the certificates?'

'He's the current president of the Australian Medical Board.'

'Impressive,' I said.

'He tells me it's nothing special. They take turns doing it.'

Eventually the 'blah blahing,' stopped and the lights in the room were turned up.

'Shhhh,' said Gloria, leaning towards us, 'here they come.' A line of people filed out onto the stage.

'That's Alistair,' Elaine whispered proudly, pointing to a tall, dark-haired man in a finely cut suit.

'Cute,' I whispered. 'I can't believe we haven't met him before.'

'Well, you know, I didn't want to rush things.'

'You spent Christmas with each other's families,' I said, a little miffed.

'Yes, but I've met them before.'

'Twenty years ago.'

Alistair's deep voice boomed out through the microphone as he started to present the registration certificates.

The rest of the room applauded politely as each name was read out, effectively muffling the gasp that Nat gave as Alistair called out Ricardo Gonzalez.

'It can't be,' she said, leaning towards the stage.

I was just as astounded as she was as we watched Ricardo shake Alistair's hand, take his doctor's registration certificate and re-join the rest of the group on the stage.

'What the fuck is going on?' Nat said to Elaine.

'How the hell would I know,' Elaine responded. 'He's your boyfriend.'

'What's wrong?' asked Gloria.

'That's Ricardo, Nat's ex, the cleaner,' Dinah told her.

'Seriously?' Gloria asked. 'He's pretty cute, for a guy.'

Even from the back of the room you could tell that Ricardo was smoking hot.

'Well,' I said to Nat, 'guess now we know what his secret was.'

I watched in dismay as Nat's blue eyes filled with tears.

'Don't cry,' I said. 'It'll all work out.'

'How?' she said. 'I behaved so horribly; accusing him of being unfaithful and kicking him out.'

'You said he left.'

'He did. But I didn't try to stop him.'

'Nat, I'm sure he'll forgive you.'

'As if he would want me when he could have anyone,' she gestured to a gaggle of female doctors clustered around the foot of the stage, all apparently staring at Ricardo.

'Well, I guess we're about to find out,' I said, indicating Elaine who was approaching Alistair.

'Shit,' said Nat, starting to stand up.

I gripped her arm firmly. 'No you don't,' I said.

We watched Elaine smoothly move through the crowd to Alistair's side. She whispered something in his ear and, taking her hand, he drew her over to Ricardo, who was talking to the other newly registered doctors. Nat tried again to break free from my grip.

'Stop it,' I advised her firmly, watching Ricardo talk to Elaine. Elaine turned towards us and pointed at Natalie, and Ricardo immediately headed in our direction.

'Well, that's got to be good,' I said to Nat.

'You don't know that,' she said, sounding distressed. 'He could be coming to ask for the rest of his things.'

Ricardo stopped a couple of metres short of us, and stood silently, staring at Nat. He opened his mouth to speak but no words came out. The look on his face revealed such intense longing that I felt my heart clench.

Nat met his eyes, a look of shame on her face. Her eyes started to well up and she looked away, blinking rapidly, to stop the tears falling. Then glancing up shyly and meeting his gaze again, she said so quietly that I had to strain to hear, 'I'm sorry.'

'Shush,' he said, closing the gap between them and pulling her into his embrace.

'No really, I am,' she said.

'Don't,' he whispered gently as he stroked her face. Then he kissed her. It was so passionate and personal I felt embarrassed witnessing it - his hands moving from her face to her hair and down to her back where he crushed her to him, her dress clenched in his fists.

Finally, they stopped - both of them panting for air - and he bent and touched his nose to hers. 'I've missed you so much,' Nat said.

'Never again,' said Ricardo, shaking his head, 'I can't be parted from you ever again.'

And the kissing resumed.

When they were at the staring-at-each-other-hand-holding stage, Alistair cleared his throat to get their attention. 'Should we all go to dinner?' he suggested.

Ricardo looked a bit uncomfortable 'I don't want to intrude,' he said, gesturing to all of us.

'Don't be silly,' I said. 'Anyway, it's for Nat's birthday.'

'Why didn't you tell me?' Nat asked him while we walked to the restaurant in Chinatown.

'Well,' he said thoughtfully, 'I didn't want to look like - how do you say it in Australia? A looser.'

'Loser,' said Nat. 'Why would you look like a loser?'

'Cleaning toilets and pretending I was a doctor.'

'But you wouldn't have been pretending.'

'How could you have been sure?'

'I would have believed you.'

'And if I didn't get Board Membership in Australia, would you still have believed me?'

'But you have a degree.'

'Anyone can forge something like that these days.'

'I see your point, but I would have believed you,' she insisted.

When I finally got home, it occurred to me that I had become the odd one out. I would probably become the hanger-on, inviting myself on my friend's dates and just generally being wherever I wasn't wanted.

'Oh well,' I said to Bad Bunny as I rolled over and punched my pillow. 'Hopefully Ricardo, Alistair or Gloria will get desperate for a bit of alone time and set me up with a yummy doctor of my own.'

But as I drifted off to sleep it was Matt's face that I saw, and it was Matt that I found myself dreaming about.

* * *

'I can't listen,' I said to Dinah.

'Shhhh, you'll miss it,' said Sue.

'I don't want to hear it,' I said.

'Well why are you in here?' she asked me kindly.

'The cake's in here,' I said, ladling some more into my mouth.

Sue smiled at me and squeezed my hand. 'I can tell you who won if you want.'

I thought about it, realising that I didn't want to hear it because if I didn't, I could pretend it wasn't real. But that wouldn't change anything. Matt was about to announce which of the five, lovely contestants he had chosen to marry. Maybe he wouldn't choose any of them. A wild fantasy popped into my mind of him denouncing all of them and instead declaring his love for me. I knew it was a long shot, but I decided to stay.

As the segment started, Sue reached over and turned up the radio. Rana raced into the tearoom and said, 'Did I miss it?'

'Just starting,' I told her from between clenched teeth. She smiled sympathetically.

The cheery radio announcer reintroduced each of the contestants and replayed the interviews. Finally, after what felt like an eternity, he said, 'All righty then, the King is ready to make his announcement. Which contestant have you decided to make your Queen?' I decided I hated the chirpy radio announcer.

None of them, I willed Matt. *None of them.*

'Contestant number three,' Matt said.

I sank back into my seat, totally deflated. He had done it, he had picked his bride and it wasn't me.

'Which one was that?' Sue asked. 'Not the pina colada chick?'

'No, that was number one,' Rana advised her.

Dinah was watching as I struggled to control my facial expressions. Reaching over she deposited another piece of cake onto my plate.

'Thanks,' I said, pushing it around with my fork. 'It was the one that thought Italy was a continent,' I advised them. I had logged onto the radio station website and, sadly, memorised all the interviews.

'The one that thought *Mission Impossible* was a James Bond movie?' Sue confirmed.

'Ahuh,' I said through a mouthful of cake. I swallowed it and then put my fork back on my plate. 'This has got to stop,' I said to Dinah while gesturing at my plate.

'No more comfort food?' she said.

'Well, not as much. I need to wean myself off it. Otherwise in a year's time I'm going to be ten-tonne-Tara again.'

She smiled sadly at me. 'Everything will work out for the best,' she said wisely.

'I know it will,' I said looking at her. 'But I also know that it won't happen by itself. That's something I learnt from The Seven Steps to Closure. I need to be proactive if I am to get better.'

'That's an important lesson,' she said.

I nodded my head. 'I just need to remember it.'

* * *

I was at Bar Blue with the gang, celebrating New Year's Eve. The end of the year had gone so quickly. That's always the way with a year though isn't it? It starts off at a crawl as you recover from Christmas and the New Year festivities, then all of a sudden the Easter eggs are on the shelves. You have a few long weekends to soften the middle of the year and then you find yourself staying up late on 30th of June trying to get your tax return done, so you can get your money back as fast as is humanly possible. You tell yourself you're only half way through the year, but the days start flicking by faster and faster. Halloween speeds by like an eerily lit orange train, and then all of a sudden the Christmas carols are playing in the department stores. *It's only the beginning of November,* you tell yourself indignantly. *Still plenty of time to get ready for Christmas.* But every year without fail, you find yourself, with a few hundred other equally frantic people, in the days before Christmas, trying to find the perfect present for everyone in your life. And every year you fail, because the perfect presents have already been purchased by the super-organised people of the world, and all that's left on the shelves are bed slippers, underwear, socks, daggy C.D's and bad paperback novels. And although you plan the perfect Christmas dinner - with wonderful bon bons and Christmas themed tableware, in the end it is easier to go to your parents' for lunch - where your poor mother slaves in the summer heat, over the biggest roast turkey you've ever seen. And by the time it is ready, no one is hungry, having filled up on grog and snacks, and everybody is too hot to eat. You don your paper hat and play with your pathetic little plastic top that you won in your bon bon. Your New Year's resolution is to be more organised and lose weight.

'This year,' I said to Gloria and Dinah, 'I am going to lose weight.'

'You mean next year,' Gloria slurred. 'Cause it's not technically this year till next year.'

I burst out giggling, 'Gloria how can it be next year when it's this year?'

She looked at me for a while; I could see her brain trying to function through the champagne-induced fog it was currently operating under.

'I don't know,' she finally said.

'You mean that you're going to lose weight next year, because you only have one hour and thirteen minutes to lose weight this year,' said Dinah.

'Yes, I see what you mean. That would be quite a weight loss challenge,' I said before breaking into such hysterical giggling that I fell off my stool and onto the floor.

'I'm okay, okay,' I announced loudly as I jumped to my feet.

I could see the bouncer on the door of Bar Blue eyeing me off, and I don't think it was my body he was looking at. I gave him a cheeky wave and a smile, really not wanting to be thrown out only an hour before the New Year countdown.

'Seriously,' I said, 'they serve you alcohol and then complain when you get drunk.'

'It's quite a conunbum, I mean cobumrum, no, no I mean co-nun-DRUM,' said Gloria triumphantly.

'Gloria,' I giggled, 'you're really funny when you're pissed.' We clutched onto each other laughing so hard we both fell onto the floor. I saw the bouncer shaking his head in dismay as Dinah helped us up.

'I'm going to be more organised,' said Dinah, after we had regained our seats.

'I'll help you,' said Gloria. She leaned towards Dinah for a kiss.

'I'm going to collect toilet rolls and make my own bon bons next Christmas,' I announced loudly, hoping to break up the snog.

Elaine and Alistair, and Nat and Ricardo were off close dancing. I'd gotten up to dance with them initially, but then the music had gotten slower and I had found myself swaying on the spot by myself, trying to work out how to leave the dance floor without looking like some sort of sad tosser. I had finally realised there was no possible way to do it without looking like a sad tosser, but that swaying on the spot by myself looked even sadder, so I had left and crashed Gloria and Dinah's private conversation. They had very kindly included me in their group, so I would be damned if they were going to spend the next hour and eleven minutes snogging in front of me. They could snog at the New Year and not before.

Much to my delight, my toilet roll announcement broke up the embrace.

'What a good idea,' said Gloria, while Dinah sniggered. 'Maybe we should do that.'

'Every year Tara plans to make her own bon bons. What happened this year?' she asked me.

'The empty toilet rolls were taking up too much space in my bathroom cupboard. I meant to collect them again at the end of the year, and then with the wedding of the year, trying to achieve closure and travelling around India with someone who will remain nameless tonight, I totally forgot.'

'What were you going to put in them?' asked Gloria.

'Lollies,' I said.

'What else?'

'Hmmm, maybe some chocolate.'

'And?'

'Well I must admit I've never thought this deeply about it.'

Dinah started to laugh.

'Hum, maybe a balloon,' I said.

'That's a good idea. You don't normally get balloons in bon bons.'

'Yeh,' I was warming to my bon bons plan, 'and maybe a card.'

'What sort of card?' asked Gloria.

'From a deck of cards.'

'What would you do with that?' said Dinah.

'Well, whoever gets the highest card gets to boss round the people under them for the day, and so on down the cards.'

'Brilliant,' enthused Gloria, 'and you have to keep your card on you at all times or you have to skol a drink.'

'Yeah. But you can force other people to swap cards with you, so that the person down the pecking order can make their way to the top.'

'How?' said Gloria.

'I don't know,' I admitted.

The three of us silently contemplated my dilemma.

'Maybe you could challenge someone to see their card and if they don't have it they have to swap with you?' suggested Gloria.

'Yeah that's it. Or you could steal it; either way, they have to skol their drink and then you get to boss them around all day.'

'What else will be in the bon bons?' asked Gloria.

'Oh I know,' I shrieked, 'fake tattoos.'

'Wow, I bet there have never been fake tattoos in bon bons before. So what else?'

'Ummmmmm. Well a hat of course. But not those stupid paper ones. No, I'll put real caps in mine.'

'Tara,' said Dinah.

'Yeeesss.'

'Exactly how big are these bon bons going to be?'

'Big. I'm going to cut the toilet rolls up and use them to make bigger ones.'

'Why don't you just buy a roll of cardboard to make them?' she asked.

'Wow. I've never thought of that.'

'And what are you going to put in them for the cracker part?' Dinah continued.

'Well... I just thought you could say BANG, when you pull them.'

'So how do you know who won?'

'The person with the biggest half,' I said seriously.

'You mean the biggest piece. Cause a half can't be bigger than the other half, otherwise it's not a half,' slurred Gloria before putting her head on the table.

'You've bon bonned her out,' said Dinah in amusement.

'That's the first time I've ever bon bonned someone. Do you think bon bonning someone could be listed as a talent?'

'What, like if you went in a Miss Universe competition?'

'Yeah,' I said, and then continued in a deep voice, 'please welcome to the stage Miss Tara Babcock, her talent is bon bonning innocent victims.'

'Would you have to bon bon someone during the competition?'

'Yes. I may need to borrow Gloria.'

Just then, the others returned from the dance floor.

'What happened to Gloria?' asked Elaine.

'Tara bon bonned her.'

'She appears to be dribbling on the table,' observed Alistair.

'I'm all right,' Gloria shrieked, sitting up so quickly that I fell off my stool in fright. Just then the music got boppier and Gloria raced to the dance floor screeching, 'I love this song - come on.'

We all followed her and engaged in wild crazy dancing. I jumped around and around with my arms stretched in the air and the music pumping through my body, feeling so lucky to have such wonderful friends.

All of a sudden, the D.J. was counting in the New Year and all my friends paired off staring into each other's eyes, getting ready for the New Year's snogging session. I found myself wondering if Nat would lend me Ricardo for a quick kiss so I wouldn't feel totally left out, but decided not to press the friendship that far. Feeling a tap on my shoulder I turned to see the bouncer standing behind me. Oh great. He was going to turf me out now? It's not like I was behaving any more badly than anyone else in the bar.

'Eight,' said the D.J.

'You're not going to,'

'Seven.'

'Kick me out now,'

'Six.'

'Are you?' Maybe Bar Blue didn't want to ruin its reputation as the hippest bar in town by allowing a single person to be seen on the floor at the countdown to the New Year.

'Five.'

'No,' he said in a broad, pommy accent.

'Four.'

'Well, what's up?'

'Three.'

'Just thought,'

'Two.'

'You might like,'

'One,'

'A bit of this.'

'Happy New Year.'

And then he kissed me. It wasn't a wonderful romantic kiss, or a wildly passionate one. But it also wasn't sloppy and didn't involve too much tongue. And while I would have preferred that it were Matt kissing me, I have to admit, it was the perfect kiss to have when you're not having a kiss.

'Thanks,' I said, smiling at him as we broke apart.

'No problem, all part of the service.' He gave me a cheeky little salute and sauntered back to his post on the front door.

'What was that?' Elaine asked me, laughing.

'Oh, that,' I said nonchalantly, 'I pre-ordered a New Year's snog. He was just delivering it.'

'That's why they won the Best Bar,' Elaine informed me quite seriously. 'They have wonderful service.'

The evening went on for a couple more hours during which more champagne was consumed and more dancing followed. It was the wee hours of the morning when I finally stumbled in my front door. The red light on my answering machine was blinking and I hit it as I carefully navigated my way to the bathroom. As I picked up my toothbrush I realised I could hear Matt's voice. Staggering, I raced back to the machine managing to connect with most of the furniture in the room. I yelped as I stubbed my toe on the couch and then banged my thigh on the table.

'Shit, shit, shit, shit,' I said as I hopped to the machine to replay the message. In my hurry I missed the replay button and hit the erase one.

'Noooooo,' I shrieked as I saw the light stop flashing. 'No, no, no, no,' I cried as I stabbed rapidly at the buttons on the machine, trying desperately to get the message to replay.

After about five minutes, I had to admit defeat. I had erased the message. All I had heard was him wishing me a happy new year. Had he said he missed me? Had he said he wished he could be with me? I couldn't be sure. Bad Bunny in tow, I dragged myself off to bed and promised myself I would ring him in the morning.

* * *

It was the morning I had been dreading. I sat with some toast and a cup of coffee, and tried to ignore the thought going round and round in my head. Today was the day Matt was getting married.

I'd tried to ring him a few times on New Year's Day, and each time gotten the currently unavailable message. After that, I had given it all up and decided that this year was the year I got over Matt. I secretly feared that my life had gotten off course and I would spend the rest of it getting over the guy who had helped me get over the guy before him. I shuddered at the thought.

I was onto my second coffee when I heard the banging on my front door.

'Seriously,' I said to Bad Bunny, who was lying in a patch of sun on the carpet, 'Why can't people just knock? Why do they always have to bang?'

I opened the door to find Elaine, slightly stooped over and puffing.

'You ran up my stairs?'

'Worse,' she said as she passed me heading for the kitchen. She helped herself to a glass of water. 'I couldn't get a park so I ran all the way down the street and then up your stairs.'

'You missed me. That's really sweet.'

'Actually I thought you might be interested in reading this.'

She pulled Benny out of her handbag and then a magazine, which she flicked onto the table. Benny ran over to sniff Bad Bunny, who opened one eye and then perceiving no threat, closed it and went back to sleep. Benny flopped down next to him in the sun.

'He's tired,' Elaine observed of Bad Bunny.

'He spent all night shagging his teddy bear.'

'I'm surprised Benny's gone anywhere near him after what happened last time.'

'It couldn't have been nice being humped in the head like that,' I agreed.

'Does he shag his bear back to front?'

'Back to front, on the side, upside down, he is quite partial to a sixty-niner though.' I gestured at the magazine. 'Not another closure article?'

'Not even close, go on read it.'

I picked up the magazine and joined her on the couch.

'*Travel Abroad*?' I asked her. 'You want me to go overseas again?'

'I think you'll find it interesting reading.'

The cover of the magazine had a beautiful photo of a location that I recognised immediately.

'That's the lily pool at the Floating Palace in Udaipur,' I said. I looked a little closer and let out a gasp. 'Oh my God, that's me.' I knelt beside the pool wrapped in a sarong, running my fingertips through the water.

'I thought it was. I couldn't be sure because it's taken from such a distance.'

I read the front cover searching for something about the photo. 'Romantic Rajasthan.' I stopped and looked at Elaine thoughtfully. 'It's Matt's article?' I asked her.

'You're not very smart this early in the morning, are you?'

'I didn't get much sleep last night. BB got up quite a rhythm and one of teddy's eyes was banging on the floor.'

'Why didn't you stop him?'

'Didn't have the heart - at least one of us was getting some.'

'If you don't read this damned article you definitely won't be getting any.'

I flicked to page 21 and began to read.

'India - a country of contradictions. After five years in India I thought I'd seen it all. I've seen riches right next to poverty, gluttony next to starvation and watched new life emerge out of a field of death. But never before, had I watched it unfold through another's eyes. Never before had I touched India, tasted India or felt India the way I did recently. Sharing India with someone special amplified my reactions to it. This new India was about quiet companionship amongst a fairy-gardenland. It was strolling hand-in-hand through abandoned forts and rambling streets. It

was watching sunsets over lakes. This India was made of magic, woven about me by a web of romance.'

The article went on for a few pages talking about our travels through Rajasthan. It never referred to me by name, instead mentioning me in an ambiguous way. I was the ghost that walked with him through his journey. Most of the spectacular photos featured me in some way, but in none of them could you have pointed at it and said, 'Hey isn't that Tara Babcock?' I was a silhouette, or slightly unfocused against a spectacular backdrop, or just so far away that I was unidentifiable.

He had written an article called Romantic Rajasthan, and when he talked about someone special adding a magical ingredient to a previously well-known dish, he was referring to me. He was getting married in, I checked my watch, forty minutes, and I was sitting on my lounge, with crumbs on my pyjamas and a full-on bed-head.

'Shit.' I jumped up and started running around my apartment.

'Tara. What are you doing?'

'Getting ready,' I said as I ran into the bathroom, and then back out as I forgot what I had gone in there for. I entered the kitchen and then ran back into the lounge.

'Tara. Stop.'

I froze looking at Elaine.

'What.... Are.... You.... Doing?'

'I have to go.'

'Go where?'

'I'm not sure. I have to stop the wedding.'

'Thank God. That's the first sane thing you've said all morning. Right - into the shower.'

I nodded stupidly and ran for the shower.

'Make it quick,' she yelled after me.

'What are you doing?' I called back.

'Getting out your clothes.'

Elaine had me out the door in less than 10 minutes. We sprinted up the road to her car and I jumped into the passenger seat as she roared away from the kerb.

'We've got twenty-five minutes,' she said.

'Where are we going?' I asked, suddenly aware that I wasn't sure where the wedding was. I know they must have mentioned it on the radio but I seemed to have blocked it totally out of my mind.

'Coogee Golf Course.' Elaine dodged around another car, narrowly missing a parked one. 'Damn Sunday drivers,' she grunted.

I checked my seatbelt was done up securely. 'It's Saturday,' I said.

'Don't get all pedantic on me.' She pulled up next to another car at the lights and revved the engine as if she were in a drag race. When the light turned green, she floored the accelerator and shot past the other car, before merging in front of it. 'Pussy,' she chuckled.

'What part of the golf course?

'Fifth hole at the stack.' She pulled on the hand break as she skidded around a corner.

'Jesus Elaine, did you just do a hand break turn?'

'Uh huh.'

'Where the hell did you learn to do that?'

'When I was in high school I lost my virginity to a racing car driver. He taught me a couple of interesting things.'

'About driving?'

'That - and he taught me how to handle a gear stick properly.'

She shot me a grin, and then put her foot to the floor as the light ahead of us turned yellow. We sailed through it just before it blinked to red. After a few minutes, I realised even with Elaine's amazing driving skills we were taking far too long to get to Coogee. The traffic was horrific and more often than not, we were stationary or crawling at a snail's pace.

I groaned, the suspense starting to get to me. Elaine checked her watch - swore - and then navigated her car up onto the curb.

'Shit,' I said as I hung onto the door.

She lent on the horn as she drove along the pavement.

'Sorry,' she yelled as we sailed past some pedestrians. 'My friend's in labour.'

'Christ,' I said, thinking of Lil. Panicking, I searched in my handbag certain I had left the pager Lil had given me on the kitchen bench. Feeling it in the palm of my hand I pulled it out and looked at it puzzled.

'I put it in there,' said Elaine. 'Thought you might need it.'

'Thanks.'

Finally we arrived in Coogee to a total gridlock.

'Oh shit, the wedding,' said Elaine.

'Yeah I know, that's why we're here,' I said, totally panicked.

'No, I mean the traffic from the wedding. I'll never get us there in time, and there's no way in hell I'm going to get a park. You're going to have to run from here. Ring me later if you need me to pick you up. Good luck.'

I jumped out of the car and started pelting down the road in the direction Elaine had pointed. I was starting to sweat not just from the running, or the heat, or the fact that I was probably too late, but from the thought of what I was attempting to do. I was going to be the one that jumped up at the part that said, 'Is there anyone here who knows why these two should not be wed?' And what was I planning to say?

'Hi, yeah I've known Matt for about two months, well actually about four if you count from the night we had casual sex, and I think that as I know him better than you that I should at least have the opportunity to date him.'

Hmmmm or, 'Matthew I think that I might have fallen in love with you and I'd like to get a chance to find out.'

Better I guess, but whichever way I looked at it, it was pretty pathetic. As Dad always said, 'If it looks like a duck, and quacks like a duck, it probably is a duck.'

I reached the front of the golf course and stopped. Where the hell did I go? How was I going to get there in time and how was I going to get past those bouncers?

The bouncers, it turned out, were the easy part. I just smiled prettily at them and waltzed on through the doors like I owned the place. As soon as I was out the other side and onto the green I broke into a trot.

'Excuse me,' I said to an old man standing by a golf cart. 'Which way is the fifth hole?'

'Well,' he began, 'If you just take your pretty self off in that direction for about fifteen minutes you can't help but eventually stumble across the fifth hole. You'll know it because there will be a whole heap of people at it, some wedding or something. The whole golf course has closed down. Nobody's allowed to hit a ball in case they hit a guest. And Saturday's my golfing day too. Sunday the missus makes me take her to the grocery store, and Mondays we play bingo. Tuesday we play Mah Jong, and Wednesdays we go down to Wollongong and visit our daughter. Thursday's we have my wife's sister over for lunch, and Fridays we go to the library, so you can see, that only leaves me Saturday to play golf.'

I was standing with my mouth wide open trying to find an entrance into the conversation that would allow me to politely excuse myself and start the fifteen-minute stroll to the fifth hole. I didn't have two minutes let alone fifteen, what was I going to do? The old dude was still going when I had my idea.

'And they are doing a photo shoot of some politician up at the sixth hole. How they're doing a photo shoot for a golfing magazine without hitting a ball I'll never know. What are they going to take a photo of?'

'Oh look,' I said, pointing behind him, 'there's Elvis.'

The old man swung his head around, and I jumped into his golf cart looking for the key. I saw a button which said Start and pressed it.

'Where's Elvis?' he said. 'I can't see him.'

The buggy roared to life and putting my foot to the floor I zoomed off before the man turned back around. 'Hey,' I heard him yell, 'where's Elvis gone?'

'I'm going to find him for you,' I yelled back.

'Thank youoooooo.' I could hear his reply echoing after me as I shot along the course.

If I hadn't been so nervous I would have been enjoying myself immensely. No one had ever told me how much fun these things were. Plus the view out over the water was spectacular. I made a mental note to see if Elaine wanted to learn to play golf. We could spend all day whizzing around in these things and then head off to the club for some drinkies afterwards.

Finally in the distance I saw a huge crowd. I pulled the buggy to a halt on top of a hill overlooking the wedding and could see Matt standing at an altar, next to a woman in white. She was enormous. And when I say enormous I mean huge. Humungous. A planet. While Matt towered above her, she dwarfed him in width. I felt a smile twitch the corner of my mouth. I would have loved to have seen the look on his face when he first saw her. Obviously one of the three questions he should have asked was, 'How much do you weigh?' Or better yet, 'Have you ever been mistaken for a whale?'

My smile was wiped right off my face when I heard the minister's next words. 'I now pronounce you man and wife.'

Fuck! Fuck, fuck, fuck, fuck, fuck, fuckity, fuckfuck. I was too late. I couldn't believe it.

I saw Matt turn to the beached white whale and, lifting her veil, lean down to kiss her. I squeezed my eyes shut, unable to watch it. *If I just close my eyes for long enough*, I thought reassuringly, *they'll all be gone when I open them, and then I can pretend that nothing ever happened.*

It was the noise that made me open my eyes. A weird sound getting louder and louder, closer and closer, making me unsuccessfully search my memory of sounds to determine what it was.

THWAAAAACKKKKKK.

Then, a noise like a whip cracking, as something small and very, very hard pummelled into my thigh. I let out a huge bellow of pain, causing the entire crowd at the wedding to look up the hill. Letting out another cry I collapsed to the ground, clutching my leg. I rolled face first into the soft grass and felt a sharp pain in my mouth as I rolled onto my side.

'Aiyeeeeee.' I let out another loud cry, following it with, 'Pfhwwhhwww,' as I tried unsuccessfully to spit out whatever was in my mouth. It seemed to have attached itself to my tongue.

I could hear someone saying, 'Sir, I think you've hit somebody.'

And then a familiar voice say, 'Have I? Damn, what were they doing up the top? I thought they'd all be down at the wedding.'

I stuck my tongue out a far as it would go and looked down at it, cross-eyed, turning my head to get some better light. Oh Fuck. I had a bee stuck to the end of my tongue. A bee had stung me on the tongue. What the fuck was a bee doing here? It was a golf course - there was no clover or flowers for miles to attract a bee. And then I realised....... the flowers from the wedding. I had gotten stung on the tongue by a bee from the radio slut's bouquet. Fucking baby's breath. This was just great.

Very carefully, breathing through my panic, I grasped the bee while resisting the urge to squeal at the feel of it wriggling between my fingers, and I plucked it from my tongue. I examined him. (I was definitely thinking of the bee as a him.) He was missing his sting which could only mean one thing. It was still in my tongue. I whimpered a little, resisting the natural urge to put my tongue back in my mouth to swallow, and poked it out as far as it would go.

'Chooor, get a load of this,' I heard someone say, with a laugh in their voice.

'What's she doing?' someone else asked.

Ignoring them, I focused on my tongue trying to get the sting before it pumped more venom into me. And then I heard two different men say my name in two entirely different ways; one affectionate and amused, the other annoyed and intolerant, and the old man whose golf cart I had stolen's, words popped back into my head.

'Some politician having a photo shoot for a golfing magazine.'

Oh great. That was all I needed. My first meeting with Jake since I had left, and I had to be sitting on a golf course with a dead leg and a rapidly swelling tongue.

Matt leant down in front of me and shook his head, obviously amused by what he saw.

'Tara?'

In answer I held up the bee in my hand and pointed to my tongue.

'He bit you on the tongue?'

'Stung you mean,' I heard Jake say spitefully, 'bees don't bite.'

'Did you hear that? She got stung on the tongue by a bee,' said someone from the rapidly expanding crowd.

'First she got hit in the leg by a golf ball,' someone else said.

'Blimey. That's a bad day. That's a day you shouldn't have bothered getting out of bed for.'

I was definitely inclined to agree with whoever that was.

Ignoring them, Matt reached out and gently turned my head so he could see my tongue from side on. 'There it is,' he said and plucked it out.

I lay down in relief, fighting the tears that were threatening to come. The media was all around me joking, laughing and taking photos. It was my worst nightmare come true. Actually, it was worse that my worst nightmare. Never could my imagination have conjured up a scene that had me witness the man I thought I loved marry a stranger, before being whacked in the leg by a golf ball, (hit by my ex-husband, the Mayor of Sydney while he posed for a magazine cover), which made me fall to the ground and get a bee in my mouth, (probably from the bouquet of the stranger the man I loved had just married), which then stung me. It was the oxymoron of my motorbike fantasy.

'Hey look, she can't fit her tongue in her mouth any more,' someone said in amusement.

It was true. I groaned softly. My tongue was swelling at a fast pace. It filled my mouth and the very tip was being forced beyond my lips. This was my punishment for laughing at how fat radio slut was. Why did I always get punished while no one who did nasty things to me seemed to?

Matt leant down and took a closer look at me. 'Can you breathe?' he asked in concern.

Of course I could until he asked me. Then I got into such a panic that I couldn't get enough oxygen into my lungs. I started flapping my hands around while I sucked in lungful after lungful of air.

'Ten bucks says she passes out,' someone - I think it was the golf caddy - said.

'Nar that's not a fair bet, look at her, if she doesn't pass out it'll be a miracle.'

'All right, ten bucks says she doesn't make it,' he amended.

'What? Like dead doesn't make it?'

'Yeah.'

'All right, I'll take that bet,' said his friend.

I gave the two men as nasty a look as I could summon as I continued to pant and gasp for breath.

'Ignore them,' said Matt, standing up and flipping open his mobile phone. 'Ambulance,' I heard him say, and then, 'hello we're on the fifth hole at the Coogee Golf Course. We have a female here, thirty years of age, who's been stung on her tongue by a bee.' He paused. 'No, this is not a joke. Her tongue is swelling rapidly and she is in need of urgent medical attention.'

Urgent Medical Attention? I didn't want to die. *I'm too young*, I thought, *I have too much to live for.*

Even as I thought it I realised it was true. So I might not have a husband any more. So the man I thought I loved had just married someone else. I had friends and a loving family, and a good job. I looked sadly at Matt, mentally saying good-bye, preparing myself for a future without him.

I fought back the tears threatening to spill down my face knowing if I started crying I wouldn't be able to stop. And then I probably wouldn't be able to breathe. I would choke to death on my own tongue right there in front of Jake and Matt.

I breathed deeply, snorting air through my nose while I wondered if Matt could perform an emergency laryngotomy.

Matt put his phone in his pocket and stalked over to Jake. 'Nice work numbnuts,' he said.

'How do you know my wife?' I heard Jake ask rudely.

'I don't know your wife.'

'But you know her name.'

'Oh, you mean your ex-wife,' said Matt, emphasising the ex.

'Yes, I mean my ex-wife of course.'

'I don't see how that's any of your business,' Matt said smugly.

'What do you mean it's none of my business?' Jake was not pretty when he was angry.

'I'm sorry. What part of none of your business don't you understand?' asked Matt.

'I just want to know how you and Tara know each other,' Jake said through clenched teeth.

'Well I want to know what the hell you were doing hitting that golf ball?' retorted Matt.

The two of them were faced off across from each other like a pair of roosters. If I hadn't been in such pain from my leg and my tongue I would have been quite chuffed.

'I'm here with *Golfing Australia*,' said Jake.

'Yes I know. As I understood it, it was a photo shoot and not an action video you were doing,' Matt said sarcastically.

'It's a little hard to do a photo shoot for a golfing magazine and not hit a ball,' Jake said sullenly.

'No balls were to be hit. Those were the rules.'

'Don't you tell me what to do.'

'She wouldn't be in this predicament if it wasn't for you and your ego,' Matt said, gesturing at me.

They looked to be getting to the shoving part of the argument. I could see the media horde frantically taking notes. Thankfully, at that moment, the ambulance appeared in the distance, and the two of them backed away from each other.

'How are you?' Matt asked, kneeling down next to me.

'Itty ood,' I said as clearly as I could, smiling with false bravado. It was so wonderful just to be near him, to see his face again. I tried to forget I had just witnessed him marry someone else.

The ambulance officer approached the crowd and said, 'So what's this about a bee stinging someone on the tongue?' The crowd opened up a little and someone pointed at me. He took one look and burst out laughing. 'Charlie,' he called to his partner. 'Quick. You gotta check this out. We thought they were joking when we got the call,' he confided in me.

I tried to be pleased for him but as it was my tongue now protruding out of my mouth, and my face which was starting to swell up like a balloon, I was finding it hard to share his delight.

'Eeelllp,' I managed to squeak.

'Get the ice and some Phenergan,' he called out again.

'Ohh,' I heard someone in the crowd say, 'she sounds just like a little mouse.'

'Will she be all right?' asked Matt.

God bless him, he seemed really concerned. I couldn't believe he was married.

'Don't you worry mate, she'll be as right as rain.'

That made me feel a little better.

'Come on let's get you to the ambulance.' He pulled me to my feet at which point I let out a primordial moan and collapsed back to the ground.

'What's wrong with her?' he asked in confusion.

'She got hit in the leg by a golf ball,' Matt explained.

'Blimey,' said the Ambo. 'You've had a nasty day haven't you?'

I nodded my head sadly as a tear slipped down one cheek. Matt reached out and brushed it away. He looked really upset.

I could see Jake hovering and wondered what the hell he was still doing there. I thought about telling him to piss off but knew I couldn't manage it. 'Iff off,' probably just would have had them all in stitches.

Charlie came back from the cab with a stretcher and he and Steve - the first ambulance officer whose name I had spied embroidered on his uniform, helped me onto the stretcher.

Matt was standing next to the ambulance as they loaded me into the back.

'Don't worry gov,' Charlie said, in a thick English accent, 'we'll take real good care of her.'

'I'm going with her,' I heard Jake say.

'Fwark oaff,' I said in alarm. The last thing I wanted was Jake's company. I wanted to be left alone with my misery to examine my life and work out where I had gone wrong. I mean, given today's events I must have taken a wrong turn at some important fork in my life. As it was probably the first day that I met him, I really didn't want him anywhere near me during my trip down memory lane.

'No,' said Matt. 'I'm going with her.'

'Don't you think you should be with your new bride?' Jake said and then sniggered.

Matt looked over his shoulder at the crowd that awaited his return. He sighed and shook his head and then leaned over and kissed me on the cheek. I was wondering if he would have kissed me on the lips if they weren't so grossly swollen when he whispered in my ear, 'You know none of this was real?'

What? Did he mean I was still asleep in bed and this was all a very bad dream? That would make a hell of a lot of sense.

He looked into my eyes and seeing my confusion said quietly, 'Tara. It's just a radio stunt. It's not a real wedding.'

Then he was gone, leaving me staring after him, too stunned to be relieved.

Charlie pushed me back into the ambulance and Jake clambered in after me.

'Cancel all my afternoon appointments, I'll ring you when I'm finished,' he said to his aide.

'You owe me ten bucks,' I heard the aide say to the caddy.

'No I don't.'

'Well she's not dead is she?'

'Not dead yet, you never know what will happen when she gets to the hospital - if they get to the hospital.'

Thankfully at that point the ambulance door was shut, blocking out the rest of the conversation.

I closed my eyes and pretended to sleep. I couldn't stand the thought of Jake being that close to me, so instead I thought about Matt. I held onto the feel of the brush of his lips on my cheek and his last words.

Quite quickly, I was wheeled into the Emergency Ward where I probably would have had to wait forever - even though I was starting to resemble a puffer fish, if it weren't for the presence of my dear ex-husband.

'Oh Lord Mayor,' I heard a nurse simper, 'come straight through.'

The doctor was on speed dial as well and no sooner had the nurse left than he arrived and Steve and Charlie finished the handover.

The doctor ordered some ice packs, gave me another couple of shots of something, one which he said would help me sleep for a while, and then started up a conversation with Jake about the state of Sydney's emergency departments. I remembered feeling slightly smug that not everybody was Jake's biggest fan, and then I was sound asleep.

When I woke, I lay still for a few seconds, getting my bearings, before reaching up to gingerly feel my face. I heard Jake say, 'The swelling's gone down.'

Ahh, fuck. The stupid bastard was still there. And I was hoping he would have gotten bored with not being adored and wandered off. I opened my eyes and looked at him. Why hadn't I ever noticed how cold his eyes were?

He stood up and looked outside the little curtained area I was stationed in. Oh goody, maybe he was going. But no, he came back and, pulling his seat even closer, leant towards me. I found myself wiggling over to get as far from him as possible.

Ouch. My leg still hurt. I bet it had a nasty bruise. I was dying to check it out, but there was no way I was pulling down my pants in front of him.

'Tara,' he said softly.

I ignored him.

'Tara,' he said loudly enough that I had to acknowledge him.

'What?' I asked annoyed.

He lowered his voice again and whispered, 'I've missed you.'

I looked at him, stunned. That was not at all what I had been expecting. 'Bullshit.'

'I have.'

'I guess that's why you never called me,' I said coldly.

'I couldn't?'

'Why not?'

'You have to understand.' The tone of his voice was reminiscent of other fights we had had.

'Stop,' I said, firmly. 'I don't have to understand anything except the fact that you were screwing my cousin.'

'It wasn't like that,' he said.

I laughed in disbelief. I was going to ask what it was like but I stopped when I realised that I didn't want to hear it. I didn't want to hear his bullshit, make-believe, poor-Jake story. Not now. I realised that I didn't care any more - that I was free, and I started to laugh. I was finally free. It felt so good. I stretched my emotional wings, flexing them in all directions. Yep, they were healed.

'What are you laughing at?' he asked, clearly annoyed.

'You.'

'You have to believe me,' he said, pathetically.

I looked at him. How ironic, I was finally hearing the words I had longed to hear, but now I didn't want them.

He continued, somewhat bolstered by my silence. 'You look fantastic.'

I snorted in disbelief. I looked like someone with a very fat face. I wondered how much of this had to do with the fact that Matt and I obviously had some sort of connection?

'Maybe we could meet up for a drink sometime.' I felt my eyebrows shoot up beyond my fringe. This was obviously a case of not wanting someone else to play with his toy. 'For old time's sake,' he continued.

And then I heard a pager beeping. It took me a few seconds to realise that it was the one in my handbag. I looked around frantically for my bag, finally spying it on the back of Jake's seat.

'My handbag please,' I said, holding out my hand.

'It's been making that noise for a while now,' he informed me.

'Shit. Why didn't you wake me?'

'You looked so peaceful.'

'Yeah, I was dreaming of Matt,' I longed to say, but didn't feel like getting into an argument at the moment.

I found my pager and checked it. *In Birthing Suite, room 23.* It was Lil. Thankfully I had ended up in the same hospital.

I swung myself off the bed, wincing as I stood up.

'Where are you going?' Jake asked.

'Lil's in labour.' I headed off to the elevators. After 6 births I knew my way to the birthing rooms from every part of the hospital. I could hear Jake following me as I hobbled along the corridor.

'Tara,' he called, 'wait.'

'What the hell for?' I asked over my shoulder.

'We need to talk.'

'No. We don't. We stopped needing to talk when our divorce came through.' I hit the up button on the elevator and miraculously the doors on one of them popped immediately open.

'I haven't finished yet,' Jake said in an angry voice as he followed me into the elevator.

I could see a very pregnant lady in a wheelchair being pushed towards us. Jake leant over and hit the close door button. I smacked his hand away and pushed the door open button. The doors, which had started to close, sprung back.

'Thank you so much,' panted the lady.

'Look honey,' said her husband, 'it's the Lord Mayor.'

'Oh, thank you so much Sir,' she amended.

'No problem always eager to help,' said Jake.

I rolled my eyes but managed to bite my tongue, which given the fact it was still a little swollen wasn't that hard.

We arrived on the maternity floor and Jake magnanimously let the other couple off first. I gingerly stepped off after them towards Lil's room.

'Tara, wait,' he said imperiously.

'Jake, Lil's in labour I have to go.'

'Tara, I still love you,' he said softly.

I froze and pivoted to look at him.

'Things haven't been the same since you left,' he continued.

I shook my head in disbelief, snorted, and continued down the corridor.

'Promise you'll at least meet me for a drink,' he said.

'I will do no such thing,' I said in horror.

It's hard to make a dignified exit when you're limping. It's also hard to make a dignified exit when the person you are exiting from follows you. He grabbed my arm and said, 'Well what about dinner? You could come round one night while Tash is away.'

I couldn't believe what I was hearing. Was this how it had started between him and Tash? I shook him off my arm in disgust and kept going.

It was as we drew even with the nurse's station that everything crystallised for me and finally, I understood.

'Oh Lord Mayor,' said one of the nurses, 'so good to see you again.'

Another one standing up to get his attention called out, 'Congratulations on your wife's pregnancy, Sir.'

Tash was pregnant?

I swung instinctively as fast as I could - felt my arm whipping around and then the stunning impact of my open hand slapping his cheek as hard as I could. I saw him stagger slightly from the force of the blow, a hurt look on his face; a look that once would have made me feel miserable and sorry.

I turned to the stunned nurses, giggling a little madly as I remembered the closure exercise I had once done. Wiping my hands together I smiled brightly at them and said, 'And that, my friends is closure.'

Looking back at Jake I put on my best Arnold Schwarzenegger voice and said, 'Hasta la vista baby.' I started laughing, so overcome by the humour of the situation that I only just managed to utter, 'Frankly my dear, I don't give a damn.'

Jake was slowly backing away from me, a look of bewilderment on his face. Turning back to the nurses, who were looking concerned, I coolly informed them, 'Tomorrow is another day.'

And then I looked at Jake, letting my full contempt for him show on my face. I could feel my lip curling scornfully as I said, 'Goodbye and thanks for all the fish.' And then turning my back on him for the last time I stalked off to find Lil.

It was all in all, I decided as I opened the door to her room, a pretty good ending to a rather shitty day.

* * *

Lil was sitting on the bed flicking through a magazine when I arrived. 'Wow,' she said, 'you made excellent time.'

'I was in the Emergency Ward. Sorry, I would have been here earlier but I was asleep and I didn't hear the pager.'

'Emergency Ward? What happened?'

I put my bag on the little table in the room and then moved over and sat next to her on the bed.

'What happened to your face?' she asked.

'Bee stung me on the tongue,' I informed her.

'Why are you limping?'

'Golf ball hit me in the leg.'

'Hence the Emergency Ward,' she said, shaking her head in disbelief.

'Yep.'

She opened her mouth to speak and then paused as a pained expression came over her face. When her contraction had finished, she smiled and continued flicking through the magazine.

'Who's got the girls?' I asked her.

'Martin's parents.'

'Martin?'

'In bloody Japan, can you believe it?' she said. 'I think he does it on purpose. Ever since the first birth I'm sure he's bid to be away for the rest.'

'You did give him a pretty hard time during the first birth,' I said, smiling at the memory.

'Yes, well, that one really hurt.'

'And of course there was the fact that he passed out at the end,' I added.

'And totally stole the attention of all the midwives so I had to deliver alone,' Lil said in mock rage.

'And then they had to stitch him up,' I reminded her.

'You'd think he was the one that had just given birth by the way he was behaving.'

'I think it was the happy gas they gave him.'

'And then he wouldn't give it up, so I had to be stitched up without it.'

We both laughed at the memory.

'Thank God you were there,' she said.

'Yeah, so I could hold Martin's hand. How far apart are the contractions?'

'Ten minutes,' she said calmly.

'Why didn't you page me earlier?'

'Well what with the radio comp and everything I thought you might be otherwise preoccupied?'

'I was,' I said.

'Well that explains the golf ball in the leg, but the bee on the tongue?'

'I ate the bee as I fell to the ground after the ball hit me in the leg.'

'Interesting twist on the usual boring golfing stories,' she said in amusement.

'You *know* I like to be different. And,' I added, my voice as neutral as possible for maximum effect, 'guess who hit the golf ball that got me?'

'Ummm. Come on give me a hint. Not Matt?'

'Think Sydney Royalty.'

'Nooooooo. Not Jake,' she said.

'The one and only.' I held my nails out to look at them and then buffed them on the front of my shirt. 'And guess who insisted on riding in the ambulance to the hospital with me?'

'Jake?' she said.

'Uhuh and guess who just told me that he still loved me?'

'Jake?' Her voice went up an octave in her excitement. She put her hand up to halt me while she had another contraction and then nodded for me to continue.

'And guess whose wife is expecting a baby?'

'Noooooo,' she said in a low scandalised voice.

'And guess whose face I just had the pleasure of slapping?'

She squealed in excitement. 'Aw. While I've been here having contractions you've been out there having all the fun.'

'But wait there's more...'

'Tell me, tell me.'

'It's about the wedding,' I said.

'Did it happen?'

I nodded my head gravely. 'I got there too late to stop it.'

'Why aren't you devastated?' she asked sympathetically.

'It wasn't real,' I said.

'Not real?' she asked in confusion.

'Nope. Fake. A radio stunt.'

'Oh my God. That's great. But, if it was a fake, why didn't he ring you?'

'I don't know,' I said. I felt my good mood evaporating slightly, but then I remembered the two missed calls and the magazine article in my bag.

'But look at this,' I said pulling the copy of *Travel Abroad* out and handing it to her.

'Romantic Rajasthan,' she read. 'That's a beautiful photo.'

'Look closer,' I said.

'Is that you?'

'Uhuh.'

'So this article is about you?'

'Sort of. It's about finding romance in the middle of India,' I said.

She looked for a minute like she was having another contraction, but then I realised she was crying. 'It's the hormones,' she explained. 'They make me so emotional. I'm really happy for you, honey.'

'Is that why you're crying?'

'Tears of joy.'

And then she did have another contraction.

It was the wee hours of the morning by the time I finally got home. Bad Bunny was happy to see me and hopped straight to the fridge, where he sat thumping his back foot impatiently until I got his dinner. We sat on the couch together while I had a cup of tea and scratched his furry belly.

Lil had been amazing. She said it helped that all her muscles had been stretched by the six previous labours, but it was still awe-inspiring watching her give birth. To think that she had created life - that this tiny being had grown from a single cell inside her. It really was miraculous. Maybe it was the lack of sleep or the day's events finally catching up with me, but I had wept as I watched the dark head, followed by the perfect little body, emerge from within her; so tiny, so pretty, so delicate. She had reached out her little fist and clasped my finger while she stretched and yawned. I had been instantly captivated and it had reawakened my own yearnings for a child that I had repressed all those years ago.

'There's no hurry,' I said to Bad Bunny as I put him to bed with his teddy bear. He promptly mounted the bear and began to hump him.

'Don't do anything I wouldn't do,' I told them drowsily as I drifted off to sleep.

* * *

The phone woke me the next day. It was Elaine. 'Quick, get up and put on Channel 7,' she barked down the phone.

'Good morning to you too,' I said, as I crawled out of bed and flicked on the television. I stopped talking when I saw Matt being interviewed. I felt my breath catch in my throat at the sight of him, and could feel a tingle on my cheek where he had brushed his lips yesterday.

'And so you just came back from India?' the reporter asked him.

'Yes, I only arrived back a couple of days ago.'

'That's weird,' I said to Elaine, 'we got back weeks ago.'

'Well, actually I got back weeks ago,' he continued, 'but then got asked to go back and write an article on Mumbai after the terrorist attacks. I've been helping with the rebuilding, and I wanted to check on two special little orphans.'

'So he was in India the whole time,' Elaine said to me.

'That would account for the bad phone reception.'

Just then my mobile phone rang. It was Nat. 'Are you watching the tele?'

'Yep. Elaine beat you to it.'

I sat on the couch with a phone pressed to each ear while the interview continued.

'And your latest article - Romantic Rajasthan, I'm guessing that's about someone special to you?'

'This guy's a regular rocket scientist,' said Elaine.

'Yes, very special,' replied Matt.

Nat and Elaine both squealed into my ears.

'Hang on,' said Nat, 'my mobile's ringing.' Her voice went muffled as she said, 'Hello,' then she was back. 'It's Dinah.'

'And can you tell us the name of this special woman?' the interviewer continued.

'Not at the moment, no,' said Matt.

'Did she know about the radio wedding competition?'

'Unfortunately I had been signed into a secrecy contract before I even met her. So no, she didn't know.'

'I'm guessing that didn't go down too well,' said the interviewer.

'Not really.' Matt smiled.

'Will you be seeing her again?'

'Hopefully really soon I'll get the chance to take her out to dinner and explain the whole thing.'

There was a knock at my door.

'There's someone at my door,' I told Elaine and Nat.

'There's someone at her door,' I heard Nat tell Dinah.

'Answer it,' said Elaine.

I backed to the door not wanting to miss any of the interview. Christ, I hoped they weren't about to show footage of me with a swollen tongue, or mention my relationship to Jake.

I stuck one phone under my chin and opened the door. Matt was standing there with a bunch of flowers in one hand and my missing reef sandals in the other.

'My shoes,' I said, 'they turned up.'

'Not quite the initial response I was hoping for,' he said.

I looked from him to the television with a confused expression on my face.

'It was filmed yesterday,' he said. 'I called in a favour.'

'She's opened the door,' said Nat to Dinah.

'Who is it?' I could hear Elaine asking.

'Tara, what's going on?' asked Nat.

'Excuse me for one moment,' I said politely to Matt.

'It's Matt. At the door now,' I hissed into the phones. 'Gotta go.' I hung up on both of them and stuck the phones in my pockets.

'Sorry about that,' I said.

'Quite all right,' he said, and then nodded towards the television. 'So how about it?'

'How about what?' I asked stupidly.

'Dinner, to let me explain, and to say I'm sorry for putting you through that.'

'Do I have to wait that long?' I asked.

'For an explanation or for the apology?'

'No silly, for a kiss.'

He smiled a sexy, slightly-relieved smile. 'So I don't even need to grovel?'

'Grovel if you want. But can you do it really quickly so we can get to the kiss and makeup part. That's my favourite.'

'Mine too,' he said as he pulled me into his arms. 'I'm sorry.'

'S okay' I mumbled as I buried my head in his chest and sucked back a few sniffles that were attempting to break free. 'I should have trusted you.'

'I should have told you, but I was signed into a confidentiality contract, and to be honest, when I was with you I totally forgot about it. I never wanted to do it, but I owed my mate - who's the station producer - a favour. Ratings have been a little low, and he thought this would help.'

He pulled back a little and studied my face. 'How's your mouth?' he asked me.

'Perfect, why?'

'It's just that I don't want to hurt you,' he said.

'I'm going to hurt you if you don't get on with it.'

He laughed his wonderful full-bodied laugh and said, 'I've missed you so much.'

And then he kissed me - a deep, long kiss that went on and on as we pulled each other closer and closer. Eventually, he broke away and I smiled up at him with what I am sure was a dazed expression on my face.

'Ahhh, Tara,' he said.

'Hmmmmmm,' I said dreamily.

'There seems to be something attached to my foot.'

I looked down to see Bad Bunny with his front paws wrapped around Matt's ankle. He was giving the tip of his shoe a right ol' rogering.

I reached down and scooped him up. 'Free shoe shine with every visit,' I said. 'Would you like the other one done?'

'Maybe later,' he laughed, 'but right now, if you don't mind, I'd like to shine your shoes.'

'Be my guest,' I said, opening up my door a little wider. 'You know how much I love my shoes.'

Chapter Nine

Eighteen Months Later

I gazed at my reflection in the mirror. My hair - now shoulder length - was piled on top of my head in curls. There were little diamantes sprinkled through them. Tristan had out done himself. My makeup was perfect, my gown was beautiful, and I wasn't even nervous. I turned to Nat.

'You look gorgeous, ' she said in a slightly teary voice.

'And you,' I said, 'look so ravishing that I doubt Ricardo is going to make it through the vows before he kisses you.'

She blushed a deep shade of red. 'I can't believe I'm getting married.'

'I know. I can't believe how much has happened in the last year and a half.'

Nat's Mum entered the room. 'They're ready dear,' she said, kissing her carefully on the cheek. Nat's Dad hovered behind her Mum, looking emotional.

We looked at each other, both trying not to cry, and then the music commenced and I was walking down the aisle, with Nat and her Dad behind me. I could see Ricardo standing at the altar - looking gorgeous of course. He was obviously nervous because he was playing with his bow tie.

Right next to him was Matt. My Matt. Looking extremely yummy in his suit.

I was still shocked by the intensity of my desire for him. Seeing him standing there, I just wanted to rip off his suit and have my wicked way with him. I'm sure the minister would not approve at all. Maybe I had been spending too much time with Bad Bunny, who had finally managed to wear out teddy beyond my abilities to repair. I had bought him a stuffed black rabbit, Bonny, whom he was crazy about.

I could see Elaine snivelling around a tissue she was holding up to her eyes in an attempt to catch the tears before they ruined her makeup. Her left hand, with its simple wedding band, lay across her bulging belly. She and Alistair were expecting twins in only eight weeks. Benny was in for a huge shock.

Next to them were Dinah and Gloria, still madly in love. They had bought a house together, which my Mum had happily filled with psychologically deranged animals.

I could see my Mum and Dad in their best outfits. Dad hadn't even complained once about having to get suited up for the wedding. They were sitting over on the groom's side. When I had asked why they had decided to sit there, Mum had informed me that they had wanted Ricardo to feel that he had some family here. Nat had cried when I told her.

Tristan was sitting next to Dinah and Gloria with his new boyfriend, Richard. They had been together for nearly a year now and we had high hopes for the two of them.

Matt and I were off tomorrow on a month long holiday. We were doing a camel camping trek in Morocco, which Matt assured me I would love. (I wasn't so sure about the whole camel thing, what with all the spitting and everything. It had disaster written all over it.) From there we were heading to Spain for ten days before finally meeting up with Nat and Ricardo on their honeymoon in the Greek Islands.

I had packed plenty of spare shoes.

* * *

About Donna Joy Usher

 Born in Brisbane, Donna Joy Usher started her working life as a dentist. After 15 years of drilling and filling she discovered there was more to life, and put pen to paper. Now she drills by day and writes by night. When not doing either of those things she likes spending time with her husband and two little dogs, fishing and camping, motorbike riding, stand-up paddle boarding, traveling and drinking wine on her deck.

Her debut novel, *The Seven Steps to Closure*, took gold in the humour category of the 2012 elit Publishing Awards and was shortlisted for the Shirley You Jest 2012 Book Awards and the 2013 Indie Excellence Awards. She has also reached the status of Amazon Best-Selling Author.

She has lived in a myriad of places: Melbourne, Perth, England, Rockhampton, Roxby Downs, Sydney, Cairns and is now situated on the New South Wales Central Coast.

Other Books by Donna Joy Usher

THE CHANEL SERIES

Book One - Cocoa and Chanel

Faced with the unattractive options of an affair with her boss's husband or the unknown, Chanel Smith chooses the unknown and unwittingly traps herself into joining the New South Wales Police Force. More interested in fashion than felony, Chanel staggers through training and finds herself posted to the forces most notorious crime hot spot: Kings Cross. Against her wishes she becomes entangled in a case of the worst kind, a serial killer targeting young women in The Cross.

As she is drawn further into the seedy underworld of The Cross in her attempt to unravel the truth, Chanel makes new friends, new enemies and draws the attention of the killer. Can she solve the case in time, or will she become the killer's next victim?

Cocoa and Chanel is now available for sale as an eBook and in paperback on Amazon.com.

THE WAR FAERY SERIES

Book One – Away with the Faeries

Isadora Scrumpleton is a witch with problems. She is rapidly approaching her 18th birthday and still hasn't been chosen by a familiar - a fate that would leave her powerless within the witching community and which she deems worse than death.

When she learns that not only is she part faery, but that her faery self has been secretly dating the heir to the faery throne in her dreams, her problems really begin.

Spurned by the faery Queen, lost within the witching world she struggles to come to terms with her new powers and her budding relationship with Aethan. Unable to remember her night forays with him she thinks they may be better off apart.

When he is kidnapped by the evil Goblin Queen – Galanta - she is forced to make a decision that will change not only her own destiny but the destiny of the world.

If you are interested in hearing when the War Faery Series are published please contact me though my website www.donnajoyusher.com

SELF-PUBLISHING: How to Publish Like a Pro for a Fraction of the Cost

ANYBODY CAN SELF-PUBLISH - BUT NOT EVERYBODY DOES IT WELL

Want to self-publish your book but concerned about the cost involved? Frustrated with 'how to' books, that tell you *what* to do, but not *how* to do it? Bamboozled by the number of self-publishing options available?

SELF-PUBLISHING: How to Publish Like a Pro for a Fraction of the Cost contains everything a DIY author needs:

- The crucial self-publishing options available.
- Things you need to do *before* you self-publish.
- How to self-publish for $35 and have your book available for sale on Amazon, Smashwords, Kobo, Barnes and Noble, Sony, and iBookstore amongst others.
- How to format your 2007 or 2010 Word Document to look like a professionally printed book.
- How to format your eBook.
- How to format for Smashwords' Meatgrinder.
- How to load your files into Amazon, CreateSpace and Smashwords.

This book is ideal for all authors, especially those with limited computer skills, who want to produce a professional looking product and reap the rewards.

DONNA JOY USHER is the award-winning, Amazon best-selling author of *The Seven Steps to Closure* and *Cocoa and Chanel*. She is a self-taught, self-publishing author, who is passionate about helping others achieve success.

Available on Amazon as an eBook November 2013.

CPSIA information can be obtained at www.ICGtesting.com
Printed in the USA
LVOW07s1327070316

478092LV00002B/86/P

9 780987 320704